Incident at Tybee Island

by
Rowan Wolfe

ROOFTOP
publishing

RoofTop Publishing™
1663 Liberty Drive, Suite 200
Bloomington, IN 47403
Phone: 1-800-839-8640

First published by RoofTop Publishing 5/11/06

ISBN: 1-6000-8001-4 (sc)

Library of Congress Control Number: 2006901119

Printed in the United States of America
Bloomington, Indiana

This book is printed on acid-free paper.

To Colonel Howard Richardson, U.S.A.F. (Retired)

Robert J. Lagerstrom

&

Clarence Stewart

The original crew of the B-47 and F-86L.

Without them

Incident at Tybee Island

would never have been written.

*

And to the men and women of our

United States military,

some of whom have made the ultimate

sacrifice to ensure our continued freedom.

For your courage and dedication,

I salute you!

www.rowanwolfe.com

Acknowledgments

Without Colonel Howard Richardson, USAF (Ret), Robert Lagerstrom, and Clarence Stewart, there would be no *Incident at Tybee Island.* For your generous contributions, gentlemen, I thank you.

My father taught me to always ask if I didn't know or couldn't find the answer, and if I was going to ask, I should preferably ask an expert. I've questioned a lot of experts for my crime/military thrillers, and without their help, my research would have been far less accurate.

Therefore, my thanks to the wonderful folks of U.S. Army Special Forces at Fort Bragg, North Carolina, who, for security reasons, will have to remain anonymous. And to Tony, who went to those places he cannot name to do things he's not allowed to talk about.

To Chief Robert M. Stewart of South Carolina Law Enforcement Division, for granting me access. And Inspector Richard E. Hunton, Jr. for his extraordinary expertise and time to make the homicide in Camden, South Carolina, really authentic. Thanks also to Lieutenant Joseph M. Leatherman and Lieutenant Amanda Simmons of SLED, who supplied me with even more information.

My thanks also to Captain Allen Trapp and Lieutenant Herbie Frasier of Camden Police Department for a really great and informative day, and lunch at Gadgets.

To Lieutenant Colonel Jay, my "military encyclopedia," without whose seemingly endless knowledge, I'd be still doing research.

Thanks also to Tybee Island Police Department, Captain Mike Smith, B.J. Riffel, and all my friends on Tybee who make it such a special place.

To Gary, my proofreader, for his eagle eye.

And special thanks too, to my extended family of Mike, Nancy, Mark, Tracy, and Morgan for their encouragement and support.

And last, and by no means least, my wonderful "Corgi kids." A breed not known for their patience, they accepted my extraordinarily long hours at a computer and only interrupted when it was time to eat. Imagine that?

Chapter One

Off the Coast of Georgia
Tuesday, February 4, 1958

At approximately 1830 hours, when the 19th Bombardment Wing B-47 Stratojet took off from Homestead Air Force Base, Florida, it carried a Mark 15 thermonuclear bomb to add authenticity to the simulated combat mission. The weather forecast had been typical: a chilly February night but with almost unlimited visibility. After a scheduled air refueling, the B-47 flew north, almost reaching the Canadian border, before it turned back toward the designated target. Over Radford, Virginia, the crew "released" their deadly cargo.

All that now remained was to rid themselves of the chasing F-86 fighters posing as the enemy and escape to the Carolinas. Using electronic countermeasures, or ECMs, plus some high-speed evasive maneuvers to throw off the fighters, the B-47 reached "friendly territory." Climbing to a cruising altitude of 39,000 feet, the bomber turned for home.

Up to this point, the mission had gone according to plan, and for the first time in hours, the crew relaxed. Except for Captain Jack Worcek. Despite the cold, sweat trickled down Worcek's face. His frame of mind was not improved by a raging case of hemorrhoids, or that he'd been a last-minute substitute for the regular radar navigator of the three-man crew. The B-47 was the first supersonic swept-wing bomber with a well-founded reputation for being a difficult-to-handle erratic boneshaker even under good conditions. The airplane now reminded Worcek, who was raised on a Texas ranch, of a bucking bronco.

The burning and itching were so bad that his knuckles were white as he gripped the metal tubing of the navigator's seat. *Goddamnit! I gotta see a doc when we land.*

In the tight constraints of the crew compartment, Worcek tried to lean forward in an attempt to get some relief. As he did, he saw a gray shape.

A jarring impact, a fiery flash, and a sound that resembled an airplane exploding immediately followed. It was over in less than a second. The searing pain in Worcek's back was not. It was the last thing he remembered...

He was therefore unaware that the mid-air collision with the F-86L had severed the releasable fuel tank beside the B-47's #6 engine on the right wing. But rather than give the order to eject, the pilot descended to 20,000 feet. After careful consideration, to save the airplane and anyone on the ground, somewhere over the Atlantic, he jettisoned the remaining left fuel tank. And the bomb.

Worcek also wasn't aware that at 0126 on Wednesday, February 5th, the crippled B-47 landed safely at Hunter Air Force Base, near Savannah. Or that one of the ambulances among the many waiting emergency vehicles sped him away on a stretcher to a local hospital.

On regaining consciousness, twenty-four hours later, Worcek was told that his fellow crewmembers and the pilot of the F-86L had also survived. He made no comment. He didn't comment either when he was later informed he'd been awarded a Commendation Medal.

Six months after that fateful night, Worcek finally left the hospital in a wheelchair on his way to a rehabilitation center, his Air Force career all but over. He was still unable to walk, but during his time in intensive care, the nursing staff did cure his acute outbreak of hemorrhoids.

Chapter Two

Michael Correa's Office, G Street, Washington, D.C.
Wednesday, September 4, 2002

The secure phone rang.

"Still taking your daily run with Dan?" asked the familiar voice of Brigadier General Joshua Collins.

"Yes, sir."

"Good. Then meet me at Lincoln Memorial at 1300."

"I'll be there."

A clandestine meeting? Michael thought as he replaced the receiver. *Now what's so important?*

The Lincoln Memorial, Washington, D.C.

At precisely 1300 hours, Collins, the director of the Joint Special Operations Group, or JSOG, was already waiting by the steps to the memorial, trying unsuccessfully to keep cool. Wearing sunglasses and a baseball cap to cover his thinning hair, Michael guessed correctly that his former commanding officer and mentor was as uncomfortable in his civilian clothes as he looked.

"We've got a potential situation," Collins said without preamble. "But then I expect you realized that."

"Yes, sir."

Collins nodded to the man at Michael's side. "This is need to know, Whitney. You'll be briefed later." He faced Michael. "Let's walk. I'm beginning to think the eggheads are right about this global warming."

Following at a discreet distance, former Secret Service agent Dan Whitney stayed out of earshot, but the two men were never out of his sight. To the casual observer, they could have been father and son, except that Collins was three inches shorter than Michael, and his loose-fitting shirt made him look even stockier.

"What do you know about Tybee Island?" Collins asked.

"It's east of Savannah, Georgia, sir."

"Precisely." Collins went on to explain the events of February 4th, 1958. "The Air Force immediately went looking," he continued, "but they never did find the jettisoned bomb. The search was finally called off and the incident basically forgotten. Until last year. Apparently, a property developer wanted to build upscale homes on Tybee, and the thought that a nuclear device could be a stone's throw from his investment didn't sit too well. He musta pulled someone's strings, as the Air Force recently completed a second search. With all our technology, it was considered an easy mission. Wrong. The divers came up empty, because someone had beaten them to it. And recently, according to the report. We need to find who got to it first. No need to tell you, Michael, that this is top priority. If word leaks out, we could have a whole-scale panic on our hands."

"How dangerous is this bomb?"

"It isn't, without the device to arm it. Which is why the original search and recovery was abandoned. But with the collapse of the old Soviet Union, they became a veritable Kmart for anyone with money. Submarines, tanks, missiles, nuclear triggers—you name it. Scary thought, eh?"

"Very," Michael replied. "Where do I start?"

"By the time you get back to your office, a file will have been delivered. All the information we've got is there. In light of 9/11, we could be looking at another very explosive situation. Literally."

Michael shuddered and not from a sudden breeze. "Report directly to you?"

They'd reached the Roosevelt Memorial, and Collins stopped, lowering his voice. "Not anymore. You're in charge. The president's fully aware of what's going on. He asked that you personally handle it." Collins handed Michael a business card with a telephone number. "Your direct line to the White House Communications Center. Use it. But keep me briefed. And anything else you need, ask."

Michael pocketed the card. "Is my father in the loop?"

"Not yet. Although I foresee a time when CIA might be involved. For the time being, this comes solely under a JSOG mandate." Collins began to leave. Then stopped. "Find it, Michael, before some lunatic spawns Armageddon."

"What about our current investigation?"

"This takes top priority. The president agrees. You can always go back to it. Got that?"

Michael only nodded.

As soon as Collins was out of sight, Dan reached Michael's side. "Bad news?" he asked.

"The worst," Michael replied. "Let's run. I've got to think."

Instead of following his father, Francis, to the U.S. Naval Academy in Annapolis, Maryland, Michael surprised everyone who knew him by accepting an appointment to equally prestigious West Point. "I'd love to be a fly on the wall in the Correa household during the annual Army/Navy Game" and "I'll bet he did it to spite his father" were some of the comments after his graduation. But Michael didn't choose the Army to "spite" his ex-Navy pilot father. His only goal was special warfare. At six feet one and 220 pounds, Michael knew he'd face strong competition from other midshipmen at the Naval Academy vying for one of the sixteen annual billets available for SEALs. The Army offered him more opportunities. So, under the watchful eye of his father's longtime friend Joshua Collins, Michael became the eyes and ears for Washington; they called him "the mind" or "the snoop" because he could provide the final "go, no-go" on any action. He'd succeeded, almost too well, and been suitably rewarded. Already on the fast track, in an unprecedented promotion, he became a major while still only twenty-four. His annual salary was far in excess of the standard pay scale, although it would take more than a genius to unravel the paper trail to the original source. Then, when it looked as though his career was heading straight to the top, Michael uncovered a presidential plan to illegally obtain Russian oil that almost ignited World War III. Having survived a harrowing ordeal, plus several attempts on his life, he eventually told Collins, "I've had enough." But Collins had no intention of letting his best covert ops specialist actually retire. It took many months, much persuading, and a new president in the White House to get Michael to return. When he did, it was as a supposed civilian to head a specially created division attached to the Department of Justice. Michael's title was now Director of Contracts and Evaluations.

"We thought it sounded nicely ambiguous," Collins said. And to make sure Michael retained an official military status, he added, "You're now a lieutenant colonel in the Reserves. That means you can officially get dirty on weekends, etc. Congratulations on the promotion."

Michael's Office, G Street, Washington, D.C.
A short time later

Molly Davies looked up as Michael and Dan came through the door to the suite of offices.

"This came for you, sir," she said, holding up a plain oversized envelope with *Top Secret* clearly stamped in large letters. "No interruptions for the rest of the day?"

"Correct, Molly. Unless it's the general or my father," Michael replied.

"Or the president," she added.

Michael took the file. "Him too. Where's Brian?"

"On his way."

The door to Michael's office closed behind him.

This isn't good, Molly thought. *He never said "please" or "thank you." That's not like him.*

Once called "an old battleaxe" by Michael's ex-wife, Molly Davies had been chosen as Michael's executive assistant for a reason. Long ago, she and her late husband had been Washington, D.C. police officers, until he was fatally shot during a botched bank robbery. Back then, knowing that a woman's chance for promotion was slim to none, Molly quit the force, but the thought of ever leaving the District of Columbia never crossed her mind. Instead, she went to secretarial school, and after graduating with honors, she joined the Civil Service. It didn't take long for her to be promoted to an executive assistant. Administrations came and went, but Molly remained part of the political scene. She never remarried, and over the years, she got a reputation for keeping her mouth shut and her eyes and ears open. To Collins, she was the ideal candidate—totally trustworthy and mature enough not to distract Michael, whose reputation as a ladies' man was well founded, until he'd met Kathryn Sullivan.

Even so, I'm still not taking any chances, Collins thought at the time. Having worked for members of both political parties on the Hill, Molly was nearing retirement when she accepted the transfer. But after only a few months with her new boss, all thoughts of soon moving to Florida and playing golf every day vanished.

Molly quickly proved to Michael that she was indispensable, and he now considered her an integral part of his team. Dan Whitney, the Secret Service agent assigned to Michael, had also been Collins' choice.

At first, Michael vehemently objected. "I don't need a babysitter."

"I know," Collins replied. "Whitney's a rising star. He turned down a promotion to be with you. The guy's good. And loyal too. I thought, after you get to know each other, he might prove very useful."

"Really?"

"Trust me on this, Michael. You have to look official, even if you're not."

As Collins predicted, Dan proved to be very useful, and a mutual respect turned into friendship.

Brian Mullen had been Michael's choice for his team. A homicide detective from Dallas, Texas, he'd made national headlines during a high-profile murder trial. When the trial ended, Brian welcomed the offer for a change of scene with a big fat paycheck.

"I'm a forty-seven-year-old cop, with twenty-four years on the job, hon," Brian told his longtime live-in girlfriend, Pauline. "When do you think I'm goin' to get another chance like this?"

Their move to Washington, D.C., was accomplished in record time, and since his first day with Michael, Brian had yet to regret his decision.

Brian now knocked on Michael's office door, and without waiting for a response, he lumbered inside.

"Molly said to come straight in," he said, taking the chair next to Dan. "Guess we've got another crisis?"

"That's one way of putting it," Michael replied. "What I'm about to say gets top priority. Everything else gets put on the back burner." He then repeated his recent conversation with Collins.

"The general got any idea of a possible target?" Brian asked when Michael finished.

"No. It wasn't discussed."

"You reckon it was al Qaeda?"

"They're top of my list."

"And mine," Dan added.

"Read the file," Michael continued, handing them each a copy. "Then we'll talk."

When Brian finished reading, he looked up. "Where's Tybee Island?"

"Just east of Savannah, Georgia," Michael said.

"That's not good," Brian continued. "Didn't we see a report in April about some secret summit meetin' in Lebanon, and how container ports were bein' used as a possible entry point for more terrorists? We could be dealin' with another twenty-five members of Hezbollah, the Islamic Jihad, or even Hamas, if our intel's correct."

"Which is why I need you on Tybee. ASAP."

Brian snorted. "Like I've said before, it's a good thing I don't own a dog with all this travelin' I do."

"I said you wouldn't be bored."

"You got that right too." Brian got to his feet. "What cover?"

"Your choice. I've got the utmost faith in you."

With his hand on the doorknob, Brian looked back. "Guaranteed, it won't be as a suntanned tourist. Not in September. Typical Air Force, droppin' it in the Atlantic."

"Spoken like a true Marine," Michael commented as the door closed. And he wasn't about to tell Brian that he was wrong about the weather or remind him that the crew of the B-47 had been deservedly decorated for landing the crippled plane.

Instead, he faced Dan. "Time to get Molly involved. Agreed?"

"Agreed. She's going to have to know sooner or later. Better sooner."

Having just been fully briefed, Molly closed her eyes. "The Pentagon, the World Trade Center, and Flight 93 in Pennsylvania, and now this," she muttered. She faced Michael. "How long's this going on, sir? When we're all dead and the United States is just a memory?"

"That's the terrorists' goal. Our mission's to stop them. And we are going to stop them. You can quote me on that."

Molly blew her nose. "Please forgive my un-professionalism."

"Don't apologize. When you're ready, we've got work to do."

She sat more upright. "I'm ready, sir."

Brian crossed the spacious reception area that doubled as Molly's office and entered a small room he shared with Dan. The dark cherry furniture was immaculate, and the desktop was clear of any clutter. There were a few scenic pictures on the walls, but for the most part, the office looked unused. Brian turned on the TV to Fox News, now a habit at Michael's insistence, and opened the doors to a large wall unit that housed a computer docking station, scanner, and printer. Brian had disliked computers, but with all the access codes at Michael's disposal to secure and classified sites, it took much of the legwork out of the investigative process. These days, Brian rarely went anywhere without his laptop.

Almost an hour later, he was back in Michael's office.

Michael looked up. "You haven't left yet?" He paused. "You won the lottery?"

Brian waved some papers. "Close. I did some surfin'. Tybee Island seems to have its fair share of domestics and DUIs, but there hasn't bin a homicide since '94. Until this year. I highlighted the date."

"Do we know who?"

Brian handed Michael the sheets of paper. "Sometimes the media have their uses."

The homicide had made the front page of the *Savannah Morning News*, dated July 10, 2002. It read:

> TYBEE ISLAND: The body of a white male believed to be in his twenties was found early yesterday by a member of the Maritime Rescue Squad, in the vicinity of Lazaretto Creek Marina on Old US Highway 80. It is not yet known whether the man was a local resident or a tourist. The Tybee Island Police Department are releasing very few details, until the victim's next of kin can be notified. However, they did say that they are treating the death as suspicious. The last known homicide on the local island, popular with vacationers, was in 1994, when ...

Michael stopped reading and turned to the second page, dated the following day.

> TYBEE ISLAND: The body of a man found in the early hours of Tuesday morning has now been positively identified as twenty-four-year-old Peter Gibson, formerly of Newport, Rhode Island. Gibson began working last December as a captain for local charter boat owner Chuck Maizer. All Maizer would say was that Gibson was a good employee, well liked and to the best of his knowledge had no known enemies. Ed Sims, who found the body, has been a member of the Maritime Rescue Squad for the last eighteen months, but he refused to comment as to what he and several other members of the squad were doing in the area at the time.
>
> Although police admit the crime was particularly gruesome, they are not releasing any details. However, they are appealing to members of the public who were at Cafe Loco or in the area of Lazaretto Creek Marina on the night of Tuesday, July 9, 2002, to come forward. "We've got no suspects at this time," a police spokesman said. According to the same spokesman, after the medical examiner has completed the autopsy, the body will be released to relatives for burial. Funeral arrangements are not yet known. So far,

all attempts to contact Gibson's relatives in Rhode Island have been unsuccessful.

If you have any information, please call the Tybee Island Police Department at 786 ...

Michael was about to turn to page three.

"Don't bother," Brian said. "They got nothin' more."

"Good work. Thanks, Brian."

"Don't thank me yet," he added, as Michael's office door closed behind him.

Michael looked again at the date. *A dead boat captain so soon before the Air Force resumed their search. Coincidence? No way.*

Getting a flight was still easy, as long as you arrived at the airport two hours ahead of departure. Brian was late, but used the remaining downtime to read again his copy of the file and develop a plan of action.

With no direct flights available to Savannah from Reagan National, the half-full US Airways nonstop flight left on schedule for Charleston, South Carolina, at 7:35 p.m. With only a carry-on bag, Brian was behind the wheel of his full-size rental car and heading south before 10:00 p.m.

Ocean Plaza Beach Resort, 15th Street & Oceanfront, Tybee Island, Georgia

It was almost midnight when he checked in at the hotel at the south end of the island. With no time to get a fake identity, Brian used his real name—only this Brian Mullen was a recently retired Texan oil executive and prospective buyer of a new luxury beachfront home. *That'll explain my accent and the boots if anyone asks.*

In his room, Brian made good use of the minibar. Then ignoring the NO SMOKING signs, he lit a small cigar, a habit he'd acquired from Michael, and stretched out on the king-size bed.

Sleep was the farthest thing from his mind, and it was well after 2:00 a.m. when Brian finally turned off the light.

Ocean Plaza Beach Resort, 15th Street & Oceanfront, Tybee Island, Georgia
Thursday, September 5, 2002

Brian awoke before the alarm, and hitting the remote for the TV, he rolled out of bed. *Good Morning America* was in its first half-hour when he opened the drapes.

That's one helluva view, he thought as a gray Atlantic rolled as far as the eye could see. The only thing separating him from the ocean was a parking lot with more cars than he expected, small sand dunes, and a beach. An overcast sky merged with the expanse of water, making it difficult to pinpoint the horizon, but beyond the small pier, he thought he could make out an island. Reluctantly, he turned away and began to dress.

Tybee Island Police Department, Van Horn Street, Tybee Island, Georgia

At the north end of the island, Brian sat before Police Chief Sam Jenkins, grateful for the hotel's large breakfast and travel mug of strong hot coffee. He already knew that the island's police department was small, and he suspected that they'd be suspicious. He was right. Jenkins was somewhat guarded when Brian had introduced himself and asked to see their report on the July 9th homicide.

Sam Jenkins sat in an ordinary office chair, behind an equally ordinary desk, ignoring Brian as he studied the business card. Without being invited, Brian took the only other chair in the small unpretentious office. *A workin' cop. My type,* Brian thought. *Don't play hardball. Yet.*

"You understand why I'm checking," Jenkins said, reaching for his telephone.

Brian forced a smile. "Sure do. Go right ahead. If Michael Correa isn't available, I'll give you another number." He took a sip of coffee. "Guess you know the name. His father's director of the CIA."

Brian gave Jenkins a lot of credit when he didn't react, and the one-sided conversation was brief.

Jenkins replaced the receiver. "Okay, Mr. Mullen, you'll get a copy of the report. Although I'm curious why the Justice Department's interested in a local homicide."

Time to trade. Silently, Brian opened his briefcase and handed Jenkins some photographs. He was now grateful that before he'd left D.C., he'd made copies of known or suspected terrorists, plus an identikit version of what they could look like if they'd changed their appearance.

"We think that one of those individuals, or an accomplice, is your killer. When they found what they were lookin' for, they had a witness. He had to be eliminated."

Jenkins studied the faces and pointed to several. "I've seen these. Who hasn't? You're suggesting terrorists on Tybee? What were they looking for?"

Brian remained silent.

Jenkins sat back. "Shit! Not the Tybee bomb. again? The Air Force was only here last month."

"We know."

Jenkins gave Brian a very direct look. "They didn't find it?"

"Sorry, Chief, I'm not at liberty to say."

Jenkins closed his eyes. "Fuck," he muttered.

"That was our reaction," Brian said.

Outside the two small gray-painted buildings, one of which doubled as the Tybee Island courthouse and jail, Brian climbed into the white Ford Crown Victoria.

"The chief said to give you full cooperation," Detective Rick Rollins said.

Brian was already thumbing through the police report as the cruiser left the department. "Thanks. How far's the crime scene?"

"Less than ten minutes," Rollins replied. "It's a small island."

The signs to the side road leading to Lazaretto Creek Marina advertised Dolphin Cruises and the Cafe Loco.

Brian's first thought as he stepped from the cruiser in a sandy area that doubled as a parking lot was that the entire complex looked like a no-frills workplace.

"Popular with tourists?" Brian asked.

"And the locals," Rollins replied. "Cafe Loco's worth a visit." He then turned to what appeared to be a derelict building with badly peeling cream paint and old sheets of plywood nailed across the windows. "That's where the victim was found."

In an area of scrub and undergrowth to the right of the building, Brian saw a large abandoned propane tank.

Rollins pointed to the far side of the rusty old tank. "There."

As Brian expected, there was nothing left to see. The police tape had long gone, and summer showers had washed any remaining blood into the sandy soil. And according to the report, there'd been a lot of blood. The victim's throat had been slashed so viciously that it had almost severed his head.

Brian looked up at the rickety screen porch that ran almost the length of the building. "Tell me again who found him."

"Ed Sims." According to Detective Rollins, the local Maritime Rescue Squad used the building to meet on the second Tuesday of every month. No one, including the twenty or so guys from the squad, knew why, except it was an excuse to get drunk. At twenty-five, Sims was one of the youngest in the group, and having had his fill of Red Dog, he'd stumbled into the dark. He was about to throw up when he tripped over the victim.

"He lost more than the beer," Rollins added.

Brian didn't doubt it.

"It was obvious the individual was deceased," Rollins continued. "But they dialed 911. The call goes to Chatham County and then routed to our dispatcher. That's when the patrol officer responded. I followed a short time later."

Brian checked the report. The response time from the original call had been less than seven minutes. *Impressive.*

Rollins glanced at his watch as the sun began to break through the clouds. "If you want to see Chuck, we'd better get going. He's probably got a cruise this morning."

Brian was surprised. "I thought the summer season was officially over?"

"With our weather, the tourists are always here."

That would explain the hotel parkin' lot, Brian thought.

All they found at Chuck Maizer's office was a motley collection of friendly dogs, an assortment of fat cats, and a large parrot in a cage.

"All strays. Left mostly by tourists," Rollins explained, tickling a large mixed-breed dog of unknown age behind its ear. "Chuck's got a real soft side. He's probably at the boat. It's this way."

Rollins gave Brian some background on Chuck Maizer as they passed Cafe Loco by way of a long boardwalk leading to the dock.

An island native, Maizer had enlisted in the Navy at seventeen. After ten years of active duty, he'd returned to Tybee, married a local girl, and beginning with his father's single fishing boat, he'd built a successful charter business, catering to tourists and locals alike.

"Chuck's a fixture around here," Rollins added. "Nice guy."

At the dock, a bright yellow boat with a canopy and the words *Dolphin III* painted in black on the hull was empty. But on the sundeck of a good-looking sportfisherman moored farther away, a man was bending over.

He straightened as Brian and Rollins approached.

With the introductions over, Chuck Maizer, a small wiry man in his late sixties, Brian guessed, studied Brian's card.

"So the bigwigs in Washington thought we could use some help," he said.

"Chief said 'full cooperation,' Chuck," Rollins replied.

"If it's okay with Sam, it's okay with me. Whatta you need, Mr. Mullen?"

"It's Brian. And everythin' you can tell me."

From a face of permanently suntanned skin, Maizer had a very white smile. "That's no D.C. accent."

"Texas," Brian replied. "Former Marine. Dallas cop for twenty-four years, thirteen as a homicide detective."

Maizer pocketed the business card. "I've got a charter at one, Brian. You've got 'til then. Otherwise, you might wanna come back."

He went over the whole scenario again, but there was nothing he could add to the report he'd given the police. Peter Gibson had personally arranged everything, and Maizer never saw the person who chartered the sportfisherman. He did know it was a man and that he'd paid a sizable cash deposit. The boat left very early on the morning of Thursday, July 4th, and was gone four days. On the morning of the fifth day, the boat was back at the dock, but there was no sign of Gibson or the charter. "I guessed I'd read him wrong," Maizer continued, "and that Pete had taken off with the rest of the money. That was until Ed found him. Not the kinda thing that happens around here. Real shame."

"When did you hire Gibson?"

Maizer sat on the gunwale. "He showed up last November. Told me he'd spent the last two years doing boat deliveries up and down the East Coast. He'd just delivered a boat from the Caribbean to a marina in Savannah and wanted to know if I had any work. Said he didn't want to spend another winter up north. He'd gotten a captain's license, and all the references he gave me checked out. So I hired him for a month to see how he'd do. He seemed honest, reliable, and the customers liked him. At the beginning of December, I hired him full time. When he wasn't out on charters, he worked on the boats. Hell, he even spent Christmas Day with me and the missus."

The sound of voices made Maizer stop. "That's my one o'clock," he added.

"Thanks for your time," Brian said as a small group of tourists came toward them. "If you think of anythin', however insignificant, let me know?"

Back at the police department, Brian shook Rollins's hand. "I appreciate your help," he said.

Rollins returned the firm grip. "Sorry you had a wasted journey."

Brian only shrugged before getting into his rental car and driving away.

Lazaretto Creek Marina, Old US Highway 80, Tybee Island, Georgia
A short time later

Brian drove back to the marina, and leaving the car at the sandy area in front of the ships store, he wandered along the boardwalk toward the dock. The yellow-hulled dolphin cruise boat was gone, but coming toward him was a small figure carrying a fishing pole. The boy had a pronounced swagger to his loping gait, and Brian couldn't help wondering how such an extraordinarily long neck could carry the very round head. His first thought was *ET?*

The boy stopped, scrutinizing Brian with dark eyes that mirrored a wisdom far beyond their years. "You're the dude from D.C.," he said, not moving.

"That's right." Brian held out his hand. "Brian Mullen."

The boy took Brian's paw. "Otis Johnson."

"Nice to meet you, Otis. Bin fishin'?"

Otis stared into the small pail. "Maybe. Guess you're doing your own fishing."

Brian chuckled. "Sure am."

"Not having any luck, are you?" Otis added.

"You got that right. But then you look like a real smart fella."

Shit! Flattery ain't goin' to work with this kid, Brian thought as Otis gave him a very direct look, the whites of his eyes in stark contrast to skin that reminded Brian of full-bodied Colombian coffee beans.

"Maybe I am," Otis replied. He shifted his feet. "So, Mr. Brian, how much is what I know worth?"

"How's about I buy you an ice cream?"

Otis snorted. "I ain't stupid, Mr. Brian. Show me your money, and then maybe we'll trade."

"If you know somethin', why not tell the local cops? You musta known they needed help."

Otis's expression was all Brian needed as a reply. It then crossed his mind to give him a lecture on withholding information, but he thought better of it.

"I'm a kid," Otis said. "Never knew my old man. The old lady's doing ten years for slingin' dope again. My sister's the local ho." He stopped. "So the cops ain't gonna pay me."

"And you think I am?" Brian turned to go.

"I saw five of them," Otis added hurriedly. "A-rabs, or something like."

Brian turned back. "Go on."

"My money?"

"Maybe. Dependin' on what you tell me."

When Brian left the marina more than an hour later, Otis was full of ice cream and twenty dollars richer, and there was a very good chance he'd be taking a VIP trip to Washington, D.C. Sitting on the steps to the dilapidated building where Peter Gibson's body was found, Otis slowly devoured the ice-cream cone with a remarkably pink tongue, unable to take his eyes off the twenty-dollar bill in Brian's hand.

"I'm listenin', anytime you're ready," Brian said.

Otis licked the last drop of ice cream from none-too-clean fingers. "It was real early in the morning ..." he began.

According to the story that unfolded, interspersed with two more ice-cream cones, Otis's sister was "entertaining" one of her many "boyfriends" on the night of Sunday, July 7th. It was a habit, Brian learned, that if the noise in the trailer got too loud, Otis would slip away into the night. As he spent all his free time at the marina, it was the obvious place to go. He'd seen the sportfisherman return to the dock and tie up. Five men, including Gibson, had gotten off and met with another man who'd driven a large dark pickup into the parking area only minutes before. "They musta had cell phones," Otis said. "The timing was too good."

Got that right, kid, Brian thought.

Otis had the sense to hide, and from his vantage point, it sounded to Brian as though he saw almost everything. All six men then carried what looked like diving tanks off the boat to the pickup.

"They was running their mouths in some strange language, when one of them said, 'Speak English.' He sounded real pissed."

They'd all returned to the boat and carried off more gear. Otis didn't know what. They went back for a third time for bags that looked like luggage. After throwing them into the pickup, they covered everything with a tarp.

The one who seemed to be in charge then handed something to Gibson. As he did, one of the others hit Gibson over the head. They caught him before he fell, and two of them dragged him out of sight to the side of the dilapidated building. A short time later, they came back without him. The five remaining men then returned to the boat for a fourth time.

"It seemed like they was there forever," Otis added. "I didn't dare move, so I don't know what they was doing."

I do, Brian thought. *Wipin' the boat clean, seeing as no identifiable fingerprints were ever found.*

Finally, returning empty-handed to the pickup, four of them drove away.

"I thought you said there were five of them, includin' the driver of the pickup?" Brian said.

"There were. I guess one of 'em stayed with their boat."

"I'm confused. Their boat?"

"Yeah, their boat. The one from the trailer."

"What trailer?"

Otis sighed. "The boat trailer the pickup was towing."

"The trailer was empty?"

"It was when they left. The boat ramp's the other side of the bridge."

After much questioning and waving the twenty-dollar bill, Otis finally admitted that he'd seen what looked like the same pickup truck with a trailer launch a boat from the public ramp earlier in the day.

Brian then discovered that after the pickup left, Otis went to find Gibson. At this point, Otis became the kid that he was, and he began to shake as he turned his back on Brian to wipe away tears.

"I've never seen anyone dead," he said quietly. "And I don't want to anymore. There was blood all over. It was real bad. Pete was my friend."

Otis couldn't tell Brian what color the pickup was, except it was dark and a dually, and he was too far away to get a license plate.

"You shoulda told the police, son," Brian said when Otis finally finished.

"Think they'd believe me? No way." The arrogance was back. "So what you gonna do? I'm too young for jail, and I've already bin in juvy. Piece of cake. Food's not bad either."

Brian ignored him. "How old are you?"

Otis straightened. "Almost thirteen."

Having cross-examined Otis for another thirty minutes, Brian concluded that he was either the best liar Brian had ever encountered or he was telling the truth. Brian was inclined to believe the latter, although the thought that five possible terrorists could be on the loose sent shivers down his spine. When asked again what Otis thought the leader of the group had handed Gibson, Otis replied, "A wad of money." When Gibson fell, some of the bills had fallen from his hand, but the leader quickly scooped them up and stuffed them in his pocket.

Brian handed Otis the photographs he'd shown Chief Jenkins. "Any of these look familiar?"

Otis studied the faces for some time, then pointed. "That one. Sorta."

"Sorta?"

"The leader didn't have no beard."

Brian waited until he'd reached the public boat ramp across from Lazaretto Creek Marina before calling Michael.

Michael listened without interrupting until Brian finished.

"Why does the kid think these guys were like Arabs?" Michael asked.

"Says he watches TV. He's seen all the news shows, and his teacher at school gave them a lesson on the Muslim religion. The kid's no dummy. He's a real smartass, and he's either a real pro, or he's tellin' the truth."

"At least he'd got the sense to hide."

"That's what I thought. Otherwise, the homicide rate for Tybee Island would have doubled for this year."

"He really ID'd Hamza Jarrah?"

"Sorta. He wasn't sure."

"He thinks there were five of them?"

"He was pretty sure. One who drove the pickup, one who left in the boat they launched, and three who went out with Gibson."

"Get the kid up here?" Michael asked.

"I'm goin' back to see Rollins in the mornin'. I've got some more questions. And I'll get some background on the family. Let me decide then?"

"Fine. Right now, any lead, however small, is worth pursuing."

"If they came in through Savannah, maybe it's worth checkin' rental companies for large dark dually pickups with boat trailers?"

"Dan'll start when we hang up," Michael said. "But my gut says he won't find anything."

"But I might. There's a Coast Guard station here."

"Call me later."

Coast Guard Station Tybee
A short time later

Regardless of flashing his ID, Brian was told by the petty officer in charge for the day that he'd have to get authorization from Sector Charleston before giving out any information.

Thinking he'd have to come back in the morning, Brian was surprised when all it took was a couple of phone calls.

"Anythin' unusual about July 7th?" Brian asked the petty officer after the last call was made.

After checking the log, the petty officer pointed. "This I remember. There was an anonymous tip about a bomb on board a ship in the Savannah River. Everyone was involved. We responded, along with the Savannah police, the Chatham County police, the Department of Natural Resources, the ATF,[1] and Coast Guard Investigations. Tied us up for hours."

"Did you find a bomb?"

"No."

That figures.

"But these days, you can't be too careful," the petty officer added.

Brian thanked him for his time and left.

Sounds as if these guys are not only organized but smart too, Brian thought as he drove back to the hotel. *That's real bad news.*

Ocean Plaza Beach Resort, 15th Street & Oceanfront, Tybee Island, Georgia
Late afternoon

In his hotel room, Brian stretched out on the bed and began to re-read the files in his briefcase. When he reached the section on the 1958 jettisoned bomb, he stopped.

It weighed 7,600 pounds. How the hell are you goin' to retrieve somethin' that size? he thought. *Not with a coupla divers, that's for sure. And without attractin' attention?*

Two hours later, Brian left the hotel, still deep in thought.

Skipper's, Butler Avenue, Tybee Island, Georgia

After a short walk, Brian was now seated on a stool in the local bar/restaurant, having just finished a large Black Angus steak. He ordered a second beer and took a good look around. It was obvious from the dark wood interior, the several TVs tuned to ESPN and the Weather Channel, and the general conversations going on around him that this was a locals' hangout. And from what Brian could tell, the natives seemed friendly.

---

[1]   Bureau of Alcohol, Tobacco, Firearms and Explosives.

"Guess you liked the steak?" said the man seated next to him as the barmaid removed Brian's empty plate.

"Sure did," Brian replied. "Hit the mark."

"Next time, try the seafood. They've got good seafood. Visitor, are you?"

"Hopin' to buy a place here," Brian lied, holding out his hand. "Brian Mullen."

His handshake was returned with a crushing grip. "D.J. Perkins. Tybee's a real special place. You'll like it here."

"Already do." Brian waved at the barmaid. "Another round for D.J."

"Coming right up," she replied.

Much later, and well over the legal limit, both men stood on the sidewalk.

"You drivin'?" Brian asked.

D.J. shook his head. "Live a coupla blocks from here. Nice meeting you, Brian. See you around."

"Hope so," Brian replied.

On his way back to the hotel, Brian was grinning. *Sometimes, all you need is a little luck.*

Ocean Plaza Beach Resort, 15th Street & Oceanfront, Tybee Island, Georgia

Although it was late, Brian called Michael.

"I know how they did it," Brian said.

"How who did what?" was the sleepy reply.

"How the bad guys got the bomb."

Michael was suddenly wide-awake. "How?"

"I met this guy D.J. in a local bar," Brian began. "Turns out, he's a shrimp boat captain. Bin fishin' the waters here for thirty years ..."

Brian had artfully steered his conversation with D.J. Perkins, laced with a never-ending supply of beer, onto the subject of the Tybee Island bomb.

D.J. chuckled. "Savannah's got that book, *Midnight* something. We've got the bomb."

"You get much interest?"

"It comes and goes. We've got a few local activist types who get a bee in their bonnet from time to time. Try to whip folks into a frenzy. Most of us take no notice. There's this guy in Statesboro, 'bout an hour from here, he's retired military, who keeps showing up, trying to find it. He should ask me."

"You know where it is?"

D.J. took a long swig of his beer. "In Wassau Sound. It's no big secret. Most of us who fish these waters commercially will tell you that."

"So if I was a bad guy, how would I get it without attractin' attention?"

"Use a shrimp boat. They've got all the hauling capacity you'd ever need, depending on the time of year."

Brian remained casual. "July?"

At that point, D.J. told him that July was in the middle of the brown shrimp season. "See shrimp boats out all the time. Closer to shore too."

"In the daytime?"

"Sure. Depending on the tides." D.J. gesticulated at the barmaid. "Got a tide chart under the counter?" he asked.

Moments later, he was holding a small booklet. "Pick a date."

"July seventh," Brian said.

D.J. pointed at a page. "High tide was at 7:16 p.m.; 8.64 feet. That's exactly what you'd need. And still plenty of daylight."

According to D.J., once the bomb was aboard the shrimp boat, it would be easy to transfer to a much smaller boat. When Brian asked about the weight, D.J. replied, "I'd use additional air-filled pontoons. That would solve the weight problem, if you weren't going far."

"Anyone you know who'd do that?" Brian asked.

"Not personally. But if the price was right, there's a couple I could maybe name."

"Then let's drink to us good guys," Brian said, holding up his beer.

"Amen to that," D.J. replied and took a large gulp.

"Did you get names?" Michael asked now.

"Didn't want to blow my cover. I know where to find him, if we need him. I had to satisfy my curiosity."

"So now that your curiosity's been satisfied, are you going to sleep any better?" Michael asked.

"Doubtful."

"Know the feeling. So if that's how they did it, where did they take it?"

"A 7,600-pound nuclear device hidden inside a boat on a trailer. It could be anywhere."

"That's what scares me," Michael replied.

Tybee Island, Georgia
Friday, September 6, 2002

Leisha Johnson opened the door to the trailer. Tall and slim to the point of scrawny, she wasn't at all what Brian expected. He was the first to admit that he was no fashion expert, but Leisha's several elaborate chains and long Indian-style turquoise earrings didn't seem appropriate with her fake camouflage capri pants and matching tee shirt.

Brian half expected her to be chewing gum as she casually leaned against the doorframe, looking down. "So you're the white dude from D.C."

Brian offered his hand. "I am. Brian Mullen, Ms. Johnson."

Her dark, almond-shaped eyes never left his as she returned his handshake. Her long slender hand, with green-frosted nails, reminded him of talons.

"What can I do for you, Mr. Mullen?" Her question was loaded with innuendo.

Brian played it straight. "I'd like your permission to take Otis back to Washington with me, ma'am. I think he can help with our investigation."

His politeness helped. But it was the cash incentive he was finally forced to offer Leisha, and not his negotiating technique, that eventually persuaded her to let Otis go.

At the Charleston airport terminal, Brian kept telling himself that Otis was only a kid, and a poorly educated one at that. He'd been initially concerned about taking Otis out of school, but according to Detective Rollins, when Otis wasn't on suspension, he was AWOL.

"I reckon he's after an entry in the *Guinness Book of World Records* for the least number of school days ever attended," Rollins said.

Brian wasn't sure whether it was Otis or Leisha who had chosen Otis's traveling outfit, but the sight of him dressed in denim shorts with the crotch at his knees, an over-shirt many sizes too large, and badly worn sneakers made Brian cringe. Otis now seemed in total awe of his surroundings, and temporarily, to Brian's relief, his constant questions had stopped.

"He ain't bin farther than Savannah, Mr. Brian," Leisha said. "You make damn sure nothin' happens to him."

Washington, D.C.
Early afternoon

By the time Brian reached the parking lot at Reagan National, it was almost 2:30 p.m.

Before he drove away, he called the office.

"Michael's not here," Molly told him. "He asked if you would keep the boy with you and bring him in tomorrow morning."

Brian wanted to make a scathing comment about babysitting, but with Otis in the car, he didn't.

With Otis's approval, Brian had gone through the contents of the small shopping bag that he carried. All Otis had with him was a toothbrush, a half-used tube of toothpaste, and one pair of underwear and socks.

"Change of plan," Brian said, putting the car in gear. "We're goin' shoppin'."

By the time they left the Fashion Center at Pentagon City, Otis was dressed in jeans, a brightly striped golf shirt, and new sneakers. The bags that Brian carried also contained more clothes and underwear. Brian had insisted on the sweatshirt.

"This ain't Tybee," he said. "It gets cool here at night. Trust me. You'll need it."

With more time to kill before Pauline got home, Brian decided on a short trolleybus tour. Otis didn't object.

After driving over the bridge into D.C., Brian left the car in the office parking lot and walked to the trolleybus stop. The afternoon rush was in full swing, and Otis seemed strangely silent. He stayed that way on the tour, and the only comment he made was when they caught a brief glimpse of the White House.

"It's small, ain't it?" he whispered.

"It's small, isn't it," Brian corrected.

Otis looked up. "You say 'ain't.'"

Brian couldn't argue and decided he'd better watch his language in the future. Otis's temporary silence didn't mean his brain had stopped working.

Brian and Pauline's apartment, Massachusetts Avenue, Washington, D.C.
Later that night

Otis ate with an appetite that made Brian and Pauline wonder when he'd last had a decent meal. Although his table manners left a lot to be desired.

"That were real good, Miss Pauline," Otis said at the end of dinner. Then, sitting back, he rubbed his small bulging stomach and belched loudly.

Brian was about to reprimand him, but Pauline quickly shook her head. "Why don't you both go watch some TV? I'll make coffee and do the dishes."

In the family room, Brian pressed the TV remote. "What do you like to watch?"

Otis shrugged. "Dunno. My sister's boyfriends show up at all times, and I get kicked out or have to go to bed."

After Pauline placed a mug of coffee next to Brian's chair, he lit a cigar.

"Can I have one?" Otis asked.

"Sure," Brian said, handing him the cigar and ignoring Pauline's look.

Otis took a deep puff. His violent coughing was instantaneous, and his eyes rolled, convincing Brian that if Otis's skin hadn't been so dark, he would have turned green.

Silently, Brian took back the cigar. "Maybe when you're older?"

Otis could only nod in agreement.

At 10:00 p.m., Pauline took him to the spare bedroom.

"Sleep well," she said. "And don't forget to wash your face and hands, and clean your teeth. If you need anything in the night, please knock on our door."

Otis hesitated. "You got your own room?"

She pointed. "Just down the hall."

"You make a lot of noise when you fuck?"

Pauline was caught off-guard. She recovered quickly. "Not that you'd hear."

Otis turned away. "Then I'll sleep okay."

"Good night, Otis."

"Good night, Miss Pauline."

Michael's Office, G Street, Washington, D.C.
Saturday, September 7, 2002

On a Saturday, Pennsylvania Avenue was much quieter than on a workday, except for the tourists.

At 9:00 a.m., Brian and Otis entered the suite of offices, surprised to find Molly there.

"Michael said to go straight in," she said after meeting Otis. "I'll bring coffee, and I've also got soda and cookies."

Michael held out his hand. "Nice to meet you, Otis. I'm Michael Correa."

Otis returned the handshake. "You're the boss man?"

Michael laughed. "You could say that."

"So how come you're younger than Mr. Brian?"

"What did I tell you about good manners?" Brian said, before Michael could reply.

"Sorry," Otis mumbled.

"Are you ready to look at some photographs, Otis?" Michael asked.

"Sure. Ain't ... isn't that why I's here?"

Sitting on the overstuffed leather Chesterfield, a soda and cookies within arm's reach, Otis studied page after page of the faces of known or suspected terrorists. To make sure Otis wasn't going to waste their time, Brian showed him the photographs again before leaving Tybee Island.

"That's him," Otis said, pointing at Jarrah. "He was the leader."

"You're sure?" Brian asked.

"Course, I'm sure. He were the one that said, 'Speak English.'"

But to make doubly sure Otis had correctly identified Jarrah, Michael had inserted several versions of a clean-shaven identikit picture among the other faces. Otis found them all.

After forty-five minutes, he yawned.

"Had enough?" Michael asked.

Otis looked around. "I'm okay. Mr. Brian said you're an Army colonel."

"That's right."

"Where's your uniform?"

"I'm doing a civilian job right now. So I don't have to wear one."

That seemed to satisfy Otis, who got to his feet and stood in front of a large map of the United States on one wall. "Where are we?"

Michael pointed. "Here." He then showed Otis where Tybee Island was located. "Were you born there?"

Otis stared harder at the map. "A hospital in Savannah. Where was you born?"

Michael pointed to New York State. "A small town right here."

"Is your old man still around?"

"Yes. He's director of the CIA. Do you know what that is?"

"Central Intelligence Agency."

Michael and Brian were surprised.

"Do you know what the initials FBI stand for?" Michael continued.

"Federal Bureau of Investigation."

"The other member of the team is a former Secret Service agent. Do you know what they do?"

"They guard the president."

"Correct. And other things."

Otis turned away from the map and stared at the interior door. "Is the old woman outside your mother?"

Michael fought to keep a straight face. "No. Mrs. Davies is my executive assistant. She used to be a police officer."

"Like Mr. Brian?"

"Not exactly. He was a homicide detective."

Otis turned to Brian. "You've seen lots of dead people?"

"More than my share," Brian replied. "Ready to get back to work?"

Otis nodded, and sitting back on the sofa, he began to turn pages again.

Otis was drinking his second soda, and the plate of cookies was empty.

"Didn't he eat breakfast?" Michael whispered.

"He ate more than I did," Brian said quietly. "The kid's got hollow legs."

"I don't think we're going to get any more out of him."

Suddenly, Otis looked up. "This looks like one of them."

Don't speak too soon, Brian thought.

"Show me," Michael said.

Otis pointed. "He looks like the one who bashed Pete."

"I thought you were hiding?"

"I were. But him and another of them dragged Pete away. When they came back, this one lit a cigarette. I saw the scar."

Michael took the page and studied the photograph of As'ad Rashid. The ugly deep gash on his cheekbone reminded him of a lightning bolt. "Which side?"

Otis closed his eyes. "Left."

"Anything else?"

"He was the only one with a beard." Otis pointed at some other photographs. "It weren't as long as these. It were shorter."

Otis was given the afternoon off, and Brian had no alternative but to resume his babysitting duties.

At the Air and Space Museum, Otis devoured a bacon cheeseburger in the cafeteria, and afterward, Brian bought tickets to the IMAX theater.

I'm sure the kid won't have seen anythin' like this, he thought. *And unless somethin' changes, not likely to.*

They had time to kill before the movie, and Otis seemed fascinated by the airplanes hanging from the ceiling.

"How come you're so sure it was the man in the photograph you saw?" Brian asked at one point.

Otis was still looking up and didn't take his eyes off the Kitty Hawk. "I'd seen him before."

"When?"

"I dunno. A few weeks."

"He was at the marina?"

"Yeah. With Pete."

"Why didn't you tell us?"

Otis finally turned. "You didn't ask."

"I'm askin' now."

Brian found a quiet corner and flipped open his cell phone. "Otis says Jarrah was on Tybee about a month before," he told Michael. "I can't confirm, right now. I gotta go see a movie."

Chapter Three

Brian found a chair in the small office as Maizer flipped slowly through a well-worn datebook on his crowded desk. Maizer had been out on a charter until late the previous day, so after finally returning Otis to his sister, Brian spent another night at the Ocean Plaza.

Maizer now thumbed again through the pages. "You did say June?"

"The kid said a few weeks."

Maizer shook his head. "Got a vivid imagination, that boy. Pity he can't put it to good use in school."

Maizer handed Brian the book. "You look. I don't see anything relevant."

There were two columns per page. One for Maizer, the other for Gibson, and most of the entries had either the names or initials of clients.

Brian studied one page twice, before pointing at the entry. "What's that?"

Maizer took the book. "Pete had a two-man/three-day dive charter."

"How did they pay?"

"Cash."

"You get a lot of cash charters?"

Maizer didn't reply.

"I'm not the IRS," Brian added. "I don't care if you keep two sets of books. But I gotta know if this is what I'm lookin' for."

Maizer hesitated before reaching into a lower desk drawer. "What's the date again?"

"June 11th to June 13th."

29

"June 11th? That's when my latest grandson was born. Me and the missus was at the hospital most of the day."

"So you never saw the charter?"

"No."

Goddamnit! But to make doubly sure, Brian handed Maizer an identikit photograph of Jarrah's clean-shaven face that Otis identified more than once. "This man?"

Maizer shook his head. "Can't help you, Mr. Mullen. I would if I could."

Brian believed him, and in his mind, he'd reached a dead end.

He voiced that opinion to Michael on his way back to the airport in Charleston, South Carolina.

"Not necessarily," Michael said. "If they were diving to locate the bomb, they had to be trained."

"Gibson was a certified diver."

"I know. But it's a big bomb. More than a one-man job."

"Point taken."

Michael's Office, G Street, Washington, D.C.
Later that afternoon

By 3:00 p.m., Brian was back at his desk.

"Where do you want me to start?" he'd asked Michael a few minutes earlier.

"Help Dan out by calling rental car companies in Savannah. Maybe we'll get lucky."

"It's goin' to take time to go through all this rental info when the paperwork arrives," Brian said, hanging up from the last call on Dan's list. "I didn't know so many companies rented pickups. But no dually. If necessary, tomorrow we widen the net," he added, picking up his overnight bag. "I'm goin' home."

"Otis coulda been mistaken," Dan said.

"I don't think so."

"He get back okay?"

Brian stopped in the doorway. "Yeah. Great kid, when you get to know him."

Brian & Pauline's Apartment, Massachusetts Avenue, Washington, D.C.
That night

"I want to make an honest woman of you," Brian said suddenly.

Pauline looked up from the law book she was studying. "You already did, remember?"

Brian immediately knew she was referring to the first time they'd met.

Late one night, desperate and penniless, Pauline had approached Brian on a Dallas street and clumsily offered her favors. Although Brian took her to jail, the following afternoon, he paid her fine and then waited for her on the courthouse steps.

"Where are you goin'?" he asked.

She shook her head. "I don't know. A shelter maybe."

Good instincts told him she wasn't really a hooker, so for reasons he could never explain, he took her home.

As Brian was already divorced, the house was a pigsty, and he was suddenly ashamed. Pauline didn't seem to care.

The following morning, Brian left her at the house, rationalizing that if she robbed him, it would be no great loss.

But she didn't rob him. Over the first few weeks, Brian constantly expected to come home and find her gone. But Pauline used the money he gave her only for groceries and cleaning materials. The neighbors even began to remark that the house was looking great again as Pauline began putting her energies into tidying up the outside.

Brian didn't think she could surprise him anymore. When six months later she greeted him with the news that she'd found a job, Brian took her out for a celebration dinner. Later that night, he took her very willingly to his bed for the first time, and he was again surprised that although she wasn't a virgin, she was very inexperienced.

At the end of her first week at the hair and beauty salon, her mouse-brown hair disappeared for good, and Pauline had been blonde ever since. The salon owner, finding Pauline to be very astute and trustworthy, trained her well. When several years later the woman met a wealthy widower at the racetrack and eventually moved with him to Florida, she kept the business and made Pauline the manager.

In all the years they'd been together, Brian's only regret was that Pauline had refused point-blank to marry him. Apart from that, in Brian's eyes, he'd found his perfect mate, as long ago he'd gotten over the doubts and fears that Pauline would leave him for a man her own age.

"I didn't mean that," Brian said now. "It's bin fourteen years. With us movin' up here, I thought you might wanna finally make it legal. Seein' as you now work for a lawyer."

"You're proposing?"

"Guess I am. There's no need for a big fuss. Just Michael and Kathryn as witnesses."

Pauline closed the book. "Not a good idea."

"Us gettin' married?"

"No. Michael and Kathryn as witnesses."

"Why's that? They're practically family."

"Kathryn moved out."

From Brian's reaction, Pauline knew he had no clue. "You're kiddin'? When?"

"Two months ago. Michael didn't tell you?"

Brian shook his head.

"You spend more time together than we do," Pauline continued. "Men. How typical."

"Do you know why?"

"Yes. But I'm not sure I should tell you, if you really didn't know."

"Give me a break. This could be important. Who am I goin' to tell?"

"Molly and Dan for starters."

"Wrong. But I'll bet Tom Morgan knows."

"Not necessarily."

"C'mon, hon. Give."

Having easily passed the Washington, D.C., bar exam, Kathryn Sullivan had recently opened her own law practice when she'd first met Pauline. And although Pauline knew nothing about working for a lawyer, Kathryn's intuition told her that Pauline would still make the perfect assistant. Her intuition hadn't let her down. So much so, Pauline was now studying for her associate law degree. Even though she'd originally dropped out of high school, during her years in Dallas, Pauline finally got her high school diploma and then went on to get a degree in business administration. In the two years that Kathryn's law practice had been open, the two women had also become friends.

In an effort to study in peace, Pauline began arriving at the two-room office in downtown D.C. around 7:00 a.m. This way, she could hit the books for an hour before Kathryn typically arrived. Therefore, she'd been surprised one Monday morning in July to find Kathryn already at her desk, a mug of coffee in front of her, circling ads in the real estate section of Saturday's *Washington Post.*

"Are we moving to bigger offices?" Pauline asked.

"I'm looking for a small apartment to rent."

Pauline was astonished. She knew Michael owned a two-bedroom townhouse in the old section of Alexandria that the couple used during the week. Pauline was about to be astonished again as Kathryn reached into her briefcase for a pack of cigarettes.

"I've left Michael." She lit a cigarette, inhaling deeply. "Stupid. I quit years ago. But it now seems to be helping."

"After I get coffee, tell me what I can do."

"He's changed," Kathryn said when Pauline returned.

Although Michael never carried out his threat to resign his Army commission, he did take time off, and they'd spent the next few months cruising Chesapeake Bay on Michael's boat and settling into what Kathryn thought was a happy routine at his house on Maryland's Eastern Shore.

But according to Kathryn, he began to get more and more restless. Until Joshua Collins arrived that day to offer him his current job.

"I really thought it would help," she added, "and to a point, it did. But then he began to shut down again. This past weekend was the final straw. After Josh left to go back to his mother, I casually mentioned how nice it would be to have a family of our own someday. Michael exploded. He said he already had a son, and he didn't want any more kids, or another wife."

"Looking back, I didn't handle it well," Kathryn continued. "But although I said a lot of things in anger, he made it crystal clear that our relationship's going no further. I'm thirty-one. I want to get married and have a family. Is that so unusual?"

"No, it isn't," Pauline said. "I'm sure this'll all blow over, and he'll come to his senses in a few days."

"It's not the first time," Kathryn admitted. "But it is the last." She picked up the paper again. "Want to start calling the ads I've circled?"

Kathryn spent a week in a hotel before finding a small converted row house in Georgetown, courtesy of a client. "I was looking for a small efficiency to rent, not a house to buy," she told Pauline. "But this deal is too good to pass up. He needs the cash, and I need a roof over my head. Plus, it's a better investment than the stock market."

"Kathryn's living in Georgetown?" Brian asked now. "That can't be cheap."

"Seeing as she inherited millions when her grandmother died in '98, I don't think money's the problem," Pauline said. "The house was empty, so she moved in the following week."

"What was Michael's reaction?"

"How should I know? Kathryn says he's never called, and she certainly hasn't called him."

Brian got to his feet, and taking Pauline's hand, he then knelt in front of her. "We got sidetracked," he said. "Now, will you marry me?"

"I've always thought Mrs. Pauline Mullen sounded really good. So the answer's yes, if you're really sure?"

"I've had long enough to think about it. Course I'm sure."

Michael's Office, G Street, Washington, D.C.
Friday, September 13, 2002

Despite Brian's objection that it was a total waste of their time, he and Dan spent the remainder of the week chasing down leads of all pickup trucks from Savannah area rental car companies.

By late afternoon on this fourth day, they were no further on. With the information now in their possession, they'd first checked all the driver's license numbers with DMV. None of the faces remotely resembled Jarrah or anyone else of Middle Eastern descent.

In one case, they'd actually spoken with a thirty-two-year-old Hispanic man. But he'd rented a pickup to move furniture to a new apartment. They'd even confirmed it with his landlord, who lived in the same converted building.

"I've known Jesus for years," the landlord told them. "A quiet family man and a good worker. He's as honest as the day is long."

"It was a long shot," Dan commented, replacing the receiver.

"Like I said, if Otis said it was a dually, we're lookin' for a dually," Brian said. "How many thirteen-year-old boys do you think can't tell the difference?"

"Not many."

"I rest my case."

At 5:00 p.m., Brian and Dan were in Michael's office, giving him a report on their nonexistent findings.

"Go home," Michael said. "We'll meet on Monday at 0830. Let's take the weekend to come up with another approach. I want your ideas. Right now, chasing down rental pickups is all I can come up with. Unless they bought one?"

"It would help if we knew make and model," was Brian's reply.

Chapter Four

Michael's Office, G Street, Washington, D.C.
Monday, September 16, 2002

Michael was making notes on a flip chart when his secure line rang at 8:45 a.m.

"Get your butt to Bradenton, Florida, ASAP," Collins said. "Over the weekend, two off-duty MPs saw a suspicious Middle-Eastern-looking individual in a local bar near Bragg. Some kinda skirmish ensued. But before civilian law enforcement arrived to break it up, the MPs found a Florida address in this individual's pocket. They had the good sense to pass it on. We're about to do a joint raid with local SWAT and FBI. I want you there."

"I'll be on the first flight I can get."

"Not necessary. There's a plane waiting at Andrews. You'll fly to MacDill and pick up a car. Bradenton's roughly fifty miles south. And, Michael? Take Mullen and Whitney with you."

"Anything else I should know?"

"You'll be given a file before you board. Photographs of more suspected terrorists. If you need one, you'll get a more thorough briefing later."

Cherry Blossom Avenue, Bradenton, Florida
Late morning

"Behind you, Michael," Dan said quietly.

He turned to see a very large woman staring openly from behind the picture window of the house opposite. "Perfect. Nosy neighbors."

"Let's hope," Dan added.

Five minutes later, Renee Waterhouse was still in her living room, but now she was staring through her glasses at the photographs Michael had handed her.

"I recognize him," she said, pointing to one of the faces. "That's Philip."

Michael hid his surprise. "Philip who?"

In her sixties, her muumuu doing little to hide her sagging flesh, Renee gestured at #1037. "Philip Armond, my neighbor."

She then seemed unable to take her eyes off the scene outside. Men in clearly marked FBI and SWAT flak jackets and carrying an array of automatic weapons swarmed the street, now filled with armored troop carriers and unmarked cars, their sirens silent but lights still flashing.

Eventually, Renee turned back. "I don't understand what's going on. What's happening?"

Michael gestured at a chair. "What do you know about Philip?"

Reluctantly, Renee sat. "They seem like a nice young couple."

"Couple?"

"Yes, couple. Sabrina, his wife. Oh, and the two children. The youngest was born earlier this year. Cute little girl. They named her Susie. Her brother's adorable. John. Such a pretty child and so well behaved."

"How old is he?"

"I seem to remember Sabrina telling me he was about four when they moved in."

"How long have they lived there?"

Renee tried unsuccessfully to peer through the window again. "Gerry, my husband, and I went on a Caribbean cruise. That was two years ago June, when I retired. Philip and Sabrina moved in right before we left."

"They've been neighbors for over two years?" Michael asked. *Shit! This's worse than I thought.*

Renee's several chins wobbled. "That's right. More than two years."

"What else?"

"Like what? They're a regular couple. She drives a green minivan. Takes John to school every morning. Sometimes she'll come straight back; other times, I guess she goes shopping. Grocery and the like. Just regular folks."

"What about Philip?"

"He told me he's a pilot."

"He told you?"

Renee shifted in her chair. "Yes, he told me. We're neighbors. I don't ignore my neighbors. My Gerry said he'd have to have a good job to afford the car he drove."

"Do you know the make or model?"

"You'll have to ask Gerry. I've got no interest in cars. It's foreign, I do know that."

"Is Philip away a lot?"

"I suppose. I don't keep a diary of his movements, if that's what you're asking."

Pity, Michael and Dan thought.

Suddenly, Renee stood, making Dan wonder how someone so large could have such small feet. "Will you please tell me what's going on? This's a nice neighborhood. Nothing ever happens here." She went again to the window. "Look at all this. Men with guns. All those cars. Why are they inside the house?" She turned to Michael. "I think you owe me an explanation. Where are the Armonds?"

"I don't know, ma'am. I was hoping you might."

"Well, I don't. I last saw them on Friday, so they're probably on vacation." Renee's eyes narrowed. "Didn't you introduce yourself as Lieutenant Colonel?" She looked again at the card Michael had handed her. "Where's your uniform, if you're really in the military?"

"We don't always wear uniforms, ma'am."

It had taken longer than Michael expected, but by the time he and Dan finally left Renee Waterhouse alone, he knew a lot more about "Philip and Sabrina Armond." According to Renee, a former supervisor with the Sarasota Department of Planning and Zoning, the Armonds led a quiet life with very few visitors. "They coulda had more, but I don't spend that much time home," Renee added. "I'm enjoying being retired, but that doesn't mean I'm a couch potato. Sabrina always smiles and waves when she sees me." She paused. "It never seemed strange, but now I come to think about it, I never see her in anything but tent dresses. Mind you, she's always well dressed. It's just that I never see her in shorts or anything. I think she's a bit shy."

"Why's that?" Michael asked.

"I've never been invited over. They keep themselves to themselves."

"What about your husband?"

"He's retired too," she continued. "But he couldn't take being home every day, so he got himself a part-time job. He's there now; otherwise, he'd be here to see all this ... I've gotta call him."

"Later. Where's there?"

"The central library. He was a high-school English teacher. Still loves his books."

Out of earshot of her house, Michael stopped.

"Finally, Dan, a break. Check the airports. With the Feds finding the house empty, my guess is they've split up. I'll bet Sabrina Armond, or whatever the hell her name is, has taken the kids and literally took off. I want to know where they went and what name they used. Find the green minivan. I'll bet she's dumped it."

"And after lunch?"

Michael raised an eyebrow. "Take Brian with you."

"Thank you. Two heads, etcetera."

"Get outta here. Now. I'm off to see Gerry Waterhouse before anyone else gets to him."

Manatee County Central Library, 1ˢᵗ Avenue, Bradenton, Florida
Late afternoon

Michael found Gerry Waterhouse, and as he suspected, his wife had already called.

Outside, on a bench in the shade, Michael showed Waterhouse his ID and gave him a brief explanation. "... and anything you can tell me, however insignificant, could be helpful," Michael added. "For instance, the car he drives?"

"Nice BMW," Waterhouse said. "White with leather. The 7 Series. But then airline pilots get well paid. He can afford it."

"Do you know what airline?"

"I think he said American, but don't quote me." To Michael's surprise, Waterhouse lit a cigarette. "Secret smoker," he said. "Renee thinks I've quit. It's at times like these, I know I'm not ready. Dumb at my age." He faced Michael. "You hear about this sort of thing. You never think you'll be involved in some way."

Waterhouse only confirmed what his wife told Michael. He hadn't thought it unusual until this moment that at least one of the Armonds and the children weren't there. Michael wasn't about to tell him that according to Brian, who'd accompanied the FBI raid, whoever lived at #1037 appeared to have left in a hurry.

"Perhaps they took a vacation," Waterhouse continued. "With all the airline layoffs and the hours Philip worked, that would be my guess. Philip said Sabrina was Italian, so maybe they've taken the children to Italy, seeing as we never saw family visit."

"Who did you see?"

"The occasional man. Nothing odd. I thought they were probably Philip's airline buddies." He lowered his voice. "If I'm right about all this, none of them had long beards and flowing robes, if that's what you're trying to find out." He paused. "I'm aware of recent events, Colonel Correa. I'm a reasonably well-educated man."

"I don't doubt it, Mr. Waterhouse." Michael then handed him the same photographs he'd shown his wife. "Do any of these men look familiar?"

Waterhouse studied the faces. "I recognize this man. Hamza Jarrah. Only I know him as Philip Armond. I don't know about the others. Like I said, they were all clean-shaven and wore Western-style clothes."

"Any female visitors?"

"Not that I remember. But I suspect you've already asked Renee. Unfortunately, I wasn't into neighbor watching. Got better things to do with my time."

Damn it! Another dead end.

"Maybe that's now changed," Waterhouse added.

"What about your other neighbors?" Michael continued. "Would they know anything?"

"You'll have to ask them," Waterhouse said. "Everyone thinks Florida's full of old people waiting to die. It isn't. All my neighbors have regular jobs. Unless there's something I don't know about, we're the only retirees on the block. And we don't stay home that often, either. That'll get you old and dead real fast. Renee and I like to keep active."

Michael's Office, G Street, Washington, D.C.
Thursday, September 19, 2002

Less than forty-eight hours later, copies of the statements given to the FBI from the Armonds' other neighbors were delivered to Michael's office. They had nothing to add.

After thoroughly searching the house, Brian and the FBI agents came to the conclusion that whoever lived there wasn't coming back. Food, including leftovers, was still in the refrigerator, and although children's toys were in the house and yard, there were no clothes to be found, kids' or adults'. They did find some smudged adult fingerprints, but none that were good enough to be identified. Some small fingerprints belonging to a child were saved for possible future use. Although the books, magazines, and some papers were removed, Michael understood it would be some time before any relevant information might be forthcoming. If there was anything to find.

Dan eventually found the locked green minivan in long-term parking at the airport with the help of the Tampa Police Department and airport security.

But there was no sign of a white BMW 7 Series. As no fingerprints were found in the minivan, everyone involved concluded that they were dealing with professionals. The DNA from a few hairs found, after the minivan was impounded and sent to a local lab for analysis, later produced zero results.

When the passenger lists from the airlines were studied, there was no record of a woman, a child and baby, a single man, or any other combination, taking a flight from Tampa over the weekend or on the several days following.

With every relevant agency involved, the information was gathered quickly. It came as no surprise that American Airlines had never heard of a Philip Armond, and his photograph didn't match anyone in their aircrew personnel records. What did surprise everyone was that both Philip and Sabrina Armond had valid Florida driver's licenses and social security numbers, obtained in July 2000. According to DMV records, they were both new licenses and not re-registered from another state. They had both passed the driving test. The good news was that Michael now had a picture of the woman. The bad news was that after enlarging it and studying it for some time, he came to the conclusion that she was probably wearing a curly dark wig and that her oversized tinted glasses were unnecessary.

Brian agreed.

FBI agents later showed the photograph to Gerry and Renee Waterhouse, and her only comment was, "That doesn't look like her."

The Armonds also had a joint bank account at a Bradenton branch of Sun Trust, which they opened a few days after moving into the house on Cherry Blossom Avenue. Although either could sign, only Sabrina Armond's signature appeared on the canceled checks. When questioned, the tellers couldn't remember seeing her. "They use the night safe for the deposits and their ATM card for cash withdrawals."

The only deposits to the account were once a month for cash, and no checks were ever included. The utility bills were always paid on time, as was a regular monthly check first posted three months after the Armonds moved in. The payee was later identified as the home's owner, and the checks were his monthly rent. When questioned at length, he admitted he never got references, as a two-month security deposit, plus three months' rent in advance, had been too much of a temptation. "They seemed like a quiet, respectable family," he said. "Always paid on time and kept the place nice too. I've got no complaints."

When asked how the Armonds found the rental, he replied, "A sign in the front yard."

It was only Sabrina Armond's signature on the two consecutive one-year leases, but when it came time to renew in June 2002, the landlord was told the husband could be transferred to Europe, so they paid for another three months in advance, with an option to extend. Consequently, he wasn't expecting another check until October and had no idea the Armonds had gone.

To cover all the bases, they even checked the names Philip and Sabrina Armond, and Hamza Jarrah with the Immigration and Naturalization Service. Having gone back to 1999, they had no record of them ever entering the U.S. legally. "Illegal entry's another matter. Good luck."

The only option remaining was to trace the vehicles. The list of dealerships selling BMWs in all fifty states was huge, and they'd no idea whether the car was new or used. It could also have been stolen and repainted. The minivan was no help either; the VIN had been removed.

"That's the sign of a real professional," the technician in charge said. "We'll never trace it."

At this point, a raid that had begun with such promise hit a dead end. Again. And Michael's frustration grew.

Michael's Office, G Street, Washington, D.C.
Friday, September 20, 2002

At 10:30 a.m., Brian and Dan were called into Michael's office, where they found him studying the flip chart.

"It's like a goddamn maze," Michael said. "Every lead takes us nowhere."

He pointed at Jarrah's name. "I say we concentrate on him. As we now know he was living in Bradenton for the last two years, I asked Molly earlier to get a list of diving schools in the area. Call them. I doubt he was trained in the desert. Agreed?"

"Agreed," Brian replied. "It's as good a place as any to start."

By 4:00 p.m., Dan and Brian had either faxed or e-mailed the identikit photograph of a westernized Jarrah to the local diving schools. They'd spoken to secretaries, and in one case the owner, but none of them had any record of a Philip Armond ever applying for his diving certification.

"What does that mean?" Brian asked a secretary at one of the diving schools.

"All our students have to pass the final exam. Then they're registered as certified divers."

"There's a paper trail?"

"Of course. Otherwise, anyone could say they're a certified diver."

"And if they took the course but never the exam, then what?"

"They wouldn't be certified, would they?"

Makes sense, Brian thought.

"... and please see if anyone there recognizes the photograph?" Brian heard Dan say from his desk before hanging up the telephone.

Brian turned. "Well?"

Dan shrugged. "Same as you. No record. Maybe we widen the net?"

"Or we get lucky that someone at the schools recognizes him. Jarrah's smart. Why leave a paper trail to follow?"

"Keep dialing?"

"Got nothin' better to do."

Two hours later, they'd covered an area as far as Tampa to the north and Fort Myers to the south.

"I can't see him goin' that far," Brian commented.

When they were able to talk to a real person, it resulted in the same reply: "No record." In two cases, they had to leave messages on answering machines.

"Didn't realize divin' was that popular," Brian said, hanging up from the last call on their list. He got to his feet. "That's it for today," he added. "Now we wait and pray."

Chapter Five

Michael's Office, G Street, Washington, D.C.
Monday, September 23, 2002

"There's a call for you on line two," Molly told Brian at 9:20 a.m. "A Jeff Osborne from the Blue Water Diving School in Sarasota."

Immediately, Brian hit the flashing button. "Mullen."

"I saw a picture of Philip Armond in the office this morning. I was told I should call," Osborne began. He went on to explain that he'd found the faxed photograph while searching for an up-to-date instruction schedule on the secretary's desk.

"You coulda blown me away," Osborne added, Brian not quite able to place his accent. "What's the DoJ² want with him?"

Brian ignored the question. "Did he take the final exam?" he asked.

"No. He shoulda. The guy was good."

"Do you know why he didn't?"

"Said he got recalled to the airline. The exam dates kept clashing with his flying roster."

"Tell me about him."

"He's a nice guy. Friendly. Generous. Hell, he's got this great boat that we take out when he isn't flying and my teaching schedule permits. We have a good time together."

"There's nothing odd about him?"

"No. I'm a former Army Ranger. We're trained for that kinda thing. Why'd you ask?"

Brian stayed silent.

---

2   Department of Justice.

"Oh, fuck," he heard Osborne mutter after a pause.

"Stay on the line," Brian said. "There's someone else here you should talk to."

"I'm going to Florida to meet with Osborne," Michael said a short time later.

"Thought you might," Brian replied. "Seein' as you outrank him, give him hell."

Dockside Bar and Grill, Main Street, Sarasota, Florida
Later that night

As there were no direct flights from Washington, D.C., to Sarasota, Michael had taken the opportunity to read Osborne's military file before landing in Tampa. Enlisting at eighteen, Osborne had been a good soldier. After Ranger School, he'd seen action in several overseas theaters during his military career and had been decorated. Born and raised in Boston, Massachusetts, after his retirement, he'd moved south.

"To get away from the cold," Osborne explained in a relatively quiet corner booth, when Michael asked.

Another one, Michael thought. *Gibson did the same thing. Must be a New England trait.*

"A couple of winters in Bosnia will do that to you, sir," Osborne added.

Michael understood, too clearly.

Osborne sipped a beer. Well built and deeply tanned, he was in his early forties. "I'm real sorry about Armond, sir," he said. "I feel like a real dumb bastard."

Michael shrugged. "We're just beginning to find out how good these guys are. You weren't to know. But I would like to hear everything about him."

Osborne finished the beer in one gulp. "When he first signed up for my beginner's course, he told me he was Italian. The way he looked, I'd got no reason to think otherwise. His English was perfect. I did comment on that. He said all good European schools taught English as a second language and that his teacher had been this snooty Englishwoman."

Michael stopped a passing waitress to order two more beers.

"He was real determined," Osborne continued after the waitress had left. "Had to be the best and didn't mind working at it. The European work ethic, I guess."

Money was no problem to Armond, according to Osborne. He took lessons three times a week to start and insisted, against Osborne's advice, on buying all the diving gear. "Top of the line too."

"We suggest that our students rent the equipment, in case they've got no aptitude for serious diving," Osborne continued. "But Philip brushed me off. Said he knew it was what he wanted."

After a few weeks of lessons, they began to have a drink together after the diving sessions. Armond did admit to Osborne that he was married, but Osborne never saw a wife. "Got the impression his marriage wasn't that great. He never talked about her."

"Or the children?"

"He's got kids? I didn't know that. Now, I'm surprised."

"Not the fatherly type?"

"Hell, no. Acted more like he was single and on the prowl. A wife he wants to forget, I can understand. But kids? That's not right."

Armond was halfway through the intermediary course when he introduced Osborne to two of his "airline buddies." "One of them hated it," Osborne added. "After that first lesson, I never saw him again. But the following week, another one shows up. He was okay."

"You've got the names?" Michael asked.

"Better." Osborne handed Michael two sheets of paper with not only their names, but also addresses, telephone numbers, even copies of the driver's license and a credit card.

"Guess they're all fake," he added.

Michael didn't disagree but hoped he was one big step closer.

Philip's two friends completed the intermediary course. "But only one of them took the advanced course with Philip."

"Do you know why?"

"He told me he was flying again. A regular route in Europe."

Europe, my ass, Michael thought and reminded himself to check the flying angle.

Osborne pointed to one of the pieces of paper. "That one dropped out three lessons shy of the final exam."

"Recalled to fly?"

Osborne nodded. "The airlines were all rehiring. It didn't seem odd at the time. But he did come out with us on the boat a few times after the course finished."

"Tell me about this boat."

"A fifty-two-foot Egg Harbor sportfish. Know how much those suckers cost?"

"Yes."

"I didn't think I'd see Armond again. Then he suddenly shows up one afternoon at the diving school. Says he's bought a boat. It was used, he says, but in real great shape."

"Was it?"

"It looked new. And he knew how to handle it." Osborne paused. "Come to think of it, I made some comment about it. Armond just smiled and said something like, 'I'm full of surprises.' I'm beginning to understand what he meant."

Me too, Michael thought. *And there's another angle we've got to explore.* "How long had it been since you'd seen him?"

"Six, seven months maybe."

"I'll need dates. As close as you can get."

"Sure. If you're still coming to the school in the morning, I'll check my old calendar. I didn't think to bring it."

In his hotel room, with the realization that he was beginning to learn a lot more about Hamza Jarrah a.k.a. Philip Armond, Michael made notes from his interview with Osborne.

It was after midnight, so he stopped himself from calling either Brian or Dan.

It'll wait until tomorrow, Michel thought as he climbed into bed and turned out the light. *With luck, I'll have got even more for them.*

Blue Water Diving School, S. Tamiani Trail, Sarasota, Florida
Tuesday, September 24, 2002

Owner Ignatius "Iggy" Patterson took Michael's hand in a vice-like grip.

"Can't believe 9/11 was a year ago this month, Colonel Correa," he said, barely glancing at Michael's ID. "As a former SEAL, I'll do everything I can to help catch these bastards." He waved Michael to a chair. "Full cooperation, sir," he added, taking a seat behind his desk.

Michael looked around the office, which was plastered with framed photographs, and mentally kicked himself for not doing a quick background check on Patterson.

"My father's former Navy," Michael said. "Fighter pilot."

Patterson's eyes narrowed as he looked again at Michael's business card. "Former Navy. Last name Correa. Your dad the returning director of CIA by any chance?"

"Affirmative."

Patterson sat back. "Small world. We met during the Cuban Missile Crisis. Had a little thing going, if you get my drift? Say hello from me when you next talk to him."

Michael was surprised. "I'll be sure to tell him."

"Do that. Want some coffee?"

"Thanks."

"I'd have called you myself, but I didn't see the fax until after Osborne called your office. I've been down in the Keys with some students. Only just got back." Patterson picked up the identikit photograph. "We've all seen the FBI's Most Wanted List, and now that I really look at this, I'm feeling real dumb for not recognizing him. Getting too old, I guess. Whatta you need to know?"

"Anything you can tell me."

But Patterson had little to add to what Michael already knew. In Michael's mind, the only important piece of information was that Patterson knew the owner of the marina where Armond kept the boat.

"Nice, well-kept place," he said, already reaching for the telephone. "So, when you're finished with Osborne, I'll take you over and introduce you. It's not far. Maybe Slim Nulty can help—Hello, Slim? It's Iggy ..."

"Slim?" Michael asked when Patterson hung up.

"You'll see."

"Before we get Osborne in here, is he trustworthy?"

"Totally. I've normally got three diving instructors. All former military. Two are still here. The third one's in the Reserves. He's away at annual training right now. Hope he comes back soon. Business is picking up again."

On his way to the marina, the only additional piece of information Michael had was the amount of time that passed before Armond reappeared at the diving school.

"It was seven months," Osborne said, pointing at a date on an old calendar. "Monday, December 6, 2001. That's the day we went out on his boat for the first time. He showed up around Thanksgiving to ask if I wanted to go. I'm usually off on Mondays, that's how I remember."

"And you last saw him?"

"'Bout the end of August, I guess."

"If you think of anything else, or happen to see him, call me," Michael said as they shook hands.

"Count on it, sir," Osborne replied.

Fairwinds Marina, Marina Plaza, Sarasota, Florida
A short time later

With the intention of returning directly to the Tampa airport, Michael followed Patterson to the marina. After passing through the security gate, Michael parked his rental car and took a good look around.

The manicured complex, with palm trees and other lush foliage, had several long docks. Flower-filled planters decorated each one, and there didn't appear to be a boat under thirty feet in any of the slips. The gray clapboard clubhouse had a wide walk-around deck, and where the deck wasn't covered in a royal-blue awning, the white circular tables and chairs were protected by matching patio umbrellas. Beyond the clubhouse, Michael could just see an in-ground pool.

"Nice setup," he said.

"Slim runs a tight ship," Patterson replied. "Cause any trouble, and you're outta here. Some folks will pay well for the security and surroundings."

Slim Nulty was in his air-conditioned office. Michael guessed he weighed at least 350 pounds, his huge torso covered in a garish Hawaiian shirt. He attempted to get to his feet, holding out a hand that reminded Michael of a slab of beef.

"Nice to meet you, Colonel Correa. Take a seat."

As Michael and Patterson both sat, Nulty dropped heavily onto his chair.

Michael pushed his ID across the desk. "I understand from Mr. Patterson that a Philip Armond has a slip here for a fifty-two-foot Egg Harbor."

"Had."

Michael raised an eyebrow.

"Marina rules: Owners are to tell us if they're leaving for a week or more. The boat left on September 15th and hasn't come back."

Shit! Michael thought. *That's the day before the raid. He was warned, damn it!* "Did he tell you?"

"No."

"Is his car still here?"

Michael could tell Nulty was having trouble breathing.

"I doubt it. Same rule applies, so security knows. But you're welcome to check the parking lot."

"What about his slip?"

"It's paid through the end of the year." Nulty tried to take a deep breath. "We're now using it for guests, until he comes back."

He won't be coming back, Michael thought.

He'd noticed the oxygen tank by the side of the desk, and before Nulty said any more, he placed a clear mask attached to the bottle over his nose and mouth, gesturing for Michael to wait.

A couple of minutes passed.

"You okay, Slim?" Patterson asked as Nulty removed the mask.

He nodded. "Emphysema, Colonel," he said slowly. "My weight doesn't help."

"If this wasn't so important, I'd do it some other time."

"Ask your questions," Nulty said, handing Michael two pieces of paper. "Those help?"

Michael looked at a copy of the original contract for the slip, dated Thursday, November 8, 2001, and the renewal contract two months later.

Nulty's breathing got worse again, but he motioned for Michael to continue. Instead of verbally replying to Michael's questions, Nulty wrote his answers on a notepad. From the speed and clarity of his writing, Michael assumed he'd had lots of practice.

Back outside, having thanked Nulty for his cooperation, Michael faced Patterson. "You've known him long?"

"Over twenty-five years. A former police officer. Got hit by a car in the line of duty. That was his downfall. He quit the force, took over the marina, and began eating. Two packs a day didn't help."

"How bad is he?"

"I've seen him worse. These attacks last hours, sometimes days. But they're getting more frequent. Shame," Patterson added quietly. "He's a good guy."

After thoroughly checking the parking lot, there was no sign of a BMW 7 Series, white or any other color.

On his return flight to Reagan National, Michael took the time to go over his notes. Nulty had admitted that a "To Whom It May Concern" letter of reference on American Airlines stationery, now known to be a forgery, and a large cash deposit persuaded him to accept Armond as a marina club member without further references. "Money's money," he'd written.

The Egg Harbor arrived in its slip on November 15, 2001, exactly a week after Armond signed the first contract. Regardless of expense, the boat was meticulously maintained, and Nulty hadn't thought it out of the ordinary, until now, that Armond insisted the fuel tanks were always kept full. At that point, he produced copies of Armond's fuel dock receipts. "Money was never an issue," he wrote.

Armond used the clubhouse for an occasional drink, but he rarely used the restaurant. When he did, he was alone, and paid the required minimum monthly charge without complaint.

Nulty never saw a woman or children with him. "Most members with kids socialize and use the pool," he wrote. Armond never did. In fact, he didn't even know Armond had a wife. There was nothing on his application to even suggest he was married. The spouse/children information had been left blank. Michael saw he'd used the Cherry Blossom Avenue, Bradenton, address. But it wasn't until he checked the file on Jarrah that he was able to confirm the telephone numbers didn't match.

He quickly found the copy of the sign-up sheet from the diving school. The telephone number Jarrah gave was different again. *How many cell phones is he using?* Michael thought.

Michael's Office, G Street, Washington, D.C.
Friday, September 27, 2002

After his return from Florida and throughout the remainder of the week, Molly watched as Michael's frustration continued to grow.

The driver's licenses belonging to Jarrah's "airline buddies" turned out to be good fakes. All they were left with were two faces that didn't match any of the photographs of known terrorists. The telephone numbers Jarrah used on his applications were from stolen cell phones, and to Michael's annoyance, they hadn't been used after reported missing.

With the cooperation of the Italian authorities, the search began for a Sabrina Armond. The chances of finding her, or discovering that she really existed, were slim to none, and everyone involved knew it.

Convinced that Jarrah was given advance warning to leave the Bradenton house, Michael spoke to the FBI agent who'd interviewed the man arrested in the bar near Fort Bragg, North Carolina.

"He didn't say anything," the agent said. "We don't even know if he spoke English."

"Let me have a go at him?"

"I wish I could."

"Meaning?"

"He hung himself in his cell. No one knows how."

Michael could hardly believe it. "What about phone calls?"

"According to our information, none were made."

After slamming down the receiver, even Molly overheard Michael's string of expletives.

"I'm bettin' he used a cell phone or pager before he was picked up," Brian said later.

Michael could find no reason to disagree.

By the middle of the afternoon, Michael had reached his breaking point. The flip chart had been added to and reworked so many times that he'd used all the pages.

Molly got him a new one, and he'd been working at it ever since. He'd even missed his daily run with Dan. *That's a mistake,* she thought.

At 4:00 p.m., Brian and Dan were studying the new chart.

"Tell me what I've missed," Michael said, flopping into his chair. "I'm going round in goddamn circles, with no way out."

Brian flipped to a clean sheet and drew three columns. He then wrote the names "Hamza Jarrah a.k.a. Philip Armond," "Sabrina Armond a.k.a.?" and "Peter Gibson" above each column.

"These three individuals are all connected. We know that for a fact. In police work, when I hit a brick wall, I go back to the beginnin' and start all over."

"I'm not cut out for this," Michael said. "I'm military intelligence, not a detective. They picked the wrong man."

"Bullshit," Brian replied. "They picked the right man. You've just got too much goin' on. Can't see the forest for the trees." He turned back to the chart. "That's why you've got me. Begin with Jarrah. What do we know is fact?"

By the end of the day, and several sheets of paper later, the information at their disposal was neatly recorded on the chart.

Brian finally put down the pen and stood back. "That's where we start," he said. "Three individuals, and there's three of us. We take copies of that information home, and over the weekend, we can work on it. Maybe by Monday mornin', we'll have got some fresh ideas. Right now, we need a break." He turned to Michael. "You included."

Michael didn't move from his chair. "Fine. Send Molly in on your way out. She can type up this chart, and when she's finished, go home."

"You, too," Dan said as they left.

Michael waited until the Friday night rush was over before driving to Eagles Nest, his home on Maryland's Eastern Shore. *Brian's right,* he thought, crossing the Chesapeake Bay Bridge well before midnight. *Some downtime will clear my head.*

By the time he was walking down the dock to his boat, he was unconvinced that President Makepeace had chosen the right man. *I shoulda quit and left it at that.*

Chapter Six

Michael's Office, G Street, Washington, D.C.
Monday, September 30, 2002

After catching up on much-needed sleep, Michael's mood had improved. But before he even reached his desk, his intercom buzzed.

"There's an Ian McDonald from the British Embassy on line two for you, sir," Molly said. "He said to tell you it's about Sabrina."

"Trace the call," he replied and then waited twenty-five seconds before hitting the button for line two. "Correa."

"You're a hard man to find," said a very British voice. "You are Lieutenant Colonel Michael Correa, son of CIA Director Francis Correa?"

"Yes."

"Thank God. We need to meet."

"We do? Why?"

"A common bond, old boy. You're looking for Sabrina. So am I. Thought we could trade information, seeing as we're on the same side. Your choice of venue."

Michael checked his watch. "The Roosevelt Memorial. 1400."

"I'll be there," McDonald said and hung up.

Almost immediately, Michael's door opened.

"The call came from the British Embassy," Brian said.

"Then find out who the hell this guy is. You've got less than five hours."

"I'm on it."

Michael closed his eyes as his door clicked shut. *Let this be our break.*

With a vast network of classified information at their disposal, it hadn't taken Brian very long to find Ian McDonald.

"He's MI-6," Brian said, handing Michael an information sheet with an old photograph. "So what do the Brits want with Sabrina?"

Michael studied the photograph of a slightly built man in a British army uniform. "Hopefully, I'll be able to tell you in a couple of hours."

The Roosevelt Memorial, Washington, D.C.

Michael slowed to a walk as the memorial came into sight, and as he wiped his face with a towel slung around his neck, he scanned a small group of tourists.

In his early fifties, Ian McDonald was easy to recognize, sitting on a bench, dressed in an immaculate dark-brown suit, white shirt, and regimental striped tie. On seeing Michael, McDonald stood, and "dapper" was the word that immediately sprang to mind.

"Delighted you dressed for the occasion, old boy," McDonald said, holding out his hand, while eyeing Michael's sweat-stained tank top, running shorts, and sneakers. "You Yanks really take this keep-fit thing seriously."

Michael returned the firm handshake, choosing not to comment. "Let's walk," he said instead. "What do you know about Sabrina?"

"She's one of mine," McDonald replied. "Recruited her in '94, when she was nineteen."

Michael was stunned. "She's a British agent?"

"And a damn good one. At least she was, until she disappeared."

"When did she last make contact?"

"September 15th. Called from the airport in Tampa. Said she was coming in and bringing the children. The connecting British Airways flight was out of New York. We confirmed seating for one adult and two children, but she never boarded the flight. Since then, nothing."

Michael headed for the steps at the side of the Jefferson Memorial. "My car's waiting. Let's take a ride."

The gray Lexus was in a no-parking zone, and as Michael approached, Dan got out of the driver's seat.

Michael made the introductions. "Dan's former Secret Service and part of the team," Michael added. "So you can talk freely."

Before sliding into the rear seat, Michael pulled on sweat pants and a top. "We can talk while Dan drives. Or go back to my office. It's a secure environment."

McDonald raised an eyebrow. "In Washington, D.C.?"

"It's secure," Michael repeated. He wasn't about to tell McDonald that the entire space was swept every morning, and if the offices were left empty at any time during the day, they were swept again. "Why did you recruit Sabrina?"

McDonald had done his homework. He now knew that if anyone could be trusted with the information he was about to divulge, it was the man next to him, regardless, in McDonald's mind, of his somewhat-cavalier appearance.

"Someone had to," he said. "After the Cold War ended, you Yanks cut back on all human intel. Bloody stupid idea. Anyone with half a brain could see the United States was a sitting duck. The Middle East has been a hotbed for extremists even before Suez." He stopped, glancing at Michael. "Long before you were born."

"I know about it," Michael replied. "I can even find it on a map."

McDonald chuckled. "Not many of your fellow countrymen can say that."

"I'm not disagreeing. Sabrina?"

"Real name: Samin Fareed. Born Tehran 1975. Only daughter of Farrokh Fareed, a good friend of ours. Educated primarily in Great Britain, followed by four years at the Wharton School of Business in Pennsylvania to get her BS. We picked her up at Heathrow on one of her first trips home. Made her an offer she couldn't refuse. She's been with us ever since."

"What offer?"

"Not important, old boy. Suffice to say, up until the time we lost contact, she'd been most successful."

"How?"

"She seduced and married that bastard Jarrah, the terrorist you know as Philip Armond. Even had two children to protect her cover."

"And when did you intend sharing this information?" Michael asked.

McDonald didn't fail to detect the coldness in Michael's voice. "After you Yanks, we lost the most victims in the attack on the World Trade Center. Regardless of all the political reasons for Prime Minister Blair wholeheartedly supporting the U.S. position—" He stopped in mid-sentence.

"Let's face it," he continued, "we've been around for a very long time. The United States is the world's superpower, even if half the members of the U.N. think you're a bunch of rich spoiled brats. But we didn't conquer most of the world at one time or another by being dimwits. We'd rather stand side by side with you than against you. Now we want Jarrah as much as you do."

"He was involved with 9/11?"

"Hard to tell. He's dangerous, even if he wasn't. Whatever he's up to, it won't be pretty."

"How did you find me?"

"Wasn't easy. You've no idea how many phone calls were made. Finally, I received a call from the prime minister's residence, and there he handed me your name and number. Said President Makepeace gave it to him. I was then informed that your president had a hand in creating your current position. Must be nice to have friends in very high places."

"And don't forget my father," Michael added.

McDonald faced him, ignoring the sarcasm. "We're both Army guys. We know how this works. We've both been in the trenches, so to speak. Therefore, I understand your reluctance. When I get back to the embassy, I'll arrange to have a dossier on Samin Fareed for you. It should be ready by tomorrow, if you're available. How's that?"

"Fine," Michael replied.

As per Michael's instructions, Dan waited until McDonald entered the British Embassy before driving away.

"Do you trust him?" Dan finally asked.

"Not as far as I could throw him," Michael said. "Time to see what my father knows. But first I've got to shower and change."

Less than an hour later, Michael was speaking to his father on a secure line.

"Ian McDonald," Michael said.

"The British spymaster," Francis replied. "A well-educated weasel. Highly successful army career. Ex-SAS. Now a big wheel within the U.K. intelligence community. Gets results. But keeps very low key. Normally."

"What do you mean 'normally'?"

Francis chuckled. "Not often he makes a public appearance. I'm assuming that his visit with you was worthwhile?"

"For whom?"

"You, of course. Pick his brains. I'm guessing that he needs you more than you need him."

"How did you know?"

"The president asked my opinion. I said that CIA was better kept out of it. There's no love lost between us and MI-6. And don't ask. It's a long story, which one day I'll tell you. And if you want my personal opinion, you've handled worse than McDonald. I told the president that too."

"He admitted Sabrina Armond was one of his. Don't you find that odd?"

Francis laughed. "He's playing you. Is she?"

"I've no way of knowing."

"Precisely."

"Meaning?"

"He took the gamble that you were either trying to find her or that he knows where she is but can't get to her. I'm guessing the former, unless our intel's worse than we thought. Regardless, you played right into his hands. So knowing that she could be a British agent, you'll be doubling your efforts to get to her first. I told you, he's a weasel. A very smart one. He's got no authority in this country. He knows it. You know it. I'll bet that after your meeting tomorrow, he'll fly home then wait for you to do his dirty work."

"Now I'm confused. Is she an agent or not?"

"How the hell should I know? You still need to find her. And does it matter?"

Michael paused. "I guess not."

"I'm betting she's still here."

"Do you know that for a fact?"

Francis checked his desk calendar. "No. But it's been fifteen days since McDonald says he lost contact. Guaranteed, he's already checked with his overseas sources to see if she's surfaced. If not, why wait so long to see you? I think you're on the right track."

"Thanks, Dad."

"You're welcome," Francis replied before hanging up.

"You look like a bull hog in a pen-load of sows," Brian commented a few minutes later.

Michael then repeated his conversation with McDonald and his father.

"This's gettin' interestin'," Brian said when he'd finished. "We've got a possible female British agent in the mix. Wonder what's comin' next?"

Me, too, Michael thought.

"Like I've said," Brian added as he was leaving. "All we gotta have is some luck."

Chapter Seven

The Mall, Washington, D.C.
Tuesday, October 1, 2002

From a bench, a more casually dressed McDonald was feeding pigeons from a brown paper bag. There was no recognition as Michael sat down.

"Not running today, old boy?" McDonald asked, throwing some more seed to a group of birds.

Michael wanted to tell him he was only thirty-five and certainly not his "old boy."

"Too early," he said.

"What you need is in that *Washington Post*," McDonald continued, not looking at the newspaper between them on the bench. "If and when you find her, let me know." He threw some more seed. "No need to add that joint cooperation is imperative for future relations."

"I get the picture."

"I really do hope so … for your sake."

Michael reached for the newspaper and began to read the front page.

After a few minutes, he folded the paper, and getting to his feet, he strolled away with it in his hand.

There had been no further conversation with the man from MI-6.

Michael's Office, G Street, Washington, D.C.
That night

It was late when Michael stretched out on the large leather sofa.

"They must think you're worth it," his father commented, on seeing the office for the first time.

Michael originally thought that his expensively furnished suite of offices was also a little excessive, but at times like these, he was grateful for the overstuffed Chesterfield and fully stocked liquor cabinet.

With a generous glass of Glenfiddich in one hand and his copy of McDonald's dossier in the other, he began to read.

Samin Fareed, a.k.a. Sabrina Armond, was the only daughter of a wealthy Iranian rug merchant. Not the kind of merchant found in a local bazaar, but one of a generations-old international business that dealt all over the world in high-quality merchandise. Her grandfather and father had been educated in Europe, and for reasons that weren't stated, Fareed was sent to a girls-only private boarding school in Great Britain, before being accepted to the University of Pennsylvania Wharton School of Business. Four years later, she graduated with a BS in accounting.

For the family business? Michael wondered.

After spending the remaining summer in the U.S., Fareed returned home to her family in Tehran. At this point, Michael made a note in the margin to try to find out why she'd stayed in the U.S. Both boarding school and university records showed that Fareed was an excellent student, popular with her peers, and a good athlete. Although a Muslim, there was no reference to her being a devout follower of Islam or ever attending any mosques. In fact, she appeared totally westernized and was fluent in English, French, and Italian.

Michael took a gulp of the scotch. *And there's the Italian connection.*

The report was then missing three crucial years, for when Fareed next surfaced, it was as Sabrina Armond, wife and mother, living as a homemaker in Bradenton, Florida.

What the hell happened? How did she end up marrying a fanatic like Jarrah?

He read the notes again and did a quick calculation to confirm. *That's not right, unless Renee Waterhouse made a mistake. If the oldest child was four, how come there's no mention of her being pregnant in her last year at Wharton?*

He underlined the note in the margin twice before studying the enlargements of the few available photographs taken during Fareed's boarding school and university days. Her nose was slightly hooked, her eyes almond-shaped, her forehead proud, and her mouth too wide. *But altogether, she's a raven-haired beauty.* Short of plastic surgery, he knew there'd be nothing she could do about her nose, but Michael wondered what the five-foot-five woman would look like as a blonde with dark-brown eyes. *Or maybe a redhead? We've got to find her.*

He then picked up the intelligence report on Hamza Jarrah, a.k.a. Philip Armond, compiled hours before by Molly. She'd used all their firsthand information, plus additional data from other sources and their many months of research. Jarrah's file wasn't any thicker than Fareed's, but now included on the FBI's Most Wanted List, his face was becoming very well known. With all the media coverage, plus millions of dollars being offered as a reward for information on his known whereabouts, Michael was surprised that no one had yet come forward.

Although born into a middle-class family in Riyadh, Saudi Arabia, Jarrah witnessed firsthand the huge discrepancy between rich and poor. The rich got richer from money supplied by the West, and the so-called decadent American lifestyle was everywhere, advertised in brash neon. All reports showed that Jarrah was considered by those who knew him to be a quiet, polite boy who showed no tendencies whatsoever toward his later hatred and fanaticism. He practiced his Muslim religion, but not fervently. His education was typical for the son of a respected banker, and after his high-school graduation, he took several menial jobs before leaving Riyadh for Germany. Michael reckoned it was there he saw firsthand the West in all its "decadent" glory.

It didn't stop you from becoming part of it, did it? Michael thought. *Even if it is an act. Tomorrow, we begin again.*

When he finally got to bed, he lay in the dark and stared at the ceiling. The feeling that Samin Fareed, a.k.a. Sabrina Armond, was the key in this investigation wouldn't go away.

How? I've got nothing on which to base that assumption. Maybe she's an unwitting pawn? But if that's true, why hasn't she come forward? Fear? Or some other reason?

By the time he fell asleep, none of his questions had been satisfactorily answered.

Michael's Office, G Street, Washington, D.C.
Wednesday, October 2, 2002

"Don't sit down," Michael said as Brian entered the room. "Do a background check on Peter Gibson. It's not making any sense. How did these guys find him? And if he was on the up and up, as everyone seems to think, why didn't he blow the whistle. Agreed?"

"Agreed. But we're gonna need help. We're stretched too thin. Dan's chasin' down Egg Harbors sold in 2001. I'm off to Philadelphia in the mornin', and Molly's workin' around the clock." Brian rubbed his eyes. "If these bags get any bigger, I'll be usin' 'em to carry the supermarket shoppin'. Time to call in reinforcements maybe?"

"Like who?"

"Kathryn."

"Bad idea."

Brian hesitated. "I know you split up."

"How?"

"I had to pry it outta Pauline when I proposed ..." Brian began.

"Congratulations," Michael said when Brian finished. "When's the big day?"

"Haven't got a ring or set a date yet. Bin too busy. Are you goin' to call Kathryn? You're both adults. And I'm not tryin' to play Cupid."

"Smart. I'll think about it."

"Do that." Brian turned to leave. "But don't think too long."

The door closed.

The last time Michael saw Kathryn, she'd accused him of taking her for granted. He said very little, which only fueled her anger. Words like "uncommunicative" and "thoughtless" were included in a tirade of very unlawyer-like language.

"If you can't stand the heat, get out of the kitchen," Michael snapped, before finally striding down the dock to the boat.

"You're an arrogant, selfish bastard!" Kathryn shouted after him.

Michael stayed on board for several hours and realized that regardless of the circumstances, he'd probably be the one apologizing. But Kathryn saved him the trouble. By the time he returned to the house, she'd packed her clothes and gone. There was no note, and he wasn't sure whether he was relieved or disappointed when she didn't call either. Days turned into weeks, and it had now been more than three months since they'd spoken.

Brian's right. But I don't want to do this, he thought now, reaching for the telephone to dial a very familiar number.

"Attorney Sullivan's office," Pauline answered. "May I help you?"

"Pauline, it's Michael. I need to speak with Kathryn."

"Hi, Michael. I'll see if she's available."

"Tell her it's work-related," he added quickly.

There were several seconds of silence, then a click.

There was no greeting. "What kind of work?" Kathryn asked.

"My kind," Michael replied. "Can you spare Pauline? We need help and someone I can trust."

"How long do you need her?"

"Two days. Maybe more. There's some urgency."

"I'm assuming this's serious?"

"Affirmative."

"Would two heads be better?"

"What about your clients?"

"Nothing that can't wait."

"How soon can you be here?"

"We're leaving now."

Michael's dark suit jacket was flung over an arm of the Chesterfield, his shirt unbuttoned, and his tie hanging loosely when Kathryn and Pauline entered his office.

He looked up from his reading to see that Kathryn was a brunette again. Her hair fell almost to her shoulders, and her classic tailored dress made her look even slimmer. *She's lost more weight.* Michael wanted to tell her how good she looked. He didn't.

"Thanks for coming," he said, waving them to the two chairs in front of him. "As usual, I'm breaking the rules."

As Kathryn and Pauline sat, he handed a file to each of them. "That's all we've got on the late Peter Gibson. I need to know his life story. I've got a generous budget, so no detail left out. However insignificant. Dig deep."

"Can we know why?" Kathryn asked.

"We think that somewhere in his background there's a link to known terrorists. I suspect he wasn't picked at random."

"You did say 'late'?" Pauline asked.

"In July, Gibson was found murdered near Savannah, Georgia. Tybee Island to be exact. He was working there as a charter boat captain. We've now got a witness who can link him to our suspects."

Kathryn had been scanning the brief file. She stood. "We'll get started immediately."

"No need to say 'be discreet.'"

Kathryn turned with her hand on the doorknob. "Attorney/client privilege. Remember?"

"Thanks," Michael said. "Keep me posted?"

"Of course."

"Why the hurry to leave?" Pauline asked as they exited the building.

"No reason," Kathryn replied.

That's a lie. "I thought Michael looked tired."

"He's consumed with work, as usual."

"But he still looks good?"

Kathryn stopped on the sidewalk. "I know what you're doing. I've been trying to forget him, and you're not helping."

"I just thought ..."

"Well, don't! I've got to get on with my life. Even you agreed. Looks aren't everything."

"I know that."

"Then let's change the subject. We've got work to do."

Wharton School of Business, Philadelphia, Pennsylvania
Thursday, October 3, 2002

Except for his military service, Brian had spent his life in Texas until he'd accepted Michael's job offer. He'd yet to regret his decision, even though he liked to give Michael a hard time over the amount of traveling involved. For the most part, Brian enjoyed it. *Any excuse to get out of D.C.,* he thought on his drive to Philadelphia.

On a sunny and pleasant fall day, the traffic on I-95 moved quickly, and the added bonus was finding a metered parking space directly outside the Huntsman building on 38th and Spruce.

After showing his ID and introducing himself, Brian took a seat in the office of the director of Student Services and Administrations.

The director opened a file on his desk. "I'm not going to ask why the Department of Justice is looking for Samin Fareed, Mr. Mullen. I'm sure you've got your reasons. This is Miss Fareed's admissions file, not that I think it's much help. I was director when she enrolled in 1994. An exceptionally good student. You said she's missing? And her family's got no idea where she is?"

"We've exhausted all possibilities," Brian lied. "We were hopin' we might find a lead here."

The director handed Brian the file. "A photocopy for you. And I took the liberty of arranging for you to see Samin's associate director, Davis Livingston. If anyone on the faculty knows about his students' extracurricular activities, it's him."

Let's hope, Brian thought, as the director reached for the telephone.

After telling Davis Livingston that Brian had arrived, the director then gave Brian directions to his office.

Brian shook the director's hand. "Really appreciate the help."

"I do hope you find her," he said.

Appearing to be an afterthought, Brian handed him a business card. "If anyone else should come askin' about Miss Fareed, I'd like you to call us on any of those numbers. It's real important."

"Don't worry, Mr. Mullen. I'll call immediately."

With the directions memorized, Brian wound his way through the campus of old buildings to the associate director's second-floor office. The plaque on the door read "Dr. T. Davis Livingston."

Brian knocked.

"It's open," said a muffled male voice.

A crumpled checked shirt and cord pants hung from Davis Livingston's tall, lanky frame, and Brian guessed he was in his early forties as Livingston held out his hand.

Brian returned the handshake. "Dr. Livingston, I presume?" he said, his ID in full view.

"That ceased to be funny a long time ago, Mr. Mullen," Livingston replied, studying the ID closely before gesturing to a chair. "Take a seat."

Sitting behind his cluttered desk, Livingston leaned back and crossed his long legs. "I understand from the director that you're trying to find Samin Fareed?"

"Correct."

Large green eyes focused on Brian, giving him the impression that despite Livingston's casual posture and unkempt attire, he was incredibly astute. "Must be important for you to end up here?"

"You could say that."

Livingston looked slowly around his very untidy office before focusing again on Brian. "Samin was a Muslim. Is this what this is about? The federal government now targeting anyone who doesn't fit the politically correct profile? She was an authentic foreign student with all the right legal documents."

Brian was now convinced that if Livingston had been old enough, he'd probably have led Vietnam War protests.

Brian held his tongue. "Miss Fareed's missin'," he said. "We've got no leads, and we need to find her. Sooner rather than later."

Livingston suddenly leaned forward, his voice hard. "You think she's a terrorist."

Brian wasn't about to tell him anything. "No. But we do need to find her. So any information you can give me could help trace her whereabouts."

"Why should I believe you?"

"Why would I lie?"

"Do you think she's in danger?"

"No."

Livingston rolled his chair away from the desk and stood. "What did the director tell you?"

"Nothin'. He gave me a copy of her admissions file and said I should talk to you."

Livingston pulled a crumpled pack of cigarettes from his pants pocket. "Do you mind? It's strictly against regs."

Livingston had just added another piece of information to Brian's mental profile. "Go ahead," Brian said.

Livingston opened a window and lit a cigarette. "Thanks." He turned back toward Brian. "Samin was a perfect student," he continued. "So typical of most foreigners. She came here to study and get a degree. Unlike so many of our kids who think university is just party time."

"You got to know her well?"

"I suppose. She got a great all-around education at her private English boarding school and could already speak fluent French and Italian. Consequently, she was very surprised at her roommate." Before Brian could ask, Livingston added, "I don't expect the director mentioned her?"

Brian shook his head.

"No, I didn't think so. Susan Irene Sybil Matthews. Named after her mother and grandmothers, poor kid. Consequently, she was known to everyone, including her family, as Sis. Except she's now Sis Matthews hyphenated Boyd. I got invited to the big society wedding. The Matthews family have been very generous over the years with their endowments to Wharton, which is why Sis was 'invited' to attend the school."

Brian caught on quickly. "Grades not good enough?"

Livingston began to relax and finally laughed. "She was an academic disaster. Kept reminding me of those old Goldie Hawn movies. Dumb blonde personified."

"And she was Miss Fareed's roommate? Any reason?"

"Luck of the draw. Not at first for Samin—we all called her Sam—but they became really good friends. Sis actually graduated with decent grades. Must have come as quite a shock to her father. It was Sam's influence, of course. In the end, Sis really wanted to go out into the business world, but daddy had other ideas. A year after graduation, she married this supposed wiz-kid son of a major Matthews' competitor. A very old-fashioned way to cement a corporate merger, don't you think? The arrogant jerk was a Princeton grad, and now he's got some vice president's position in the Matthews' corporate conglomerate."

Livingston reached into a desk drawer and then handed Brian a cream and gold matted photograph. "Sis is now a mother. The old barefoot and pregnant routine. The complete yuppie housewife. I wouldn't be surprised if she's driving a minivan. What a waste."

Every time Brian thought he was beginning to like Livingston, he said something to make Brian immediately change his mind.

Instead of commenting, Brian concentrated on the studio portrait of a very attractive blonde cradling a newborn baby. It was dated November 12, 1999.

"Pretty woman," he said, handing it back.

Livingston took another look before returning the photograph to the drawer. "Yes, she is. And so is Sam. They made quite a striking pair on campus."

"Where does Sis live now?"

"Here in Pennsylvania. Bedminster, to be precise. I'll bet she's got one of those really small executive-style homes, a few miles from daddy's estate. The house was a wedding gift, I believe. Probably to ensure that any future heirs to the Matthews' empire would grow up close to the doting grandparents."

Brian ignored Livingston's obvious contempt. "Another silver-spoon kid destined for Wharton?"

Livingston grinned. "Precisely. But give old man Matthews his due. Sam spent almost every weekend at the Matthews' estate during her time here. She's an exceptional horsewoman, I was told. Sis once said that her father believed Sam was born in the saddle. When the ladies weren't studying, they were horseback riding. As Matthews also owns a stud farm and show horses, I assume she must have been good. He gave her free rein."

Brian didn't laugh. "Any boyfriends?"

"No time, apparently."

"You stay in contact with Sis?"

"A card at Christmas, with the increasingly popular mass-produced account of their year. Before the baby was born, an occasional letter."

"And Miss Fareed?"

Livingston scratched his unruly hair. "A couple of Christmas cards. The last one came from Germany, I believe."

"Can you remember when?"

"It was at least a couple of years ago. Since then, nothing."

"And Sis has never mentioned her?"

"Not that I can remember."

"Is that odd?"

"Not really. I'm here to advise the undergraduate students. Then they graduate, go out into the big wide world, and I never hear from them again. There are exceptions, of course."

"But Miss Fareed wasn't one of them?"

"Unfortunately not."

"Tell me more about Sis."

Thirty minutes later, Brian had a reasonably clear picture of Susan Irene Sybil Matthews hyphenated Boyd.

"Thanks for your time," he said to Livingston as he was leaving. Brian then pointed to the brass name plaque on the door. "What's the T for?"

"Trevor," Livingston replied. "English/Welsh ancestors. Davis is bad enough. I get called David a lot. Parents have no clue when they christen their kids. Can you imagine what I got called at school with the first name Trevor?"

Couldn't have happened to a nicer guy, Brian thought on his way back to his car.

He called Michael. "We could be one step closer," Brian said. "But the information comes from an academic bleedin' heart liberal Democrat who probably has a shrine to Stalin hidden in his basement and marches with the anti-abortion nuts every chance he gets."

"Sounds like your type."

Brian went on to give Michael a brief account of his meeting with Livingston, adding, "As this Sis Boyd lives not far from here, I thought I'd go check it out."

"Do that," Michael said, "and keep me posted."

Bedminster, Pennsylvania
Later the same day

It didn't take Brian long to realize he was heading into Pennsylvania horse country. The landscape became a continuous vista of rolling green fields, trees, planked fencing, and grazing animals.

He had to stop three times to check his map, and when he did eventually find the Matthews-Boyd home, it wasn't at all what he was expecting. From the contemptuous comment Livingston made, Brian had been searching for a builders' development of ostentatious homes and not a large, old, stone farmhouse set halfway up a hill. From what little Brian could see, the farmhouse had been tastefully extended and modernized, and he assumed from its vantage point that there was a spectacular view of the valley from the oversized arched windows.

Shit, he thought, eyeing the long winding driveway and the sign attached to one of the stone entrance pillars advertising the security system. *No cover for surveillance either. Goddamnit!*

The lane was bordered on either side by tall, natural, and as Brian was to later discover, prickly hedges. There was nowhere to pull over and park, so after driving another half-mile, he turned around and came slowly back.

He'd already made the decision to risk taking some photographs as the house came into view again, but as he searched for a suitable place to stop, he saw a vehicle coming rapidly down the driveway. Hitting the brakes, Brian quickly reached for his map. Covering the steering wheel and most of his face with the map, he hoped it would look to the other driver as though he was lost.

The woman behind the wheel of a dirty black Range Rover never gave him a second glance as she swept into the lane and accelerated away at high speed.

This is my lucky day, Brian thought as he hit the gas and followed. *Sis Matthews hyphenated Boyd in person. And that's no minivan.*

If the first stoplight in Bedminster hadn't been on red, Brian knew for sure he'd have lost her. He was just able to make a mental note of her license plate before the left-turn light turned green, and she set off with a squeal of tires that left rubber.

Sure is in a hurry, Brian was thinking as he also made the turn.

There was no turn signal again from the Range Rover as it braked violently and then careened down the first right-hand side street.

Brian's turn onto the street was far less erratic, and the first thing he saw was a school sign with flashing yellow lights. *Now I get it.* Ahead of him, the Range Rover had swerved into the curb and come to a very quick stop. The driver's door opened, and Sis Matthews-Boyd jumped out, running to the passenger side rear door.

Twenty yards away, Brian came to a much gentler stop. Normally, he'd be far too close to his subject, but he could see that the last thing on her mind was a tail. She appeared to be in a frantic hurry as she lifted a little girl out of the Range Rover and reached inside again for a baby. Then, carrying the baby and holding the little girl's hand, she headed through the gate to the small school and disappeared inside.

Brian stared through the windshield. *Now ain't this interestin'.*

He'd no idea how long she'd be, so he quickly edged his car forward and took some photographs of the Range Rover and school using a digital camera with a telephoto lens.

The vehicle in front of the Range Rover began to pull away, and Brian seized his chance to take the space. He was able to study the vehicle as he passed, noting that apart from the dirt, it looked quite new. Although it already had more than its fair share of dings and scrapes. *Couldn't possibly be the way she drives?*

Brian was adjusting the telephoto lens when the door to the school opened, and Sis reappeared, this time accompanied by a small, dark-haired boy. She was still carrying the baby and holding the little girl's hand, but this time, she looked quite calm and laughed as the boy looked up and said something.

Brian took as many photographs as he could, but as Sis reached the car and helped the boy into the front passenger seat, Brian knew it was time to leave. He noticed, via his rearview mirror, that the boy was putting on his seatbelt while looking directly at Brian's car. Sis seemed far too busy buckling the other two children into child seats in the back of the Range Rover to notice.

Brian drove onto the next right-hand side street and stopped again. He was still able to see the Range Rover through the branches of the old trees that edged the school's playground. *This isn't smart,* he thought. *All I need is some eagle-eyed parent or teacher to see a middle-aged man with a camera, in a car with out-of-state tags, hangin' around a school.*

To Brian's relief, the Range Rover began moving again, a lot more sedately. It turned onto the street where Brian was stopped, and as it passed, he could clearly see the boy. At the end of the street, the right turn signal blinked on.

Keeping his distance, Brian followed.

At the light where Sis Matthews-Boyd had left rubber, she went straight this time, heading back the way she'd come. Just to make sure, Brian kept the Range Rover in sight, and when he saw the left-hand turn signal begin to blink, he knew for sure she was headed home.

Enough for one day, he thought as he continued past the turn to the lane to the Matthews' home. He stopped at a gas station a mile down the road, not only to get gas and coffee, but also to call Michael.

"... I got a real good look at the boy," Brian finished. "He's too old to be the one I saw in Livingston's photograph. I couldn't see the baby. But unless Sis Matthews-Boyd gave birth to a second child and didn't send Livingston another photo, who do the kids belong to?"

"A neighbor?"

"Could be. Except there aren't any. Well, not close anyway."

"Good work," Michael added. "By the time you get back, I'll see how much info we can get on the Matthews family. And the husband."

Brian had been looking forward to a rare evening with Pauline. "Guess I'll see you later then."

Michael's Office, G Street, Washington, D.C.
Later that night

This's another advantage to workin' for someone who's connected, Brian thought as he savored a large plate of veal Parmesan. *In Dallas, this woulda bin pizza or a salad from Subway.*

Michael insisted that they all stop working when the take-out dinner from one of Washington's better restaurants arrived.

Molly thought, as she made space for the large containers of food, that Michael's office looked like a bomb had hit it; papers were everywhere.

Dan quickly swallowed a mouthful of seafood Newburg as he reread the page of information in front of him. "Old man Matthews was a very large contributor to the president's campaign."

Michael stopped eating. "Highlight that and put it in the priority pile. Then finish your dinner."

Silence returned to the office, until a few minutes later when Molly got to her feet. "Who's ready for dessert and coffee?"

Brian groaned. "You've gotta be kiddin'. More food?"

"A very rich chocolate torte."

"If you insist," he replied. "And the coffee."

"We're all going to have to walk home," Dan said. "All I want to do now is sleep."

Michael looked up. "Later." He turned to Brian. "How do we get close to Sis Matthews-Boyd?"

"Surveillance is goin' to be a bitch. It can be done, but we need more manpower."

Michael again studied the enlargements of the digital images that Brian had taken of the house. "What about the husband?"

"I'm just about to read the info Molly found," Dan said. "Graduated Princeton in 1994, at age twenty-three. That makes him roughly thirty-one."

Leaning back in his chair, Michael closed his eyes. "Brian's right. We do need more manpower." He paused. "Hand me that sheet on Matthews, Dan."

He read carefully before checking his watch. After reaching for his secure phone, he punched in some numbers. To his surprise, the man who answered knew his name.

"I need to speak with him ASAP, in a secure environment," Michael said.

"We'll let you know where and when," was the reply.

"Thanks." Michael looked up to see Brian and Dan watching.

"Your father?" Brian asked.

"The president," Michael replied. "I'll call my father tomorrow."

Molly was finally able to view the photographs Brian had taken earlier.

She held up a print. "These children look about the same age as the ones Mrs. Waterhouse described in her statement."

All conversation stopped.

"She said there was a boy about six and a baby. What do these look like?"

Michael looked again at the photographs. "It makes sense. They were good friends. If Fareed's on the run, two kids would slow her down. Good work, Molly."

It was almost midnight when they left the building, but they knew a lot more about the Matthews' family rise to riches, begun generations before.

"Rich to richer," Dan commented at one point. Before leaving the office, Dan copied all the information they could find on Mark Boyd and took it home with him. "He's got good taste," he said. "Drives a Lexus 300."

Despite the cool night air, Michael put the top down on the Jaguar for his drive home to Alexandria.

By the time he inserted his key in the front door, he'd already developed his plan of action. The only big question mark was the president. Having closely studied all of Brian's photographs, Michael knew he had to see his father for additional manpower. The possibility of Samin Fareed's children being in Sis Matthews-Boyd's care made Sis important. But there was no way Brian and Dan could keep surveillance on her twenty-four/seven and chase down other leads.

After checking, there was no record anywhere that Sis had given birth to more than one child. The dirty Range Rover was registered to Arnold Matthews, making Michael believe that Sis was probably under her father's thumb.

If that's the case, he thought, *then that further limits our chances of getting to her.* His gut told him to concentrate on the husband, but he wasn't sure how. Yet.

Michael's brain was still working overtime, and he was now too wide-awake to sleep. He kicked off his shoes before pouring a nightcap of Glenfiddich. Having turned off his cell phone earlier, he checked it again for the umpteenth time since calling the president. This time, there was a message. *Damn!*

"The row house, 1400 tomorrow," said the male voice.

"Thank you, Mr. President," Michael replied to an empty living room before re-dialing the Communications Center number to confirm.

CIA Headquarters, Langley, Virginia
Friday, October 4, 2002

With very little sleep, Michael called his father at 7:00 a.m.

"I need to see you ASAP," he said.

"My office, anytime after 0830. I've got a meeting, but I'll tell Mary to interrupt. Okay?"

"Thanks, Dad."

Mary Howard, the director's private secretary, did get him out of his meeting, and a few minutes later, Francis Correa strode into his outer office.

"Follow me," he said to Michael, without even slowing down.

With the door now closed, Francis faced his son. "What's this about?"

Michael told him.

Francis listened without interruption. "Give me until the end of the day," he said when Michael had finished. "Have you talked to the president?"

"I'm meeting him at 1400."

"Good. Tell him everything." Francis picked up some papers from his desk. "It seems your instincts are right again." He hesitated. "I'm proud of you."

Michael was caught off-guard. "Err ... thanks, Dad."

"Gotta go," Francis added, heading for the door. "I'll make sure you get what you need."

An area of Washington, D.C.
Early afternoon

As far back as anyone could remember, there'd been speculation in the District and beyond about the secret underground passages leading to and from the White House. No official had ever confirmed or denied their existence, but a privileged few knew the truth.

President Chester Makepeace, unlike some of his predecessors, didn't use them often, and to placate the Secret Service, he rarely used the same one twice. Regardless of why the passages were used, the president's Secret Service detail naturally hated the idea. And they really hated it when the president's meetings were with Michael Correa.

At 2:00 p.m., Michael was waiting in a slum area, outside one of many boarded-up row houses. Graffiti covered the plywood sheets nailed over the windows, and many of the doors had been ripped off their hinges. Weeds grew through cracks in the broken concrete sidewalks, and trash littered the narrow street. It was definitely not a place for tourists or those who stumbled on it by mistake. It was dangerous in daylight, but at night, no D.C. cop, unless absolutely necessary, would enter the area. If Michael was in any doubt that the president of the United States would at any minute step through the dilapidated front door to #22, the black Suburban parked farther down the street gave him a rather obvious clue.

The door to #22 was just a facade, and Michael noticed that someone had once tried to get through it with an axe. He couldn't help wondering what the axe wielder's reaction had been when it hit steel six inches thick.

The door now swung quietly open, and Agent Jack Jones stepped out, followed immediately by Makepeace. Agent Jones' expression left Michael in no doubt of what he thought of this idea, and his already-bad mood wasn't helped by the sight of Michael's Jaguar XK8 convertible.

Michael jumped out as Makepeace stepped forward, his hand outstretched. "Good to see you, Michael."

"And you, sir. Thanks for seeing me on such short notice."

"Any excuse is fine. Can I drive?"

Before Agent Jones could protest, Makepeace walked to the passenger door. "Just joking," he added before sliding inside. "Can we lose them?" he asked as Michael got behind the wheel and locked the doors.

"Probably, sir. But not a good idea. I don't want to be number one on the Secret Service hit list." He edged away from the curb, the Suburban already much closer. "But I could give them a good run for their money."

Makepeace, looking very un-presidential in a flat cap, old jeans, work boots, and a windbreaker, laughed. "Another reason I like you. You're sure I can't drive?"

"Sorry, sir. But if you'd like to close Andrews for an hour, you could take her for a spin there."

"Don't tempt me," Makepeace said. "If we weren't on high alert status, I'd take you up on that offer. Being president has its drawbacks. Remember that."

Michael wasn't sure what he meant and kept quiet.

A genuine war hero, Makepeace had the medals to prove it. After graduating from West Point, he saw two tours of duty in Vietnam before leaving the military to serve his country in other ways. His political career had been as solid and unspectacular as the man himself. Of medium build, with a nose that had been broken and never fixed, his most outstanding feature was his cornflower-blue eyes.

In the beginning, becoming president of the United States hadn't been part of his plan. But after John William Pearson III was elected, Makepeace was overheard privately saying, "Give the man [Pearson] enough rope, and hopefully the maniac will hang himself." When Pearson was eventually removed from office, Makepeace wasn't surprised by the Republican Party's overwhelming support for the obvious and popular frontrunner. Along with the vast majority, Makepeace was surprised when the man firmly declined to run, citing family and health reasons. Makepeace was further surprised at talk of his future nomination. Unlike the flamboyant and charismatic Pearson, Chester Makepeace was an honest man of high principles and values, totally unfazed by political posturing and agendas. "He'll be a shoo-in at the next election," they muttered as Pearson's dictatorial first term abruptly ended and his vice president took over. But the vice president was forever cloaked with the same maniacal reputation as his predecessor and not for reluctantly occupying the presidency for only fourteen months. With public opinion at an all-time low, even the enthusiastic support he got from the Democratic Party to run in the 2000 election wasn't enough. The landslide victory belonged to Makepeace. Gratefully withdrawing from the limelight, the forty-fourth president was soon forgotten.

At a red light, the man behind the wheel of a Stanley Steamer van glanced at the Jaguar and then at the passenger. When he saw the black Suburban parked almost in the Jaguar's trunk, he quickly looked again. *No. It can't be,* he thought just as the light turned green, and both vehicles sped away in a passable imitation of the start to the Indianapolis 500.

"We need to get out of D.C.," Michael said, heading for Route 50. "How much time do you have, sir?"

"As much as you need, much to my secretary's chagrin. What's this about?"

"Arnold Matthews."

If Makepeace was surprised, it didn't show. "Very wealthy industrialist. One of my biggest campaign contributors. A staunch Republican family. A generous philanthropist. Keeps low key. We occasionally have dinner together. I've even spent the odd weekend at his estate in Pennsylvania. You're investigating him?"

"Do you mind?"

"Why should I? I've got the utmost faith in you, Michael. If you think he's a rat, I want to know." They reached Route 50, heading east to Annapolis. "What speed are we doing?"

"I'm nine miles over the posted limit, sir."

Makepeace grunted. "Keep it there." But Michael was getting the distinct impression that given a different set of circumstances, his passenger would have told him to hit the gas.

Michael gave him a quick glance. The president appeared to be asleep, his eyes closed, his hands resting in his lap. For a time, neither man spoke.

Eventually, Makepeace broke the silence. "Tell me what you know."

Michael began with the raid on the Armonds' house in Florida.

By the time he'd finished, he'd reached the second-to-last exit before the Chesapeake Bay Bridge.

"As much as I'd like to take you to Eagles Nest, sir, I think it's time to go back. Otherwise, we're going to get stuck in Bay Bridge traffic."

"Do it," Makepeace replied. "I'm sure by now Agent Jones is muttering a few choice words."

Michael took the Cape St. Claire exit, crossed over Route 50, and accelerated fast down the entrance ramp heading west to Washington. The Suburban kept pace, making Michael wonder how many horses were under its hood.

"Why is finding Samin Fareed, or Sabrina Armond, or whatever alias she's using, so important?" Makepeace asked.

"My gut, sir. No other reason. If she's a terrorist gone to ground, I need to find her. But if she isn't and is an innocent party, why run?"

"You say this Brit McDonald's also looking?"

"Yes, sir."

"Does State[3] know he was here?"

"I don't know, sir. I haven't asked them. But I get the impression he's trying to keep a low profile. My father knows about him."

"Then let CIA handle him. But do what you think is necessary. If Matthews or his daughter are mixed up in this, I want to know." There was a pause. "You're sure the children Mullen saw are Fareed's?"

"If we find her, we can prove it with DNA. But yes, we're satisfied they're hers."

The outskirts of D.C. appeared on the horizon.

"Take the official route back, Michael. Saves all this damn sneaking around."

"Yes, sir."

---

3 Refers to the State Department.

As they exited the Beltway, another Suburban appeared to escort them back to the White House, where Marine guards snapped to attention as the small convoy swept through the gates to a private entrance.

After 9/11, with no personal vehicles allowed within close proximity to the White House, Michael followed the lead Suburban into an underground parking garage.

Makepeace unbuckled his seatbelt but made no attempt to get out. By now, the Jaguar was surrounded by Secret Service agents.

"Ask for whatever resources you need," Makepeace said. "If there are problems, I'll make sure they go away. Have you spoken with your father recently?"

"This morning, sir."

"Is he getting you the additional manpower?"

"Yes, sir." Michael hesitated. "If you don't have a problem using CIA on U.S. soil?"

"None whatsoever. Given our current status, we need all the agencies involved. It's long overdue. And let me know if you need an introduction to Matthews. If he's dirty, I want you to personally bring me his goddamn head on a platter. Understood?"

"Yes, sir. Thank you, Mr. President."

Makepeace finally got out of the car. "Keep up the good work. It's time to smooth Agent Jones' ruffled feathers," he added before the passenger door closed.

In his rearview mirror, Michael saw two Secret Service agents watch him leave before following Makepeace toward the elevator doors.

Michael's Office, G Street, Washington, D.C.
Late afternoon

Molly appeared in Michael's office, closing the door behind her.

"There are three CIA agents outside. They said you were expecting them?"

Michael stood. "That was fast. Send them in. And tell Dan and Brian to wait. I'm going to need to see all three of you too."

Moments later, two men and a woman filed into Michael's office.

"Agent Frank Hunter, sir," said the older of the two men, who in Michael's mind could easily be mistaken for a blue-collar worker or an accountant, depending on how he was dressed. "The director told us to report to you." He turned. "These are agents Bentley and Eden."

The female agent in her late twenties stepped forward. "Susan Bentley, sir. It's a pleasure to meet you."

Dressed in what Michael considered to be a very ugly and unbecoming checked suit, she had a face devoid of makeup and nondescript mid-brown hair. *This's good,* he thought, returning a very firm handshake. *A very unmemorable woman.*

Agent Ben Eden was in his mid-thirties but looked very much younger, despite his rapidly thinning hair. Of medium height and build, there was nothing eye-catching about him either. *Just a face in a crowd,* Michael thought, shaking an equally strong hand.

With all the introductions over, each agent handed Michael a file.

"Our personnel files, sir," Ben Eden explained. "We were told you'd need to see them."

Michael sat behind his desk again and opened the first file. "Get comfortable," he said. "I've got some reading to do."

Michael never looked up as he read through the files, although he was aware that from time to time, the agents were watching him. *My father's chosen well,* he thought, getting to the end of the last file. *They've all got a lot of field experience.* All three agents had been in the Middle East. Susan Bentley even spoke Arabic and some Farsi. They'd all successfully completed several surveillance assignments, and in Michael's opinion, at least Bentley and Hunter had passable firearms experience. He wasn't sure about Eden.

Michael pushed the closed files to one side. "What were you told?"

"We were called to the director's office earlier this afternoon," Hunter replied. "He told us that our case loads had been reassigned and that our section heads had been informed. Temporarily, we'd been transferred to another agency. He then said to report to you, sir. A matter of national security."

"That's it?"

"The director made it very clear that you would brief us, sir," Eden said. "And that until further notice we were to take our orders from you."

Michael got to his feet and then leaned against the front of his desk. "You all have impressive files. On paper." He gave the agents credit when they didn't respond.

"We're not CIA," he continued. "But when necessary, we'll break the rules. I'm not hand in glove with my father. I report directly to the president. As long as that's understood and you accept those terms, I'll continue." He paused. "If not, you are free to leave. No harm, no foul."

No one moved.

"Fine." Michael then hit the intercom button. "You can come in now."

The door opened, and Molly entered, followed by Brian and Dan.

Michael made the introductions. "Welcome to the team," he said, addressing the CIA agents. "There's no rank here. Molly's my executive assistant, but she also has a high security clearance. Use her. Her knowledge of the Hill and its players, plus a great ability for research, is invaluable."

Michael sat behind his desk again. "Brian's a former homicide detective. He's the best, although I'd never tell him."

"Takes one to know one," Brian muttered.

"Dan was Secret Service," Michael continued. "Presidential detail."

"And you, sir?" Bentley asked.

"A West Pointer," Brian interrupted. "Officially out of the Army, but the best special warfare specialist they have."

Bentley's eyes widened. "Did you say Army?"

"Yes. Don't let the suit fool you."

The $1,000 suit, she thought.

"As my father's an ex-Naval aviator," Michael continued, "I thought I'd make the annual Army/Navy game a bit more interesting."

"And he's got a terrible sense of humor," Dan added.

While Michael was talking, Molly had handed everyone a file.

Michael opened his, removing the first 8 x 10 photograph of Sis Matthews-Boyd. "This's your first target," he began. "If you've got any questions during the briefing, feel free to interrupt."

"... we begin tomorrow. Saturday's just another workday," Michael said an hour later, in a briefing that had few interruptions. "Go home, pack for a minimum of a week with whatever clothes you think suitable for small town Pennsylvania. If you don't have what you need, we'll get it. We'll rendezvous here tomorrow, 0830. Then to Baltimore to collect the vehicles and meet the rest of the team. Any questions?" He picked up his briefcase. "Good. I'm going home."

"The colonel gives a good briefing," Bentley commented to Brian as they left the building together.

Brian stopped. "Don't be misled by the fancy trappin's. The president created his position 'cause he didn't want to lose him. And it's got nothin' to do with his father. Michael's all pro."

"What's his main area of expertise?"

"Killin' people," Brian lied. "See ya in the mornin'."

Susan Bentley was left on the sidewalk with a sensation of fear and excitement. *Dear God, he was serious.*

As she made her way to the nearest Metro station, she told herself to get a grip. *Why'd he have to be such a hunk?* she thought as she boarded the train.

Regardless of her rigorous training and as hard as she tried, she couldn't stop wondering whether he was as good in bed as he looked.

A Classified Address, Baltimore, Maryland
Saturday, October 5, 2002

With no commuter traffic to slow them down, it took less than an hour from D.C. for Michael and the CIA agents to arrive at a warehouse in an old industrial section of Baltimore.

From the outside, the warehouse was rundown and ill kept, making Bentley think it was abandoned. A magnetic keycard opened a rusty and dented double garage door, and as the Suburban entered, the door was already beginning to close.

The inside belied the exterior. The concrete floor was painted an immaculate pale gray, and overhead, lines of fluorescent tubes lit the two rows of vehicles parked diagonally on opposite sides.

As Michael got out, a small man in mechanic's overalls came toward him.

He stopped and saluted. "Morning, sir."

Michael returned the salute. "Morning, Boost. Everything ready?"

"Yessir!"

Michael turned to the agents. "Meet Corporal Mateo 'Boost' Aguilar, United States Marine Corps. He's our vehicle mechanic and other things."

"Boost?" Bentley repeated.

"Yes, ma'am," he replied.

"How old were you when you stole your first car, Corporal?" Michael asked.

"Seven, sir!"

"And how old were you when you first got caught?"

"Ten, sir!"

"And the last time?"

"Seventeen, sir!"

Michael faced the agents. "Lucky for us, when offered the choice of jail or the Marines, he chose the Marines. Isn't that right, Corporal?"

"Yessir!"

"Carry on."

"Yessir! Thank you, sir."

"He's a mechanical genius," Michael added, watching Aguilar leave, before facing Bentley. "There isn't a vehicle made that he can't break into. Hence the nickname Boost. New York City P.D. was very relieved when he became a Marine. Their list of stolen vehicles decreased dramatically."

Eden studied the vehicles. "And these?"

"Some we buy. The corporal still has connections. The more up-market ones are seized or confiscated by other agencies. Big drug busts and well-publicized white-collar crime. Right now, we take our pick, and the location of this warehouse is classified. Unless we're desperate, they're all legal. Look under the hood, and none of them are what they seem."

From a large corner office set high in the rafters, another man started down the wooden staircase, carrying a clipboard. He was tall and wiry, with close-cropped gray hair, and dressed in a checked shirt and khakis. Appearing to be in his middle forties, Bentley guessed correctly that he could handle himself.

"This's Master Sergeant Tom Morgan," Michael said as the man reached them. "Tom's been with me a long time; haven't you, Tom?"

"Yes, sir."

"What happened to your ponytail?"

"Cut it off, along with the beard, sir. They'll grow back. Thought it best on this mission."

"Smart."

Michael turned back to the agents. "The master sergeant's also part of the team. On this mission, he'll be working with you. Anything you need, he'll coordinate with the corporal. Understood?"

They nodded.

"Assign them their vehicles, Tom."

"Yes, sir."

Bentley, who Michael thought was greatly improved by makeup and an elegant hairstyle, was now dressed as a casual but well-to-do suburban housewife. But she seemed disappointed with her almost-new Toyota Camry.

Michael had seen them all eyeing the more exotic vehicles. "If you're there more than a week, you change appearances and vehicles," he said.

Eden, dressed in a dark suit and tie, was handed the keys to a 1999 Mitsubishi Mirage.

Hunter, looking more like a construction worker, was assigned a beaten-up Ford F-150 pickup.

"Don't feel bad," Tom said, handing him the keys. "I got the minivan."

They left at irregular intervals.

Tom was the last to leave. "Quit worrying, sir," he said to Michael. "We'll all do our jobs. Your father wouldn't send you bum agents."

"Thanks, Tom."

As the warehouse door closed behind the minivan, Boost reached Michael's side. "You got that list for me, Colonel?"

Michael handed him a piece of paper and pointed. "That's my first choice. If you can't find it, let me know."

Boost grinned. "Oh, I'll find it, sir."

"That's what bothers me. Nothing illegal. Not this time."

"Understood, sir. Color?"

"Silver gray. Or dark green."

Boost flipped open a small notebook. "According to this, the XK's going to need a service soon. How's she running?"

"Like a rocket."

From the corporal's expression, Michael knew he'd given the right answer.

Chapter Eight

The Gibsons' House, Washington Street, Newport, Rhode Island
Monday, October 7, 2002

Start at the source, Kathryn thought, after reading the sparse file on Peter Gibson. *That could be tough.* But she'd been pleasantly surprised when Gibson's mother readily agreed to see her.

"That was easy," she said to Pauline.

"Let's hope it stays that way."

The Gibson family home wasn't difficult to find, and Kathryn was relieved there was a driveway. From what she'd already seen, having driven into the old section of Newport, there appeared to be no available street parking.

As she climbed the steps to the front porch, she presumed that the house had been in the Gibson family a long time. The two-storey colonial wasn't nearly as pretentious or well kept as its neighbors, but Kathryn guessed that the land alone was worth a fortune.

Before she could ring the bell, the front door was opened by a full-figured middle-aged woman with brown wavy hair. The shorts she wore did nothing to hide legs that reminded Kathryn of tree trunks, and she concluded that the woman wasn't aware of or didn't care about her appearance.

Smiling, the woman held out her hand. "I'm Elaine Gibson. You're the lawyer?"

Kathryn returned the handshake and handed her a business card. "I am. Kathryn Sullivan, Mrs. Gibson."

"You picked a nice day to visit. Come on in. I've got lemonade ready in the sunroom."

The sunroom, converted from a rear porch, ran the width of the house. At the far end, seated in a wooden rocker, an old lady moved back and forth, staring at the view.

"Don't mind Mother," Elaine said, steering Kathryn in the opposite direction. "She's deaf and has trouble getting around these days. We've tried to get her to wear a hearing aid, but she won't, so she'll not bother us. She spends all her time in that chair when it's warm."

"I can see why," Kathryn replied, admiring the view of the water and an occasional sailboat from a padded bamboo-framed sofa.

"She used to be so active," Elaine continued. "But she was never the same after Dad passed away." She sat opposite Kathryn and poured two glasses of lemonade. "You said on the phone that you were asked to help find Pete's killer. How does a lawyer do that?"

"It's often helpful to know the victim's background. We don't think his death was random. With the present national crisis, I'm sometimes asked to assist the Department of Justice with background research. That's why I'm here. I'm also very sorry for your loss."

"Thank you. But I still don't understand why the Justice Department's involved?"

"Your son's death may be connected to an ongoing investigation concerning national security."

"No, that can't be. Not my Pete. He was such a good boy. He'd never be mixed up in anything illegal."

"Even unwittingly?"

Elaine didn't reply.

"Why don't you tell me all about him," Kathryn added.

"Pete grew up in this house," Elaine began. "His great grandfather bought it in the twenties, before property around here became as high priced as it is now. We get offers to buy the place almost on a monthly basis, but we wouldn't do anything until Mother goes."

Despite two rotating ceiling fans, the sunroom was aptly named. Taking off the jacket to her business suit, and unseen by Elaine Gibson, Kathryn turned on a micro cassette recorder hidden in her briefcase. Although she intended to take notes, she wanted to make sure nothing was missed. Kathryn sensed an initial reluctance from Elaine to talk about her dead son, but once she got started, Kathryn was grateful she'd left her return flight open. She was already getting the impression that this was going to be a very long day.

An hour later, Elaine was still talking, when a sudden sound stopped her.

Kathryn turned to see the old lady tapping the wood-planked floor with the metal tip of a walking stick.

Elaine got to her feet. "Mother's telling me it's time for lunch," she said and looked at her watch. "No wonder, it's after one. I expect you're hungry too?"

Before Kathryn could reply, Elaine added, "I made some seafood quiche and a few other things. I hope you're not allergic to seafood?"

"Not at all."

"Good. I'll be back with a tray."

Kathryn took the opportunity to stretch her legs and was about to go through a door and down some steps to the garden when she heard a woman's voice. "Ask Elaine about Ollie."

Kathryn turned back to Elaine's mother. The old lady continued to rock, but she was now looking directly at Kathryn. "Elaine's been yakking for more than an hour, and she's only up to Pete's fourth grade. At this rate, I hope you planned on spending the night."

Kathryn couldn't control a smile as the old lady gestured for her to come closer. "Elaine gets it from her father. The Gibsons can all talk the hind leg off a donkey. I've had to put up with it most of my life."

"You're not deaf?"

The old lady lowered her voice. "When it suits me. It's easier that way now. The Gibsons always were stubborn." She reached for Kathryn's hand. "You won't tell?"

"Of course not. Who's Ollie?"

The old lady turned toward the door. "Elaine mustn't see me talking to you, but my youngest daughter, Cheryl, met him in a bar. She was twenty-six at the time. I knew immediately that he was rotten, but no one would listen. He was far too young for her."

"How old was he?"

"He told us he was twenty-three, but just before they got married, I found a birth certificate in his room. He was living here at the time. He was born in 1974, so that would have made him nineteen. Pete idolized him. If anyone in the family had anything to do with his death, it's Ollie."

"How old was Peter?"

"Fifteen. A typical impressionable teenager. He didn't look on Ollie as a future uncle, more like his best friend. After Ollie showed up, he changed."

"Where's Ollie now?"

"I don't know, and I don't care. I was taught never to think ill of anyone, but Ollie's the exception. If he's not dead, I hope he's in jail. He ran out on Cheryl, just like I said he would, and took all her hard-earned money when he realized he wasn't going to get a free ride from the Gibson family." She checked the doorway again. "He was a lying, cheating son of a bitch."

"Where's Cheryl?"

"She moved out to Colorado and remarried. We didn't talk for years, but she did come back for my grandson's funeral. Ask Elaine. She knows all the details."

"Thank you very much," Kathryn said.

The old lady took Kathryn's hand again. "Find the bastard who killed my Pete. I'd like some closure before the good Lord takes me."

"I'll do what I can. That's a promise."

The old lady began to rock again. "You'll enjoy my daughter's cooking. She's a gourmet chef."

Elaine's mother hadn't been exaggerating; the best seafood quiche Kathryn had ever tasted melted in her mouth. Elaine covered the glass-top table between them with an array of food that made Kathryn realize that if Elaine tasted all the food she prepared, it was probably why she was overweight.

Making the promise to exercise twice as hard, Kathryn sampled everything. "This is just wonderful," she said between mouthfuls. "You'd make a fortune in D.C."

Elaine smiled. "We do quite well here."

"I didn't mean to imply—"

"That's okay," Elaine interrupted. "We sold the fishing business after Pete left and bought an old deli just down the street. After it was remodeled, I finally got to turn my hobby into another business. My husband now manages the place, and I do most of the specialty cooking. Let me know when you're ready for coffee? It's the house favorite. We blend our own beans."

With Elaine Gibson's permission, Kathryn lit a cigarette by the water's edge, looking back toward the house.

"Tell me about Ollie," she said and sipped from a mug of freshly brewed coffee.

"You talked to my mother."

Kathryn wasn't sure how to reply.

"It's okay," Elaine continued. "She doesn't know I know she isn't really deaf, but I guessed she'd have something to say when she said she wasn't feeling well enough to go to the senior center. They paint on Mondays. It's her favorite day. Ollie had us all fooled, except her. Mom knew right off he was bad news. Caused a lot of spats." Elaine faced Kathryn, shielding her eyes. "You probably think we're a weird family?"

"Not at all. But I think it would be a good idea for me to talk to your sister."

"Cheryl's spent years trying to forget him, so it would probably be a waste of your time, even if she'd see you. Her marriage to Ollie caused a big split in the family. Mom has always thought it was the reason Pete left home. His funeral was the first time we'd been together in a long time. Because of the big age gap, Cheryl and I have never been close, so I was surprised she came. Mom wasn't. Despite her age, she's still as smart as a whip."

By late afternoon, Kathryn had already missed the 5:10 p.m. return flight. She was having trouble keeping her eyes open, and the warmth, a full stomach, and Elaine's constant talking wasn't helping. She'd even stopped taking notes.

"... why he decided to stay down there. He began e-mailing photographs. It looked like paradise, with all that blue sky, white beaches, and palm trees. Just like you see in the travel posters."

Kathryn forced herself to concentrate. "I'm sorry, where was this?"

"The Caribbean. After Pete got his fifty-ton captain's license. When he told us he wasn't coming back last winter, 'cause of the cold, I could understand why."

"Did he send many photographs?"

"All the time. Once we got used to the computer, it was better than postcards. One time he was home, he even showed us how to save them to CDs. It's amazing. Of course, we print some for Mom—it's easier that way—but the rest I can look at any time I want, and the place isn't littered with photo albums."

Kathryn remained outwardly calm. *Finally, I could be getting somewhere.* "Did he send you any photographs from his last trip?"

After nodding, Elaine blew her nose. "They're still in the computer," she said quietly.

Keep going, Kathryn thought. "And his e-mails. Did you save those?"

She nodded again. "Yes."

"I know how difficult this must be," Kathryn added, "but I would very much like to copy the e-mails and borrow the CDs. They'll be returned, of course."

"I don't know about that."

"I'll get duplicates made in Washington and have the originals sent back to you in overnight mail. That's a promise."

Slowly, Elaine got to her feet. "If they help find Pete's killer, okay. Follow me. The computer's inside."

Kathryn was finally about to leave when Elaine's husband appeared. Her conversation with him delayed her even more, but after hearing what he had to say, she was glad she stayed.

"Ollie Stackler was a con man," Mark Gibson said. "I knew that from the first time he went out on my boat. He told me he was a good seaman, but he got as sick as a dog and lived off Dramamine. And he'd never been around boats like he told me. I put up with him for Cheryl's sake. Looking back, it was a real dumb thing to do." He began to light a pipe and motioned for Kathryn to follow him outside.

"It would be easier for them," he continued, turning to the house, "to think Stackler had something to do with my son's death, but I don't see it myself. Stackler was a landlubber, through and through. Pete got his own boat when he was nine. Paid for most of it himself with money he'd earned. His grandfather and I helped, of course. Pete was born to the water. Given the choice, Stackler wouldn't want to be within a hundred miles of it. Unless he's changed a lot. Which I doubt."

Damn, Kathryn thought at the time. *There goes that theory.*

Kathryn was now left with no alternative but to take a hotel room for the night. But in her briefcase were three CDs of Peter Gibson's photographs and all of his e-mails.

As her new departing US Airways flight was at 6:20 a.m. the following morning, she arranged for a wake-up call and promised herself an early night.

Looking over her notes before turning off the light, something told her that Orville "Ollie" Stackler could well turn out to be more than just a rotten ex-son-in-law.

En Route from Rhode Island
Tuesday, October 8, 2002

Kathryn reread her notes during the nonstop one-hour, twenty-two-minute flight to Reagan National.

Elaine Gibson confirmed that her sister had met Ollie in a local bar, and according to her, "Ollie wasn't that tall, but he was quite good looking and had a real way about him." At that point, Kathryn wrote "charismatic?" on her legal pad.

Elaine went on to say that when Cheryl first brought Stackler home, he told the family he'd hitchhiked to Newport in the hope of finding work, but no one in the family ever checked his story. Stackler found a cheap room in a local boarding house, and within a few days, he'd met Cheryl Gibson.

"My sister told me it was love at first sight," Elaine said. "She fell hard and fast." So much so, according to Elaine, that Cheryl persuaded her father to hire Stackler as a deck hand on one of his fishing boats. "Dad said he was a hard worker, but that all changed after the wedding."

Within six months of Stackler dating Cheryl, they announced their engagement. Shortly after, he moved into the Gibsons' house. "When he wasn't working or taking Cheryl out, he spent all his time with Pete," Elaine said. "It was like they were joined at the hip."

Despite her conversation with Gibson's father, Kathryn was even more convinced that Stackler could be important. *But how?*

Kathryn's Office, 16th Street, N.W., Washington, D.C.
The same morning

"You're here early," Pauline said.

"My flight just got in," Kathryn replied.

"You just got in? It went well then?"

Kathryn sipped her third coffee of the morning. "It was a very long day but not a total waste." She handed Pauline a piece of paper. "That social security number belongs to Orville Stackler. The Gibson family cannot only talk, but they also don't throw anything away. Find out everything you can about him."

Kathryn began to re-pack her briefcase. "Oh, and according to the grandmother, he was born in Bloomington, Indiana, in 1974."

"Who is he?"

"Briefly, Peter Gibson's uncle."

Pauline did a quick calculation. "Uncle?"

"Don't ask."

"Okay. Did you tape the interview?"

Kathryn held up a tape. "Unless you want to be put to sleep, I don't recommend it. I made notes. Take them. Orville Stackler's a gut thing. If you need me, I'll be at Michael's office."

Pauline raised an eyebrow.

"It's business," Kathryn added.

"Of course it is."

Michael's Office, G Street, Washington, D.C.
Thirty minutes later

"Go straight in," Molly said. "He's expecting you."

Kathryn opened Michael's office door to see him seated at his desk.

"Was the trip worth it?" he asked.

"Maybe." Kathryn sat and held up three CDs. "These have to be copied and the originals returned to Elaine Gibson in overnight mail."

Michael took the CDs. "Do I have to guess?"

Kathryn stopped herself from giving him a smart reply. "Photographs that Peter Gibson took with his digital camera and then e-mailed to his parents from his laptop."

Michael remained silent.

"You didn't find a laptop or a camera, did you?" Kathryn added.

"Not that I'm aware."

"That's what I thought. But those prove they exist."

"Or did."

"That too. There's no point in me looking at them, as I don't know what I'm looking for. But I'll read all his e-mails."

"You got those too?"

She smiled. "Of course."

"Anything else?"

"The name Orville Stackler." Kathryn then repeated some of her conversations with both of Gibson's parents.

"I don't know how to thank you," Michael said when she'd finished.

I can think of a few ways, Kathryn thought as she left his office.

"Copies of Gibson's photographs," Michael said, handing the CDs to Brian. "Start with disk three. Those are the later ones. Maybe we'll get lucky."

"Accordin' to the Tybee cops' report, no camera was found when they searched Gibson's rental."

"And neither was a laptop. Get Dan to check Gibson's credit card purchases. Maybe we can find out where and when he bought them."

Brian began to leave. "That's a start."

"And run an Orville Stackler through NCIC.[4]"

Brian stopped in the doorway. "Who?"

Michael explained.

---

4   National Crime Information Center. A computerized index of criminal justice information serving agencies in all 50 states.

"Kathryn's instincts are almost as good as yours," Brian said a few hours later. "The guy's a career criminal accordin' to his rap sheet. But I don't see how he could have anythin' to do with the Gibson homicide. He was in jail at the time."

"Is he still there?"

"Sure is. And will be for some time. He was part of a ring that got busted by the ATF for smugglin' cigarettes from North Carolina to Michigan."

"When?"

"He was arrested in May. No bail."

"That's the connection. If I'm right, at least 8 million dollars was involved, and the proceeds were being sent to Hezbollah for their terrorist activities."

"You're kiddin'?"

"No. Follow the lead, Brian. Let me know if you need help."

"I'm right on it," he said as he left.

Michael's Office, G Street, Washington, D.C.
Wednesday, October 9, 2002

It was mid-afternoon when Brian and Dan entered Michael's office.

"We've both gone over these," Brian said, handing Michael some photographs. "Some nice scenes of the marina and Tybee Island from the water, and even some shots of Gibson's passengers. And you can't see a damn face in any of 'em."

Michael studied the photographs of men in diving suits. "Deliberate?"

"That'd be my guess. 'Specially as some are blurred."

"The e-mails?"

"Nothin' there either. Just some references to demandin' rich customers when Gibson was in the Caribbean. But no names. He's mostly describin' the scenery and the nightlife, I'm guessin' for his family."

"No luck yet on the credit card receipts," Dan said before Michael could ask. "If Gibson bought the camera and laptop new, we could get lucky and get the serial numbers, if he registered them. But the numbers will have to show up on lists of stolen property to take us any farther."

"Goddamnit!"

"Before you blow a gasket," Brian said, "I'm goin' to suggest that Dan sees Stackler on Monday. We're helpin' out with surveillance on Matthews-Boyd for the next few days. The agents need a break, and you're needed here. Agreed?"

There was a long pause.

"Agreed."

"It's a helluva time for Dan to get his feet wet," Michael said to Brian when they were alone.

"Gotta happen sooner or later. Better sooner. What's the latest from the agents?"

"Nothing new," Michael continued. "So far, Sis seems to lead a quiet but normal life."

"Patience."

Michael didn't reply. Brian knew exactly what he was thinking.

Chapter Nine

Wallens Ridge, Big Stone Gap, Virginia
Monday, October 14, 2002

After spending the previous four days on surveillance in Pennsylvania, Dan drove directly to Virginia. He soon discovered that the "supermax" prison lived up to its name.

Eventually, and accompanied by a guard, Orville Stackler entered the interview room in shackles. His outward show of confidence immediately reminded Dan of Charles Manson, and although there was no physical resemblance, Dan could see why women would find Stackler attractive.

Then dismissing the guard, Dan motioned Stackler to the only other chair and slid his ID across the table.

Stackler appeared to study it. "What's the Justice Department want with me?" he asked.

"Peter Gibson."

Bright hazel eyes fixed on Dan, but he was about to discover that Stackler's apparent self-assurance was only an act.

He seemed to shrink in his seat. "I didn't know they were going to kill him. Honest."

It was the last thing Dan expected to hear. He tried to remain calm, and as he quickly reformulated his interrogation, he could hear Brian's words: "The guy's a career criminal. But he's not that smart if he keeps gettin' caught."

Stalling for more time, Dan pushed a pack of cigarettes across the table.

Stackler didn't move. "That's pretty funny, seeing as I don't smoke."

"Then use them to trade." Dan sat back. "So the cigarette scam was just for money?"

"It's as good a reason as any."

"But it got your nephew killed."

"Like I said, I didn't know nothing about that 'til after it happened. Then it was too late."

Opening an envelope, Dan slid some enlarged crime scene photographs across the table. "He was murdered. Take a good look."

Stackler turned away. "I'm not saying nothing more," he muttered. "I could be next."

"Promise him the moon, if you have to," Michael had said. "But get him to talk."

"And if we don't deliver?" Dan replied.

"What's he going to do, sue us?"

"We can protect you," Dan said now.

"How? They're everywhere."

"Who?"

"These guys."

"Explain."

"Not until I got proof you're going to move me. Today. They'll know you came to visit. So if I stay here, I'm a dead man."

"Give me something."

Stackler remained close-mouthed.

"My boss reports directly to the president," Dan added. "He'll guarantee your safety. If you've got information."

Seconds ticked by.

Finally, Dan got to his feet. "Pity you won't cooperate." He reached for his briefcase. "I was your ticket outta here."

Silently, Stackler motioned him to sit again. Then he slowly leaned across the table. "Wayne Applegate," he hissed.

"That's it?"

"If you're who you say you are, that should be enough."

Dan got to his feet again. "I'll tell the guards you're to wait here. I'll be back."

Stackler looked up. "You'd better. 'Cause I'm no good to you dead."

He's got a point, Dan thought on his way to find some privacy from which to call Michael.

"Bring him in," Michael said two hours later.

"To D.C.?"

"Affirmative. We're doing the paperwork now. Can you manage him on your own?"

"No problem. He's not the violent type."

To make sure, Stackler was driven to D.C. in shackles, but wearing his civilian clothes.

"You won't need these," he said, rattling the chains after Dan had strapped him into the rear seat.

"They stay," he replied. "And if you behave, they'll be removed at our destination."

Michael's Office, G Street, Washington, D.C.
Several hours later

Stackler wasn't sure where to look—around the sumptuous office or at the man behind the desk, dressed in a shirt and tie, and wearing a shoulder holster with the grip of a 9 mm Beretta clearly visible.

For several minutes, he questioned Michael's authority.

Finally, Michael had enough. "Tell me about Wayne Applegate," he said.

"And if I do, I won't be going back?"

"Not to Wallens Ridge. Your status depends on your information."

"Who makes that decision?"

"I do."

Stackler looked around again. "It's a long story."

"I'm not going anywhere."

"The piece of shit I was driving crapped out in this rinky-dink town in Michigan," Stackler began. "But I didn't have enough money to fix it."

Instead, according to Stackler, he left the car where it was and headed to the nearest bar. Halfway through the afternoon and several beers later, he met George.

"George who?" Michael asked.

"I never did find out. He was just George."

When the bar eventually closed, Stackler, by his own admission, was very drunk and had told George his life story. "George had done time," Stackler continued, "so he understood."

With the promise of a bed for the night, Stackler managed to climb into George's pickup before he passed out.

The following morning, waking fully clothed on a cot in a cabin, Stackler met Wayne Applegate for the first time. "He's a good ol' boy," Stackler said.

"Heads this militia group. Looks like a bulldozer in fatigues, with a ponytail and a gun on each hip."

It soon became clear that Applegate already knew Stackler's history and circumstances, and despite Stackler's thundering hangover and disheveled appearance, Applegate questioned him for some time before finally making him an offer.

"Which was?" Michael asked.

"He'd get my car fixed. And I'd pay him back by working around the compound. But he made it real clear that I wasn't to ask questions."

Michael had read Stackler's file and came to the conclusion, as Stackler began to relax, that for a high-school dropout, he had a remarkably descriptive way with words. Michael was getting a very clear picture as Stackler went on to describe "the compound." Well hidden in thick woods and far away from civilization, it consisted of several wood cabins, while camouflage netting hid an assortment of pickups and "army-type vehicles." Heavily armed men, whom Stackler described as "mercs," came and went on a routine basis. Sometimes they were gone for hours, other times, for days. Stackler counted three women. Their main purpose seemed to be keeping the cabins clean, cooking, and looking after livestock and a vegetable garden. "Didn't need no supermarkets," he said. "They even milked a couple of cows and goats." But from the sounds he heard coming from the cabins at night, the women also served another purpose.

As "Big Wayne" insisted on regular target practice, hunting deer and wild turkey wasn't only a way to supplement the food supply. It also honed the men's skills.

Stackler had been at the compound for a week before he saw "Big Wayne's lady." All he ever knew was that her name was Betty, and he described her as "a good-looking piece of ass."

In the beginning, although he was allowed to eat at the communal table, he wasn't supposed to speak unless spoken to. When he was eventually accepted, he discovered that Betty appeared to be well educated. "She drove a new white Caddy," he said. "Sorta looked out of place there, and it was always kept well hidden."

It didn't take long for Stackler to realize that anyone arriving at the compound for the first time wore a blindfold. "Guess if I hadn't passed out, I'd have worn one too."

After describing his daily routine in detail, Stackler finally began to pique Michael's interest.

"Betty seemed to come and go as she pleased. Then one day, she shows up with this Italian-looking dude." By then, Stackler had been at the compound for several months and was beginning to be integrated into the group. "You didn't piss off Big Wayne," he added. "He sure hated the government. So I just agreed with everything he said."

Smart, Michael thought.

After almost six months, Stackler was allowed to leave the compound in the company of another man from the group. "We went to the town, where I'd first met George, to pick up supplies." After several trips, Stackler was told his blindfold was no longer required.

"Then one morning, Wayne tells me to take a truck and get the supplies on my own. I guess it was my big test."

At this point, Stackler admitted, he'd been very tempted to run. "But Big Wayne got my wheels fixed, like he said, and they were back at the compound. Where was I going without them?"

After dinner one evening, Applegate took Stackler to one side and asked if he'd be interested in working for the group. "By then, I'd seen how he operates," Stackler added. "I didn't like the odds if I said no."

Having agreed, and with a large cash incentive as a bonus, Stackler was told he'd be driving a truck. "Wayne knew I'd been a trucker and still had a valid license. That's how I finally met the Italian-looking dude. Only he wasn't Italian. His name was Mohammed."

Stackler paused to see if there was any reaction. There wasn't.

"Keep going," Michael said.

"We met at a topless bar in Detroit. It was odd, 'cause Betty was there. I was told she was one of the owners. She and Mohammed had a real thing going. So I guess that's how he got to Wayne. And he sure didn't act like any Muslim. Loved his women and booze."

"Was this 'thing' with Betty genuine?"

Stackler shrugged. "Dunno. And I sure as hell wasn't going to ask." He inched forward and lowered his voice. "I hadn't been at the compound more than a few weeks when Wayne got us all together. Except the women. He'd got this guy strung up. He was covered in blood and looked half dead. Then Wayne starts up this chainsaw and tells us this is what happens if you double-cross him. He cut off the guy's hands and feet, and left him to bleed to death." He swallowed. "I can still hear the screams. Wayne left him hanging 'til he stank. Then he got cut down and fed to the hogs."

As Stackler had just answered Michael's next question concerning any possibility of finding the victim's body, he didn't comment.

"Who was he?" he asked instead.

"Dunno. Poor bastard."

Michael looked at the open file in front of him. "According to your statement, you had nothing to do with the planning of the cigarette smuggling. True?"

"Yes. I only drove the rig. I wasn't told where I was going 'til I got behind the wheel."

"And you didn't know where the rig came from?"

"No. But Mohammed was always there. That's how me and him got to talking. It took awhile, but one night, he finally asked me if I knew of anyone who could handle a boat. Money never seemed a problem to these guys, so I called Pete. He's ... was a good kid. I thought I was sending extra cash his way."

"You never asked where the cigarette money was going?"

"No way. And I didn't find out 'til after we got arrested. I thought Wayne was getting it." Stackler paused. "Eight of us pleaded guilty, but we never thought we'd end up in supermax. You know about Wallens Ridge?"

Michael nodded. Even he'd been surprised that Stacker was sent there. The prison's reputation for violence and assaults against prisoners was well documented. Men had died in custody, and recently too. The warden had been replaced. But Michael assumed that as the FBI had traced cell phone links to Hezbollah during their investigation, they considered Stackler a terrorist.

He checked the file again. "There's no mention of Applegate here."

"I'd rather do the time," Stackler said quietly. "You don't rat on Wayne and live. He'd get me, wherever I was."

"What made you change your mind?"

"Pete getting killed. He was like a brother. He was the best thing that ever happened to me. The rest of the Gibsons you can keep. The old man wanted cheap labor. Pete's mom never shut up. Grandma's a nosy old broad. And Cheryl, the one I married, no sooner was the ring on her finger when she turned into a nagging bitch."

"I'm told you left with her life savings."

"Bullshit! They like to make out they're hard done by. I took what I thought was due. Hey, even Pete left. Smart kid."

"You stayed in contact?"

"Hell, yes." Stackler looked down. "I'm no saint, Colonel. I know that. I didn't want Pete doing the dumb things I do. I just wanted to make sure he was okay."

Stackler cleared his throat. "Pete called me after the first charter. He was real up. Like a pig in shit. He said they'd paid cash, which made his new boss real happy, and they'd given him a big bonus. Pete then said the icing on the cake was that they wanted to do it again, only next time with some real fancy gear. Pete was a scuba diving instructor too. That was the last time I spoke to him. Next thing I hear, he's dead."

By the time Stackler entered his office, Michael already knew he'd only been at Wallens Ridge a few weeks and that Mohammed Ibn Khaldun was incarcerated at the same prison. "Do you still talk to him?"

"That crazy son of a bitch? No way. He now hangs out with his Muslim buddies. They're all bad news. Leaves me alone, thank God."

"Explain."

"They'd slit your throat if you look at them funny. Life is real cheap to them. Fanatics is a good word."

"But you said you spent time with him before you were arrested."

"I did. He seemed like a regular guy. I knew he was foreign, but still, a regular guy. None of this Allah shit he does now."

"Does he get visitors?"

"Hell if I know. We're not even in the same cell block."

"But you must hear things?"

"If I do, I keep them to myself."

"So he does get visitors?"

"Maybe. He uses all his telephone privileges. And no, I don't know who he calls."

Michael got to his feet. "Take a break, Stackler. Then we want you to look at some mug shots. Tell us if there's anyone you recognize."

"And after that?"

"Back to jail. One that's safe. And if your information's accurate, you'll stay there until the trial. But if I find out you've lied, or left anything out, you'll be headed back to Wallens Ridge to take your chances."

"I've told you the truth."

"I hope so. For your sake."

The FBI had considered Mohammed Ibn Khaldun small fry on their ever-increasing list of terrorist suspects, so with him now safely behind bars, Michael's only hope was that Stackler would recognize another face. He took his time in going through the photographs, but he said none of them looked familiar. "These guys all look like A-rabs," he said, reaching the last page. "Mohammed was the only A-rab I saw; the rest of 'em was white, Colonel."

"Look again," Michael instructed.

Stackler did, but he passed over the several photographs of Hamza Jarrah, a.k.a. Philip Armond, without a second glance.

Finally, Dan led him away.

Michael waited until after his door closed before getting to his feet. "Shit! But I'm inclined to believe him."

Brian stood slowly. "Me too. If Wallens Ridge is as bad as they say, even a guy like Stackler's goin' to cooperate."

Michael's Office, G Street, Washington, D.C.
Friday, October 18, 2002

Michael was replacing the receiver as Brian and Dan entered.

"That was the FBI," he said. "They've been after Applegate's paramilitary, anti-government organization for years. He's been under surveillance on and off during that time, but with what Stackler told us, they're now beefing it up again. They chose not to charge Betty Gilliam, one of the owners of the bar in Detroit. They got the feeling she knew a lot more than she was saying and thought she was running scared. She left for the Virgin Islands right after the arrests. They know where she is, but she hasn't come back yet."

"Interestin'," Brian commented.

"With the FBI covering that connection, I want us to concentrate on Sis Matthews-Boyd," Michael continued. "Agreed?"

Brian nodded. "Agreed. The agents are spread too thin. If those kids are Fareed's, she's gotta make contact sooner or later."

Michael began to shuffle papers. "That's settled. You begin on Monday, but see me before you leave."

Brian and Dan turned to go.

"Have a good weekend," Michael added, already reaching for the telephone.

"He's up to somethin'," Brian said to Dan as they got ready to leave.

Dan had been around Brian long enough to respect his judgment. "Do you know what?" he asked.

"Not yet. But guaranteed, Michael's playin' some card."

Dan slung his topcoat over his arm. "Time will tell."

"Sure will."

Michael's telephone conversation was brief, but he was smiling as he hung up.

A few minutes later, Molly was surprised to see him leaving.

"I'm going to Eagles Nest," he said. "If anyone wants me over the weekend, I'll be there."

Eagles Nest, Somewhere off Route 301, the Eastern Shore, Maryland
Saturday, October 19, 2002

The Sikorsky Sea King VH-3D helicopter landed on a large patch of freshly mown lawn to the south of the three-car garage. The rotor blades were still turning as Chester Makepeace jumped out, and ducking his head, he walked quickly toward Michael.

"Welcome to Eagles Nest, Mr. President," Michael shouted.

Makepeace straightened and looked around. "Now I understand what all the fuss is about. This is really something."

Seated on the sundeck of Michael's forty-six-foot Viking sportfisherman, moored at the long dock leading from the rear of the house, Makepeace rolled up his shirtsleeves and faced the sun, his eyes closed. "What I wouldn't give for just a few hours of this," he said. "Take her out much?"

"Not as much as I'd like, sir."

Makepeace didn't comment. "I think I've come up with a way to get you to Matthews without arousing any suspicion," he continued.

"How, sir?"

"Horses," Makepeace replied.

"I don't know anything about horses."

"You will."

Then Makepeace began to elaborate, and it was not at all what Michael was expecting.

Chapter Ten

Michael's Office, G Street, Washington, D.C.
Monday, October 21, 2002

Michael entered the outer office at 8:00 a.m.

Greeting Molly, he added, "I need to know everything there is about horses. Give me five minutes to go through the mail. Then send Brian and Dan in. You too."

A few minutes later, Michael was repeating his weekend conversation with the president.

When he finished, he was met with stunned silence.

Brian was the first to recover. "Have you ever ridden a horse?" he asked.

"A couple of times. When I was a kid."

"Then you'd better learn. Fast," Brian added.

"I've got a better idea," Michael said. "You do it. You're a Texan."

"Surprisin' as it may seem, we don't all ride horses." Brian turned to Molly. "Find him a copy of *Horses for Dummies*."

"He's going to need a lot more than that," Dan muttered.

By the time the day was over, Michael had a pile of books on his desk.

"These are the best I could find," Molly said an hour before. "I suggest you read them in order." She then handed him a list. "And those are the nearest equestrian centers."

Michael scanned the list. "You took Brian seriously?"

"Of course. Didn't you?"

That night, Michael began his reading, and once he got started, he found he actually enjoyed the learning process.

Chapter Eleven

Michael's Office, G Street, Washington, D.C.
Wednesday, October 30, 2002

Michael was still studying at night when Molly placed some videos on his desk.

"These might help too," she said. "Isn't it time to get on a horse?"

It was something Michael had originally been dreading. "Find me a good place and make an appointment."

"Fine," Molly replied. "And that's book a lesson," she added before closing his office door.

"Your first lesson's at 1430 tomorrow," she told him a few hours later. "It's just you and the instructor, and they have an indoor arena."

Michael looked up. "That's important?"

"Yes, it's important. It might be nice outside now, but you'll be learning over the winter, unless you enjoy being cold and wet."

Wouldn't be the first time, Michael thought.

"You've got to wear jeans and some hard-heeled shoes or boots," she continued. "They'll supply everything else."

Green Meadows Equestrian Center, Barn Lane, Centreville, Virginia
Thursday, October 31, 2002

Michael wasn't comfortable with either the horse or his small female instructor. He was assured that the large gray mare had taught many beginners to ride, while Sally Ridgeway reminded him of a brutal Marine drill sergeant he'd once had the misfortune to meet.

Sally looked him up and down, but it was purely professional, convincing Michael that she probably had a girlfriend. "Six feet two?" she asked.

"Close enough," he replied.

She pointed to a row of riding helmets. "Find one that fits snugly and follow me."

With a pair of suede chaps over his jeans and his helmet firmly in place, Michael finally mounted the mare. *It looked a hell of a lot easier in the videos.*

"Head up! Back straight. Keep those heels down! And stop doing your knitting with those reins, Mr. Correa!" Sally barked at him continuously for almost an hour.

Finally, he dismounted.

"My advice is to take a long soak in a hot tub. You're going to be sore."

Bullshit, Michael thought, knowing that he was physically fitter than the vast majority. Although he wasn't at what he considered peak condition, he ran almost every day and worked out with weights three times a week.

Chapter Twelve

Michael's Office, G Street, Washington, D.C.
Friday, November 1, 2002

Almost unable to sit, Michael bitterly regretted his decision to ignore Sally's advice.

"How was it?" Molly asked as he limped past her desk.

"She's a goddamn tyrant," he muttered, disappearing into his office.

Chapter Thirteen

Green Meadows Equestrian Center, Barn Lane, Centreville, Virginia
Wednesday, December 4, 2002

After twelve lessons, Michael arrived at the stables wearing tall boots, snug-fitting britches, and a sweatshirt. He held a new riding helmet and whip.

"You look the part," Sally commented. "Is there a reason why you're learning to ride in record time?"

"Call it a presidential order," he replied, leaving her speechless for once.

By now, Michael had progressed to a more spirited mount, which he handled with ease.

"How good am I?" he asked her after the lesson.

Sally could see that he was serious. "Far better than most novices, Mr. Correa. I assume you've got a reason for asking?"

"I need to fool the experts."

She'd no idea what he meant by that. "In that case, we'd better keep working."

From the first time Michael was at the stables, he'd been watched by a horse in the end stall.

"Why can't I ride that one?" he asked during his second visit.

"Oh, no, Mr. Correa; he's off-limits to you. Got a real bad temperament."

"So?"

"He's a vicious brute. He'd take off your arm if he could. Please don't go near him."

But Michael chose to ignore her. The animal piqued his interest. Without Sally's knowledge, Michael slowly made friends with the dark-brown gelding, and he'd never once attempted to bite. After weeks of gaining his trust, the horse now nuzzled Michael's arm or shoulder, and kicked at the stable door whenever Michael left.

He made some discreet inquiries. The five-year-old was half Quarter Horse, half Morgan, and it was assumed he'd been ill treated by his previous owner. He was at the stables on consignment, but so far there'd been no buyers. "And not likely to be," Michael was told.

Almost two months had passed since his meeting with the president at Eagles Nest. Michael suspected that time was running out and that he should now call Makepeace to get the introduction to Arnold Matthews.

Green Meadows Equestrian Center, Barn Lane, Centreville, Virginia
Sunday, December 8, 2002

It was early when Michael drove to the stables, relieved to find that Sally was nowhere in sight.

"I want to ride the consignment horse in the last stall," he said to one of the grooms.

"You can't," she replied. "He's off-limits to students."

"And if I was thinking of buying him?"

When he signed a disclaimer, she gave in.

With a grooming kit and the gelding's saddle and bridle, Michael entered his stall.

Thirty minutes later, he was leading the horse to a small empty paddock.

Well, here goes, he thought, swinging himself into the saddle. He stroked the horse's neck. "Okay, buddy. Let's see what you can do."

The gelding flicked his ears, listening to Michael's every word, but when Michael shortened the reins and squeezed with his legs, the equivalent of WWIII began. The gelding reared, bucked, and twisted, trying every move he knew to get Michael off his back. Several times, Michael thought he'd succeeded. All he could hear were Sally's words: "Keep your heels down! Shorten the reins!"

It seemed like an eternity, but finally the gelding stopped. He was bathed in sweat, foam was dripping from his mouth, and his sides resembled bellows.

Apart from the foam, Michael thought, *I'm as bad.*

"Mr. Correa! What the hell do you think you're doing!"

Michael turned slowly in the saddle to see Sally and a small group of riders who'd gathered to watch.

Michael stroked a very wet neck. "Okay, buddy. One more time. We're both in a lot of trouble."

This time, on Michael's commands, the gelding behaved perfectly.

When Michael finally dismounted, he loosened the girth, and pulling the reins over the gelding's head, they walked slowly to the gate.

"You're crazy!" Sally snapped. "Don't you ever—"

"Enough," Michael interrupted. "I need to rub him down."

"Wash him down first," she shouted after him.

An hour later, Michael found her in her small office.

"I won't be needing any more lessons," he said. "But thanks for all your help." He could see he'd surprised her.

He was about to surprise her even more. "I own a small farm on the Eastern Shore. So, draw up a contract of sale, and I'll write a check."

"You want to buy the consignment horse?"

"His name's now Delta," Michael replied. "How much?"

Later that afternoon, Michael called Tom Morgan. "What do you know about horses?"

"One end kicks and the other end bites."

"That's what I figured. I've bought a horse and need you to find someone reliable to look after him."

"This's a real bad line, sir. I thought you said you'd bought a horse?"

"I did."

"Call me again after you've sobered up." There was a very long pause. "You really did buy a horse, didn't you, sir?"

"Affirmative."

"Oh, fuck," Tom muttered. "Now I've heard it all."

Chapter Fourteen

Michael's Office, G Street, Washington, D.C.
Tuesday, December 17, 2002

"I've got SAC Fuller[5] on line one," Molly said soon after Michael arrived.

Michael picked up the receiver. "Tell me it's good news."

"Wish I could," Fuller replied. "We've checked every Egg Harbor dealer we could find for sales of that size boat from 1998 through 2001. New and used. We got two possibles. One's an Egyptian heart specialist living in Chicago. The other, an Iranian lawyer, now a naturalized U.S. citizen, living in Naples, Florida. We did extensive background checks. They're both clean."

"Damn it."

"It had to be a private sale," Fuller continued. "We've asked all our offices anywhere near the coast to keep a lookout in local marinas. That's the best I can do. Sorry."

"I appreciate the help."

"Let me know if there's anything else?"

"Will do. Thanks."

Goddamnit again, Michael thought, hanging up.

Finnegan's Bar, Bedminster Road, Bedminster, Pennsylvania
Later that night

The surveillance team quickly learned one thing about Mark Boyd; he stopped at the local bar almost every night. On Thursdays he was always late,

---

5 Special Agent in Charge for the FBI.

due, they discovered, to a regularly scheduled racquetball game. Although their primary target was Sis Matthews-Boyd, they hadn't ruled him out as an innocent party.

"He's got Fareed's children livin' under his roof," Brian said. "He's gotta know somethin'."

In the end, it was agreed that Dan would attempt to develop a friendship. After several weeks of showing up at the bar on a regular basis and making one beer last at least an hour at a small corner table with the best view, Dan finally graduated to a bar stool. Little by little, he'd been cultivating the barmaid Stella, who, he'd noticed, spent more time with the younger men.

In Dan's mind, Stella looked as though she'd stepped from another era. Her short curly hair was dyed Marilyn Monroe blond, and her heavy makeup was craftily applied. She was polite to the few female patrons, but it was the men on whom she lavished attention. She knew all the regulars by name, but most of the time, she called them either "dear" or "luv." And Mark Boyd seemed to be a favorite. When Stella wasn't behind the bar, she was clearing tables or carrying drink orders. She sashayed around the room, her high heels clicking on the worn vinyl tile, and Dan had to admit that for a woman in her fifties, she had a great pair of legs. Obviously, Stella knew it too. Dan had never seen her without a tight miniskirt and low-cut fitted top. He guessed she was at least a size sixteen, and that was being conservative. The regulars sat on stools at the bar, where Stella frequently leaned toward them, her deep cleavage on full display. She appeared to enjoy the ogling.

Or maybe it's just an act, Dan thought, making him wonder if she'd once been a stripper. She blew kisses from glossy lips, and Dan guessed that her perfect white smile must have cost a small fortune.

The previous week, Dan was seated at the bar when Boyd walked in, loosening his tie. Ignoring Dan, he sat on the next stool, and in an instant, Stella was in front of him. Studying him, she placed a hand with long red fingernails on his. "Hard day, luv?"

"You can tell?"

She laughed. "Stella always knows. Your usual?"

"Of course."

She turned away to mix his drink.

Dan seized his chance. "I'll get this one, Stella." He turned to Boyd. "I'm Dan Olsen," he added and held out his hand. "I keep seeing you here. Thought it was time to say hello."

"Mark Boyd." His drink arrived, and he took a huge gulp. "Stella? Dan's next round's on me."

"Thanks."

But although Boyd paid for Dan's second drink, he was more intent on having a conversation with the other man next to him. All Dan got was a good view of his back. And when it came time for Boyd to leave, Dan was all but ignored.

There's got to be a better way to get to him, he thought, running various scenarios. Having researched Boyd and his days at Princeton, he kept coming back to the same one.

After talking it over with the team, Brian told him to try it. "At this stage, whatta we got to lose?"

As Tuesday nights seemed less busy, Dan waited next to Stella's Nissan Maxima for the bar to close.

Eventually, Stella headed toward him, fumbling in her purse with her head down.

Even with the security lights, it was dark, and the last thing Dan wanted to do was scare her.

"Hi, Stella. It's Dan," he said as he got out of his car.

For a second, she stopped. "You're out late."

Dan held up his ID. "I've got good reason. We need to talk."

"Now?" Stepping toward him, she peered at the ID. Then she fumbled in her purse again, and finding a small flashlight, she looked more closely before handing it back.

"You're with the Justice Department?"

"Yes."

"Am I in trouble?"

"Not as far as I know." Dan opened the passenger door. "Why don't you get in."

Stella noted it wasn't a request and dutifully sat.

From the driver's seat, Dan opened a file and began to read. "You were born Stella Jabinsky, in Pittsburgh, Pennsylvania, on September 7, 1949. The only daughter of second-generation Polish immigrants ..."

As Dan continued to read, Stella's big brash persona melted away, leaving behind a nervous middle-aged woman.

Eventually, Dan closed the folder. "We also know you own the majority share of the bar. We've seen your tax returns. What are you skimming? Fifty thousand a year? More?"

She paled under the heavy makeup.

"We're not the IRS," Dan added. "But we do know where to find them."

She didn't look up. "What do you want?"

Stella listened to what he had to say.

"That's it?" she asked when he'd finished.

"Yes. Can you do it without arousing suspicion?"

She nodded. "No problem."

God, I hope so, Dan thought as she drove away.

The Matthews-Boyd House, Spruce Hill Lane, Bedminster, Pennsylvania
October through December 2002

Surveillance on Sis Matthews-Boyd was difficult at best. And the hours she spent at the house proved to be even more of a challenge. Sorting through the couple's trash wasn't an immediate option either. Like the rest of the nation, garbage became public property in Pennsylvania when placed at the curb, but they soon discovered that a private garbage service collected from the house.

"If she's bein' as careful as we suspect, I doubt we'd find much," Brian said after a couple of weeks.

Not wanting to involve any more people than necessary at this stage, it was decided to temporarily shelve the garbage idea, much to everyone's relief.

Using several disguises, Bentley stood close and even next to Sis in the supermarket, local bank, and library on more than one occasion. She even began using the same hairdresser, in the hope of picking up some gossip. There was none.

"... and she rarely uses her cell phone," Bentley told Brian after they'd subpoenaed her phone records.

"That's gotta tell you somethin'," he replied, when every call proved to be legitimate. "She ain't no angel. Somethin's goin' on."

After weeks of tailing Sis whenever she left the house, Brian told Michael, "Followin' her all over the goddamn place is gettin' us nowhere. We gotta get closer."

"Do whatever it takes," was the reply.

Sixty feet from the rear patio of the farmhouse was a large, majestic oak. And it would have been perfect for concealing monitoring equipment and even a member of the team in its huge branches had it not stood starkly alone and now leafless in the sweeping lawn.

"Pity their landscapin' wasn't a priority," Brian said. "There's no way we can get to it without bein' seen."

Until they got to know if Sis had a routine, the idea of using the tree was temporarily abandoned. Instead, they set up a hide, supposedly for bird watching, in the trees and underbrush that formed a rough boundary on the left of the property. But they were at least fifty yards away. The prickly hedge that edged the lane at the bottom of the driveway also bordered the other side of the house and was thick enough in places to partly conceal a second hide.

"Let's hope the kids are too young to come this far," Hunter commented from the hide on the first day.

Complete with well-used Audubon books on native species, cameras, and notepads, their high-powered binoculars and listening equipment wouldn't seem out of place if they were discovered. They worked in pairs, rotating in twelve-hour shifts, and kept in contact with their partner by way of headsets. To add more authenticity to their cover, they wore winter camouflage-patterned parkas with the logo and name of a fictitious bird-watching club stitched to a breast pocket.

Leaving vehicles parked for hours had also been a problem. Brian ruled out using the lane below them, and the only other road was two fields away at the top of the hill. There was an even better view of the valley, and over the years, an area of grass verge had been used as a vantage point. The once-muddy ruts from numerous tires were now frozen and had even been covered in a light dusting of snow. To make doubly sure they weren't disturbed, they sometimes parked a four-wheel-drive Chevy Blazer with an official-looking notice placed in the windshield. It read: "Members of the Maryland Bird Watchers Club."

Several weeks before, while Sis was out, Eden climbed the old oak, surprising Brian with his agility. He was able to secure a large but well-hidden microphone in its huge branches. But before he finished, Sis returned home.

It was dark when Eden finally climbed down from the tree.

He was hungry, thirsty, and cold.

"How's the view?" Brian asked.

Eden rubbed his arms. "Great, if you're a bird. As a kid, I was always climbing trees. Now, it stinks. I'm getting too old for this shit."

Despite Eden's efforts, the monitoring equipment in the oak was only effective if Sis was outside or just inside the French doors to the kitchen.

"We've gotta get inside," Brian said.

However, one thing became clear; Sis constantly reprimanded the children.

"She's a real tough cookie," Hunter commented.

"And he's henpecked. Poor bastard," Eden added, having just overheard part of a conversation on the patio. Sis sounded angry, but she kept her voice low as she berated her husband for never being home.

"Do you blame him?" Eden muttered through his headset.

Noticeably absent from the team's eavesdropping was any reference to the children.

"That's not right," Bentley said one evening. "Kids are usually the main topic with parents."

"I agree," Hunter replied. "But then they're not like any parents I know. She whines and bitches about having to pay the bills, cook, and clean, etc., but we've never heard that the kids are the problem. As the husband doesn't defend himself, I guess Dan was right. He's scared of her."

With no hidden microphones in the house, their analyses of the couple was based mostly on guesswork.

That was about to change.

The Matthews Estate, Deer Run Road, Bedminster, Pennsylvania *Thursday, December 19, 2002*

The double gates to Sleepy Hollow were open, and the first thing Michael saw was a large red and white sign: "Warning! Horses. Please drive slowly." Thick shrubbery and trees hid the Matthews' residence from the lane, and at any moment, Michael half expected to see Ichabod Crane come careening around a corner of the winding driveway.

Why Sleepy Hollow? he thought as the Jaguar XJR sedan came to a stop in a large area of gravel outside the L-shaped brick house. *Sleepy, maybe. So where's the hollow?*

After he rang the bell, the front door opened quickly, making Michael think that Arnold Matthews had been waiting. That surprised him.

"You must be Michael Fulton," Matthews said, pumping his hand. "Delighted to meet the son of such a good friend of the president. Come in."

Matthews was in his mid-fifties. Tall and broad shouldered, the only indication of his Irish ancestry was his thick reddish-brown hair. There was no discernable accent, and Michael guessed from the web of tiny red veins on his cheeks and nose that Matthews enjoyed his liquor. *Maybe too much?*

"Let's talk in my study," Matthews added, leading Michael through the house, which was much larger than it appeared.

Having done his homework, Michael already knew that Matthews' great-great grandfather, at age sixteen, immigrated to the U.S. during the Irish Potato Famine in 1848, although there was nothing in the records to say how he'd made a small fortune and been able to buy what was now Sleepy Hollow. However, Michael did know that the old farmhouse had been torn down at the end of the nineteenth century, and part of the present English-style Tudor mansion replaced it.

Someone liked wood, Michael thought as he kept pace with Matthews, now striding down yet another paneled hallway.

"We're here," Matthews said, flinging open a door.

"Nice room," Michael commented, eyeing the dark oak-paneled walls and plethora of gilt-framed oil paintings.

Matthews stared through the expanse of windows. "The house is a damn maze. Every generation added a bit more. It was great growing up here. Plenty of places to hide. But now it's just a pain in the ass." He signaled Michael to join him. "How's that for a view?"

Michael had to admit it was good—an endless vista of large fenced paddocks and a few horses, culminating in a large lake.

"Used to be a small pond," Matthews added. "Until my grandfather took up fishing. Didn't last long. He never caught a fish. But we got a nice lake. Do you fish, Michael?"

"Sometimes, sir."

"It's Arnold. Only my employees call me 'sir.' Want a drink?"

Play the game, Michael reminded himself. "A small scotch and water, thanks. I'm driving."

"Excellent choice," Matthews said, opening the doors to a large bar concealed behind some paneling. "I've got an Irish malt that's as smooth as a baby's bee-hind, but very much older."

It was obvious to Michael, as he sipped the vintage whiskey, that Matthews had no conception of the word "small."

"So," Matthews continued, settling into a large wing chair in front of an impressive Gothic-style fireplace. "The president tells me you're looking to buy some horseflesh. If that's so, you've come to the right place."

"You understand I'm a novice at this."

"Bullshit. According to the president, you're being far too modest."

Damn! Michael thought, initially surprised that Makepeace had arranged the meeting so quickly. *What's he got me into?* He took a sip of the whiskey before putting the glass on the leather-topped table next to his chair.

"... many do you own?" Matthews asked, jolting Michael out of his thoughts.

"One," he said. "I'm boarding him at the moment, until I find a groom."

"When you find a good one, hang on to 'em. They're like gold."

Matthews had just given Michael his opening. "You've got problems?"

Matthews finished his drink in one gulp. "Always. They're like goddamn gypsies. My head groom's been with me for years, thank God. But I pay him a fortune, and he gets free housing. He's also in charge of the hiring and firing. I can't keep up." Matthews got to his feet. "Want to tour the stables?"

Michael finished his drink. "That's why I'm here."

His tour took over two hours, and although he let Matthews do most of the talking, Michael was grateful he'd studied so hard. With a few exceptions, he was able to understand Matthews' conversation.

"... last but not least, the remainder of this year's foals," Matthews said, now leaning against a paddock railing. "There's some great bloodlines out there. But if you're in no hurry, you might want to consider one from next spring's crop."

Michael listened with half an ear as Matthews talked about the breeding history of each foal. "... and I've got a few friends coming for dinner on Saturday. I do it every year around this time. I know it's short notice, but I'd like you to meet them."

Shit! "Thanks, Arnold. That would be great."

On his way back to D.C., Michael drew a mental map of the stable's layout and concluded that if breeding horses was a hobby, Matthews wasn't playing at it. From all the activity and the number of people he'd seen working, Michael guessed it was costing him a small fortune. He'd gotten another invitation, but he hadn't seen anyone who remotely resembled Samin Fareed.

It was a real long shot, he told himself. *Maybe this's a total waste of time, money, and manpower.*

Green Meadows Equestrian Center, Barn Lane, Centreville, Virginia
Late afternoon

After changing quickly in the men's locker room, Michael took Delta for a brief ride along one of the many trails.

It was almost dark by the time he got back, and he was in the process of giving the gelding a good rubdown when Delta's head shot up, and he snorted.

Michael turned to see Sally.

"He looks good," she said. "He really responds well to you."

Michael stroked the horse. "He needed some attention."

"And someone to love him," she added. "I've been lunging[6] him daily. He's really muscling up."

"No riding?"

She gave a rare smile. "Not yet. He's got to learn to trust me first."

Michael gave Delta a final pat and closed the stable door. "I'd like to show you something. It's in my car."

Under the lights of the parking area, Sally stared at several identikit photographs of what Samin Fareed could now look like.

"Have you ever seen this woman?" Michael asked.

Sally shook her head. "Who are you? A cop?"

"Not really. But I really need to find her."

"That's why you took up riding?"

He nodded.

"I'm impressed. She hangs around the horse world?"

"It's a long shot."

"Wow. You must want to find her real bad?"

"I do."

Sally could see he was serious. "We're involved with most of the top shows. The horse world is really small. If I see her, what do you want me to do?"

Michael handed her his card. "Call any of those numbers, day or night."

Sally fingered the card. "Why didn't you tell me you were a lieutenant colonel?"

"It's not important."

---

6   To exercise a horse (usually without a rider) in a large circle at the end of a long rein.

"You really do work for the president, don't you?"

"I can't answer that."

"I think you just did," she said.

Michael began to leave.

"Anything else?" she added.

"Just make sure Delta gets the very best attention. He's a great horse. And I am going to keep him."

Michael's Office, G Street, Washington, D.C.
Friday, December 20, 2002

"Your father wants you to call him," Molly said to Michael. "He left the message yesterday."

Michael called the direct line.

Francis answered. "... and let's meet off campus. Free for lunch?"

"I can be."

"Good. The usual bar in Crystal City at 1300."

"I'll be there."

Michael was about to leave when Molly handed him a cell phone and what looked like a memo.

"I've got a phone," he said. "Is this an upgrade?"

"No. It's a second cell phone, dedicated to Fulton Industries. The landline should be up and running by Monday. That memo is a reminder to you, Brian, and Dan that if they should answer the phone, line four is now Fulton Industries and should be answered as such. And I've opened a P.O. box, in case you get mail. Your business cards will be here next week."

"Is all this necessary?"

"It is if you want to retain your cover."

Michael turned to go. "Thanks. That's very smart thinking."

Molly was still beaming as the outer door closed.

Teddy's Place, Jefferson Davis Hwy., Crystal City, Virginia
Lunchtime

Francis was already seated at a table in a back room when Michael arrived.

They ordered food and coffee from a waitress and waited until after she'd left.

"How was your meeting with Matthews?" Francis asked immediately.

"... it's taking far too long," Michael added, after updating his father. "I thought about it last night. It's a gut thing. I've got no proof that Fareed's still in the country, let alone working with horses."

"Has your gut ever been wrong?"

"Not yet."

"Then stick with it. If we thought you were making a mistake, we'd have said something by now. Trust me, Michael. Have you briefed the president?"

"No. There's nothing to tell."

"Tell him what you told me. Keep him in the loop."

"He's got far bigger things to deal with."

"You're wrong. He's counting on you. Don't let him down."

Their food arrived, and the conversation stopped until they were alone again.

"How're the additional personnel working out?" Francis asked, picking up a roast beef sandwich.

Michael told him.

He'd originally instructed the CIA agents to pack for a week's surveillance of Sis Matthews-Boyd. It had now been three months, and the only thing they'd learned was that apart from driving the dark-haired boy to his elementary school every morning and picking him up in the afternoon, she had no routine. What did surprise them was that the only times she went to Sleepy Hollow, they assumed to see her father, was on weekends. Mark Boyd stayed home with the children. The team gave Molly daily status reports. When Michael again expressed his doubts that they could be wasting their time, Brian disagreed.

"She's got a home phone and a cell phone," he said. "But I've never seen a woman spend so little time on either. We've tried to get near her, but no luck so far. We've pulled her records, but no numbers coincide. And we've got Molly checking every number. No red flags, yet. So, unless we bug her cell phone, there's no way we'll know who she's talkin' to."

"She's got a lover and uses text messaging," Michael suggested.

"With three kids? No way. She only leaves the house to go to the school, the bank, the supermarket, local library, or the hairdressers. She doesn't visit anyone, and no one goes to see her. For all her so-called money, what a life. Hubby gets home at all hours of the night. He's got no goddamn schedule, except he's outta there every mornin' at 0800, and he stops at a local bar most nights. Dan's tryin' that approach. So far, he's got nothin'. But somethin's tellin' me we stick with it."

"Mullen said that?" Francis asked now.

"Yes," Michael replied.

"He's a good man. Trust his judgment. And be patient."

"We need a break, Dad."

Francis finished his sandwich. "You'll get one. But I'm still at a loss as to why you bought a horse. When are you going to find the time to ride it?"

"I will."

"But a horse? If you wanted a pet, why not a goldfish or a dog or something?"

"He'd been ill treated."

Francis's coffee cup was halfway to his mouth when he stopped, studying his son. "Good God. You've got a soft spot ..."

"No, I haven't."

Francis laughed. "Yes, you have. Wonders never cease." He finished his coffee. "Drink up. I've got to go."

On his way back to his office, Michael called the White House Communications Center.

A male voice answered. "Good afternoon, Colonel."

"I need to update the president," Michael said. "We don't need to meet this time."

"I'll make sure he knows, sir."

Michael's secure line rang at 5:30 p.m.

"What have you got, Michael?" Makepeace asked.

Michael repeated what he'd told his father. "... and Matthews has invited me back tomorrow night. A few friends, he said."

"Excellent. Go. They're probably some of his rich horse-set cronies. What did you think of him?"

"Truthfully, sir?"

"Of course."

"He reminded me of a well-dressed thug."

Makepeace laughed. "Good analogy. But don't forget influential and very wealthy. With some equally influential and wealthy friends."

"No, sir, I won't."

"Keep up the good work. You'll get that break."

Michael hung up, and although he didn't know it at the time, he was about to get two.

Finnegan's Bar, Bedminster Road, Bedminster, Pennsylvania
Late that night

At 11:35 p.m., firmly supported by Mark Boyd, Dan staggered from the bar and into the parking lot.

"I'm okay," he slurred, reeling away from Boyd and almost falling.

Boyd grabbed for his arm again. "You've had a few too many."

"I'm fine." Dan squinted through one eye. "Where's my friggin' car?"

"You're not driving."

Dan pulled away. "Course, I am. Where's my goddamn car?"

He lurched against the side of a pickup truck, with Boyd close behind.

Dan looked around again, his legs beginning to buckle. "There it is."

Weaving erratically in the general direction of a gray Saturn, he grabbed at parked vehicles for support.

Reaching the Saturn, he made several attempts to unlock the driver's door. Each time, he missed the lock by several inches.

"You're not driving," Boyd said again.

Dan looked up. "I'm fine," he mumbled. "If I could just get this fuckin' key in the fuckin' lock." He handed the key to Boyd and slid to the ground. "You try."

Boyd pocketed the key.

"You're not letting him drive, are you?" a male voice shouted across the parking lot.

"No way!" Boyd shouted back. "Give me a hand?"

By the time the man reached Boyd, Dan was on his hands and knees, leaning against the Saturn. His shirt dangled from his pants, his hair was a mess, and he was quietly mumbling, although he made no attempt to move any farther.

"He needs to sleep that off," the man said to Boyd. "Grab his other arm."

They hauled Dan to his feet and half carried him to Boyd's immaculate Lexus.

"Make sure he don't throw up," the man continued, eyeing the car and the leather interior as they strapped him in. "Son of a bitch to get clean. And the smell—"

"I'll remember that," Boyd interrupted, getting behind the wheel.

"He just needs to …" the man added.

But Boyd had started the engine and was already on the move.

During the drive, Dan's head sagged, and every so often, he muttered something unintelligible.

The Matthews-Boyd House, Spruce Hill Lane, Bedminster, Pennsylvania
Just before midnight

Boyd drove into the oversized two-car garage, then grabbed Dan's arm to help him out.

"Keep your voice down," Boyd said quietly. "My wife's probably asleep. Can you do that?"

Dan staggered into a rubber garbage can but managed to nod.

There was a back staircase off the hall leading from the garage, and as it wasn't very wide, the climb to the landing above took time. Boyd didn't seem to care, as long as Dan kept quiet.

After Dan stumbled several times, they eventually reached the first door. Boyd helped him inside and steered him toward a single bed.

"There's a bathroom," he hissed as Dan collapsed on the bed. "For God's sake, use it. Okay?"

Dan mumbled something when Boyd pulled off his shoes. Then the light went out, and the door closed, leaving him alone.

The Happy Trails Motel, Bedminster Road, Bedminster, Pennsylvania
Midnight

"Boyd never made us," Bentley said to Brian in the motel parking lot.

"Too busy with his drunken passenger."

"It was an act, wasn't it?"

Brian shrugged. "Dan got inside. That was the plan." He turned to go. Then he stopped. "If he was actin', the Academy of Motion Pictures, Arts and Sciences needs to know."

"What now?" she asked.

"We wait. See ya in the mornin'."

The Matthews-Boyd House, Spruce Hill Lane, Bedminster, Pennsylvania
Saturday, December 21, 2002

Dan waited in the darkness for over an hour before rolling off the bed.

After checking the many pockets of his khaki pants, he padded in his socks to the closed door, a powerful but pencil-thin flashlight in one hand.

The door didn't creak, and slipping onto the landing, he quickly made his way down the back stairs.

The first thing he saw was the red light of a motion sensor blink on, and below it, an alarm pad lit up like a Christmas tree. On a pullout slide, someone had neatly listed the circuits, so to save time, Dan took a photograph with a very small camera. It wasn't the fact that Boyd had probably set the alarm from the second floor that bothered him; it was the four other motion sensors on the list with no indication of their locations.

Dan knew enough about alarms to know that when this particular system was armed, the motion sensors were in sleep mode. The motion sensors only took over when the alarm was set on exit and there was no one in the house. *Still, I've got to find them.*

As he suspected, the hallway from the garage also led to the kitchen. Although the room was huge, the colored lights from a second alarm pad made it easy to see.

Dan worked quickly and quietly, and by the time he finished, he'd been in every room on the ground floor. He located two more sensors and a third alarm pad by the front door. *Makes sense.* And during his silent tour, he'd double-checked the windows and other external doors to make sure they were actually wired. Every one was.

Finally satisfied he'd accomplished more than he'd hoped, he crept back to the bedroom and fell asleep in his clothes.

At 9:00 a.m., he reentered the kitchen. This time, two children were sitting on one side of a table in the breakfast area, food on their plates, but they appeared to be more intent on watching a flat-screen TV located in one of the many cabinets. At the large center island, Sis was holding a baby, her back to Dan.

He cleared his throat, and as she turned, the baby burped, sending a stream of yellow drool down its chin and onto a towel over her shoulder.

Sis smiled. "You must be Dan?"

He hoped she'd notice his crumpled clothes and slick wet hair and not his clear eyes. "I'm really sorry," he began.

She turned her attention back to the baby. "Please, don't apologize. Help yourself to some coffee."

"No, thanks. I should go. Can I use the phone to call a cab?"

Sis wiped the baby's mouth. "Nonsense. Mark will drive you, when he gets up. So unless you're in a hurry to leave, have some coffee."

She gestured in the direction of some glass-fronted wall cabinets. "Mugs are in there. There's juice in the refrigerator. Help yourself." She turned back to the children. "Eat your breakfast. Otherwise, I'll turn off the TV."

Immediately, they began to eat.

Sis was far too busy to notice Dan take a roundabout route to the coffee machine to deliberately break the beam of the motion sensor. As he'd suspected, with the alarm now turned off, a light on the pad began to flash.

As he poured the juice, he noticed a monthly calendar hanging in an alcove above a small built-in desk. *How could I have missed that?* And he made a mental note of several handwritten entries.

"You can go play," he heard Sis say. "Don't forget hats, jackets, and gloves, and stay where I can see you. You know the rules."

She placed the baby in a crib by the French doors that led to the flagstone patio. "I'm sorry, Dan. It's always crazy in the mornings. Now I can take a break. Join me?"

She was clearing the table as he took a seat. "Mark says you went to Princeton too," she continued. "What a coincidence. It's amazing you never met before."

Don't ask too many questions. He took a sip of coffee. "Different years." He turned to watch the children playing with a large plastic dump truck in a sandbox at the edge of the patio. "Great kids," he added.

Sis ran a hand through a mane of uncombed hair. "Thanks. But they're not all mine. I'm looking after John and the baby for a friend."

She tried unsuccessfully to wipe a fresh yellow stain off her sweater. "I can't believe Mark made you sleep in the nanny's bedroom. Not that we've got one yet. There are two lovely bedrooms for guests."

"It was great," Dan replied. "I'm really embarrassed that we had to meet like this."

"Don't be. We all drink too much from time to time. Mark explained you'd been having some problems." She looked up. "Speak of the devil."

Having quietly entered the kitchen, Mark Boyd gave his wife a dutiful kiss on the cheek. "Hi, sweetie," she added. "Sleep well?"

He didn't answer. "Ready to go?" he asked Dan.

"Sit down," Sis said, before Dan could respond. "Have your coffee, and I'll make breakfast. Unless Dan has to be somewhere?"

"Breakfast sounds good," he said quickly.

Dan drained his coffee and got to his feet. "That was great, Sis. Thanks. I'd forgotten how good home cooking tastes."

"I'm glad you enjoyed it. Mark has my permission to bring you home anytime." She smiled. "But next time, give me some notice."

"Anything you want while I'm out?" Boyd asked, pulling car keys from his pocket.

Sis shook her head. "No. But don't forget you have to pick up the babysitter at five thirty. Daddy's party. Remember?"

"You're a lucky guy," Dan commented as the Lexus sped down the driveway. "Great wife. Nice big house. Three well-behaved kids."

"They're not all mine," Boyd replied. "The boy and the baby belong to Sis's college friend. She's away on business."

"That was good of you to take them."

"Had nothing to do with me. Typical Sis. Told me after the fact."

Finnegan's Bar, Bedminster Road, Bedminster, Pennsylvania
A short time later

In the parking lot, Dan began to get out of the car. "Want one for the road?" he asked.

Boyd looked at the clock on the dashboard. "Better not. I've got to get back."

"Thanks for helping me out."

Boyd shrugged. "No problem. As it's Christmas, guess I'll see you Tuesday night."

Gravel flew from the tires as he drove away.

Dan entered the bar to find Stella alone.

"You left your jacket," she said as he sat on a stool. She lowered her voice. "In all the years I've been tending bar, I've never seen ginger ale have that effect before."

Dan only smiled.

She leaned toward him. "It worked then?"

"Better you didn't know."

She polished a glass with a towel. "I suppose it is." She looked up. "Morning, Bob."

Dan turned to see the first of the regulars come through the door. "Gotta go, Stella. Thanks again."

"You're welcome."

Dan grabbed his jacket off a hook by the door.

"See ya later, luv," Stella added.

The Happy Trails Motel, Bedminster Road, Bedminster, Pennsylvania
A few minutes later

Dan ignored the Do Not Disturb sign and entered Brian's room with a spare key.

Brian was hunched over a laptop on a table, reading from the screen.

"You hit pay dirt," he said. "How many bugs did you plant?"

"All of them. And I got photographs."

"This's gettin' better and better. How's the head?"

"Fine."

"That was an act?"

Dan only nodded.

"That's amazin'."

Dan hesitated. "My dad was an alcoholic."

Brian didn't need to know any more. "What did you find?"

"According to the kitchen calendar, the Boyds are going to old man Matthews' party tonight. Then she confirmed it ..." Dan began.

He'd almost finished, when Brian suddenly interrupted. "Shit!" He paused and checked his watch. "We gotta call Michael. Right now."

"Reason?"

Brian pointed at the screen. "Accordin' to this, Sis has just told hubby that she had his tux cleaned for tonight."

Dan quickly punched the speed dial for Michael's number on his cell phone.

He answered on the third ring.

"Have you got a tux?" Dan asked.

"Yes."

"Wear it tonight. We just found out the party's formal."

Brian waved a piece of paper under Dan's nose.

"And Brian wants to meet before you get there," he added.

"Tell him usual place, 1800."

Triple S Diner, Route 611, Bucks County, Pennsylvania
Early evening

Michael originally chose the twenty-four-hour diner as a rendezvous point because it was always busy. On a Saturday night, the huge parking lot was usually full of automobiles and some eighteen-wheelers. They'd met there twice before.

Brian was already parked at the back of the lot when Michael drove in.

"Nice wheels," Brian commented, sliding into the passenger seat of the Jaguar XJR.

"Boost has his uses."

"You sure look the part," he continued. "I'm impressed."

"In that case, I've got nothing to worry about. What you got?"

Brian told him.

"... and if we don't move tonight, it could be months before we get another chance," he finished.

"I should do it."

"You got other things goin' on. Bentley's small, and as long as the window don't stick, she'll get through it easier than any of us. Dan was smart to unlatch it and loosen the screen. She'll get access across the garage roof."

"I don't like it. What if the babysitter sets the alarm?"

"It's a risk we've gotta take. There wasn't enough time to get the disable code. Dan knows where three motion sensors are. Bentley's got to find the other one. But we'll be watchin'. All you've gotta do is tell us when the Boyds leave the party."

"And spend the evening with a lot of boring, over-dressed rich people."

"You're the best qualified."

Michael gave Brian a sideways glance. "I'll take that as a compliment. I think."

"Maybe a backhanded one. It's your call," Brian replied. "You're usually the big risk taker."

"Exactly. If I was the one breaking in while the house is occupied, I wouldn't have a problem. But I'm not."

"Bentley's okay. She thinks on her feet."

"I hope so. What about equipment?"

"Tom got what we needed."

Michael stared through the windshield. "Okay. You've got a green light. But if you have any doubts, pull her ASAP. Got that?"

"Yessir. Got that."

Brian watched Michael drive away.

What he don't know won't hurt him, he thought. *He gave us a green light. So what if it was after the fact.*

The Matthews-Boyd House, Spruce Hill Lane, Bedminster, Pennsylvania

At 5:15 p.m., Bentley was dressed in black spandex, reminding Eden of an Olympic speed skater. But instead of skates, she wore black, rubber-soled sneakers. The spandex was skintight, convincing him that if Bentley had been young enough, she wouldn't be any threat to beauty pageant contestants. Her black backpack didn't improve his image.

Eden's headset suddenly hissed. "Boyd's leaving," he heard Hunter say from his vantage point. "Subject in the kitchen with the kids. Go!"

Eden gave Bentley the thumbs-up sign and mouthed, "Good luck," before she ran, hunched over, from the cover of the nearest bushes to the corner of the garage. She reminded him of a small black beetle, until she scaled the drainpipe with ease. *I'll be damned,* Eden thought. *She's good.*

Bentley quickly crossed the garage roof and disappeared from Eden's sight. When he saw her again, she was squatting at the side of one of the two chimneys on the peak of the main roof, silhouetted by an almost-full moon.

"Great view from here," they heard her say quietly as she tied a rope around the base of the chimney and then around her waist.

Better you than me, Eden thought as, holding the rope, Bentley began to ease down the shingles, heading for the dormer to the bedroom where Dan had slept.

She was still several feet above the window when she heard Hunter. "Stop. Subject no longer in sight."

Suddenly, Bentley lost her footing on the steep pitch, and with nothing but the rope to hold onto, she slid rapidly past the dormer. The rope snapped taut a few feet shy of the edge, but it didn't prevent her legs from flying into space. Eden was convinced she was going to fall. He was also convinced that even without a spotlight on her, she couldn't have been more visible. As Bentley now dangled two floors up, being pelted by a shower of loose mortar from the old chimney, the dark-haired boy ran onto the patio in his pajamas with Sis in hot pursuit. Although Sis was wearing a slinky long black dress and spiked heels, neither the outfit nor the cold night air appeared to slow her down. They were both laughing as Sis caught the boy and scooped him into her arms.

Don't look up, Hunter and Eden thought in unison.

Sis didn't and reentered the kitchen, giving Bentley the opportunity to haul herself to partial safety.

"Subject gone again," Hunter said as Bentley maneuvered below the window. She lay on the shingles at a precarious angle but made no attempt to move any farther.

Minutes ticked by.

"Subject in the kitchen," Hunter said at last. "Go now. Be careful."

Bentley was too busy trying to regain her foothold to reply.

As quietly as she could, she pulled herself into a crouched position, and with a firm grip on the rope, she edged back toward the dormer.

She removed the loose screen without incident, but raising the bottom half of the double-hung window wasn't so easy with only one hand. The roofline was even steeper than it looked, and Bentley dared not let go of the rope. From the angle of her legs and feet, her hamstrings were stretched to their limit, and just when she thought they were about to snap, the window moved.

Now able to curl her fingers over the windowsill, she took a deep breath and let the rope drop. For a second, Eden was sure she was going to fall again, but with something substantial to hold onto, Bentley was able to push up the window far enough for her to slide inside.

Eden exhaled loudly as she disappeared.

"I'm in," Hunter and Eden heard her whisper.

Bentley immediately untied the rope, and after coiling the excess, she placed it within arm's reach on the shingles below the dormer. Then she closed the window.

In case Dan was seen, Tom Morgan tailed Boyd to the babysitter's house and had been briefing Dan every few minutes. From his vantage point on the lane above the house, Dan then relayed the messages to Hunter and Eden.

"Boyd's on his way back," Eden told Bentley. "Shouldn't be much longer."

It was another twenty-five minutes before the couple left, Sis now behind the wheel of the Lexus. Hunter and Eden had overheard her giving the babysitter, a woman in her sixties, a precise set of instructions and several telephone numbers. The woman appeared unfazed by Sis's lecture.

"Go and have a good time," they heard her say. "Everything'll be fine here. No worries."

"Let's hope," Hunter muttered.

He could see the babysitter in the kitchen, a baby monitor close at hand. "Mommy said straight to bed when this show's over," she told the other children.

"They've gone," Hunter said into the headset. "You've got less than thirty minutes."

"Copy that," Bentley replied.

Opening the door to the landing, she peered out and reminded herself that there was still one more motion sensor to find.

Carefully, she made her way along the narrow hallway. Reaching two steps that led to a huge open landing and sweeping staircase to the foyer below, she assumed that she was about to leave part of the original house.

Halfway across the landing, partly concealed by a large painting, was the other motion sensor. And beyond that was a door they'd calculated must open to the master bedroom. All Bentley had to do now was get across the landing without being seen or triggering the sensor. She hugged the wall, as best she could, and reached the door.

After slipping inside, she took a good look around.

If the bedroom was any indication, Sis wasn't the neat-nick type. There were clothes strewn everywhere. *Or maybe they were in a hurry?*

Bentley headed straight for the telephone on a nightstand by the bed, avoiding several scattered shoes. Working quickly, she inserted the tiny listening device.

She'd almost finished when her headset hissed. "Babysitter could be headed your way," Hunter said.

Bentley ducked into the master bathroom. *I hate thick carpets.* She couldn't see the bedroom door from her hiding place but suddenly sensed someone had entered the room.

"Lord. What a mess," Bentley heard a woman mutter. "She really needs a housekeeper."

I agree. But go away! And don't close the door.

A few minutes later, she heard Hunter's voice again. "All clear. You've got ten minutes."

The Matthews Estate, Deer Run Road, Bedminster, Pennsylvania
Around midnight

"Thanks for coming," Matthews said as Michael got ready to leave. "You seem to be the hit of my little party. I've gotten several requests from the ladies to make you a permanent fixture."

Michael didn't know how to respond. "I had a good time, Arnold. Thank you."

"Haven't seen my daughter that animated in a long time," Matthews continued. "She's usually the first to leave. Not tonight."

There is a God, Michael thought.

"I understand the MacFarlands invited you to their annual tournament," Matthews added. "You're going, I hope?"

"It sounds a bit out of my league."

"Bullshit. We have a great time. Novice and experts alike. And they throw one helluva party. Three days of it. You eat, drink, and ride. You should go. Cement some new business opportunities." Matthews lowered his voice. "And there's always a shitload of pretty young women. You could take your pick."

I get the picture. "I'll certainly think about it."

"You'd be doing me a favor to say yes."

Michael wasn't about to commit. "It's a long way off. They'll probably forget."

"If I know Jim and Stella, they won't forget."

Following several other vehicles down the driveway, Michael called Dan's cell phone.

"They're a couple of minutes ahead of me," he said. "ETA less than fifteen minutes."

"Copy that. How was it?"

"The food was good."

Chapter Fifteen

The Matthews-Boyd House, Spruce Hill Lane, Bedminster, Pennsylvania
Tuesday, December 24 to Tuesday, December 31, 2002

With Kathryn no longer in his life, Michael suggested that he keep surveillance on Sis Matthews-Boyd over the Christmas holiday.

"The agents need a break," he told Brian. "I've got nothing going on."

Brian was about to argue then changed his mind. "If anythin' happens, you'll call me?"

"Affirmative."

Special Operations were sometimes used to waiting around like undercover cops, so consequently, Michael enjoyed spending Christmas Eve alone in one of the bird-watching hides. It not only gave him time to think, but it was also a sharp reminder of what he used to do.

If this mission ever ends, he thought as dawn broke on Christmas Day, *I'm quitting this civilian crap and going back to active duty. I'm not cut out for a desk job. It was a mistake.*

He was convinced that Fareed would somehow make contact, regardless of her Muslim faith.

Sis isn't a Muslim, he rationalized. *Christmas is a big deal for little kids.*

He was disappointed by late on Christmas Day that neither Sis nor Mark Boyd had left the house. The only telephone calls had been from their respective families, and Sis had been far too casual, in Michael's mind, when she'd thanked her father for the large check.

Michael spent another few nights in the hide with the same result, grateful he'd brought along several novels that he'd been meaning to read and never found the time.

On the afternoon of December 31st, Brian had to almost pry him out of the hide.

"Seein' as you spent Christmas here, you gotta see your folks on New Year's Eve." He purposely paused. "And I'll bet Delta's missin' you."

Mere mention of the horse made Michael finally pack up and leave.

I knew that'd do it, Brian thought, watching him go.

The Correa Family Home, Alpine Way, Fairfax, Virginia
Tuesday evening, December 31, 2002

"There'll be no shop talk tonight," Sheila announced as Michael took off his coat in the entry hall. "It's New Year's Eve. We're going to celebrate like a normal family. Hope you're hungry?"

He kissed his stepmother on the cheek. "Starved. Where's Dad?"

"In the family room, watching the news. He's expecting you. And, Michael, remember what I said."

In 1997, unable to stomach what the previous administration had begun to do, Francis Correa resigned as director of the CIA. A man of principles, he could no longer tolerate the high price or compromise of the former president's mission. Francis retired amid fanfare and praise, but gossip and speculation had still run rife. It was generally thought that his second marriage to a woman twenty-two years his junior was his motivation. It wasn't. Sheila Correa was considered by many to be a dumb blonde, and she did nothing publicly to change that opinion. The few who'd gotten to know her knew the truth. The only heir to real estate mega-millions was an astute and highly intelligent woman under the glamorous exterior.

Shortly after Francis's resignation, the couple left the U.S. for a vineyard in Tuscany, Italy, seemingly for good. There, Francis had intended to settle into a happy and prosperous early retirement. But it didn't work out quite the way he planned, and a personal request by Chester Makepeace, shortly before taking office, persuaded Francis to return to his old job.

Sheila now watched Michael head to the family room before returning to the kitchen. *He looks tired,* she thought. *Let's hope some family time and a decent meal helps.*

As she'd predicted, father and son remained closed-mouthed throughout the evening, and she'd been the one doing most of the talking, until she'd mentioned Delta. To her surprise, Michael became quite enthusiastic. For him.

She knew enough not to ask why he'd taken up riding and bought a horse. But before they watched the ball drop in Times Square and toasted the New Year with champagne, Sheila got Michael to promise they'd go riding together.

"I didn't know you rode," he said at one point.

She laughed. "I'm full of surprises."

That's what Jarrah supposedly told Osborne.

"I owned horses, and even won ribbons, when I was younger," she continued. "I still adore them."

"Wonders never cease," Francis muttered.

"Do you know what Michael's doing?" Sheila asked, after he left.

"Some of it," Francis said.

"Is it dangerous?"

"Depends on your definition of dangerous."

She unzipped her dress. "I know, if you told me, you'd have to kill me." Stepping out of the dress, she added, "God save me from spooks," before Francis could reply.

Chapter Sixteen

Michael's Office, G Street, Washington, D.C.
Thursday, January 2, 2003

Brian had been about to leave for more surveillance duty in Pennsylvania when Michael called him in.

At 7:35 a.m., Brian was getting déjà vu as Michael studied the flip chart.

"I had the holidays to think," Michael began. "We're no goddamn farther on than when we started."

"... as it's been three months, I'm thinking of cutting back the surveillance," he concluded some time later. "Did I miss anything?"

"Nope."

With his hands behind his head, Michael leaned back in his chair and closed his eyes. "Where do we go from here?"

Brian finished his second coffee of the morning. "I've got somethin' in mind."

At the flip chart, he turned back to the original page and pointed. "Remember what I said? When you hit a wall, go back to the beginnin'. Maybe we didn't go back far enough."

"Meaning?"

"This really started when the bomb was ditched. I wanna check out the original crew."

"From 1958?" Michael did a quick calculation. "Eighty-year-old terrorists?"

"They weren't eighty back then."

"Air Force officers? And don't forget, the crew was decorated. The pilot got the Distinguished Flying Cross."

"I wasn't."

"This's stretching, even for you. Ask my father. The military did rigorous checks on personnel involved with sensitive missions. More so then than in past years."

Brian shrugged. "But you're not sayin' no?"

"Affirmative. But this has to be the longest of long shots." Michael picked up his jacket. "It's too early to run," he added. "Want to grab a late breakfast instead?"

Brian nodded. "Sure. Why not."

Chapter Seventeen

Clarksville, Texas
Wednesday, July 6, 1960

A bearded Jack Worcek left the liquor store in his wheelchair with a brown paper bag of bottles in his lap. Enough to last him three days. Six months earlier, the same bottles would have lasted him a week. After rolling across the sidewalk to a mud-splattered Ford pickup, Worcek put the bottles behind the driver's seat and heaved himself behind the wheel. Then leaning out to collapse the wheelchair, he flung it into the flatbed with one hand and drove away in a cloud of dust.

Across the street, Grigori Kolesnikov put his car in gear and followed.

A mile beyond the small town, a dirt road led to a dilapidated trailer. Kolesnikov waited until Worcek was settled under a tattered awning, taking a long gulp from one of the bottles, before he approached.

Worcek looked up and squinted at a young man dressed in a cheap-looking suit. "Who the hell are you?"

"A friend."

"You're no friend of mine."

"Perhaps we can change that." Kolesnikov gestured at an upturned wooden crate. "May I?"

Worcek pushed a matted strand of long hair over his shoulder and took another gulp from the bottle. "Help yourself. It's a free country."

Kolesnikov perched on the crate. "Is it?" He pointed at Worcek's useless legs before scanning the trailer. "A man who serves his country is left like this. It's not the kind of freedom I would want."

Worcek knew the stranger was foreign, but he didn't know from where. Nor did he care. "What's your point?"

"Money. I am here to offer you money."

From Worcek's reaction, Kolesnikov thought he'd made a mistake. Although Worcek was confined to a wheelchair and looked older than his thirty-two years, his shoulders were broad and his bare arms were solid muscle. If Worcek had legs that worked, Kolesnikov didn't doubt he'd lose a physical fight.

To Kolesnikov's relief, Worcek took another swig of liquor. "Keep talking."

Worcek continued to drink, while Kolesnikov talked.

"That's it?" Worcek asked when he finished. "I tell you where we ditched the bomb, and you'll give me five thousand dollars?"

"That is my offer."

Worcek lit a cigarette with trembling hands. "Just because I'm stuck in this goddamn chair doesn't mean I'm friggin' stupid. Five grand? You'll have to do a lot better than that. Otherwise, take a hike."

A week later, Worcek was still at his trailer, but he was now watching a brand-new TV and drinking decent liquor for a change.

Chapter Eighteen

Ranch Road, Benjamin, Texas
Wednesday, February 5, 2003

The name on the mailbox read Worcek. A long fenced driveway led from the country road, and in Brian's eyes, the property appeared to be a typical Texas homestead.

As his rental car came to a stop by the white clapboard ranch house, a weather-beaten man appeared. Wearing chaps over his jeans and carrying a cowboy hat that had seen better days, Brian guessed he was in his early forties.

"Mornin'," Brian said, getting out of the car. "I'm lookin' for Jack Worcek."

"My dad expectin' you?" the man asked.

Brian adjusted his own immaculate cowboy hat. "No. Just passin' through. Thought I'd stop by and surprise him."

Obviously satisfied, the man pointed through some trees at a small barn on a rise to the left of the main house. "He's in his workshop. Go on up."

"Thanks," Brian said.

It had taken several weeks for Brian to collect, but according to his information, Captain Jack Worcek suffered a devastating spinal injury during the B-47's midair collision. "A freak accident," the doctors said. Worcek spent months in a military hospital and another year in a veteran's rehabilitation center. While there, he endured hours of painful therapy, but in the end, it appeared he was destined to spend the rest of his life in a wheelchair. Unable, or unwilling, to stay in the Air Force, he was given a medical discharge and a small disability pension.

His string of DUIs began in the early 1960s, followed by two arrests for possession of marijuana. His third arrest, for possession of drugs with intent to distribute, landed him behind bars. He served five years and was released in 1973 at the age of forty-five. Less than a year later, he was arrested again for being drunk and disorderly. Then came an assault with a deadly weapon. Worcek served another eighteen months.

In 1976, there was an explosion, followed by a fire that gutted his trailer. Brian wasn't sure how Worcek survived, but after spending five days in a hospital being treated for second-degree burns, he was released and disappeared.

At this point, Brian assumed that Worcek must be dead. After further investigation, Brian was surprised to find that Worcek was not only alive but had married a widow, adopted her two young sons, and was now living in Benjamin, Texas. He did a quick calculation. *The lush made it to seventy-four? Jeez, that's amazin'.*

Through the barn's open door, Brian now saw a large man standing at a workbench, his back to Brian, a chisel in his hand.

"Mornin'. I'm lookin' for Jack Worcek," Brian said again. Having studied the few photographs of Worcek, he knew that regardless of his age, he'd know him when he saw him.

The man turned. "I'm Jack. Who are you?"

Flipping open his I.D., Brian handed him a business card.

"What's a Texas boy from the Justice Department in Washington, D.C. want with me?" Worcek asked, studying the card. Despite his leg braces, Worcek's whole stance had changed, and Brian quickly decided that the soft approach was no longer an option.

"Information," Brian replied, and playing a hunch, he told Worcek what he suspected.

"I'm not your guy," Worcek said when he'd finished.

"Sure you are. Just give me the name, and that'll be that. Should you decide not to cooperate, you'll find out real fast just how powerful the individual I work for is. Seein' as the statute of limitations doesn't run out on traitors, I reckon you'll be lookin' at the electric chair."

Worcek glared. "You gotta have proof first."

Brian snorted. "Think we don't? We've got a real thick file on you. We even know when you piss." He looked slowly around. "Looks like you've gotta nice life. A lovin' wife. Two hardworkin' stepsons. A successful ranch and woodworking business. Shame to throw it all away at your age." He dangled a pair of handcuffs. "What's it gonna be? The name. Or me marchin' you outta here in these."

Easing onto a tall wooden stool, Worcek stared at the rafters. "Fuck."

When he spoke again, his voice was low. "Deep down I knew that someone might come looking. Just a matter of time." He faced Brian. "I'm not proud of what I did. I was bitter and hurtin' and have a disease. Although I've bin clean and sober for twenty-six years. Some of those boys that came back from Nam know how I felt. But I can't change the past, Mr. Mullen. Even though I've often wished I could."

"But you can possibly change the future," Brian said. *Or you could have gone to the authorities long before now and saved me all this trouble.*

Worcek hesitated. "Guess it's better to finally get it off my chest. Even my family doesn't know. They won't have to know, will they?"

"Not if I leave here with what I want," Brian said. "Just tell me what happened."

After a very long pause, Worcek did just that.

Three miles from the homestead, Brian pulled over to use his cell phone.

"Tell me it's good news," Michael said on hearing his voice.

"I got the name Grigori Kolesnikov."

"That's it?"

"It's better than nothin'. If the guy hadn't stopped drinkin' and druggin' and found God, we wouldn't have that."

After he hung up, Brian pictured Worcek again. But as hard as he tried, he couldn't feel any empathy toward him. *He's still a goddamn traitor. How can you sell out your country and then drink and drug your way through ten grand? That was a lot of money back then.*

Although he hadn't talked to Collins in months, Michael decided to call him with the news.

"It's time to get your father more involved," Collins said when Michael had finished. "This sounds like something left over from the Cold War days. If I'm right, the CIA will undoubtedly have some intel you can use."

"Need to know, sir?" Michael asked.

"Not this time. Tell him everything. If he's got a problem, he can call me before I leave."

"Leave, sir?"

"We're gearing up in Iraq. It's going to get hotter. Best if I'm there."

"You want me with you?"

"Not this time. We've got it covered. You're needed here."

Goddamnit! Michael thought as he hung up.

CIA Headquarters, Langley, Virginia
Thursday, February 6, 2003

Francis held up a file. "What's your interest in a former KGB agent?"

Michael reached for the file.

"Oh, no," Francis added, keeping the file from Michael's grasp. "Not until I get answers."

When Michael finished his explanation, Francis got to his feet. "You're an idiot," he said. "I should have been told from the start."

"We wanted to keep it under wraps."

"From me? As director of the CIA, I can't be trusted? Give me a break!" Francis sat again, leaning across his desk. "What did you think I was going to do? Call the *National Enquirer* with the information?"

"It was a military matter."

"Bullshit! We're talking about a nuclear device. National security."

"The president personally asked that I handle it."

"And that precluded my involvement? I don't think so."

Michael didn't respond.

Francis took a deep breath. "Let's begin again. And this time, tell me everything."

This time, Michael didn't hold back. "... the B-47's pilot left the Air Force in 1973," he continued. "He also built his own small experimental airplanes, and when he retired to Maryland, he continued his hobby. He took off one morning in his latest experiment and was never seen alive again. Wreckage eventually washed up near Kent Island, and his decomposed body was found several months later."

"When was this?" Francis asked.

"1998. The B-47's co-pilot died in Vietnam. That left Jack Worcek. He admitted to Brian that Kolesnikov paid him for information. But then the trail ran cold."

Francis finally handed Michael the file. "I've read it. Now I know what you're looking for, I'm not sure that's going to help."

Silently, Michael took the file and began to read.

According to the CIA dossier, Kolesnikov was still a young KGB field agent when the Cold War ended. Like many operatives at the time, it took money, but not much persuasion, to turn him. For over three years, he fed his new employers accurate information, but life under Soviet rule was still harsh. Eventually, at the beginning of 1992, Kolesnikov chose to defect. He was interrogated for several weeks. Finally satisfied that the CIA had obtained all the relevant information, Kolesnikov was debriefed, given a new identity and an undisclosed lump sum to begin his new life.

At this point, Michael looked up. "He's off the payroll?"

Francis played with his pen. "Yes. George Tyson, as he's now known, had a degree in mathematics. He wanted to teach. He upgraded his degree at the University of Pennsylvania, Wharton School of Business, and for a while we monitored him. Like so many of his fellow countrymen, he embraced the American lifestyle, and we needed good teachers. But his usefulness to us was over, so we cut him loose. It's standard procedure for low-level defectors."

"Did you say the Wharton School of Business?"

"Is something wrong with your hearing?"

"No, Dad." Michael went back to reading. "It says he became a math teacher at the Lake Academy in New Canaan, Connecticut. Is he still there?"

"I've got no idea."

Michael closed the file. "Guess he didn't tell you everything. I need to find him, Dad."

"No. We need to find him, Michael. And soon."

Michael's Office, G Street, Washington, D.C.
Late that afternoon

Brian dumped his bags by the side of Molly's desk and entered Michael's office.

"Thanks for coming straight here," Michael said. "How was the flight?"

"Bumpy. Somethin's happened?"

"Maybe. Dan's on his way, if he can get through the snow. Tom's taking his place with the surveillance team. We've got bigger fish to fry."

Brian remained standing. "Sounds interestin'."

Michael repeated the conversation with his father. "... and both Fareed and the Russian attended Wharton. You know how I feel about coincidences," he finished.

"Anythin' to do with how you feel about long shots?"

"Okay, I deserved that. Good work, by the way."

"You're welcome. How old's this Russian?"

Michael looked down at the file. "Born 1938. That makes him about sixty-five. Why?"

"Just checkin'. Now we've gotta find this ex-KGB agent?"

"Looks that way."

"Connecticut in February? That's goin' to be cold."

"Affirmative. But let's do some legwork first."

"That's what I was plannin' on doin'."

Bedminster, Pennsylvania

In early January, the surveillance team moved out of the Happy Trails Motel, as their prolonged stay began to arouse suspicion.

"I'm surprised they lasted this long," Michael said when Brian voiced his concerns.

Bentley found an empty and ideally situated cottage on the edge of Bedminster. Although the cottage wasn't a rental, they traced the owner to Florida. As he was spending the winter there, he finally agreed, with a large check for his cooperation, that it could be used.

The team was now much closer geographically to the Matthews-Boyd house, but due to bad weather, monitoring Sis was sporadic at best. Although everyone was using four-wheel-drive vehicles from the warehouse in Baltimore, they'd already been snowed in for days at a time.

"Plowin' here isn't a priority," Brian told Michael. "But if we can't drive, she can't either."

Michael's Office, G Street, Washington, D.C.
Friday, February 7, 2003

Despite the cold and snow flurries, Michael and Dan took their daily run. By the time they returned to the warmth of the office, Dan had been fully briefed.

He now stared out of Michael's window as the snowflakes became larger.

"Guess I just got out in time," he said. "The barmaid told me Bedminster often gets cut off."

"When did you last speak to Mark Boyd?" Michael asked.

"Wednesday night. I told him I'd got a job interview in D.C. and might not be back for several days."

"Smart. Did he question it?"

"No way. Boyd's a pompous prick, full of his own importance. He knows I'm a down-on-his-luck Princetonian with a failed marriage that cleaned me out financially and no regular employment. But not once has he offered to help. Buys me the occasional drink and talks about himself."

"Still no mention of the children?"

"Nada. When I bring up the subject, he just says, 'They keep Sis busy, thank God.'"

"What about that dinner invitation?"

"You see the daily briefings. She's never mentioned me. Neither has Boyd. Out of sight, out of mind."

He's got a point. Michael began sifting through a pile of papers. "Let me know as soon as you've got anything."

Dan turned to go. "Will do. This KGB lead sounds hopeful."

"Knock on wood," Michael said as Dan left.

It was after 4:30 p.m. when Brian's head appeared around Michael's door.

"Gotta minute?" he asked.

Michael waved him inside.

"The Lake Academy has a web site," Brian said, handing Michael a color printed 8½ x 11 sheet of paper. "That's downloaded from their site. A nice picture of their math teacher, Professor George Tyson."

"Great."

Brian sat. "Not so fast," he began.

Brian easily found the Lake Academy web site using an Internet search engine. But when he called the school, he was given the runaround before finally speaking with the assistant principal.

"Professor Tyson's no longer with us," he was told. But when Brian pushed for the reason why and when Tyson left the school and his last known address, he was given an emphatic "I couldn't possibly give out those details. Especially over the telephone."

As patiently as he could, Brian explained again that he was from the Department of Justice. It fell on deaf ears. "Only the headmaster is authorized to divulge the personal details of staff members. I suggest you make an appointment to see him."

"Did you?" Michael asked.

"Tuesday afternoon. He's away at some headmasters' conference 'til then." Brian glanced at the falling snow. "I'm flying into JFK, weather permittin'."

Chapter Nineteen

The Lake Academy, Smith Ridge Road, New Canaan, Connecticut
Thursday, February 13, 2003

Over the previous weekend, heavy snow partially shut down several major airports, and canceled flights became commonplace. After the headmaster's return from his conference was also delayed twice, Brian finally made the decision to drive. Having been forced to change his appointment three times, by the time he left D.C. on Wednesday morning to allow himself plenty of time, Michael was like a bear with a sore head.

At the private prep school, Brian was finally seated in front of the headmaster, who shook his hand and studied his ID.

"This weather's quite something," the headmaster said. "Mind you, we're used to it."

If that means all drivin' like maniacs, I agree, Brian thought. "What can you tell me about Professor Tyson?"

"Can I know why you need to find him?"

Brian shook his head. "I'm not at liberty to divulge information from an ongoin' investigation."

"I can't imagine what it would be after all this time. George was one of our best teachers. And well liked by the faculty. The students were very upset when he resigned."

"When was this?"

"September 2001. We were barely a week into the new semester. Finding a replacement was extremely difficult on such short notice."

"Do you have an exact date?"

The headmaster looked down at an open file. "He handed me his resignation on Friday the eighth, to take effect immediately. He came back briefly the following Monday to clean out his desk."

Oh, shit! "Did he give a reason for resigning?"

"I believe he said, 'Something personal.'"

"How did he act?"

"Looking back, I think the decision was causing him great conflict. He got very emotional and left in tears."

"Has he bin back?"

"No. We mailed his last paycheck."

"Where?"

The headmaster looked down again at the file. "To his residence."

"So you don't know if he's still there?"

The headmaster shook his head. "Several of our students lost parents and other family members in the World Trade Center. Trying to cope with those terrible losses took top priority."

Brian was about to leave. "Did you know that Professor Tyson's photograph is still on your web site and listed as one of the faculty?"

"He designed the site for us and kept it current. So I'm not surprised, after what happened, that it got overlooked. Now I'm aware, I'll see that it's corrected."

"Was he good with computers?"

"Excellent."

When Brian left the school, the sun was setting, but he'd gotten Tyson's last known address and his social security number. And just to be on the safe side, he'd also gotten a copy of Tyson's Connecticut driver's license. "A school requirement," he was told.

Having been stuck in D.C. for two additional days, Brian spent the time researching the school and surrounding area. The private academy had been founded in the 1950s, and there was nothing he could find that raised a red flag. Although his eyes widened when he saw the annual fees.

Holy shit! A school for rich kids.

His drive back to the Stamford Marriott only confirmed that this was a very wealthy area. With the snow coating everything, it looked like a winter wonderland of very expensive homes.

In the hotel's lobby, Brian found a local street map and some real estate brochures.

Give me somethin' to read this evenin'.

He ate in his room, which would have boasted a great view of Long Island Sound had it not been for the snow now obliterating everything and the fact it was dark. All Brian saw from his window was an endless stream of headlights on I-95, three lanes wide in both directions, crawling at a walking pace.

"The snow's really slowed 'em down," he commented to his waiter when the food arrived.

The man took a quick glance. "It's always like that. Even when it's nice out."

Brian fully intended to find Tyson's address after dinner. But when he stepped out of the hotel's lobby to see drifting snow and deserted streets, except for snowplows and salt trucks, he changed his mind.

What's another few hours? No one's goin' anywhere in this.

From his room, Brian called Michael instead.

In Brian's mind, Michael still sounded like a bear with a sore head. His mood wasn't improved by the fact that he was now stuck in D.C., due to bad weather gridlock, and had opted to sleep at the office.

"Better than a drafty cottage in Pennsylvania," Brian said, trying to lighten his mood.

It didn't work.

"Tyson resigned and left the school right before 9/11," Brian added. "I don't think that's just another coincidence."

"Neither do I," Michael replied before hanging up.

Stamford, Connecticut
Friday, February 14, 2003

Long Island Sound was now bathed in sunlight, the snow glistening, but traffic on I-95 didn't seem to have improved.

Brian watched the morning crawl before eating a large breakfast, relieved that he'd had the sense not to hurry.

The previous night, after studying the street map, he was confident that he'd find Tyson's address with no problem. The real estate brochures had been a different story. *I thought D.C. was expensive. How does anyone afford to live here?*

He left the Marriott's parking garage at 9:35 a.m., and passing under I-95 on well-plowed streets, he headed toward the Sound. Having driven through a small industrial section, Brian was surprised to find that the single-family homes suddenly got larger and more impressive.

It's gotta be the water, he thought.

Brian soon discovered that Tyson's address was an upscale condo complex with its own marina.

Maybe math teachers at posh private schools make more than I thought?

Brian rang the bell.

He was just about to ring again when the intercom came alive.

"Who is it?" a scratchy female voice asked.

"I'm lookin' for George Tyson."

There was a coughing sound. "He doesn't live here anymore. He moved."

After a lot of persuasion and holding his ID in front of the security camera, the main door was eventually buzzed open.

The elevator to the third floor opened directly into the living space, where he found a woman in her thirties bundled in a thick bathrobe, a tissue covering a very red nose.

"I've got an awful cold," she said, taking Brian's business card. "Otherwise, I'd have been at work."

Brian tried to concentrate on the water view from the living room and ignore her fluffy white rabbit slippers with large pink ears.

He sipped a mug of very strong coffee.

"I hope it's okay?" she said. "I can't taste anything."

He smiled. "Just how I like it. Did you ever meet George Tyson?"

"Oh, yes ..." she began.

Her nose was even redder and the pile of tissues almost overflowed the wastebasket at her feet by the time Brian left, but he had the name and address of Tyson's realtor.

"She was my agent and the listing agent," she said when Brian asked how she knew. "She told me he hadn't been here long. I think she was surprised he was selling."

"When was that?"

"It'll be two years this August."

So Tyson knew in advance he'd be leavin' the school, Brian thought.

The woman's description of Tyson matched the one on the Lake Academy web site, but to be sure, Brian showed her the photograph.

She blew her nose again. "That's him. He seemed very nice. Quiet, but well educated."

"Any accent?"

"Not that I remember. Should he have had one?"

Brian didn't answer. "Anythin' else?" he asked.

"He had some lovely furniture. The place was beautifully decorated and so clean. I was surprised to find out he was a teacher." She motioned for Brian to look around. "Apart from the furniture, I haven't changed a thing. If he'd been an interior decorator, I wouldn't have been surprised. Don't you agree?"

Whether he did or didn't, Brian nodded. "He wasn't married?"

"He never mentioned a wife."

"How's about lady friends?"

"Not that I saw."

Brian had no alternative but to wait in the listing agent's real estate office.

"She's due back at 3:00 p.m.," he was told.

The reception area was warm. With another cup of coffee, he sat down to wait with a pile of homes magazines.

At 3:10 p.m., a woman pushed through the front door. Her arms were full of papers and her boots covered in snow.

"Who wants to see houses on a day like this?" she said. "They've got to be ..." She stopped on seeing Brian.

When the receptionist whispered that he'd been waiting to see her, he got a professional smile and a warm handshake.

The smile soon faded when she discovered he wasn't a prospective buyer.

Brian got the impression that he was interrupting her schedule, but he made it clear that he wasn't leaving without some information.

After sighing loudly several times and muttering quietly, she began to flip through the contents in the bottom drawer of a file cabinet.

"Now I remember him," she said, opening a file. "He owned an apartment on Strawberry Hill Avenue. Nice enough, and they sell quickly in that price range being so close to the hospital."

"Was the place he bought more expensive?"

"Very much so. Shippan Point's very popular, being so close to the water. We have no trouble selling them."

"Did he come into money?"

"It did cross my mind. If memory serves me correctly, the mortgage he needed was quite small."

"Did he tell you why he was selling?"

"I seem to remember he said he was leaving the area. I know I was surprised, seeing as he'd only been there a few months. When I explained that he might not be getting any profit, he said he didn't care. Most homeowners want top dollar, you understand. He just wanted a quick sale."

"Did he get one?"

"Yes. With closing costs and commission, he actually took a small loss. He really was in a hurry to move."

"Where did he go?"

She shook her head. "Do you know, he never told me. And he wasn't at the closing."

Shit!

"But the post office probably has a forwarding address."

Brian thanked her for her time, and with directions to the main post office, he managed to get there just before they closed.

Having checked Brian's ID thoroughly, the postmaster then confirmed that Tyson left no instructions to have his mail forwarded to a new address.

Brian drove back to his hotel.

Michael's goin' to be real pissed.

He was right. But after the expected explosion, Brian added, "As frustratin' as this is, we're on the right track. Tyson's tryin' to disappear. That's gotta tell you somethin'."

"Seems like he's succeeded," Michael said.

"Not necessarily. We found him once; we can find him again. It ain't worth me drivin' back to D.C. I still gotta check on a few more leads. Okay?"

"Fine with me."

Chapter Twenty

Stamford, Connecticut
Monday, February 17, 2003

After spending the weekend at the Marriott, Brian called Molly at 8:30 a.m. An hour later, having walked from the hotel, he was in a lawyer's office above a bank on Atlantic Street.

The attorney, whom Tyson had used for his closing, looked to Brian as though he was still in his teens. Brian even commented on it.

"I get that a lot, Mr. Mullen. I'll be thirty-one in November."

"The Dick Clarke of lawyers?"

The attorney laughed. "So I'm told." He opened a file. "According to this, after the mortgage was paid off, Mr. Tyson got a cashier's check for the balance."

"Do you know what he did with it?"

The lawyer looked down. "The check was drawn on our escrow account," he said. "As Mr. Tyson wasn't able to attend the closing, he left instructions for the money to be paid into his account at a local bank."

"Can I have a copy?"

The lawyer scribbled something on a piece of paper. "That's the best I can do. The bank's address."

"Thanks. There's nothin' more you can tell me?"

"Sorry, Mr. Mullen. I would if I could."

"Good luck," the lawyer added as Brian was leaving.

I'm goin' to need a lot more than luck, Brian thought as he stepped into the cold. *A former KGB agent wantin' to disappear. Jesus! That's goin' to be like lookin' for a needle in a haystack.*

The Lake Academy, Smith Ridge Road, New Canaan, Connecticut
That afternoon

Getting parental consent to interview Tyson's former students would have taken too long, so Brian had no alternative but to question them in the presence of the headmaster, although he doubted that any of them would be forthcoming.

"We still have twenty-one students that were in Professor Tyson's classes in 2001, Mr. Mullen," the headmaster said. "A whole class graduated, several more have moved away, and three are currently out sick."

Brian would take what he could get.

One by one, the teenagers were called to the headmaster's office. They had little to add, except one common thread: "I was real surprised" or "I couldn't believe he was leaving."

"Has he ever written? A letter or a Christmas card?" Brian kept asking.

All he got was a shake of the head or, "No, nothing."

"What's your opinion?" he asked the headmaster as the last student closed the door.

"They told the truth. They've got no reason to lie. I think we'd have known if they were."

Unfortunately, Brian agreed.

Before leaving the school's parking lot, Brian called Molly.

"I've completed the search," she said. "But records indicate that George Tyson still lives in Stamford and has a current Connecticut driver's license."

"Interestin'."

"That's what I thought. And this probably doesn't help, but way back when, before the rules changed, it would have been quite easy for him to get several identities, just in case. All he would need was a copy of a birth certificate of a deceased male born about the same time. He was Russian and former KGB. Regardless of his defection, don't you think he'd have done that?"

"It's beginnin' to look that way. Good police work."

"I still remember some of it."

"What would you do next?"

"He'd blend more with large Russian communities. Twenty years ago, he probably still had an accent."

"Anywhere particular in mind?"

"Philadelphia."

"Why there?"

"He went to Wharton, and Philly has a big Russian community. They even have a web site."

"Before you do anythin', run it by Michael. And if he's there, I need to speak with him."

"He's here. I'll put you through."

Michael said very little as Brian brought him up to date.

"... so I reckon we've gotta follow the money," Brian concluded.

"Agreed." Michael checked his watch. "It's not too late. I'll make some phone calls and get back to you."

The Marriott, Tresser Blvd., Stamford, Connecticut
Later that night

Brian's cell phone rang.

"A Bernie Kopt from the main Connecticut IRS office will meet you in the lobby at 0900 tomorrow. He's got all the authorization you'll need to access Tyson's bank accounts."

"That was fast."

"My father backed up my request for their involvement."

"Remind me to have him put in a good word for me around tax time."

"If I thought that would work, I'd be first in line."

Still, it helps to have two Correas in the game, Brian thought as he hung up.

Stamford, Connecticut
Tuesday, February 18, 2003

At exactly 9:00 a.m., Bernie Kopt met Brian in the lobby of the Marriott. The IRS agent was a small man, wearing an old tweed topcoat over a crumpled suit and knitted vest. He carried an ancient leather briefcase, and if his glasses had been held together with Scotch tape, Brian wouldn't have been surprised. After shaking Kopt's almost child-size hand, Brian wished he hadn't.

They walked to the bank. In the manager's office, Kopt finally removed his hat to reveal a mostly bald head. Thin strands of hair from a parting just above one ear appeared to be glued in place and did nothing to assure Brian of his ability.

Less than an hour later, Brian and Kopt were back at the Marriott.

Don't judge a book by its cover, Brian reminded himself as they sat in the bar drinking coffee. For despite Kopt's appearance, he'd exhibited a no-nonsense, almost aggressive attitude toward the bank manager. In no time at all, Kopt was handed all the relevant documents.

Kopt now turned to Brian. "I think I've got everything I need to track this individual for you, Mr. Mullen." He went back to studying the pages in front of him. "I think this's going to be easier than I first thought," he added, putting the duplicate bank statements into his briefcase.

"How so?"

Kopt explained.

"I'm impressed, Mr. Kopt," Brian said when he'd finished.

Kopt took a sip of coffee. "My superiors tell me that this is a matter of national security. I'll get on it right away. As soon as I know anything, what's the fastest way to reach you?"

"Any of the numbers on my card," Brian replied. "You're goin' to track this individual for us?"

"Of course. But when we find the other bank accounts, with names and addresses, the ball will be in your court."

"No problem."

"As it's my understanding this individual was former KGB, that means he probably has many different identities."

Brian nodded.

"Don't worry, Mr. Mullen," Kopt continued. "They don't call me the 'Rat Terrier' for nothing."

"I'm beginnin' to see why."

Kopt drained his coffee and got to his feet, pulling on the topcoat. "He can run, but he can't hide indefinitely from the IRS," he added, clutching his briefcase. "You've got my business card, Mr. Mullen, if you need anything more. Otherwise, I'll be in touch."

"Thanks again, Mr. Kopt."

Grateful there was no parting handshake, Brian watched him push through the lobby doors before returning to his room.

"I'm checkin' out," Brian told Molly, throwing his clothes into a travel bag. "Tell Michael I'll see him in the mornin'."

"Did you meet with the IRS agent?"

"Sure did. Looks like we're gonna get a paper trail to follow."

"That is good news."

Michael's Office, G Street, Washington, D.C.
Wednesday, February 19, 2003

"The good news: We're goin' to get a way to track Tyson," Brian said.

"And the bad?" Michael asked.

"The IRS agent found Tyson wrote checks to six different individuals until the account was empty. Then he closed it."

"Six?"

"'Fraid so."

"All possible aliases?"

"Looks that way."

"Shit," Michael muttered.

Brian continued, "Most banks have stopped returnin' customers' checks, but they do copy front and back. From the endorsements, we'll know where the checks went. Kopt reckons that Tyson probably endorsed his own checks. A handwritin' expert can confirm that."

"How long before we know?"

"Weeks. Maybe months."

"We don't have months."

Chapter Twenty-One

Michael's Office, G Street, Washington, D.C.
Monday, March 3, 2003

It had only taken ten days for the IRS agent to get back to Brian.

"My investigation isn't yet complete," Kopt said, "but so far, all indications are that the money was slowly being funneled to an account in Camden, South Carolina, in the name of Harold Wentworth. Former KGB agents are usually better than this at covering their tracks, which leaves me to believe that Tyson was in a hurry when he left Connecticut. I'm continuing to dig, of course, but my suggestion to you, Mr. Mullen, is to start looking in Camden. There's also another Wentworth account at the National Bank of South Carolina. It's a business account for Wentworth's Antiques and Collectibles. The private checking account was opened in September 2001. The business account, three weeks later. That's not that long after Tyson's Connecticut closing. I hope this is helpful?"

"It sure is."

Later that afternoon, Brian was in Michael's office, repeating the conversation with Kopt.

"It gets better," Brian added. "I checked the social security number Kopt gave me. It does belong to a Harold Wentworth, and it was issued in 1960. He must have got it around the time he first contacted Worcek. Guess he was makin' long-term plans, even back then."

"This sounds promising. Guess you're going to Camden," Michael said.

"Guess I am. Molly's checked the airlines. It's goin' to be easier to drive."

"Keep me posted. This's the first decent-sounding lead we've got in a long time."

Camden, South Carolina
Tuesday, March 4, 2003

By early afternoon, Brian was crawling in heavy traffic due to major construction on I-95 in Florence, South Carolina. When he did reach the I-20 exit, having had plenty of time to check his map, he reckoned that Camden was less than an hour away. Something was telling him that this was a promising lead as the speedometer climbed to 80 mph.

On Broad Street, near the center of Camden, Brian turned into an almost empty gravel parking lot at the side of Wentworth's clearly marked antiques store.

At the front of the store, behind the half-glass door, the red sign said "Closed," but the opening times were clearly posted. According to them, the store should have been open.

Brian peered through the large windows on either side of the door. He could make out plenty of merchandise in the dark interior, but his instincts told him something wasn't right.

He crossed the street to a similar-looking store opposite.

"Can I help you?" a middle-aged woman asked as he entered.

Brian pointed. "What's up with the store across the street? I was hopin' to see Harry Wentworth."

"Oh, dear," she said. "You're not from around here?"

"Nope."

"Was Mr. Wentworth a friend?"

Brian felt a knot in his stomach. "We'd done business in the past."

She lowered her voice. "He was murdered, not long ago. Front page headlines, as you can imagine. It was just dreadful. You never expect something like that to happen on your doorstep, and especially not in Camden. It's normally such a lovely place to live."

Brian thanked her and went back to his car. *Goddamnit! Michael's goin' to be real pissed. Next stop, the Camden cops.*

Camden Police Department, West DeKalb Street, Camden, South Carolina
A short time later

After showing his ID and briefly explaining why he wanted to discuss the Wentworth case, Brian was told that the lead investigator wouldn't be back until the morning. "Root canal," said the lady at the front desk.

"What can you tell me?"

"Not much. You'll need to speak with Lieutenant Pat Norton of our Investigative Services Division."

"Female?"

"No, Patrick. But everyone calls him Pat."

Brian handed the woman his card. "Please get him to call me. Early as possible." He underlined his cell phone number. "I'm stayin' at the Colony Inn. Tell him it's a matter of national security. Got that?"

She studied the card. "Got that, Mr. Mullen."

"How do I find Wentworth's house?"

As she gave him verbal directions, Brian wrote on a small notepad.

"Thanks," Brian replied, before he lumbered outside.

He checked his watch. It was well after 3:30 p.m., but he didn't feel inclined to check into the hotel.

Instead, he drove to Harold Wentworth's last known address.

Brian parked in the driveway of the two-storey detached home, and as he approached the front door, he could see a small remnant of yellow police tape. Tall shrubs grew halfway up the front windows, making it impossible for Brian to see inside. *A burglar's dream,* he thought as he went around the side. *When will homeowners ever learn?* Then it occurred to him that Wentworth might have left the shrubs that tall for a reason.

He was about to look through a pair of French-style doors at the rear of the house when a voice called, "Can I help you?"

Brian turned to see an older gentleman with a small dog on a leash.

Brian approached the man, his ID in clear view. "Afternoon, sir. You live here?" he asked, pointing to the house next door.

The man struggled with his glasses. Then holding Brian's ID, he looked at it closely before replying.

"I do," he said. "I thought you were another one of those pesky reporters. Swarming all over for weeks, they were." Seemingly satisfied, he handed back the ID. "You're from the Department of Justice? What possible interest could they have in Harold, apart from the fact the poor man was murdered?"

Brian had no intention of answering. "You knew him well?" he said instead.

"I wouldn't say 'well.' But we were neighbors. This's a small community, and we like to make newcomers feel welcome."

"I'd appreciate anything you can tell me."

The man turned away. "You'd better come inside then."

Brian quickly learned that Vernon Potts was a widower as he sat in an immaculate living room, with a mug of very strong tea.

"We'd lived here for thirty-five years," Potts said. "Then my wife got sick. She struggled on bravely for another three years, before passing in 1998."

"I'm sorry for your loss."

"Thank you. I thought long and hard about selling the house after she'd gone, but it would have been a mistake ..."

Brian let him ramble on for some time about his late wife and life in Camden, and two things became clear: Potts was a longtime deacon at his local church, and he kept a prize-winning rose garden. "My roses keep me going, and Lucas here," he added, tickling the small white dog behind its ear.

"You must spend a lot of time outside?"

"With my roses, yes. Every chance I get." He turned to a glass-fronted china cabinet. "All my trophies."

"Impressive."

"Do you like gardening, Mr. Mullen? ..."

Finally, Brian managed to steer the conversation around to Harold Wentworth. "What can you tell me about him?"

"Not much," Potts replied.

But by the time Brian eventually left Vernon Potts' house, he knew a lot more about Harold Wentworth than he'd expected.

According to Potts, Wentworth had moved into the house the day after the sellers moved out.

"It was September 15th, 2001," Potts said.

When Brian asked how he knew the exact date, Potts replied that it was the same day as the church cookout. "It was almost canceled because of the terrorist attacks. But we decided that's exactly what they wanted. So we held it despite them. I naturally invited Harold, but with him in the middle of moving, I understood why he declined." Potts then added that the houses in the neighborhood usually sold quickly, but Wentworth had signed a contract the day the house came on the market and moved in thirty days later. "It was very fast," he added. "Of course, the sellers were delighted."

Potts had first thought that Wentworth was an interior decorator because "by the time he finished with the interior, it was so different and quite lovely. So I wasn't that surprised when he told me he was an antique dealer."

"A confirmed bachelor, I think," Potts said, when Brian asked about visitors. He lowered his voice. "I did wonder if he was a homosexual."

"No lady friends?"

"Not that I saw. The only visitor I saw was introduced to me as his cousin." Potts tried to remember his name. "It'll come to me," he added after Brian pushed him. "I had to sign for a parcel from Federal Express when they were out. It was addressed to the cousin."

Potts had first thought the cousin was Wentworth's business partner. But after several weeks, he never saw him again.

"Can you describe this man?" Brian asked.

"Clearly," Potts replied. "There was no family resemblance. I thought that odd."

Me too.

"And especially as his English seemed somewhat sporadic."

Hello. "Any idea what nationality?"

"European, I thought. Maybe Polish or one of the Slavic countries."

"Russian?"

"Yes, I suppose he could have been … Denis, that was it. Denis Savin. Yes, S-A-V-I-N. But that doesn't sound at all Russian, does it?"

Brian didn't comment. "Did the police ask about this cousin?"

"Naturally, I told them, but they didn't seem interested."

The Colony Inn, West DeKalb Street, Camden, South Carolina
Later that night

Brian called Michael from his room with the news. As expected, he got an expletive-driven reaction.

"What the hell's going on?" Michael said when Brian had finished. "If Wentworth was Tyson, his murder can't be another coincidence. Damn it! We're still no closer."

"Trust me; we're on the right track."

"And how far behind?"

"Maybe not that far." Brian then related his conversation with Potts. "… it was dark when I left Potts' house," he added. "Too dark to go snoopin'. I reckon the old man's lonely. I'm thinkin' this Savin character's worth pursuin'."

"We've got nothing else," Michael muttered.

"Yet. Wait 'til I talk to the Camden cops. And the old guy says he'll cooperate in an identikit of the so-called cousin. So we oughta get someone down here ASAP. Plus, I reckon he'd welcome the company."

"Agreed. I'll let you know when."

Camden Police Department, West DeKalb Street, Camden, South Carolina
Wednesday, March 5, 2003

Lieutenant Pat Norton's left cheek was slightly swollen.

"How's the root canal?" Brian asked after the introductions were over.

"Better than the abscessed tooth," Norton replied. "Grab that chair."

Brian pulled a spare chair to the side of the desk.

"What's the DoJ's interest in a small-town homicide, however nasty?"

"Nasty?"

Norton gave a slight cough. "The victim's throat had been slit. One swipe, the M.E. said, with a very sharp blade. Done by a professional, he thought. It almost severed his head."

This sounds familiar. "Go on."

"It started as a missing persons case ..." Norton began.

The owner of the shop opposite Wentworth's had called the police department on Thursday, January 9th, 2003, to tell them that his antique and collectibles store had been closed for a week.

"I know he goes away on buying trips," she added, "but he always tells me when he's going and leaves a key. I've tried his unlisted home number, but the answering machine isn't working. I've asked around. No one who knows him has seen him either or knows where he is. I think you should do something to find him."

A patrol officer had been dispatched to investigate. He found the store locked, but nothing from the outside appeared to be wrong. At Wentworth's home, the next-door neighbor met him in the driveway.

"That was fast," Vernon Potts said. "I was only talking to someone at the police station a few minutes ago."

"Why did you call, sir?"

"Look. There's at least seven newspapers on the lawn, and Mr. Wentworth's mailbox is almost full. He always cancels the newspapers if he's going away and gets the post office to hold his mail. I've looked through the garage's side window. His car's still there. Something isn't right."

I wonder why Potts forgot to tell me that, Brian thought.

At that point, there was little the police could do. However, they did check with the one locally based cab company to see if Wentworth had left Camden by cab. The answer was, "No." The following day, the owner of the shop opposite called the police department again.

"A shipment of overseas furniture has arrived for Mr. Wentworth. I can't find him, so what am I supposed to do? The driver says Mr. Wentworth knew it was coming today, because he'd called them to change the date, and as it's paid for, he's not taking it back without Mr. Wentworth's authorization."

In the end, the police got the woman to reluctantly agree to sign for the shipment, and it was off-loaded into her storeroom.

"Has she still got it?" Brian asked.

"Yes," Norton replied. "Until any next of kin can be traced, she's stuck with it."

With still no sign of Wentworth, Norton took his investigation to the next level and broke into Wentworth's house, although he wasn't prepared for what he found.

"See for yourself," he said, passing Brian a stack of 3 x 5 color photographs. "The place was trashed."

Brian began to thumb through them. "You're not kiddin'."

He took a good look at the first photograph of the kitchen. A large arc of blood spatter covered the tile backsplash below the upper cabinets on one side of the kitchen. The countertop was almost as bloody, and some of the close-ups showed partial bloody handprints. On the tile floor below the counter, two trails of smeared blood led to the back door. The largest pool of blood was just inside the door.

"When I saw that," Norton added, "the case became a possible homicide. It looks like he was killed in the kitchen and dragged to the door. When the body was eventually found, the blood on the heels of his shoes corresponded with the two trails. We determined that there could have been more than one perpetrator. An individual or individuals wrapped him in something before taking the body outside. There was no sign of any blood beyond the door."

"Not a drop?"

"Nada. At that point, we called South Carolina Law Enforcement Division."

Brian began studying the crime scene photographs. "How long have you bin an investigator?"

"Two years."

"First homicide?"

"Yes. It shows?"

"No. But the first one's always tough. You never get used to them. Just learn to detach. Kids are the worst." Brian held up the autopsy report from the Charleston, South Carolina medical examiner. "Where was the body found?"

"Near a lake, about sixty-five miles from here."

"What did you conclude from that?"

"They hoped the victim would never be found, and the case would remain unsolved."

"How was the body discovered?"

"A snowbird traveling back north with his dog. I guess next time he'll find a restroom. The M.E. estimated that the victim had been dead for over a month."

"Where's the body now?"

"Buried."

Brian opened his briefcase and took out the picture of Tyson from the Lake Academy's web site. He handed it to Norton. "This look like the same guy to you?"

"Could be. Add blond hair, beard, and mustache, and I say it's the same guy." Norton paused. "Who was he?"

"Someone of interest."

"And now that he's dead?"

"Nothin's changed."

"Camden's a quiet little town, with more than its fair share of tourists."

"And your point is?"

"I'm shocked, I guess."

Brian closed Norton's file. "I need copies of this."

Norton reached for the telephone. "SLED's[7] got the complete file."

"Where are they?" Brian asked before Norton could dial.

"Columbia. Forty-five minutes away."

"Then tell them I'm on my way."

Brian called Michael from the car. "Norton's got keys to the house. But we gotta get a second search warrant executed to make it legal."

"How long's that going to take?"

"Norton's drawin' up the warrant as I speak. He almost shit a brick when I told him it was terrorist-related. With that as probable cause, and if he can find the original judge, could be as soon as tomorrow. Your clout might help."

"Fine. I thought you said Norton had keys?"

Patience, Michael. "He does. And yes, it crossed my mind. But if we do an illegal search, it could come back to bite us on the ass."

Michael sighed. "Point taken. I'll get right on it. What's this judge's name and number?"

Brian told him, adding, "Dependin' on what I get from SLED, it'll go faster if we get them involved again."

"Do it."

---

7   South Carolina Law Enforcement Division. For more information on this state
    agency: www.sled.state.sc.us.

"Before you call the judge, call SLED."

"We're Justice."

"And as a former cop, trust me. Call the chief. We need his authorization. And cooperation."

"I'll do it. And keep me posted."

South Carolina Law Enforcement Division, Broad River Road, Columbia, South Carolina
Later that afternoon

A lady seated behind a thick glass partition in the entrance lobby of the main building checked an appointment list.

"Lieutenant LaRoche's expecting you," she said after Brian showed his ID and introduced himself. "I'll let him know you're here."

A few minutes later, a tall man with broad shoulders and close-cropped brown hair appeared through a side door.

With the introductions over, Brian followed LaRoche to the Forensic Science building. After signing in and getting his Visitor's Pass, Brian was shown to a door marked "Classroom."

"I was the primary investigator," LaRoche said, handing Brian a file. "The chief says it's okay for you to see that. Everything we got is in there. There were no leads. So what's Justice's interest?"

Brian sat at one of the several long tables and opened the file. "We suspect the victim had ties to al Qaeda."

"In that case, take all the time you need, Mr. Mullen. I'll answer any questions I can. Call me on this number. I'll be upstairs."

"It's Brian. And thanks."

"I'm John," he said, closing the door.

Brian studied the file for over an hour. SLED had done a thorough investigation, considering they had little to work with. With no evidence of a forced entry, they concluded that the victim probably knew his attacker/ attackers. There were many more photographs of the crime scene and the trashed interior of the house, but no obvious signs of a struggle. Only two sets of fingerprints were found in the house. Identical prints were also found in the car.

Brian had hoped the car would produce a lead. *Shit! There goes that theory,* he thought. Both sets of prints were then run through South Carolina's AFIS,[8] and when no matches were found, they increased their search using

---

8   Automated Fingerprint Identification System.

the FBI's AFIS. They got the same zero result. Consequently, they could only assume that one set belonged to the victim, as the same fingerprints were found on invoices at Wentworth's antique shop. The DNA analysis from the blood samples came from one unidentified person they still couldn't confirm as Wentworth. Local research for any dental and/or medical records hadn't turned up anything, and even though he had a South Carolina driver's license, they'd gotten nothing else. It was only after Wentworth was found dead that they had a positive ID. Not that it helped.

The list of telephone calls from Wentworth's home and business proved to be legitimate. If he'd been using a cell phone, there was no trace. LaRoche had even briefly checked the overseas crates of furniture, still stored at the antique shop across the street. According to his report, the contents appeared to correspond to the manifest. The only item the SLED investigators finally removed from Wentworth's house was a desktop computer. After examination, they found that part of the hard drive had been wiped clean using DoD[9]-type software. But with no leads, and a far more computer literate public, it hadn't raised any red flags.

Brian dialed LaRoche's extension.

"Nice work," Brian said when LaRoche appeared a few minutes later and held up a picture of Tyson from the Lake Academy's web site. "Look like the same guy?"

LaRoche thumbed through the autopsy photographs. "I'd say so."

"There's no mention of his hair being dyed?"

"They probably weren't looking. Cause of death was obvious."

Brian opened a South Carolina map. "Where was the body found?"

LaRoche pointed. "Right there. Off 301."

"Lake Marion?"

"Close. The victim was discovered at the bottom of an embankment in the Santee National Wildlife Refuge. No attempt had been made to hide it. If it hadn't been for the snowbird and his dog, it could have remained undetected for years."

A body dump that far south? Shit! Where the hell were they headed? Or is it just a red herrin' to throw us off? Brian got to his feet. "We're goin' to have to process the crime scene again."

"For what?"

"A goddamn needle in a haystack," Brian replied. "These bastards are good, but we're better."

---

9   Department of Defense.

On his way back to Camden, Brian called Michael with an update.

"... and Norton called," he added. "The judge signed off on the second warrant. I've just gotten off the phone with LaRoche, the original SLED lead investigator. He's meetin' us tomorrow mornin' with the rest of his team. How soon can you get here?"

"Tonight, sometime. This sounds promising."

Let's hope, for all our sakes, Brian thought as he hung up.

The Colony Inn, West DeKalb Street, Camden, South Carolina
Thursday, March 6, 2003

At Brian's suggestion, Lieutenant Pat Norton was to be included in the second investigation. "He's young and a bit green," Brian told Michael the previous night. "But he's got the makin's of a good cop. We could use an extra pair of hands."

Michael agreed.

Even so, Brian was surprised to see Michael and Norton already seated at a circular table by the window eating breakfast when he appeared with Dan at 8:00 a.m.

After introducing Dan and more breakfasts ordered, Michael pushed his now-empty plate to one side. "I cleared it with Norton's chief last night. Until I say so, he's now officially attached to us."

"Welcome aboard," Dan said.

"Likewise," Brian added.

Wentworth's House, Mill Street, Camden, South Carolina
Forty minutes later

With military precision, Dan thought, a small convoy consisting of two Dodge extended-cab pickups and another Suburban followed them onto Wentworth's street.

It's goin' to look like a Suburban owners' club convention or a goddamn party, Brian thought as all five vehicles stopped at Wentworth's house. *Nothin' like keepin' a low profile.*

On Michael's direction, their Suburbans parked in the driveway.

Two men got out of the Dodge pickups and approached Michael.

The older of the two appeared to be in his early thirties. "Lieutenant LaRoche," he said, extending his hand. "Nice to meet you, Colonel."

"It's Michael," he replied, returning a firm grip.

LaRoche turned to the man beside him. "Agent Charlie Boswick. He worked with me on the first investigation."

A very attractive blonde who'd been driving the SLED Suburban stepped forward. "Lynn Tillman," she said, taking Michael's offered hand.

"The lieutenant's our computer genius," LaRoche added.

"Good," Michael replied. "The more experts, the better."

They entered the house using the spare key Norton had kept after changing the locks.

Off to the right, the living room was clearly visible from the hall. Whoever trashed the room didn't take the time to unzip the pillows. The expensive-looking fabrics had been slashed, and part of the stuffing removed, which was not going to help the examination process.

Brian stared at the mess and could hear Potts' words, "... the inside's quite lovely." "It's not lovely now," Brian muttered.

"Did you say something?" LaRoche asked.

"Just talkin' to myself. What was your take on this?"

"First impression was home invasion gone wrong. With no fingerprints other than Wentworth's and another individual we've never managed to identify, it was headed to the cold cases."

"Not anymore. Apart from the computer, was anythin' else removed?"

"Not by us. If something's missing, we wouldn't know."

Brian scanned the room again. "Was this how you found it?"

Norton nodded.

LaRoche looked around. "As far as I can tell."

And a lot of Camden cops stomping around, Brian thought.

The kitchen no longer looked like a crime scene, and a faint smell from a strong cleaning agent still lingered.

"Who did this?" LaRoche asked.

"We did," Norton replied. "Department policy."

"We'd have left it." LaRoche then spread their original photographs on a countertop. "All that's left of the crime scene, sir," he said to Michael.

"There was no sign of a struggle?"

"We believe that the victim was approached from behind. He didn't have time to react." LaRoche pointed to a photograph showing bloody smears on one countertop. "As his hands were covered in his own blood, the M.E. concluded that he grabbed at his throat and then the counter before falling."

Brian was also studying the photographs again. "Looks about right."

Michael handed Dan a fingerprint card from the SLED file. "Check those against the ones we brought with us. Let's make doubly sure it's the same guy before we waste any more time."

"I'll get right on it," Dan said.

"You know the victim?" LaRoche asked as they heard the front door close.

"Not as Wentworth," Michael replied, already beginning to leave the room. "I want to take a good look around."

They toured the rest of the house. Every room, including the two upstairs bathroom cabinets, had been ransacked.

"What they were looking for is a mystery to us," LaRoche said, walking back into the master bedroom.

Michael faced him. "Whatever it is, we're going to find it. And we're not leaving until we do. Begin your investigation again, remembering that we're dealing with some very smart individuals. Use my guys. We've been on their trail for too long. If anyone needs me, I'll be in the kitchen."

LaRoche watched Michael leave. "Guess he's used to giving orders."

"It's nothin' personal," Brian said. "He's Special Forces. They're not as patient as cops. We know somethin' big's goin' down, and he's real pissed that every lead we've gotten so far has dead-ended."

"Then let's get started."

As Brian was about to leave the bedroom, Norton stopped him. "Do you really think Wentworth was part of al Qaeda?" he asked quietly.

"That's why we're here."

Dan found Michael in the kitchen.

"I got a positive match from SLED's prints," he said quietly. "Wentworth was Kolesnikov."

"So we're on the right track?"

"I'd say definitely."

"It's about time."

While the SLED team, along with Brian and Norton, began the investigation process again, Dan now scanned the set of unknown fingerprints into a laptop using a secure telephone link from inside one of the two Suburbans parked in the victim's driveway.

As the Camden police and SLED didn't find a match, it was Michael's hope that accessing worldwide databases would produce results.

"We've got lots of high-tech toys," he told LaRoche.

By the time Michael finished going through the SLED file, Brian and Norton were in the dining room, while LaRoche and Boswick were methodically working the living room in a grid pattern.

In the farthest corner, dozens of books littered the oriental carpet where a bookcase had been overturned. Every book cover was now being dusted for prints. The spine was then checked before the book was opened in case anything had been hidden. When they'd finished, it was returned to the bookcase.

Michael watched from the open doorway. "Anything?" he asked.

LaRoche shook his head. "Not yet. But knowing what I know now, I reckon it's way too clean."

"What can I do?"

"Lynn's in the family room. I'm sure she'd appreciate some help."

"Fine," Michael said, pulling on latex gloves as he disappeared.

Lieutenant Lynn Tillman was on her hands and knees in a small room off the hallway, surrounded by a sea of papers, two upturned file cabinets, a large TV face down, and various electronic components. Covering the chaos were several wall units.

She looked up. "And I thought my office was messy."

Michael looked around. "His computer was taken from here?"

She went back to work. "I guess so. It was delivered to me. I wasn't on site during the first investigation." She waved her hand. "Somewhere over there, I saw a crappy HP printer."

"Need help?"

"You bet."

As Michael stepped around her to begin lifting the wall units off the pile, he asked about Wentworth's hard drive having been partially wiped clean. "It didn't make you suspicious?" he added.

She continued to sort papers into piles. "If you know where to look, there's some pretty sophisticated software out there for civilians. Or he could have a friend with connections." She paused. "That's no help, is it?"

"Affirmative."

"Look on the bright side," she continued. "From what I can tell, he had a well-organized filing system, if I could only find the corresponding folders."

"What else did you find?"

She closed her eyes. "He surfed eBay. Sometimes bought stuff. Antiques and collectibles, from what I could tell. Booked trips online. Hotels, cars, etc. Played a few computer games. Nothing out of the ordinary."

"Trips to where?"

"Boston, New York, Chicago, Miami. LaRoche told me that he went away on buying trips."

"Nothing overseas?"

"No."

"What about e-mail?"

"All business-related."

"Nothing personal?"

"Nope."

"Didn't you find that odd?"

"He was a single man in his sixties, from what I was told. A loner. No chat rooms either."

"Damn," Michael muttered.

They worked in silence for almost two hours. Then Michael stepped carefully back across the room. "I'm going to check on Dan. Take a break."

He was gone before she could reply.

Inside the Suburban, Dan was still engrossed with the laptop.

"Yes!" he exclaimed as Michael opened the door. "Great timing. Look at this. We've got an Interpol match to the unsub.[10]"

Michael studied the screen. "What's a Russian scientist doing in the Interpol database?"

"Suspected terrorist ties."

"Shit. Does it say what kind of scientist?"

"No. But what's the betting he's a nuclear physicist?"

"I hope he's not." Michael pointed at the screen. "Print that mug shot and show it to the old man next door. See if he recognizes him before we waste time on an identikit. Then get hold of Interpol and find out everything you can about Dr. Dimitri Sadilov."

Vernon Potts wasn't home the first time Dan tried the doorbell.

On his way back to the Suburban, he called Molly. *Two heads,* he thought, before telling her to begin a background search of Sadilov.

After he'd hung up from that brief conversation, Dan then dialed an overseas number.

On his way back to the family room, Michael stopped to check on LaRoche. He and Boswick had closely examined three-quarters of the books.

---

10 Unknown Subject.

It took time to thumb through all the pages, but they knew it had to be done.

"Find any books in Russian?" Michael asked.

LaRoche shook his head.

He was too careful for that, Michael thought.

According to LaRoche, Wentworth's reading material fell mainly into two categories. Mystery/thrillers by authors like Clancy, Grisham, Cornwell, and Follett. However, by far the largest category was reference books on antique furniture, porcelain, silver, a two-volume set of a 2001 Davenport's Guide, and some glossy auction catalogs.

Window dressing? Michael thought. *Or was he really knowledgeable?*

In the dining room, Brian and Norton were working side by side. Brian had already bagged some small particles of what appeared to be mud from the oriental carpet, while Norton had examined the upturned chairs inch by inch. After finding a few hairs, they too were individually bagged and labeled before he began on the sideboard. It was laborious work.

On seeing Michael, Norton commented on that fact.

Brian didn't stop working. "Slow and methodical. A real pain in the ass sometimes. Right, Michael?"

"Right," he replied.

From his temporary office inside the Suburban, Dan saw Potts return home at 3:30 p.m.

By the time Dan was crossing the lawn in front of Wentworth's house, the old man was already walking back down his driveway with a small white dog on a leash.

"Mr. Potts?" Dan called out.

He stopped.

After struggling with his glasses to closely check Dan's ID, Dan wasted no time. "Do you know this man?"

Potts had to replace his glasses before staring at the face. "I don't think so." He looked up. "Are you a colleague of Mr. Mullen's?"

"Yes, sir."

Potts gesticulated at the three Suburbans and the two pickups. "Is Mr. Mullen here too?"

"Yes. And our boss."

Potts adjusted his glasses and looked again at the face. "Why's the Department of Justice so interested in Harold's murder?"

"I'm not at liberty to say."

"Well, I guess it must be important." He pointed at the image. "Is this supposed to be Mr. Savin?"

"You don't recognize him?"

Potts replaced his glasses in their case. "Not looking like that." He began to turn away. "That man's got a full head of hair. Mr. Savin was as bald as a coot. 'Bullet head,' I called him. But not to his face, of course. I've never understood why bald men have to grow beards. Dumb, if you ask me. Now, I've got to take Lucas for his walk. He's been in the house since early this morning."

Before Dan could say any more, Potts continued down the driveway.

Back inside the Suburban, Dan downloaded Sadilov's picture into computer imaging software and began removing the full head of hair. He'd just finished adding a beard when there was a tap on the driver's door window.

Dan opened the rear door and stepped out.

Potts tried to peer inside the vehicle. "That's quite a setup you've got there, Mr. Whitney," he commented, still trying to look around Dan.

"Want to take a closer look?"

"Thank you. Can Lucas come too?"

In the rear of the Suburban, Potts and the dog sat together. As Potts was putting on his glasses again, making Dan wonder why he bothered to take them off, he turned the laptop toward him.

"That's almost him," Potts said, peering at the screen.

"Almost?"

"Can you give him a mustache?"

Dan went back to work.

Potts seemed to be enjoying himself. "The beard wasn't nearly that bushy."

Dan made the changes.

Potts took his time. "That's definitely him," he eventually said.

"How can you be so sure?"

"It wasn't that long ago."

"When exactly?"

"November, last year. He arrived around Halloween. I remember him saying that he was surprised it was such a celebrated occasion in the U.S."

"Thank you, Mr. Potts."

He didn't seem in a hurry to leave. "Glad I could be of help." He took a good look around the Suburban's interior. "I've never seen anything like this. What haven't you got?"

"A kitchen sink," Dan said. "Can you get out okay? I've got to get back to work."

Reluctantly, Potts left, with the dog following.

Dan waited until the old man disappeared before taking a sheet of paper off the printer. Then he locked the vehicle and headed inside the house.

LaRoche and Boswick were still in the living room.

"Next time I want my apartment cleaned, I'll know who to call," Dan said from the hall. "Where's Michael?"

"Family room," LaRoche replied.

Lynn was handing Michael small stacks of manila folders to refill the now-upright file cabinets.

Dan held up the identikit face. "Potts ID'd Sadilov as Savin."

Michael turned, dropping a bundle of files into a drawer. "He's sure?"

"Very. Like Brian said, he's a lonely old man. So he could have strung this out for days if he'd wanted."

"Test him like we did Otis," Michael continued. "See how good he is at finding Sadilov in a shitload of faces. The Camden cops can—"

The doorbell effectively stopped him in mid-sentence.

Brian peered through the dining room window. "It's Potts," he called out.

"Damn it," Michael said. "I'll go."

He opened the front door.

Potts looked up. "Is Mr. Mullen here?" He pointed to a tray on the porch. "I brought some tea over. I thought you could probably use a cup?"

Michael stepped outside, closing the door behind him. "I'm Michael Correa," he said, handing Potts his card.

Potts struggled with his glasses before studying the card. "You look far too young to be a colonel. I must be getting old."

"It's lieutenant colonel, Mr. Potts."

"But still." Potts looked down at the tray and then at the five vehicles. "Did I bring enough mugs, Colonel? I thought they'd be easier. I apologize that the teapot doesn't match. It was the largest one I could find. And if there isn't enough milk and sugar, let me know?"

Michael opened the door, sliding the tray inside. Then he closed it again.

"Thanks for bringing it over, Mr. Potts. We could use a break." He lit a small cigar and moved away from the house, effectively forcing Potts to follow.

"Is it going well?" Potts asked.

Here we go. "Fine, thanks."

"How long do you think you'll be here?"

"It's too early to tell."

Potts cleared his throat. "The Camden police told the newspapers that they suspected Mr. Wentworth's murder was a burglary gone wrong, but that's not what you think, is it? Otherwise, you wouldn't all be here."

Michael tapped the ash off his cigar. *Let it go, old man.* "I can't divulge any information."

"I understand," Potts continued. "But if it was a burglary, do you think there's a chance they'll come back? Lucas is a good watchdog, but ..."

So that's it. "Don't worry. No one's coming back."

"Oh, thank you," Potts said. "I hope you understand my concern?"

Michael stubbed out the remaining cigar. "No problem." He turned away. "Thanks again for the tea. Someone will return the tray."

Back inside, Lynn was leaning against the family room wall, sipping from a mug.

"This hits the spot," she said on seeing Michael. She scanned the room. "It's a big improvement on this morning. Thanks for the help."

"You're welcome," he said. "But we didn't find anything."

"Patience."

"I'm told it's not my strong point."

You got that right. "None of us are perfect." *Not even you.* She finished the tea in one gulp and got back on the floor. "CDs next." She viewed the scattered cases. "Looks like he had a really diverse taste in music. But why did he have to be a collector? There must be hundreds here, now that we can finally see them."

Michael pulled on latex gloves and knelt beside her. "Categories again?"

"Sounds like a plan." She flipped open the first CD. "Check for contents," she added. "It'll speed up the process."

"Suits me," Michael said.

With some of the furniture roughly back in place, they now had enough room on the carpet to make several piles. Rock and roll, country, and vocals.

"Where do you want Vivaldi?" Michael asked after twenty minutes.

"I could give you a smart answer."

He grinned. "Later."

"Deal. You found classical? New category, I guess."

Michael flipped open the CD. "Not necessarily." He held the disc between two fingers. "It appears to be unmarked."

"Really? Now isn't that interesting."

Michael began to stand. "Somewhere, I saw a CD player."

Lynn was already on her feet. "No need. I've got equipment in my vehicle. I'll be back."

She reappeared a few minutes later, carrying a large black canvas tote.

"My portable bag of tricks," she said, unloading a laptop onto the partially cleared desk. "You're not the only ones with toys."

After loading the CD, her fingers flew across the keyboard, too fast for Michael to follow.

The screen kept flashing. Then suddenly a slide show of small photographs appeared.

"Does that look anything like Vivaldi to you?"

"No." As the slide show began, Michael added, "They look like vacation shots of Rome."

"They do, don't they." Lynn faced him. "This could take awhile."

Michael caught on quickly. "Keep sorting."

"Please."

To Michael, the wait and her silence were agonizing, but his search had produced two more classical CDs with unmarked discs inside. Beethoven and Tárrega. With a pattern emerging, he began looking for more. He had just found a CD of music by Elgar when Lynn finally spoke.

"Almost got you, you bastards." She faced Michael. "Sorry." She turned back to the laptop. "Look at this."

Michael studied the screen. "An encrypted file."

"Correct. There's one embedded in each of the photographs. You were right. These guys are smart."

"I'll get Dan."

She turned. "No need. I've got encryption software. This shouldn't take too long, unless they were really sophisticated."

A short time later, LaRoche appeared. "We're done for the day, Michael," he said. "We've got evidence bags to process, but we'll be back tomorrow. Okay?"

"Fine."

"Are you coming, Lynn?" LaRoche added.

She didn't look up. "Later."

"Find anything?" Michael asked as LaRoche turned to leave.

"More partial prints. Possible soil particles. And some hairs."

"That's it?"

"That's it. We've got to be dealing with pros."

From the dining room, Brian watched the two SLED pickups pull away from the curb.

"Call it a day," Michael said from the doorway. "And take Dan with you."

"What about you?"

"Lynn and I will follow."

"Sure you will," Brian muttered.

Michael ignored him. "Someone take the tea tray back to Potts and arrange to have the house secured overnight."

"Should we put the tape back up?" Norton asked.

"No point in attractin' any more attention," Brian said before Michael could reply. "Don't worry; I'll take care of it."

Back in the family room, Michael stared at the laptop screen.

"Is that what you're looking for?" Lynn asked, stretching her arms.

He scanned the e-mail. "You are a genius."

"Hardly. They used a simple encryption code. From what I've seen so far, you're only going to get incoming e-mails, unless we can find copies of his replies." She turned back to the e-mail. "Although, that could be enough."

"Can you print them out?"

"I'll do better than that. I'll give them to you on a CD."

Dusk was turning into night.

She yawned and got to her feet. "I'm tired."

"Too tired for dinner?"

She tried unsuccessfully not to respond too quickly. "That would be great, thank you. Except I haven't got a change of clothes," she added, glancing down at her uniform.

"No problem. It's 1800 now. How about 2030? I'll pick you up."

"But I live in Columbia."

"So? I just need an address. You choose the restaurant."

On the drive back from Camden, Lynn decided that there was a very fine line between assurance and arrogance. She concluded that Michael fit the former category. Just. He'd never asked about a husband or boyfriends, and just because he didn't wear a wedding ring didn't mean he wasn't married. In fact, she found it difficult to believe that he wasn't. *And it's only dinner*, she told herself, changing her mind several times on what to wear.

The Outback Steakhouse, Two Notch Road, Columbia, South Carolina
Later that night

Michael swept into the parking lot of Lynn's condo complex at exactly 8:30 p.m.

Dressed in a lightweight turtleneck, sport jacket, and slacks, he turned a lot of female heads as they waited for a table.

He said very little, until they were seated in a corner booth.

"I hope this is okay?" Lynn asked. "I felt like a good steak, and they stay open late."

Michael began to read the menu. "Steak's perfect."

She didn't look up. "What was Brian and Dan's reaction to the news?"

"What news?"

"The e-mails."

"They don't know."

"You didn't tell them?"

Michael closed the menu. "Affirmative."

This's like trying to get blood out of a stone.

"No more shop talk," he continued. "If I'd wanted that, I'd have asked Brian and Dan to dinner."

So, this is a social occasion. "Then you won't mind me asking if there's a Mrs. Correa?"

"Used to be. A long time ago. A three-year relationship ended last July. Since then, nothing."

"I didn't mean to interrogate you."

"Trust me," he said. "You weren't."

The way he said it sent a shiver down her spine.

Although Lynn thought they'd gotten off to a rocky start, throughout dinner, Michael proved, in her mind, to be as charming as his looks. He told terrible jokes that she found genuinely funny, and at one point, as she was wiping tears from her eyes, she said, "Stop. I've probably got mascara all over my face."

"You haven't," he said. "I don't know why you wore makeup. You're beautiful without it."

You did notice. "And the uniform's so sexy."

Michael finished his one and only glass of wine. "I've seen a lot worse. And clothes only hide so much."

"Do go on."

He sat back. "I'm in the intelligence business." He smiled. "We're trained observers."

I'm interested in you too. "I'm betting you're a good poker player?"

"Moderate success, when I have the time."

"And what does 'moderate' mean?"

"I win more than I lose."

Yes, I'll bet you do.

Back at Lynn's condo, she invited him in for coffee and was very disappointed when he politely refused.

"It's late," Michael added. "And we've got another long day ahead of us."

"Take a rain check?"

"Count on it," he said before driving away.

The Colony Inn, West DeKalb Street, Camden, South Carolina
Friday, March 7, 2003

"So how was your night with the sexy blonde bombshell from SLED?" Brian asked before biting into a large slice of toast.

Michael drained his coffee. "We had dinner." He got to his feet. "Get a ride with Dan. I'm leaving."

Michael passed Dan making his way to the table with barely an acknowledgment.

"What's up with the boss man?" Dan asked as he sat down.

Brian finished his toast. "Guess I hit that nerve again. Mentioned his evenin' with Lieutenant Lynn."

"Didn't it go well?"

"Who the hell knows?"

Wentworth's House, Mill Street, Camden, South Carolina
A short time later

Lynn was unloading equipment from her Suburban when Boswick drove up.

He took a quick look around as he approached. "See you survived the night with the pretty boy colonel."

"Get lost," she replied.

He followed her across the lawn. "So what's it like shacking up with the son of the CIA's director?"

She stopped. "What did you say?"

"You heard me."

She dropped the large canvas tote she was carrying and took a step forward. "If you weren't such a juvenile jerk, I'd beat the crap out of you," she hissed.

Boswick laughed and feigned a boxing stance. "Bring it on, Lieutenant."

Lynn grabbed the bag and turned away. "You're not getting into my pants, Charlie. Now or ever. Got that?"

"So, apart from looks, position, and privilege, what's he got that I haven't?"

She faced him as Norton opened the front door. "Don't make me answer that. Good morning, Pat."

"'Morning, Lieutenant."

She disappeared inside.

"Goddamn it," Boswick muttered as he followed.

"You need to find another technique, Charlie," Norton said quietly as Boswick entered the hall. "I can guarantee that yours isn't working."

"You got that right."

Lynn was already at her laptop, a thermos of coffee on the desk, when Michael entered the room.

"Thanks for last night," she said. "The Beethoven CD has photographs of Berlin."

"You're welcome." Michael pointed at the Tárrega CD. "Want to bet that's vacation shots of Barcelona or Madrid?"

Lynn began to type. "I'm sure you're right. Does that mean they've got a European network?"

"Looks that way."

He saw her shudder, but she made no comment.

Except for a five-minute break for coffee, they worked without interruption until noon. By then, Michael had opened every CD, and Lynn now had three more waiting to be scanned. The genuine CDs were now back on their racks.

Michael put away the last CD. "I'm calling a meeting," he said. "Kitchen, in a couple of minutes."

"Bring me up to date," Michael began when everyone was assembled. "LaRoche first." LaRoche had spent the morning working the master bedroom, while Brian and Norton took the guestroom. They had found a few more partial prints and hairs, especially from the shower and bath drains.

"Boswick sprayed the victim's vehicle with Luminol again," LaRoche added. "There's no sign of any blood."

"I went through a first aid kit and the CD holder," Boswick added. "There's nothing there."

"I'm betting the CDs are all classical," Michael said. "Beethoven, Vivaldi, Tárrega, and Elgar."

Boswick blinked. "You'd already checked?"

"No."

Then Michael explained.

"We're going to lunch and finishing up this afternoon," he added before facing Lynn. "By day's end, we should have all the e-mails on CD. Correct?"

"I don't see why not."

"What's in these e-mails?" Brian asked.

"There are too many to read thoroughly," Lynn replied. "But no mention of names and places, from what little I've seen. They're probably too careful for that."

"Finally, Michael in a good mood again," Brian said to Dan as they left the house.

"With good cause," Dan replied. "This sounds like the break we've been waiting for."

Gadgets, DeKalb Street, Camden, South Carolina
Lunchtime

They followed Norton a short distance to the local bar/restaurant that from the parking lot reminded Brian of a barn.

"The food's good and inexpensive," Norton told them. "Local law enforcement like eating there."

They devoured burgers and tall glasses of iced tea, with the minimum of conversation.

When Boswick lit a cigarette, Michael got to his feet.

"I'm going outside for a cigar." Then, looking directly at Lynn, he added, "I need to talk to you, Lieutenant."

"Your colonel's quite the ladies' man," LaRoche said quietly, watching them leave. "Our single guys, and a few married ones, have been trying to get to first base with her for years."

Dan followed Brian's lead and remained silent.

"Guess this isn't the first time?" LaRoche added.

"I was told that his unit got his leftovers," Brian said. "End of subject."

In the parking lot, Michael leaned against the side of the Suburban and lit a small cigar.

"Realistically, will I have all the encrypted e-mails by day's end?"

Lynn looked up. "I don't see why not. I'll get it done, even if I have to work through the night."

"Late dinner, then?"

"Absolutely. And this time, I brought a change of clothes."

Michael puffed on the cigar. "What I had in mind didn't include clothes."

She stepped closer. "Really, Colonel, I'm shocked."

"Careful," he added, stubbing out the cigar in the gravel. "We're being watched."

She turned toward the restaurant as the rest of the team came through the doors. "They're worse than little kids," she muttered. "Nosy bastards." She opened the rear door of the Suburban. "I'll ride in the back."

"Good idea," Michael replied, sliding behind the wheel.

Wentworth's House, Mill Street, Camden, South Carolina
Early evening

LaRoche and Boswick left around 4:00 p.m.

"We've done all we can here, Michael," La Roche said. "We'll process the evidence and get back to you with our findings."

"How long?"

"Knowing the urgency, a week, maybe a little more." LaRoche picked up several black canvas bags. "What about the victim's store?"

"I'll take a look tomorrow. If I need you, I'll call."

"Do that," LaRoche replied. "We're not far away. Nice working with you."

"Same here," Michael said. "And thanks again."

At 6:30 p.m., Lynn handed Michael two CDs in plastic cases.

"That's it," she said. "But it's still bugging me that we didn't find his replies."

"It's a great start. Thank you. And at least we'll be able to track them by the e-mail addresses."

She flashed a smile. "You're more than welcome. But that's all you're getting. They used anonymous re-mailers."

"Meaning?"

"They used the servers of legitimate and some not-so-legitimate companies in countries all over the world. Some none too friendly to the U.S. That's how these companies make their money and stay in business. There is no trace. That's the whole point. Sorry."

"Damn," Michael muttered.

Michael found Dan in the back of the Suburban.

"Guard these with your life," he said, handing Dan the CDs.

"No problem. What now?"

"It's up to you. We've still got the rooms. Leave now. Or leave tomorrow."

Dan glanced at his watch. "Now. That way, I can be in the office early. What about you?"

"I'm staying. I want to check the antique shop in the morning."

"And Brian?"

"He's staying too. Call me as soon as you find anything."

"That's a given."

Michael was grateful as he walked back to the house that no mention had been made of Lynn. *Dan's too smart for that,* he thought.

As he entered, Brian was coming down the stairs.

"Norton's gone back to the department with the mug shots they lent us. He'll be back later," he said. "Potts ID'd Savin, several times. Did Dan tell you?"

"No. But I'm not surprised." Michael started up the stairs. "I'm going to take a final look." He stopped. "Wentworth's store in the morning. Okay with you?"

"Wouldn't miss it."

"Take Norton to dinner. I've got plans."

He disappeared before Brian could comment.

Michael entered the master bedroom at the top of the stairs. The bed linens were now heaped in the center of the four-poster bed. Clothes were in one huge pile on the carpet, although the antique dresser drawers had been returned to their rightful places. There was something about the room that seemed familiar. Michael had the same feeling the previous day. But he still couldn't say why.

He looked around the guestroom and bathroom before returning to the master bedroom. He studied the room from the doorway. Then it hit him.

Against a far wall was a drop-front oak desk. His mother owned a similar one, with secret drawers, that she'd bought in England before Michael was born. As a child, Michael had played with it.

He strode across the room and dropped the front onto its pullout slides. The inside of the desk was compartmentalized with small drawers and curved partitions for envelopes and papers. The drawers in the center were much larger. Michael quickly removed them, and saying a prayer, he pulled on the thin wood that separated them. The divider slid out, complete with a false back, revealing two much smaller drawers with ancient leather pulls.

The top drawer was empty, but the bottom one contained a modern-looking key. Using latex gloves, he bagged the key before putting back the drawers and closing the desk.

He suddenly felt movement behind him and turned to see Lynn.

"Perfect," he said, reaching her side, and pulled her farther into the room. Then he kissed her with a hunger that even surprised him. It was what she'd been wanting for the last twenty-four hours, and Michael didn't disappoint.

"You still up there, Michael?" they heard Brian shout.

He ended the kiss. "I couldn't wait," he whispered in her ear. "On my way," he shouted back.

Lynn looked down. "I'll go first." She had a broad smile. "You need some time."

"I can't control it," Michael said quietly as she left the room.

I doubt that you've ever been out of control in your life, she was thinking before she saw Brian in the hallway. "Michael's just finishing up. He'll be down in a minute."

Brian didn't comment.

"We done here?" he asked when Michael appeared.

"For now."

"Then I'm lockin' up. I'm meetin' Norton later, to give back the house key."

"Fine. Breakfast, 0800." Almost as an afterthought, Michael tossed Brian the keys to his Suburban. "You'll need these."

Then he opened the front door, with Lynn following.

"Dan left his hotel key in an envelope at the front desk," Brian said, making Michael stop. "In case you need an extra room."

Michael raised his hand in acknowledgment and faded into the darkness beyond the house.

Brian watched from the window. Moments later, the taillights from Lynn's SLED Suburban rounded the far street corner and disappeared from view.

I hope she gives you a good time, he thought as he turned away.

The Colony Inn, West DeKalb Street, Camden, South Carolina
A short time later

With their anticipation in maximum overdrive, Michael was barely able to slam his hotel room door shut with his foot.

There was no denying the chemistry between them, and the kiss he gave her was long and by far the best she could remember.

"What about dinner?" he finally asked.

She looked up. "I can eat tomorrow. Right now, all I want is you."

He chuckled, and after lifting her off her feet, he dropped her gently in the middle of the king-sized bed. "Lady, you've got me."

Their clothes soon littered the bedroom carpet, and during the next few hours, Michael proved that he had, in her opinion, an almost insatiable appetite. He initially made love with an aggression that surprised her, but as the hours passed, he became far more gentle and caring. Although the list of Lynn's lovers wasn't long, she soon discovered that Michael was in a league all his own.

Around 3:00 a.m., before falling into a deep contented sleep, she came to the realization that he used sex as a release mechanism.

That's just fine with me, she thought as, wrapped in his arms, she snuggled closer.

The Colony Inn, West DeKalb Street, Camden, South Carolina
Saturday, March 8, 2003

Lynn was vaguely aware of the sound of a shower, and when she did open her eyes, it was to see Michael fully dressed.

"What time is it?" she asked.

"0730."

"Oh, no." She leapt naked out of bed and flew past him into the bathroom.

"It's Saturday," he said loudly to the closed door.

The door opened a crack. "It is?"

"Yes," he replied, handing her her clothes.

The door closed again. And when it reopened a few minutes later, she was dressed in jeans and a sweatshirt, but her long hair was still tousled.

"You're beautiful," Michael said.

She wasn't sure how to respond. "Thank you," seemed appropriate.

"I had a great time," he added. "Can I call you?"

"I'd like that. You've got my home number." She turned for the door. "I'd better go."

Then she stopped. "Do I get a goodbye kiss?"

Michael kissed her gently. "It's not goodbye."

He watched the door close and turned back to his kit bag.

She was horrified to see Brian in the parking lot.

"Mornin', Lynn," he called out.

Shit! She waved. "Good morning, Brian."

As he approached, she got the distinct impression that he'd been waiting for her.

"I wanted to thank you," he said on reaching her Suburban. "If it hadn't bin for you, we'd never have found those e-mails."

She opened the driver's door. "I was happy to help. I know how frustrating this must have been."

"Women have always bin attracted to Michael," he continued, catching her off-guard with his rapid change of subject. "As far back as anyone can remember."

Not again! She turned, intent on giving him an ear full.

"Hear me out," Brian added quickly. "Before you rush to any conclusions."

"Go ahead."

"Women and Michael. Like moths to a flame. But it takes someone special to get his attention. If you get my meanin'?"

She visibly relaxed. "I understand." She hesitated. "I know he was married. But why did his last relationship end?"

"He told you about that?"

"Yes."

"She wanted a weddin' ring and babies." He paused. "You're a smart woman. You've probably noticed that he's not ready to settle down."

"I've noticed." She slid behind the wheel. "Is his father really the director of the CIA?"

"Sure is." Brian chuckled. "Guess you two didn't talk much last night. And if you're goin' to ask if that helped his career, it didn't. He made it all on his own."

"Thank you, Brian. It's been a pleasure."

"You take care," he said before lumbering away.

At the breakfast table, Michael didn't look up as Brian took the seat opposite.

"Are you interfering with my love life again?" he asked.

"Course not." Brian helped himself to a pot of coffee. "She's a helluva smart lady. University educated. Master's degree."

"Your point is?"

"You could do a lot worse."

Michael leaned back in his chair. "I still can't picture you as Cupid." He pushed the evidence bag across the table. "What do you make of that?"

Brian peered inside the bag. "It's a key." He closed the bag. "Has it bin dusted for prints?"

"Not yet."

"Where did you find it?"

Michael told him.

"Well, well," Brian said when he'd finished. "How old's this desk?"

"My mother's was nineteenth century. Around 1830, I think. This looked about the same."

"Early version of a safe?"

"They must have thought so."

"We shouldn't be processing evidence in a parking lot," Brian said from the back of the Suburban a short time later. "If this key was ever called into play, they could make a case for contamination."

"I don't care," Michael replied. "Just tell me if the print matches Wentworth's."

Brian didn't look up from a small but powerful magnifying glass. "You got your match," he said moments later. "Perfect right thumb print."

Michael opened the driver's door. "Then let's go find what it fits."

Wentworth's Antique Shop, Broad Street, Camden, South Carolina
Twenty minutes later

Michael parked in the gravel lot at the side of the building and entered the store through the front door.

Once inside, they turned on the lights but kept the "Closed" notice in place. As it wasn't yet 9:00 a.m., and the stores around Wentworth's didn't typically open until 10:00 a.m., they hoped to have an hour of uninterrupted searching.

"Look at all this stuff," Brian commented.

"A modern key narrows it down. Any ideas?"

Brian shrugged. "Think like a bad guy. A smart bad guy."

Michael looked across the large room, full to overflowing with furniture and collectibles, thankful he was tall. "That's the best you can do?"

"He's former KGB. You're the intelligence expert. I'm only the cop."

Michael maneuvered around a table and chairs. "I'll take the office. You start here."

Their first interruption came at 10:05 a.m.

A middle-aged man in a brightly patterned shirt, accompanied by a woman, rang the bell. When he got no response, the man rang again.

"Here we go," Brian muttered, making his way to the glass front door. He pointed at the sign. "Store's closed," he said loudly.

"What time will you be open?" the man shouted back.

Brian held up his badge. "We won't. Try across the street."

The man was about to reply, when the woman tugged on his sleeve.

Brian mouthed, "Thank you," at her and turned away.

He watched them enter the store opposite before resuming his search.

By 11:00 a.m., he'd had four more similar interruptions.

To hell with this, he thought, turning off the lights before threading his way to the office.

He found Michael seated at the desk, going through drawers.

"Sold anything?" Michael asked.

"Funny. But I reckon there's money to be made in this kinda business."

"If you know what you're doing. Yes."

"It just looks old to me."

Michael got to his feet. "Want to carry on here? The desk's been searched inside and out."

"Fine. Let me show you how far I got."

Michael continued to search the furniture where Brian had left off, and by noon, he'd covered over half the store, with zero results.

"Gadgets?" Michael said, appearing in the office.

Brian closed the top drawer to the single file cabinet. "Why not? I think better on a full stomach."

Gadgets, DeKalb Street, Camden, South Carolina
A short time later

Michael watched as Brian devoured the last french fry from his plate. "What are we missing?" he said. "Why do I think it's staring us in the face."

Brian drained his iced tea. "Don't see how. With all the furniture and knickknacks, it's hard to see anythin'."

Michael grinned. "That's it."

"It is?"

He leaned forward. "The woman across the street has been forced to store more crates of furniture. If Wentworth had taken delivery, where was he going to put it?"

"Good point."

Michael stood. "Ready? Before we waste more time, let's go see her."

"I'm not disagreein'," Brian said as they reached the Suburban. "But those crates arrived after Wentworth was murdered. How's that hidden key connected?"

Michael slid behind the wheel. "One step at a time."

The Camden Antique Mart, Broad Street, Camden, South Carolina
Early afternoon

After Michael flashed his ID and explained who he was, the owner looked very relieved.

"I thought I'd been forgotten," she said. "I keep calling the Camden police, and they keep telling me there's nothing they can do. Are you here to arrange the removal?"

"I'd like to see the crates and the manifest before making that decision, ma'am," he replied.

"This way. I really need the space." She stopped. "Unless, you can give me the authorization to sell it?" Her voice dropped to a whisper. "Harold had very good taste and knew where to buy."

"I'll let you know, ma'am."

At a large wooden storage shed behind her store, she unlocked the door.

"I've got to get back to customers," she said. "The manifest's on the first crate. Light switch is inside the door. Help yourselves."

Brian flipped the switch and came face to face with a mountain of crates. "Holy shit. No wonder the poor woman's goin' nuts."

Michael scanned the manifest. "It says there are thirty-five of them."

"We'll be here for a week."

"No, we won't."

"How come?"

"Follow me."

Back inside the store, Michael told the owner that he was arranging to have the crates removed. "... You'll get a copy of my authorization, if anyone should ask," he concluded.

She seemed half relieved, half disappointed.

"When?"

All she could get out of him was, "Soon, ma'am."

Wentworth's Antique Shop, Broad Street, Camden, South Carolina
A few minutes later

"What we goin' to do with a shitload of crates?" Brian asked when they were out of earshot.

"There's a large warehouse in Baltimore. Unless you want them in your office?"

"Baltimore sounds better. Boost's goin' to love that. I'm goin' back to search the office." Threading his way through the furniture, Brian then stopped. "Should we call the hotel for another night?"

"It crossed my mind." Michael suddenly noticed the sign, "We have no public restrooms." "There's no bathroom?"

"Sure there is. Hidden behind that curtain in the office."

The small bathroom was spotlessly clean. As Michael stood at the toilet, he glanced across at the pedestal sink. Next to it, covered in what appeared to be a towel atop a lacy-looking tablecloth, was a piece of dark wood furniture. He could just see the bottoms of the tapered legs.

What's that doing in the bathroom? he thought as he flushed.

He removed the towel and the lacy cloth. *It's a Victrola.* He tried unsuccessfully to open the doors before looking more closely. *The lock's been replaced.* Then removing the key from the evidence bag in his pocket, he wasn't that surprised when it fit.

Inside the cabinet, all but two of the record compartments were empty. Pulling on latex gloves, he removed an unmarked videotape from one and a Wayne Newton CD from the other.

He couldn't help smiling as he flipped open the CD. It was also unmarked. *Guess he threw the original away.*

"We need a VCR," Michael said from the bathroom doorway, holding up the tape.

Brian turned. "You took a leak and found that? That's goin' to take some explainin'."

Michael handed him the CD. "And that."

"Where? Don't tell me. Not the toilet tank?"

"No. The Victrola."

"What the hell's that?"

"Old-fashioned record player to you. The cabinet next to the sink."

Brian slowly shook his head. "You were right. In plain sight." He flipped open his cell phone. "I'm callin' Norton. They've got to have a VCR at the department."

Camden Police Department, West DeKalb Street, Camden, South Carolina
Thirty minutes later

They stared at the images on the TV screen.

Norton, who'd been mowing his mother's lawn and was dressed in cutoff jeans and a sweat-soaked tee shirt, finally had to sit down.

Michael and Brian made no comment as a terrified man, along with a teenage boy and girl, were forced to watch the rape of a woman Brian assumed was the mother.

There had been audio, but Michael had the presence of mind to turn it off. The graphic scene was bad enough.

At the point on the tape when the hooded men finished with the woman and made a grab for the girl, Michael hit the STOP button.

"Enough," he said, turning to a pale Norton. "We all get the message."

"That looked like Savin, with hair," Norton said quietly.

"It was," Michael replied. "Now we know how they got his cooperation."

Norton studied his grass-stained sneakers. "I've never seen anything like it."

"Welcome to the world of international terrorism," Michael continued. "You okay?"

He nodded. "Hell of a way to spend a Saturday afternoon."

"Thanks for coming in on such short notice," Brian added. "And for the use of the department's equipment."

"No problem." Norton got to his feet. "I hope you catch the bastards."

Michael picked up the videotape. "We will."

"I'm drivin'," Brian said in the police department parking lot. "You look beat."

Michael threw him the keys without comment.

"We outta here?" Brian continued, putting the Suburban into reverse.

"Gone," Michael replied, raking back the passenger seat. "D.C. next stop."

He was asleep before Brian reached the entrance ramp to I-20.

When Michael awoke, Brian was on an exit ramp, and it was dark.

"D.C. already?"

"Denny's," Brian replied. "Back over the interstate to that truck stop. We're just south of Richmond."

They took a booth and ordered from a waitress.

"Did you recognize their language?" Brian asked, knowing Michael spoke several.

"Before I turned off the audio, I heard Russian and French."

"No kiddin'? Can you interpret?"

"I'll have a damn good try before calling someone in."

Now deep in thought, their remaining conversation was minimal at best.

Brian dropped off Michael at his townhouse in Alexandria around 11:00 p.m.

"I'll take the Metro in the morning," he said before closing the passenger door.

From the privacy of his living room, and with a strong nightcap and a good cigar, Michael watched and listened to the entire videotape.

When he finally fell into bed, he tried unsuccessfully to replay the pleasurable hours spent with Lynn, as the graphic images from his recent viewing constantly interrupted.

Michael's Townhouse, Duke Street, Old Town, Alexandria, Virginia
Sunday, March 9, 2003

When Michael saw his image in the mirror at 8:00 a.m., he went immediately to the kitchen to brew a strong pot of Blue Mountain coffee.

After showering, but still in a bathrobe, he poured a mug before calling Brian.

"Where are you?" he asked.

"On my way in."

"I watched the tape last night."

"Got a feelin' you would. And?"

"I don't know if the blood spatter on the lens at the end was real or done for effect."

"Sick bastards."

"I thought I'd work on it here."

"I'll come over."

"No need. I'll be in touch."

As he sat in his favorite leather chair, opposite the flat-screen TV, Michael thought of Lynn. *Don't be an idiot. Call her later,* he thought and pressed the PLAY button on the remote.

Although he believed in a God, Michael wasn't at all religious in the true sense of the word, but somehow viewing the graphic images on a Sunday morning seemed all the more repugnant.

He stopped the tape. Then with a pen and notepad, he began the tape again; only this time, he listened instead of watched.

He hit the PAUSE and REPLAY buttons many times, but at the end of two hours, he'd managed to translate the majority of the conversation.

Good enough, he said to himself after playing the tape for a final time. Then he locked it inside a concealed wall safe.

After calling Lynn, their conversation light and full of innuendo, Michael felt better.

It was only after he'd cleaned up his notes, transferred them to his laptop, and printing three copies that he called Brian again. "Are you still at the office?"

"Sure am."

"I'm on my way in."

"I'll be here."

Michael's Office, G Street, Washington, D.C.
Middle of the afternoon

Brian had opened the door at 9:00 a.m., surprised to see Molly at her desk.

"What are you doin' here?" he said. "It's Sunday."

"I could ask you the same question. And keep your voice down. Dan's asleep in Michael's office."

"How long's he bin here?"

"I don't know. I found a note on my desk a few minutes ago."

She followed Brian into the office he shared with Dan. "My guess is, all night," she continued. "What happened in Camden? And where's Michael?"

Brian gave her a brief outline of events, purposely leaving out the part about the videotape.

"I guess Dan drove straight here," he continued, pointing to Dan's overnight and garment bag by the side of his desk. "He musta worked all night."

"Then let him sleep. Having one bear with a sore head is enough."

Brian grinned. "Michael's a changed man."

"Really? Do tell."

Dan had only just woken up when Michael walked in.

"You look like shit," Michael said.

"Thanks."

He turned to Molly. "You shouldn't be here. It's Sunday. Go home."

"I told her that at 0930," Brian said. "She ignored me."

Michael put his hands on her desk and leaned toward her. "I'm ordering you to leave."

"Fine. So I assume the background info on Dr. Dimitri Sadilov wasn't that important after all?"

He straightened. "Okay, you win. Brief us. Then go home. Deal?"

"Deal," she said.

They all went through the pages of information that Molly compiled. Then, as promised, she left.

Michael waited until he heard the outer office door close. "Before we discuss Molly's research," he said, and pushing Sadilov's info to one side, he handed Brian and Dan some more sheets of paper. "Read this."

Dan finished first. "Jesus. This reads like an X-rated movie script. What the hell is it?"

Michael explained.

"Where's the tape now?" Dan asked when he'd finished.

"In a safe place. And unless it's really necessary, I don't want Molly knowing."

"It's real bad," Brian added.

"You saw it?"

"Part of it. That was enough. I thought Norton was goin' to pass out." Brian turned to Michael. "You reckon your translation's good enough?"

"I do now. They spoke French and Russian. That seemed odd, until I saw Molly's info." Michael picked up her notes and turned to the last page. "Says here that Sadilov's lived in France for the last fifteen years. He married a Frenchwoman. If you see the tape again, it's clear that they only spoke French to the wife and kids."

"Then the woman was Sadilov's wife?"

Michael only nodded.

"Shit."

Michael gathered up the papers. "If you want to see the tape, Dan, I'm leaving now. Brian, go home. Or follow us. Your choice."

"I'm comin'," he replied.

"I'll grab my gear," Dan added, leaving the room.

"Hope you've got some strong liquor?" Brian said.

"Ten-year-old Glenfiddich. And some very smooth cigars."

"Good. We're probably goin' to need 'em."

How right you are, Michael thought as he flipped off the lights.

Michael's Townhouse, Duke Street, Old Town, Alexandria, Virginia
Early evening

They watched the tape.

When it finished, Brian silently held up an empty whiskey glass, rattling the ice cubes, which Michael immediately filled.

Dan could only stare at the carpet, muttering, "God almighty," more than once.

Brian lit a cigar. "If you're goin' to puke, use the bathroom. Michael's got a nice place."

"I'm okay. But I'll take a refill. And a cigar."

"Didn't know you smoked?"

"I do now," Dan replied.

Brian got to his feet. "Most guys I know who get together on a Sunday evenin' with booze and smokes, play cards and watch porno flicks," he said, attempting to lighten the mood.

"I wish we were. How many times did you watch it, Michael?"

"Too many."

By the time they'd viewed the tape over and over again, using both Michael's translation and Molly's background information, they concluded that the Sadilov family had been attacked in their home in northern France. It was only after Sadilov's fourteen-year-old daughter had been raped and brutalized, in full view of the family and the camera, that Sadilov had agreed to help them. The piercing screams of both mother and daughter made Michael mute the tape on the third viewing. But none of them could decide if the blood seen at the end was from someone's throat being slit.

"If it was for real, who was it?" Michael asked.

Brian grunted. "My money's on the son."

"I think Brian's right," Dan said. "We saw how they got at both mother and daughter. They need Sadilov alive. Maybe killing the son was to cement his cooperation. Mother and daughter next if he failed to produce."

Michael faced Dan. "Call Interpol tomorrow. Find out if there was a murder in Haguenau around that time. And if they know where the family is."

"You've got it."

"The tape's stamped Sunday, October 20, 2002," Michael continued. "According to Potts, Savin, as he became, spent almost a month with Wentworth last November. Why?"

"If Brian can go through more of the e-mails, maybe we'll get that answered," Dan said.

"That reminds me," Michael added. "We found another unmarked CD. Call Lynn?"

"I can decrypt it. Unless you need the excuse?"

"I don't need any excuses," he replied.

Despite several cups of coffee and food that had been delivered, Brian and Dan were both well over the legal limit. Brian called a cab. Dan crashed in Michael's guestroom.

"You can drive the Suburban back to the office in the mornin'," Brian told Dan before he left. "But check your blood alcohol before you do."

"I just need a good night's sleep."

"Don't we all," Brian said before the door closed.

Chapter Twenty-Two

Michael's Office, G Street, Washington, D.C.
Monday, March 10, 2003

Michael and Dan arrived together, but it was Molly and Brian who followed Michael into his office.

"Who's first?" he asked.

"I'll be faster," Molly said, handing him two pages of typed notes. "That's the list of calls while you were away. I've dealt with most of them, as you can see. I told the White House you wouldn't be back until this week, but I suggest you call today."

She pointed. "That call came in on your Fulton Industries line. A Mrs. Stella MacFarland. She said she met you at Arnold Matthews' Christmas party, and wanted to know if you'd got the invitation, as she hadn't heard."

Molly handed him an expensive-looking ivory-colored envelope with a card inside.

"I told her you were away on business, then I found that in the P.O. box. I think you should call her. She seemed very insistent."

"Damn," Michael said, scanning the invitation. "It's that horse weekend they mentioned. I hoped I'd been forgotten."

Fat chance of that. Molly began to leave. "You should go," she said from the doorway. "You need the break. And even if you don't think you do, Delta would probably enjoy it."

Then the door closed.

Brian sat opposite. "She's right."

"Thanks, Dad. They live in Georgia."

"Then you'll have to drive through South Carolina."

Michael didn't react. "Haven't you got e-mails to read?"

"Yes, but I've already found somethin' interestin'."

Michael took off his jacket. "Really? White House first. Then I'll buzz you."

Brian lumbered to the door. "I'll be here."

Michael watched the door close before dialing the number.

The now-familiar male voice answered. "Good morning, Colonel. Do you need to speak with the president?"

"If he's available. Yes," he said, still not knowing the man's name, but only too aware that he should never ask.

There was a series of clicks. "Michael?"

"Good morning, Mr. President."

"Heard you were in South Carolina. Successful I hope?"

"Yes, sir."

"I want to hear about it," Makepeace said.

Michael gave the president a short but concise briefing, all the while trying to think up ways of avoiding any mention of the videotape. But he couldn't.

"What's on this videotape?" Makepeace eventually asked.

Michael had no alternative. "We suspect Sadilov's abduction."

"I want to see it."

"I strongly recommend that you don't, sir."

"Your objection's noted, Michael, and overruled. Where's the tape now?"

"In my possession, sir."

"In D.C.?"

"No, sir."

"Can you have it here tomorrow?"

"Yes, sir."

"Then my aide will arrange the time. That okay with you?"

"Yes, sir."

"See you then, Michael."

"Thank you, Mr. President."

There was a click, and the line went dead.

Shit! Michael thought. *This isn't good.*

He buzzed Brian, who appeared moments later.

Brian sat again. "Dan's bin talkin' to his buddy at Interpol. It sounds like he might be gettin' somewhere." He looked at his notes. "Seein' as we might be short on time, I cross-checked some dates from the e-mails ..." he began.

Arriving in the office before 7:00 a.m., Brian immediately started to print the e-mails from the first CD that Lynn had given them. One date in particular caught his eye. September 11, 2001. The content of the text didn't seem unusual, until he got to the part that stated, "The big party went better than we expected."

Big party? That's what you bastards called it? he thought.

E-mails months before made reference to "an engagement Berlin," followed a few weeks later by "a honeymoon Florida." *That's gotta be when Jarrah and Fareed got together.*

With a format developing, it made sorting and reading the e-mails a very much faster process.

On July 8, 2002, an e-mail stated that the "big package had been collected." *That's the Tybee bomb,* but Brian couldn't find any remote indication of where it was now.

At that point in his search, the second CD had stopped printing. Brian scanned the last dates first. In October 2002, there were several e-mails about "your relative," but nowhere was there mention of Sadilov by name. The last e-mail dated the first week of January 2003 appeared to be arranging a visit. Then all e-mails stopped.

"They musta had somethin' to do with Wentworth's murder," Brian said now. "No point in sending messages to a dead man."

"Good work," Michael replied. "What next?"

"We need to go through all of 'em with a fine-toothed comb."

"Affirmative. I'll get Molly to help, if you're sure there's no reference to that tape?"

Brian shook his head. "They're too smart for that."

At noon, Dan found Michael, Brian, and Molly surrounded by papers.

"I've got something," Dan said, waving what looked like a map before glancing pointedly at Molly.

Michael caught on quickly. "Time for lunch. We'll order in."

"I'll take care of it," Molly said, leaving his office.

Dan immediately closed the door.

Molly turned on her way to her desk. *All you had to do was ask me to leave. I wonder what's so important that they can't share? Typical men.*

Dan spread out a map of France and pointed to a town east of Paris. "That's Haguenau, in the Alsace region. It's where the Sadilovs live."

"It's real close to Germany," Brian commented.

"Exactly," Dan replied. "That's why Sadilov appeared on Interpol's radar screen."

While with the Secret Service, Dan had just been told of his promotion to Presidential Detail when he attended an international law enforcement conference in D.C. It was there he met Henri Bruyere, and the two men became friends. They stayed in touch, and over the next few years, Dan discovered that Bruyere was forward thinking and violently disagreed with his country's views on global terrorism being just an American problem. When Interpol's Fusion Task Force was created in September 2002, Bruyere readily accepted the post of assistant director. Although based in Lyon, the FTF monitored most of Europe. During a surveillance mission in Berlin, a German-based colleague finally identified Sadilov in a photograph with a suspected terrorist. As Sadilov lived in France, he brought it to Bruyere's attention.

When Dan called him from Camden the previous week, Sadilov's name was already familiar. The following day, Dan sent Bruyere the identikit that Potts had identified as Savin.

Early that morning, Dan called again, in reference to the videotape.

"Bruyere's just called back," Dan said now, always grateful that his friend spoke perfect English. "It's not good news."

"I'm listening," Michael replied.

According to Dan, after Sadilov was identified in Berlin, he was put under surveillance.

"It's one of the many problems we have, now that the borders are open," Bruyere told him. "People come and go as they please, and we have a hard time tracking them."

Sadilov made two trips to Berlin that they knew about. The second time, he was photographed with another man neither the German nor French authorities could identify.

"That's just arrived," Dan continued, handing Michael a grainy copy of a black and white photograph. There was little to see of the face of the man talking to Sadilov on a busy Berlin street. "It's like one of Brian's long shots," he added, "but I'm guessing that's Jarrah."

Michael studied the photograph before passing it to Brian. "My gut says you're right. Which means we really need to find Fareed. Go on."

According to Bruyere, the French authorities continued to monitor Sadilov, who worked at the university in Strasbourg, but after his second Berlin meeting, Sadilov went back to a regular work routine. At the end of October, the entire family disappeared. With manpower at a premium, Bruyere had no alternative but to pull the surveillance team at the end of November, although many hours were spent looking at surveillance tapes from airports. "They just vanished," Bruyere said. "Until now. What are they doing in America?"

When Dan explained that they only knew about Sadilov, Bruyere immediately contacted the local authorities in Haguenau.

"Although he had no probable cause to search the house, until I called," Dan continued. "The blood on the video wasn't fake. They've just found the decomposing body of a teenage boy inside the house. Bruyere says he's been told it looks like it's been there for several months. But there's no sign of the wife and daughter. They're working the crime scene as I speak. He'll call with any more info."

"Goddamnit," Michael said. "Does this sound familiar?"

"With one exception. Bruyere says the reason it didn't raise red flags when the Sadilovs vanished was that newspapers and utilities to the house were all canceled. So no mail. They thought the Sadilovs had moved."

"A car?"

"Yes. But it's never been found."

"So unlike Wentworth, this was preplanned."

"Looks that way."

Michael got to his feet. "I'll brief Molly when lunch arrives. Still no need to mention the tape."

By the time the day was over, they understood a lot more clearly how to interpret the e-mails.

Before Michael finally left the office, he called Tom Morgan.

"I thought you'd forgotten me, sir," Tom said on hearing Michael's voice. "Delta too."

"There's a lot going on, Tom. I'll try to get out to the house next weekend. In the meantime, I've a job for Boost and maybe you."

"I'm listening," Tom said.

"I need an eighteen-wheeler in Camden, South Carolina ..." Michael began.

"What's in these crates?" Tom asked when Michael had finished.

"According to the manifest, furniture and collectibles."

"But you don't believe it?"

"It could be legit. But seeing as the man they belonged to was former KGB with known ties to al Qaeda, draw your own conclusions."

"I'll get right on it," Tom replied. "Two extra men should do it."

"Trustworthy."

Tom chuckled. "That's a given, sir."

The White House, Pennsylvania Avenue, Washington, D.C.
Tuesday, March 11, 2003

At 8:50 a.m., Michael drove through a private entrance and parked in a familiar underground parking garage.

A Secret Service agent was already waiting. "Morning, Colonel," he said as Michael got out of his car. "Follow me, please, sir."

In the elevator, they went down, and several levels later, the doors opened to a wide, brightly lit corridor. On seeing Michael, a Marine, guarding a pair of half glass and metal doors, snapped to attention. The guard quickly scanned Michael's briefcase before buzzing him through. From all the signs, it was obvious that they were entering a classified area.

At an unmarked door, the Secret Service agent stepped inside. "The president will be with you shortly," he said, closing the door and leaving Michael alone.

He looked around the small screening room, complete with several rows of plush movie theater seating. Michael hoped that they would be viewing the video on a small TV, but someone had already lowered a large screen from the ceiling.

He was wondering how he could get Makepeace to use a smaller format when the door opened.

The president half appeared in the doorway. "Absolutely no one enters this room until I say so," he said to someone in the corridor before closing the door and facing Michael. "Good to see you, Michael," he added, warmly shaking his hand.

"And you, sir."

Watching the video on a large screen made it seem even more graphic. Michael kept the sound low, but there was no mistaking the pain and terror.

Makepeace sat through the entire tape without comment, and Michael was more than relieved when it ended.

Silently, he got to his feet and removed the tape, and when he turned back, Makepeace had his head in his hands.

"See what you mean," he said quietly. "Vietnam was a war. This's worse." He looked up. "Who else has viewed it?"

"Mullen and Whitney, sir."

"Keep it that way, for now."

"I intend to, sir."

"Was that real blood at the end?"

"Unfortunately, yes. It was confirmed yesterday by our contact at Interpol. They found the boy ..." Michael began.

When he finished, Makepeace began to pace the room. "I want these bastards caught. I don't care how you do it. Dead or alive." Michael couldn't miss the president's emphasis on the word "dead." "How close are you?"

"Closer. Thanks to a lieutenant at SLED, who discovered the encrypted e-mails embedded in the photographs."

"What's his name?"

"It's a her, sir. Lieutenant Lynn Tillman."

Makepeace stopped. "Married?"

"No, sir."

"Is she pretty?"

"I think so, sir."

Makepeace finally smiled. "Are you seeing her?"

He's worse than my father. "When I can, sir."

"Good. And when this is over, I want to meet her. Bring her to the White House. That's an order."

"Understood, sir. Thank you."

Makepeace began to leave, then stopped. "Have you seen Matthews lately?"

Oh, shit. "No, sir."

"Well, I have. He asked if I'd seen you recently and whether I knew if you were going to Georgia. I got the impression that this weekend get-together was sometime this month?"

"It is, sir."

"Excellent. You're going, I hope? Unless Matthews and his daughter are off the hook?"

"No, sir, they're not."

Makepeace could almost sense Michael's reluctance. "Then I want you there."

"Is that another order, sir?"

"Yes, Colonel, it is."

"Very good, sir."

Makepeace shook Michael's hand again. "You're doing a phenomenal job. Keep it up." His voice dropped. "When you catch them, I want them to suffer. Understood?"

"Understood perfectly, sir."

No sooner had Makepeace left the room than the Secret Service agent reappeared to escort Michael from the building.

Michael's Office, G Street, Washington, D.C.
A short time later

Michael was already loosening his tie when he entered the main reception area.

Regardless of that fact, Molly thought he looked like a male model in a very expensive dark gray suit.

"Call that MacFarland woman for me," he said after a cursory greeting. "Tell her I accept the invitation." Before Molly could reply, he added, "And tell Dan I'm going for a run, if he wants to come." Then he disappeared into his office and closed the door.

When he reappeared, he was dressed in running clothes.

"It's raining, if you hadn't noticed," Dan said, tying the laces to his shoes.

"I doubt we'll shrink," Michael replied and left the office.

"I can tell his meeting with the president went well," Dan said quietly to Molly before following.

They ran to the Roosevelt Memorial, and although it was lunchtime, it was strangely quiet. Michael slowed and stopped. "Take a break?"

"Fine with me."

Dan drank from the water fountain. The rain had temporarily ended, but angry clouds scudded across the sky, and the wind chilled flesh to the bone. "It didn't go well …?" he began.

It was too cold to sit or to stand still, so as they walked around the Basin, Michael repeated his conversation with Makepeace.

Dan chuckled. "So he wants to meet Lynn?" he asked when Michael finished.

"Looks that way." Michael hesitated. "How come you're the only one who's got no interest in my women?"

"Only seems that way," Dan replied. "I find out by letting others ask the questions."

Michael feigned a punch.

Dan sidestepped and laughed. "I know it pisses you off. But they have the best intentions."

"Could have fooled me."

"Go to Georgia," Dan continued. "You never know; you might rattle Matthews' cage, or his daughter's. I assume she's going?"

"It never crossed my mind," Michael said truthfully. "And I can hardly ask."

"Quit worrying. We'll hold down the fort, unless there's a big break. Go have some fun." Dan began to jog. "Race you to that cherry tree."

"Which goddamn tree? The Basin's full of them."

By the time they got back to the office, Michael was in a far better frame of mind.

Reading through the latest weekly update on Sis Matthews-Boyd from the agents in Bedminster hadn't been a priority, but as he now scanned their report, he saw the word "Georgia."

Immediately taking his feet off the desk, he began to read. The phone tap was producing results, although nothing remotely related to Fareed. In one conversation, it appeared that Sis was going with her father to the MacFarlands' weekend party, and they were arguing over which horses to take. The agents had made a note that said it sounded as if Sis had a cold.

Great, Michael thought and buzzed Molly. "Look up Georgia weather for me," he said.

"I'll get right on it."

She entered his office a few minutes later. "Seventies during the day. Sixties at night." She turned to go. "It's a long way to tow a horse trailer. When are you leaving?"

Michael glanced at his calendar. "Next Thursday. Unless something comes up."

Michael's Office, G Street, Washington, D.C.
Friday, March 14, 2003

Tom Morgan called at 11:30 a.m.

"You might want to leave the office early," he said to Michael. "We began unpacking the crates this morning."

"They're in Baltimore?"

"Sure. Picked 'em up yesterday."

"And?"

"I don't think AK-47s and C-4 are considered antiques yet."

"I'm on my way."

A Classified Address, Baltimore, Maryland
Early afternoon

At the warehouse, Michael had no alternative but to leave the Jaguar just inside the door. Ahead of him, between the two rows of neatly parked vehicles, were the crates from Camden.

Tom appeared from around the small mountain. "Afternoon, sir. We're finding all sorts of goodies. This way."

Behind the pile stood an assortment of antique furniture, some large vases, and statues.

"That's what we've unpacked, so far," Tom said. Then he pointed to the far end of the warehouse. "The really collectible items are in that old service bay. Not that I think a concrete block wall's going to save us if it goes up."

"If what goes up?"

"Oh," Tom continued. "We've found a coupla handheld rocket launchers since I called and some nice shiny rockets to go with them. Then there's a whole slew of hand grenades." Tom continued his way down the warehouse. "And we've only just begun." They reached the service bay. "Take a look."

"Shit," Michael said, scanning the pile. "So much for security. How the hell did this get through customs?"

"That's easy," Tom replied, pulling a sheet of paper from his pocket. "The woman in Camden gave me this. It's the first page of the manifest. It fell off when she took delivery, so she put it away and forgot about it. The Camden cops never saw it. She only just remembered as we were leaving."

Michael studied the sheet. The manifest of goods was listed as household items, addressed to Wentworth at his home.

"Port of departure was London, England," Tom added. "The shipment was cleared by British customs; that's probably why it never got the once-over here."

"And port of entry was Savannah. Damn! How did we miss that?"

"I reckon someone's pockets got well lined," Tom added.

Michael turned back to the pile. "You're probably right. Where's Boost?"

"Picking up a late lunch."

"Then let's get started."

"Oh, no," Tom said. "You go home, sir. Spend some time with Delta. We've got a system going. If we need you, I'll call."

Reluctantly, Michael agreed.

Eagles Nest, Somewhere off Route 301, the Eastern Shore, Maryland
Early evening

Tom was right, Michael thought on seeing Delta. The horse appeared to have missed him and was so full of energy, it made for a very spirited ride. Although Michael gave him a thorough workout, he decided that both horse and rider needed to go back to basic training.

We've got less than a week, he was thinking as he rubbed down Delta in his stable.

Delta suddenly snorted and stamped his foot.

"Long ride?" Tom asked from the doorway.

"A few hours. You're finished?"

"Just about. I think we're going to have to call the folks at Picatinny.[11] If we get the local bomb squad involved, it's going to raise a shitload of red flags."

Michael finished with the horse and gave him an apple wedge. "Affirmative. Want a beer?"

"Wouldn't say no, sir."

They took some beers to the end of the dock.

"The boat's in dry dock," Tom said, taking a gulp of beer.

Michael chuckled, looking at the empty space usually occupied by his forty-six-foot Viking sportfisherman. "That's stating the obvious," he said. "Leave it there, for now. Boating's the last thing on my mind."

"It's a real nice evening, sir," Tom continued, scanning the clear horizon.

"Fine," Michael replied. "Get the boat. You use it. What else did you find?"

Tom handed Michael a list. "Were they planning on starting a war?"

Michael scanned the list. "Looks that way."

"Is the woman who stored it in any danger?"

"It's crossed my mind. She told the Camden cops that Wentworth changed the date of delivery. It's beginning to make sense. That shipment was probably his failsafe."

"Didn't work, did it?"

---

11 One-of-a-kind, 6,500-acre facility in New Jersey that provides most of the lethal mechanisms for Army weapon systems and those of other military services.

"Affirmative."

"Maybe they found another source?"

"That's what worries me."

Tom finished his beer and opened another. "What do you want done with the furniture? It looks like nice stuff."

"From what little I saw, it is." Michael got to his feet. "I'll let you know on Monday. Fancy a steak?"

"Sounds great, sir."

Chapter Twenty-Three

Michael's Office, G Street, Washington, D.C.
Wednesday, March 19, 2003

"Lieutenant LaRoche is on line one," Molly said at 3:30 p.m.

"Put him through," Michael replied.

"I've got the DNA results back," LaRoche said on hearing Michael's voice. "One set definitely matches Wentworth, or whoever he is. The other set is an unsub. Do you want me to fax them to you?"

"Thanks. I'd appreciate it."

As soon as the fax arrived, Michael called Dan into his office.

"Get this to Bruyere, ASAP," Michael said. "Unlike some agencies I could name, we share information."

"DNA from SLED? That was fast."

"Yes. When Bruyere gets the DNA results from the boy in Haguenau, at least he'll have some kind of comparison."

"I'm right on it," Dan said, leaving the office.

Michael leaned back and put his feet on the desk, staring at the calendar. *I leave for Georgia in the morning? I really don't want to do this.*

En Route to Georgia
Thursday, March 20, 2003

Michael packed the night before but purposely made a late start to avoid the worst of the commuter traffic.

"It's either that or leave at o-dark-thirty," he told Tom.

"Wouldn't be the first time, sir," Tom replied. "I think you're being smart."

At 9:00 a.m., Michael was crossing the Chesapeake Bay Bridge in a new Suburban, towing Delta in a matching two-horse trailer. He knew from experience that although it looked like a longer route on a map, I-95 was faster than taking 301 to Norfolk, Virginia. *As long as I don't hit traffic.*

The daily parking lot on the Beltway around D.C. was almost over, and he got through Richmond, Virginia, in record time.

South of Richmond, he called Lynn.

"Where are you?" she asked, glancing at the clock in her office. It read 11:00 a.m.

"I-95."

"That narrows it down."

"Heading south."

"To see me?"

"Hopefully. If you can spare the time?"

"For you, I can. When?"

"Later today."

Nothing like some notice. "You're coming to the condo?"

"Not exactly. There's not enough space to park."

Lynn imagined her SLED-owned Suburban in the condo's parking lot. "You're driving a big rig?"

"Close. And I'm not alone."

Shit!

"There's a truck stop off exit 119 in Manning," Michael continued. "I thought I'd stop there."

"That's an easy drive from Columbia," she said. "Through Sumter."

"How long do you need?"

"An hour."

"Talk to you later then," Michael replied and hung up.

She stared at the phone. *Not a romantic bone in your body.*

Michael's cell phone rang.

"Matthews is going. Sis isn't," Dan said. "And neither are the children, according to the agents' latest info. Her cold got a lot worse. She's real pissed and had a big blow up with hubby. Apparently, he'd arranged to see friends in New York this weekend."

"She'd planned on taking the children?"

"Appears that way."

"What's wrong with the babysitter?"

"Never mentioned."

Michael hung up and reminded himself that when he saw Matthews, he wasn't supposed to know any of this. Matthews had given him the impression that this was definitely an "adults only" weekend. Not knowing what to expect or who else had been invited, Michael couldn't say for sure if young children being there would seem out of place.

Forget it, he told himself. *They're not going. So what's the problem?*

But as he continued south, the nagging feeling that something didn't sound right wouldn't go away.

Manning Travel Center, I-95 & SR 261, Manning, South Carolina
Late afternoon

After Michael's second call, Lynn told a sergeant that she wouldn't be back and flew out of the office at 3:00 p.m., rushing home to shower and change.

When she did arrive at the truck stop, Michael was easy to find, walking a good-looking brown horse, covered in a dark blue travel rug, his legs wrapped in matching bandages.

She parked in front of the Suburban and horse trailer, and walked slowly toward him.

"Who's your friend?" she asked.

"His name's Delta."

The gelding eyed her suspiciously but cautiously let her stroke his nose.

"You're full of surprises," she added. "I didn't know you rode horses. What's the occasion?"

"It's work related," Michael replied. Then because of who she was and who she worked for, he briefly explained.

"And I thought the DoJ had a secret mounted division," she said when he finished. "Whose idea was this?"

"My boss."

"He's some kind of horse nut?"

"Not that I'm aware."

"He lives in horse country then?"

Tell her. "A big white house in the center of D.C."

Her eyes widened. "You work for the president?"

"Yes. And he wants to meet you."

"I need to sit down," Lynn said. "How does he know about me?"

"I told him."

She stroked Delta's neck. "Why didn't you tell me this before?"

He shrugged. "There was no point. I'm classified. My job's classified. I'm sure SLED did a background check."

She nodded. "You're right. There was virtually nothing. There was some brief history. West Point. Special Forces. Then a large gap until you became a civilian. Although it did say you're a lieutenant colonel in the Reserves. You are, aren't you?"

"Officially, yes."

"And unofficially?"

"You don't want to know."

As if on cue, Delta stamped his foot. "I need to walk him some more," Michael said. "Coming?"

Michael's idea of a quiet dinner together was takeout from the truck stop, eaten inside the two-horse trailer.

"It's not like leaving a dog in your car," he said in way of explanation.

"I understand completely," Lynn replied. "If Delta was mine, I wouldn't leave him alone either."

She finished a Styrofoam cup of coffee. "When are you leaving?"

"In the morning."

"You're staying here the night?"

He nodded. "I hoped you would too."

"You sure know how to treat a girl."

"I'll make it up to you. I promise."

Coming from anyone else that statement would have been laughable, but in Michael's case, she believed him.

"Where's the bed?"

Michael pointed at the empty stall. "There."

He made sure all the trailer's doors were closed and locked before he lay next to her on the makeshift bed. Lynn had to admit, as her clothes came off, that the horse blanket, surrounded by straw bales, with an unzipped sleeping bag on top was not only comfortable, but reminded her of a nest.

"Love nest," she murmured, running her hands down Michael's naked back.

He raised his head. "What?"

"Nothing." She giggled. "I can't stop thinking about horses and sex."

"Example?"

"There's a gelding on that side, but I'm with a stallion. You know how it goes."

Michael laughed. "I get the picture. So before you run through the entire list, let me show you what stallions do to beautiful fillies."

"Yes, please," she said.

Michael was as amorous as ever, and throughout the night, Lynn was grateful that the truck stop never slept. Big rigs with noisy diesel engines and sometimes the crunching of gears came and went on a regular basis, hopefully, she thought, obliterating their sounds of pleasure.

Delta sometimes munched on a hay net and occasionally gave a low snort, but for the most part, he slept. Unlike his human companions.

Manning Travel Center, I-95 & SR 261, Manning, South Carolina
Friday, March 21, 2003

Lynn awoke early to a very strong odor. From the gloom in the trailer, she assumed it was still relatively dark outside, but she could vaguely see Michael pulling on clothes.

"Delta took a dump," he said before she could speak. "It's a morning thing."

He zipped up his jeans, and stepping over her, he reappeared in Delta's stall. "Breakfast? After I shower."

She could only nod.

Then he disappeared, along with the majority of the smell.

She watched surreptitiously as Michael devoured a large plate of steak and eggs, while keeping an eye on the trailer from their window seat.

Even though the dawn was just breaking, the restaurant was alive with truckers and the smells of cooking and cigarette smoke.

Having refused his offer of a towel and the use of the truck stop's female facilities, as she finished her scrambled eggs, all she wanted to do was go home and shower.

He finished his orange juice. "Are you okay? You seem very quiet."

She managed a smile. "I'm fine."

That means she's not fine. "Talk to me."

She shrugged. "We keep meeting in such odd places." She lowered her voice. "We have incredible sex. Then you leave."

He grinned. "I enjoyed it too. As for leaving, I'm probably an idiot for thinking that some time together is better than none."

"It is," she said quickly.

"The job comes first, right now. I thought you'd understand, better than most women."

"I do." She made an effort to be more lighthearted. "I guess waking up to the smell of horse shit affected my mood."

"Understood."

"Will I see you on the way back?"

"Doubtful," Michael replied, picking up the check. "I'll be driving straight through."

At the trailer, he checked on Delta before opening the Suburban's door. Then he hugged her and gave her a perfunctory kiss.

"Good luck," she said as the Suburban sprang to life.

"It's going to be a complete waste of time," he replied.

Little did he know, as Lynn watched him leave, that he'd never been so wrong.

Michael was making excellent time as he cruised south. But it wasn't until he saw the sign and crossed over Lake Marion that he realized where he was.

This is roughly where Wentworth's body was found. Where were they going?

When he reached the first exit sign to Savannah, it finally hit him. *Savannah and Tybee Island. What if they never left the area and the bomb's still here?*

At that moment, he was very tempted to turn around and head back to D.C.

Highland Farm, Youman's Road, Colonels Island, Georgia
Late morning

The blacktop road from the Midway exit off I-95 gave way to hard-packed sand.

I bet this is fun when it rains, Michael thought, following the twists and turns past single-family homes with spectacular views of the water.

Around a bend, Michael saw the fancy double iron gates.

At the end of the driveway, a small man wearing britches and boots, who introduced himself as Willie, the head groom, directed Michael to park the Suburban under the shade of some trees behind a long stable block. "Just follow the signs, sir," he said.

Delta seemed happy to be out of the trailer. He snorted and looked around, his ears pricked.

Michael stroked the gelding's neck. "Like what you see, buddy? Lots of space to run."

"Would you like some help, Mr. Fulton?"

Delta's head shot up, and Michael turned to see a slim young woman a few yards away, dressed in a sleeveless shirt, jeans, and short riding boots.

Delta snorted again and took several paces backward. Michael continued to stroke and speak softly to the horse, rapidly trying to gather his thoughts.

He'd kept a photograph of Samin Fareed by his bed. It was usually the last thing he saw before going to sleep and the first thing he saw in the morning. Her image was indelibly etched. Regardless of how creative she'd been in changing her appearance, he was sure he'd know her anywhere. Even with short, curly blonde hair. For months, he'd imagined all kinds of scenarios and what he'd say if he ever found her. He pictured her squarely in his gun sight before squeezing the trigger, but never walking toward him on a warm sunny morning at a millionaire's waterfront estate in coastal Georgia.

Stay cool. Don't blow this. "He's not good with strangers," Michael replied. That wasn't what he'd been expecting to say either.

"I'm sorry if I startled you," she added and took a step toward Delta, her hand out. "Easy, fella. I'm not going to hurt you."

Just thousands of innocent Americans, Michael thought.

To his surprise, Delta let her stroke his nose then his neck.

"He's beautiful," she continued, stepping back. "Part Quarter Horse, part ...?"

"Morgan, I was told."

"Yes, of course. He's still a baby."

"He's five. Miss?"

She stroked Delta again and held out her free hand. "Samantha Conti. But my friends call me Sam, Mr. Fulton."

Michael returned a firm handshake, further surprised that she knew his name. "It's Michael, Sam."

She glanced over her shoulder. "Maybe when no one's around. But the MacFarlands have a very strict policy about their guests and the staff."

I get the picture. And thanks for the opening. "You've worked for them long?"

"Long enough."

"Meaning you're about to quit?"

"Oh, no. I meant I've been here long enough to know the rules and regulations. Especially this weekend. It's a huge deal." She turned her attention back to the horse. "We have a stall ready for him. Would you like me to take him for you?"

"You can tell I'm a novice?"

"Not at all. I didn't mean to imply ..." She paused. "It's just that certain guests are assigned a personal groom. That's all."

"I made the list?"

She smiled. "Top spot."

"I'm not sure whether that's good or bad news."

"It's good news. You're a VIP. Are you going to let me have him?"

Michael handed her the halter rope. "His name's Delta."

"If you leave your car keys, someone will get your bags and unhitch the trailer," she continued. "If you'd like to follow me?"

You've got no idea what you just said, Michael thought as they started for the stable block, Delta between them.

At the stable yard, she pointed. "He'll be in the end stall. It's quieter down there."

"I'll come with you," Michael said.

"There's no need." She began to turn away, Delta following. "You're expected at the main house," she added, successfully ending the conversation.

Damn!

"You can check on him later," she called out.

He raised his hand in acknowledgment. *Bet on it.*

As a teenager, Michael's mother insisted he spend part of his summer vacations with her in Britain and Europe. "It's all part of your education," she said. "You'll thank me one day."

Michael hadn't believed her. Until now.

A woman, who introduced herself as the housekeeper, met him, and as he followed her, what he could see of the MacFarlands' house reminded him of all the ancestral and historic homes he'd been forced to tour. And it was becoming obvious how Jim MacFarland had spent some of his millions.

"Mrs. MacFarland, Mr. Fulton's here," the housekeeper announced in the doorway to a huge indoor swimming pool. One outside wall was made entirely of glass, and lush tropical foliage grew in massive planters amongst the tables and chairs, grouped on the wide tile surround. It looked and felt, in Michael's mind, like an oversized greenhouse.

Stella MacFarland swung her legs off a sun lounger and came toward him, her flimsy thigh-length robe doing little to hide her curves. She immediately reminded Michael of a younger version of his stepmother.

She held out her hand. "I'm delighted to see you again, Michael. I'm so happy y'all were able to get here early." Her Southern drawl was very pronounced.

He returned the handshake, being scrutinized by clear gray eyes. "Good to see you too, Stella. Thanks for the invitation."

"Do join me," she added, patting an adjacent lounger. "Some homemade lemonade perhaps?" She waved her arm in the direction of a long table covered with a crisp white tablecloth and vases of fresh cut flowers. "Luncheon's buffet style. Do please help yourself, whenever you're ready."

She moved slowly and gracefully, and seated again on the lounger, she flicked open her robe, confirming that her bikini was extremely small.

A pair of oversized bronze cranes spewed an endless stream of water from their beaks into the pool, and over the sound of the ornate fountain, Michael tried to make polite conversation. As he drank a tall glass of lemonade, he suspected Stella MacFarland's glass contained something a little stronger.

He began to plan a way to escape.

"... for a swim? You're more than welcome," she said, interrupting his thoughts. "By now your bags should be in your room. I'll get a member of the staff to show you where it is. We have maps on a table in the foyer, but I somehow doubt you'll need one."

The emphasis on "doubt you'll need one" did not go unnoticed.

Michael got to his feet. "A swim sounds good. Thanks."

"Oh, you're more than welcome. You'll find robes in your suite."

Michael wasn't surprised that his bedroom had a four-poster bed and was bigger than some D.C. apartments. He was surprised that his suitcases had been unpacked and his clothes put neatly away. His laptop case had been placed on a side table, and he quickly double-checked both combination locks. Nothing had been touched.

Michael swam laps, using the time to think. He was trying to stop himself from immediately arresting Fareed and leaving, even though his gut was telling him not to move too soon. *You attract more flies with honey,* he kept repeating. *We need this woman. Patience. What's a few more hours?* He was aware that more guests had arrived and that he was being watched. He had to remind himself that he was there on the president's orders, regardless of the fact that this was ostensibly a social occasion and not a covert operation. He would have much preferred the latter.

Eventually, he climbed out of the pool and grabbed a towel.

Stella MacFarland was alone again. "You sure keep in shape. I like that in a man."

Michael was beginning to think he should have brought Bentley as cover for a girlfriend or new wife. Lynn would have been perfect.

"I try," he said, putting on the robe.

"And succeed, from what I can see. Drink?"

He scanned a well-stocked cart of liquor. "No thanks. I'd better change."

"Don't bother on my account."

Michael's senses went on high alert. *Red light. But I'll play the game.* He leaned toward her. "I don't get involved with married women," he said quietly. "However tempting."

She touched his forearm. "Do you blame me?"

I'm off-limits, lady. "What if I'm gay?"

Stella laughed. "And I'm the man in the moon. That excuse won't save you this weekend."

Shit! Michael picked up his towel. "What time's dinner?"

"Cocktails at six. Dinner at eight. It's very informal tonight. Most of the guests arrive tomorrow. Then all hell lets loose."

I hope not. "See you later."

She watched him go. "Real tasty," she muttered, taking another long swig of her drink.

In his bedroom, he found a schedule of weekend events and times had been placed on his laptop case, warning him to be extra careful.

He showered, the bathroom reminding him of a five-star hotel. Nothing had been left to chance, making him wonder if some houseguests left with the expensive toiletries in their luggage.

After dressing, he removed a Smith and Wesson .38 caliber snub-nose revolver and ankle holster from the laptop case and strapped it on.

Feeling more secure, he didn't lock the bedroom door, but he did manage to leave the house without being seen.

The Suburban, minus the trailer, was now parked in the huge area of gravel by the front door, its windshield and headlights free of bugs. *They really go all out,* he thought.

At the stable block, a temporary nameplate had been attached to the door of Delta's stall. Under the horse's name, it said, "Owner: Michael Fulton. Groom: Sam Conti." To Michael's relief, Delta appeared to have settled and was munching on a hay net. But he was disappointed that Fareed was nowhere in sight. The stables seemed deserted, except for the horses. *1730. Maybe they all eat early?*

On seeing Michael, Delta stopped eating, and Michael remained with him for a few minutes before deciding it would be a good time to do some snooping.

By the time he reentered the main house, he knew the layout of the stables. He was trying to decide if there was a way he could avoid cocktails when the housekeeper appeared.

"You're expected in the sunroom, Mr. Fulton," she said. "Shall I show you the way?"

Damn it! "I know the way, thanks," Michael replied. "I'm probably late. Time keeping isn't my strong point."

The housekeeper wasn't sure why she didn't believe him.

For the next several hours, he tried unsuccessfully to keep a low profile. Arnold Matthews' arrival didn't help. He seemed genuinely delighted to see Michael, who was then barraged with questions, not only during cocktails but throughout dinner, from the small group of guests who'd also arrived early. He had to keep telling himself that they were just a group of very rich, spoiled people and naturally inquisitive with a newcomer to their elite circle.

"How's Sis?" Michael asked Matthews at one point during dinner.

"Upset she couldn't be here. Terrible cold. And now the kids have got it." He picked up his wine glass. "I told her we didn't want their germs."

"She was bringing the children?" Michael asked casually.

Matthews nodded. "Damn stupid idea. This's neither the time nor place for them. Don't know what she was thinking."

I do, Michael thought.

"Do you like a good cigar, Michael?" Jim MacFarland asked when dinner was over.

"Yes, Jim. I do."

McFarland got to his feet. "Then follow me."

Saved, Michael thought.

He was wrong.

With a very smooth Davidoff Grand Cru, Michael leaned back in a leather chair, smoke curling to the ceiling of a room that was a very passable imitation of an exclusive gentlemen's club.

"Without stating the obvious," MacFarland said, taking the seat opposite, "you've sure got a way with the ladies. Arnold's right. Looks like we're in for a helluva weekend." He leaned forward. "What's your secret?"

"There isn't one."

"Well, just remember to leave some gals for us. There's some pretty young fillies due tomorrow. Cognac? It's vintage."

Michael stubbed out the remaining cigar and got to his feet. "Thanks, Jim, but no. I've been up since 5:00 a.m. Time to get some sleep. Good night."

Without waiting for MacFarland's response, Michael left the room.

He escaped to the stables.

Low wattage security lights illuminated the concrete walkway in front of the stalls, and in the dim light, Michael could see that Delta appeared to be sleeping. Not wanting to disturb the horse, he moved into the shadows, and leaning against a paddock railing, he relit the half-smoked cigar.

He'd almost finished it when he sensed movement, and it was automatic to reach for the Smith and Wesson.

"Mr. Fulton?"

He now knew the voice, and adjusting his pants leg to make sure the holster was covered, he turned to face Samin Fareed. "I thought it was Michael?"

She reached his side. "I wasn't sure."

"I'm sure. Unless you prefer Miss Conti?"

"I prefer Sam. Want to start over?"

He nodded. But before he could continue, she slipped back into the shadows.

Careful.

She reached his side again. "Good evening, Michael."

He stared into the darkness. "That still sounds very formal."

She laughed and moved close enough for him to smell a fresh clean scent. "Hi, Michael. How's it going?"

He faced her. *You're flirting with a possible terrorist, you dumb shit.* "Better. But you need to practice."

She studied him. "How do you suggest I do that?"

"Ride with me in the morning."

"I can't."

"Why not? You don't ride?"

"Of course, I do. My father says I was born in the saddle."

Take it slow. "So what's the problem?" Michael didn't give her time to reply. "Maybe I assumed you'd want to."

"I do," she said quietly. "But the staff aren't supposed to mix with the guests. Remember?"

"Forget that. I'm used to getting my own way."

"I got that impression. But I could lose my job."

"You won't. But if you do, Delta needs a good groom." *What the hell am I saying?*

"What makes you think I'm any good?"

"Instinct."

They were inches apart.

"I've got to go," Michael added. "See you here at seven?"

She stepped back. "I'll be ready."

"Good night, Sam."

"Good night, Michael," she replied.

Spotlights flooded the perimeter of the house as Michael searched for another entrance.

At a rear kitchen door, he slipped inside. As he suspected, in a house of that size, there would be more than just the main staircase. He found some back stairs and made his way quietly to his room.

Once inside, he let out a long breath.

After undressing, he lay awake, trying to plan his next move.

If you take her into custody, you'll blow your cover. Bad idea. But she was right there. You could still avoid this weekend. You need her cooperation, and fast. He'd gotten no answers. All Michael did know was that he should trust his instinct and call Brian in the morning.

When he eventually fell asleep, it was with the image of Samin Fareed stroking Delta's nose.

Highland Farm, Youman's Road, Colonels Island, Georgia
Saturday, March 22, 2003

That early in the morning, Michael wasn't surprised to be eating alone in the enormous dining room. Having caught the kitchen staff unprepared, they kept apologizing when he insisted that toast and coffee was all he wanted.

At the stables, a little after 7:00 a.m., Willie, the head groom, failed in his attempt to stop Michael riding with Sam.

"... It's their rules," he finished lamely as Michael swung into the saddle.

"And I'm breaking them. Not you," he said. "So I'll be the one taking any heat."

Michael purposely rode off the MacFarlands' property, and as he reached the dirt road, he slowed, waiting for Sam to catch up.

Even with his limited experience, he could tell that she was perfectly at home in the saddle.

Her first question concerned Delta.

Tell her the truth, he thought. *It's easier that way.* "I found him in Virginia ..." Michael began.

"That's terrible," she said when he finished. "People who mistreat animals should be strung up."

Along with your husband. And possibly you. "I agree. He's been better since I moved him to my place in Maryland."

"You live in Maryland?"

"Yes. I'm not far from either D.C. or Philadelphia." He was hoping for some kind of reaction. He didn't get it. Instead, she silently encouraged her horse to trot, leaving Michael with no alternative but to follow.

Delta was in high spirits, and a recently mowed long field in front of him was just too tempting.

"Bet I can beat you," Michael said as Delta began to dance.

"You'll have to catch me first," Sam replied and suddenly took off, sod flying from her horse's hoofs.

I already have, he thought, wheeling Delta around and letting the reins slide through his fingers. The horse needed no more encouragement. Instantly, he gave chase, and at full gallop, he ate up the ground. By the halfway point, both horses were almost neck and neck.

"He's fast," she shouted as Michael drew level.

Instead of replying, he urged Delta forward, and the horse responded as if someone had kicked him into overdrive.

With a commanding lead at the end of the field, Michael rapidly slowed Delta to a walk. The horse's speed had been exhilarating, and although his nostrils were flared and his sides heaving, he'd hardly broken a sweat.

Sam was laughing as she reached them. "Wow! That was unbelievable. Are you sure he wasn't a racehorse?"

Michael stroked Delta's hot neck. "I doubt it. Want to try again?"

She shook her head. "We've already been gone too long, and it's at least a thirty-minute ride back. We've got to cool them off." She began to move away, turning in the saddle. "He needs to be fresh for the polo match this afternoon."

Michael pressed Delta forward. "What polo match?"

"It's on your schedule. I'm told they do it every year."

"You weren't here last year?"

"No. I only started working for the MacFarlands in November."

That fits. Now play dumb. "From your accent, I'm guessing you're English? So you must know all about polo."

"I was only educated there," she said. "But I do know about polo. It's like playing very fast croquet or field hockey on horseback."

"Go on. I need all the help I can get."

Sam gave him a lesson in polo 101. When she got to the part about "stomping divots" in between "chukkas," Michael began to laugh.

"I'm serious."

"I can see you are. What's a chukka?"

"A Hindu word," she said. "Periods, to you. When each period ends, the spectators walk the field, replacing the divots. It's tradition."

"I'm sure it is."

"You'll see."

The stables came into view.

It's now or never. Michael reined Delta to a halt. "Is there a Mr. Conti?"

Sam stopped. "Just my father," she replied without hesitation.

Michael remained casual. "You're not married?"

"Not yet."

"Boyfriends?"

"None."

"Any kids?"

She laughed. "No kids. I'm old fashioned enough to think that marriage comes first."

If she's lying, she's really good, he thought. Then he reminded himself that she worked for McDonald. At least, according to McDonald.

"Why all the questions?" she added.

Michael leaned forward in the saddle, running a hand down Delta's neck. "I was going to ask you to dinner. But if you're seeing someone—"

"I accept," she said, stopping him in mid-sentence. "And there hasn't been a 'someone' for a long time. What about you? Are you married?"

"Not anymore. But I've got a son. He lives with his mother."

"I'm surprised someone hasn't snapped you up."

"Someone tried. I guess I'm not the marrying kind."

"Or you haven't found the right woman."

"That too."

After handing over Delta to Sam at the stables, Michael didn't reenter the house but used a spare key to the Suburban and drove from the estate in his riding clothes.

He headed toward Midway, fifteen miles away, and when he was sure he was safe from prying eyes, he turned onto a small side road. Stopping under the shade of some trees, he flipped open his cell phone and hit the speed dial for Brian's number.

"I've found Fareed," Michael said.

"No kiddin'? When?"

"Yesterday. She's the groom assigned to me for the weekend."

"I'm leavin' right now."

"No. You're not."

"You're bringin' her in on your own?"

"Not yet."

"Why?"

"Because she could still be an innocent party—"

"Like hell she is," Brian interrupted.

Michael's voice turned hard. "I rarely pull rank, but I'm pulling it now. We need her cooperation. Whatever form it takes. Forget about handcuffs and thumb screws. As you keep pointing out, I'm in the intelligence business. I'm fully aware of the importance of this mission. If the president trusts me, why can't you?"

"That was hittin' low," Brian muttered.

"I don't care," Michael snapped. "I'm ordering you to stay put. Is that clearly understood?"

"Understood."

"It better be. Now, do you want to know why?"

This better be good. "Sure. I'm listenin'."

"We went riding together, this morning ..." Michael began.

"Let me get this straight," Brian said when he'd finished. "She says she's never bin married and has no kids?"

"Affirmative. Which would explain why the dates don't jibe."

"Who do the kids belong to?"

"God knows. But we've got to find out."

"Agreed. And she told you she went to school in Britain?"

"She sounds like a Brit. That was her reason."

"Interestin'."

"Run a background check on a Samantha Conti. I want to know what comes up."

"Got it."

"And one more thing," Michael said. "I crossed over Lake Marion on the way here ..."

"Savannah, Tybee Island, and she's in the area," Brian repeated when he'd finished. "I see what you mean."

"It can't be a coincidence."

"I agree. What now?"

"I'm not sure. I'll call you later. It's safer that way. Got to go. I'm playing polo this afternoon."

"You're doin' what?" Brian's question was to dial tone. *Say what you want, but women are your Achilles' heel. Damn it, Michael! You're playin' a real dangerous game.*

No sooner had Michael entered the house than the housekeeper appeared.

"Lunch is being served in the tent," she said, pointing in the general direction of the paddocks.

"Thanks," he said, turning to go. "Should I change?"

She eyed his riding clothes. "Not if you're playing this afternoon."

From the size of the crowd, as Michael approached the tent, he guessed that the MacFarlands' guests had more than tripled in number since the previous night. When he looked in the general direction of Delta's trailer, it had all but disappeared amongst a varied assortment of large horse carriers.

They really take this seriously, he thought as Stella MacFarland saw him.

"Michael! We thought we'd lost you." She grabbed his arm. "There's lots of people I want you to meet. Champagne or beer?"

"Beer," he replied.

"This way," she added, heading straight for a group of young women.

Suddenly, Arnold Matthews blocked their path. "Not so fast," he said, handing Michael a beer. "My need is greater than yours, Stella."

Before she could protest, Matthews had firmly steered Michael away.

"I want to get to you before Jim does," Matthews continued. "Play on my team? We intend to whip their ass, like we did last year."

Michael took a swig of beer. "Then you'd better let me play for Jim."

"No way." Matthews finished his drink. "I saw your horse, this morning. Built for this game."

"I've never played."

"You'll do fine." Matthews lowered his voice. "We don't necessarily stick to the rules."

So that's how it is. "Don't say I didn't warn you."

Matthews laughed loudly and grabbed another drink from a passing waitress. "I'm off to tell Jim the good news."

Michael headed for the food, hoping he'd escaped Stella's clutches, but she caught him again.

"Now where were we," she said, navigating through the crowd.

For the next hour, he was introduced to countless single women, none of whom were dressed for riding horses, and the majority of the MacFarlands' close friends. Some names and faces he recognized from the corporate and political world, but thankfully, none of them knew him.

Alcohol was flowing freely, and from the amount of liquor being consumed, Michael was reasonably sure he'd be the only sober rider. He did manage to eat and was finishing a bowl of strawberries and ice cream when a loud clanging bell quieted the crowd, much to his relief.

Then he heard Jim MacFarland's booming voice. "Let the games begin. Gentlemen, time to saddle up."

The crowd began to take their places around the field, and as they dispersed, he saw Sam holding Delta, away from the other horses.

"Remember, it's a mallet, not a stick," she said quietly as he swung into the saddle.

"Thanks."

"Ready?" Matthews asked.

"No."

Matthews grinned. "All we have to do is get a little ball through their goalposts. Nothing to it."

To Michael, it first seemed that there were far too many riders erratically swinging mallets from the backs of galloping horses for this to be considered a game. It looked more like war. Then wondering how many of the players would jump into the night from an airplane at twenty thousand feet into hostile territory below, knowing that your government would deny any knowledge of your existence if you were somehow caught, he decided that polo couldn't possibly be as dangerous, or difficult. However, hitting the ball was. He failed miserably at his first few attempts, until Matthews shouted, "Forget the horse. Concentrate on the ball."

To Michael's surprise, Delta instinctively knew what to do. His speed and turning ability, for the most part, kept Michael out of trouble, and before the first chukka ended, he scored his first goal.

"Beginner's luck," he said when Matthews enthusiastically congratulated him.

"Bullshit," Matthews replied. "You're a natural." He studied Delta, now being walked by Sam. "Let me know if you decide to sell. I'm interested."

At dinner that night, Michael was toasted several times by a very drunk Arnold Matthews for scoring the winning goal. As the guests at the table seemed equally intoxicated, no one noticed his increasing discomfort.

"Our hero," Matthews slurred at the end of the meal on reaching Michael's chair. "It's party time."

"I'll pass, Arnold. Thanks."

"Nonsense. The evening's just getting started, and you're the guest of honor."

Michael could hear the president's words, "He's my biggest campaign contributor." "Lead the way," he said, getting to his feet.

Matthews wobbled to the door. "I knew you'd change your mind."

In a house that size, Michael wasn't sure why he was surprised that the MacFarlands had a ballroom. Except now it looked more like a disco, complete with a disc jockey, colored flashing lights, and a bar. Tables and chairs lined the perimeter, and the dance floor was already filling up as the music blared.

"I'm going to get a drink," Matthews said. "Want one?"

Michael was about to say, "No, thanks," but Matthews was already weaving his way to the bar.

"I know who you are," said a female voice at Michael's shoulder.

He turned to face a well-preserved woman, he guessed in her fifties, whom he couldn't remember meeting.

"Stella was right," she continued. "You are a hunk." She held out a long slim hand, covered in diamonds the size of rocks. "Bonnie Chase. And you're Michael Fulton."

Before he could reply, she moved closer and lowered her voice. "I'm in between lovers, if you're interested?"

Oh, fuck! "There's no Mr. Chase?"

She laughed and waved the other bejeweled hand. "Who do you think buys me these? Of course, there's a Mr. Chase. Right now, the bastard's shacked up at our place in West Palm with a waitress he met in Atlanta. He's been there three weeks. That's probably good for at least another ten carats."

"Should I be sorry?"

"Lord no! He's hopeless in bed. Always was. If he'd been a horse, they'd have had him gelded."

Michael didn't know how to respond. Or if he should.

"I think I've shocked you," she added.

"No," he lied. "But aren't we all here to ride?"

She moved even closer, brushing his arm. "We are, darling. But most of the riding's done between the sheets."

That's it! I'm outta here.

He began to thread his way through the crowded room when Stella stepped in front of him. "You're not leaving, I hope?"

"What gave you that idea?"

"I saw you with Bonnie. She's quite something, isn't she?"

"That's not the way I'd put it."

Stella sipped an oversized martini, looking at him over the rim. "They're running a book to see who you'll end up with. As the hostess, I deserve a little inside information."

"Hold onto your money."

She laughed. "But it's all in good fun. The pot can get quite large. Bonnie's got experience on her side. You could do a lot worse."

"Don't bet on it."

Her expression changed. "You really need to lighten up. Or is a dyed-blonde stable hand really more appealing?"

"As this room's full of bottle blondes, draw you're own conclusion. Excuse me."

He headed for the nearest exit, leaving her speechless.

That wasn't very smart, he thought, lighting a cigar on the terrace. *But I'm not cut out for this bullshit.*

He headed for the stables, where the noise of music and loud voices coming from the visiting horse carriers was almost as bad.

Delta seemed to be resting and quite content, but Michael checked him out anyway.

Finally running his hands down the horse's legs, he was relieved to find no hot spots from his afternoon exertion. He gave the horse a final pat and turned to leave.

"He's fine," a familiar voice said from the shadows, making him jump.

As he came face to face with Sam, he told himself that he was stupid to let down his guard. Either that or he was losing his edge.

"How's the party?" she asked.

"Not my kind of thing."

"I'm not one for parties either." She hesitated. "Would you like some coffee?"

"Tea would be better."

"I make excellent tea," she replied. "It's this way."

Michael was soon to discover that she lived in a trailer, thankfully situated well away from all the nighttime revelry.

She made no apologies for her somewhat cramped living space, which was clean and very neat. As she boiled a teakettle on the propane stove, he looked around. There wasn't a single picture or framed photograph that he could see. In fact, the trailer appeared almost too sanitized.

With mugs of tea, they sat on the steps, enjoying the cool night air.

"There's going to be a lot of sore heads in the morning," she said as squeals of laughter penetrated the darkness.

Michael lit a cigar. "I agree."

They talked for almost two hours, but not once did she mention Wharton, Sis, or anything remotely connected to Jarrah.

Michael finished his second mug of tea and got to his feet. "It's late. I've got to go. Thanks for the great tea and conversation."

Sam stood on the bottom step, almost level with him. "I had a lovely time. Thank you for coming." It was obvious as she moved even closer that she wanted him to kiss her.

Michael hoped she wouldn't notice, as he kissed her on the cheek, that his body was telling him one thing, while his instincts and training were telling him exactly the opposite.

With his internal battle still raging, he disappeared into the dark. Backlit from the lights in the trailer, she looked and smelled far too tempting. Still on the verge of mentally saying, "To hell with it," he didn't look back, for fear of changing his mind.

Now's not the time, he kept telling himself as he headed toward the main house.

As he approached, he could hear the party was still in full swing. There was music, laughter, and loud voices, not only coming from the MacFarlands' ballroom, but also from the terrace. Some guests were even in the outdoor pool.

The kitchen was alive with staff too busy cooking something that smelled remarkably like breakfast to pay him any attention.

In the hallway beyond the kitchen, he slipped up the back stairs to his room and locked the door.

As he lay on the bed, staring at the ceiling, he still hadn't formulated a plan on how to get Sam away from the estate without raising any red flags. Or blowing his cover.

He could imagine, too clearly, Brian and Dan in an unmarked car, hustling her away in handcuffs, while he was left behind to explain.

I've got to come up with something better than that, he was thinking as his eyes closed.

Highland Farm, Youman's Road, Colonels Island, Georgia
Sunday, March 23, 2003

The house was so quiet, it could have been deserted, Michael thought as he came down the main staircase. Turning toward the dining room, Stella suddenly appeared.

"I want to sincerely apologize for yesterday and last night," she said quietly before Michael could speak. "Everyone's sleeping off hangovers, so I'd be very grateful if you'd join me for breakfast?"

"Of course."

Instead of entering the dining room, he followed her to a screened porch off the indoor pool. They gave their breakfast order to the only staff member he'd seen so far and then sat at a small table.

"You must think we're terrible?" she added. "We're really not. Once a year, Jimmy insists we throw this party. It's become a tradition and began long before I ever met and married him." She looked to be on the verge of tears.

"I don't think you're terrible," Michael replied. "I was rude. And that's inexcusable."

"Friends?"

"Friends," he repeated and gave her a smile.

"Oh, I'm so glad. Jimmy was furious with me last night. He thinks the world of the president, and how this could reflect badly with your father and you being such close friends of his."

"It won't," he said. "I understand why people in the public eye need to let their hair down in private." He leaned across the table. "What you see at Highland Farm stays at Highland Farm."

Stella laughed. "Thank you. The president was right. You are charming." She finished her coffee. "Would you like to go riding with me?"

Michael glanced at his jeans and cowboy boots. "I'll have to change."

"Nonsense. We've got chaps at the stables."

Sam was grooming Delta when Michael and Stella arrived, and the only words she spoke to him were, "Good morning, Mr. Fulton."

He played along and managed a brief, "Thank you, Sam," as he rode away.

Michael immediately recognized Stella's horse as the one Sam had ridden the day before. "That's a nice-looking mare," he said.

Stella beamed. "She was a wedding present from Jimmy."

"How long have you been married?"

"Almost five years." She faced him. "I hope you've noticed I'm very much younger?"

He grinned. "Difficult to miss."

"Jimmy's children from his first marriage are almost as old as I am. But I love the old guy to bits." She hesitated. "He never told me what you actually do."

"I'm in commodities," Michael said. "Both here and overseas."

"Jimmy mentioned your father, although I don't think he's ever met him. Is he still involved in the business?"

"Very much so."

"I'm guessing you're quite successful?"

"I like to think I am."

Michael decided that this double-meaning conversation had gone on long enough.

"How did you meet Jim?" he asked, hoping for a lengthy reply that would give him time to think.

He hardly listened as she went into a long explanation that involved a convention in Atlanta, politics, and horse shows. Once on the subject of horses, she rambled on.

"... the polo match is dangerous, but I personally think that the games this afternoon are a lot worse. That's why I always invite our neighbor, Peter Hughes. He's a doctor and such a charmin' man, and hopefully he won't be kept too busy."

Michael was jolted out of his thoughts. "You have a doctor on standby?"

She laughed. "As a precaution, you understand. He rides with us too. But all the people who didn't participate at polo get their chance to show off today. From previous experience, I think they're all quite mad."

"What exactly are these games?"

Stella described a few and ended with, "... barrel races. Now, you'd be really good at that."

"I would?"

"I watched Delta yesterday. He's perfect. Fast, and he can turn on a dime."

Thank you, Stella, Michael said to himself.

"We'd better get back," she continued. "Don't want to be late for the Bloody Mary brunch."

He laughed. "Did I hear you correctly?"

She had a broad smile. "Lots of terrible hangovers this morning. But don't worry; Bonnie's a very late riser. She won't bother you again."

How right you are, he thought.

Back in the paddocks after brunch, Michael was convinced that three-quarters of the guests were still as drunk as the night before. There was a lot of good-natured ribbing, much laughter, and very large bets were being placed, though he doubted the world's starving millions would find such extravagance funny.

"Don't overstress him," Sam said quietly as Michael swung into the saddle. "It's not usually this hot, and he's still a baby. Stick to the barrel race, and he'll cream the competition."

As Michael rode away, he was thinking that Sam should be riding instead of him. She certainly looked the part, dressed in cream britches and boots, with a distinctive Hermes silk scarf tied loosely over her short-sleeved shirt.

While other games were being played in other paddocks, the barrel race seemed to draw the most spectators. Having seen the first heat run, Michael could see why. One horse stumbled and fell, and another rider just fell off.

Dr. Hughes is having a busy afternoon, Michael thought.

Then it was his turn.

As Sam predicted, Delta won easily.

He also won his quarter and semifinals.

The final race consisted of five horses and riders, and Michael drew the center lane.

Delta's anticipation was so great that Michael was having trouble keeping him behind the start line, but when the flag dropped, Delta sprang into an almost immediate gallop. He raced down the paddock to the barrel, and as he reached it, Michael's toes slipped out of the stirrups. Delta almost went to his knees on the very fast turn, while Michael flew over his shoulder, hit the grass hard, and rolled several times. Then he lay still.

He could hear people suddenly shouting and then movement nearby, but he didn't attempt to raise his head. Over the noise, he thought he heard Sam saying loudly, "Leave him. I'll get him. You're going to frighten him more. He'll come to me."

Michael became aware that someone was bending down. "He's out cold," a man's voice said. "Don't move him. Give me some room."

A few minutes later, Michael groaned and opened his eyes. "Where's Delta?" he said and tried unsuccessfully to sit up. "Is he okay?"

"I'm a doctor," the man said. "Lie still. Your horse is fine."

"I want to see him."

The doctor pointed. "He's over there with your groom."

Michael squinted. "Where?"

"What day is it?"

"I don't know."

The doctor held up five fingers. "How many?"

"Three."

"He's got a concussion," the doctor said and made Michael move his arms and legs. "No bones broken, that I can tell."

"Thank goodness." Michael recognized Stella's voice. "Let's get him to the house."

Michael was put to bed in a darkened room, with a cold compress on his forehead.

"I don't think it's too serious," the doctor said. "But I could do a more thorough examination at the hospital, if you want?"

"No hospital," Michael managed to say.

"Just keep him quiet then," the doctor added. "I'll check in later."

Then a door closed.

They came back every half-hour. Michael wanted to tell them to leave him alone. Dinner that night was a light broth, when what he really wanted was a decent steak.

Later that evening, he became very belligerent, saying repeatedly that he had to get home. When he finally tried to get out of bed and told them he was going, the doctor gave him a shot that kept him quiet for the rest of the night.

Chapter Twenty-Four

Highland Farm, Youman's Road, Colonels Island, Georgia
Monday, March 24, 2003

Michael awoke to find Stella in his room.

He groaned as he sat up. "What time is it?"

"A little after eight."

Michael swung his legs out of bed and only managed to stand by holding onto one the bed's four posts. "I've got to go."

"Jim and I discussed it last night," she said. "We think you should stay. But if Dr. Hughes says it's okay, you can go, but only if someone drives you."

"I'm not leaving Delta."

"We understand that."

"He's very difficult to handle."

"We know that too." She set a tray on the nightstand. "Try and eat some breakfast. I'm calling the doctor right now."

After some more arguing and uncharacteristic behavior on Michael's part, the doctor reluctantly agreed that he could leave.

When the Suburban, towing the two-horse trailer with Delta inside, finally left Highland Farm, Michael was in the passenger seat, wearing dark glasses, and Samin Fareed was behind the wheel.

At the first rest area on I-95, Michael told Sam to stop, and when he headed for the men's room, he felt sure she was watching.

As soon as he was out of her sight, he called Brian.

"I was beginnin' to think somethin' had happened," Brian said.

"It did."

Then Michael explained.

When he returned to the Suburban, Sam was inside the trailer.

Michael gave Delta a hug. "Thanks for the help," he whispered and stroked the horse's nose. "You okay, buddy?"

"He's fine," Sam said. "And you sound a lot better."

He turned. "I am. In fact, I'll be driving." He held out his hand. "My keys, Sam."

She began to protest.

Michael held up his spare key.

Reluctantly, she handed him the set she'd been using. "I've never seen anyone recover so fast."

"Call it a miracle," he replied.

She couldn't take her eyes off him as they left the rest area and got back on I-95, heading north.

He'd already discovered that she was very intelligent, and she was about to prove it again.

"There's nothing wrong with you, is there?" she asked.

"Correct."

There was silence. Then, "Why the charade?"

He kept his eyes on the highway. "I invited you to dinner. There was no other way I could think of to get you off the estate." *That part's true.* "I keep my promises."

She began to laugh. "That's the nicest thing anyone's done for me in a very long time. Thank you."

"Don't thank me yet. How come the MacFarlands agreed to let you drive?"

"Jim and Stella arrived at the stables early this morning ..." she began.

They were still arguing about whether or not to let Michael leave when Jim MacFarland opened Delta's stable door and stepped inside.

"I don't know what all the fuss is about." He reached for Delta's halter. "He's not that..." He never finished the sentence. Delta snorted and reared, his front hoofs missing MacFarland by inches.

He made a hasty retreat.

"See," Stella said. "I tried to warn you."

At that point, according to Sam, Willie, the head groom, intervened. "Apart from Mr. Fulton, Sam's the only one I've seen who can handle him."

Stella's temper then surfaced and phrases like "what will the president think?" "injured on our property," and "dead horse" were included in her tirade.

"Jim then told me to pack," Sam said. "And here I am."

"When do they expect you back?"

She shrugged. "Stella said it was up to me. I wasn't to leave until I was sure you were all right."

Michael grinned. "So there's no hurry?"

"Not according to Stella."

Eagles Nest, Somewhere off Route 301, the Eastern Shore, Maryland
Later that night

They'd eaten on the road, and although Michael made good time, it was well after dark before Delta was safely in his own stable.

They ate a late snack at the breakfast bar in the kitchen/family room.

"I need to unpack," Sam said, picking up her empty plate and sliding off a barstool.

As she passed him, Michael grabbed her arm. "Where's Jarrah?"

Her reaction couldn't have been worse if he'd slapped her.

"I don't know. How do you know about him?" The plate crashed to the tile floor as she struggled from his grip and backed away. "Who are you?"

"Lieutenant Colonel Michael Correa. I'm with the Department of Justice."

She backed farther away.

Michael's whole stance and demeanor had changed, and his 9 mm Beretta was pointing directly at her forehead. "One more time, Sam. Where's Jarrah?"

She collided with the sofa, forcing her to sit, and she didn't doubt for a second that he'd have no compunction in killing her. "You lied to me?"

The gun didn't move from its target. "And you didn't? Where is he?"

"I don't know," she said quietly. "I don't want to know. The man's a sadistic fanatic."

Michael took a step forward, the Beretta as steady as a rock. "That's not a nice way to describe your husband."

She didn't look up. "I'm not married. Not to him or anyone. I told you that."

McDonald said she married him. Risk it. "How do you explain your marriage certificate?"

Her eyes widened. "How much do you know?"

"A lot. The marriage certificate?"

She swallowed. "A fake, like the passports."

"And the children?"

"The boy was left at the apartment in Berlin, just before we came to America. I don't know where he came from. I was never told."

Michael moved closer. "You expect me to believe that?"

"I'm telling you the truth. A man brought him. I never saw his face. Jarrah came home with the baby while we were living in Florida. We'd been there almost twenty months. All he said was, 'You've got another child.' I knew better than to ask questions."

"So you've got no idea who the parents are?"

"No. And I'm not sure I want to know."

"Why didn't you go to McDonald?"

She blinked. "You know about him too?"

"He came to find you. We met."

"I hate him almost as much as I hate Jarrah." Some of her poise returned. "He's a double-crossing, two-faced weasel."

"That was my opinion."

"It was?"

Michael nodded. "He said he recruited you."

Her voice strengthened. "Hah! Blackmail's more like it." She paused. "That's why you think I'm a terrorist?"

"Did I mention the word?"

"No. But you asked about Jarrah. I just assumed."

"Always dangerous. Aren't you?"

"Oh, God, Michael, no. I'm not ... I'm not. This's a nightmare. Please believe me. Please, Michael. I'm not who you think I am."

He lowered the Beretta. "Then who are you?"

She sat more upright. "Samin Fareed."

Michael sat in a wing chair diagonally across from her but purposely rested the Beretta in his lap. "Start at the beginning. And don't leave anything out."

"I was born in Tehran. My father is an international rug dealer. Both he and my grandfather were educated in Great Britain, so as I'm an only child, I was sent to an English boarding school ..." she began.

A lot of what Sam told him confirmed what Michael already knew. After only one semester at Wharton, she flew home for the holidays. What he didn't know was that according to her, on her return to the U.S., via

London's Heathrow airport, she was stopped from boarding her British Airways connecting flight by customs officials who accused her of smuggling drugs. "I've never even smoked pot," she said.

She was strip-searched and held for hours in a windowless room with very little to eat or drink.

"Then Ian McDonald showed up," she added. "He said I was looking at spending the next twenty-five years in an English prison."

He'd then produced some of the drugs they supposedly found in her luggage, and his interrogation of her had lasted several more hours. By the time McDonald finished, she was hungry, thirsty, and suffering from sleep deprivation, and Michael understood only too well why she'd probably have agreed to anything. McDonald also explained in lurid detail what would happen to her in prison.

"Be grateful it's not one in your own country," he said at one point. "Even if you're not a virgin, a beautiful young woman like you would soon become a regular favorite with the guards." Sam knew what he meant by "favorite" and became even more terrified.

In the four years Sam was at Wharton, she flew back and forth to Tehran at least twice a year. Each time, McDonald was waiting for her when she flew into Heathrow, either flying on to Tehran or back to the U.S.

"He never mentioned drugs again," she said. "It was always a friendly conversation about how I was doing in school and life in the U.S. in general."

After graduation, Sam spent the remaining summer with Sis Matthews. At this point, Michael made a mental note that this was the first time Sam had mentioned Sis.

When Sam finally flew home, McDonald had again been waiting for her at Heathrow. This time, he told her what he wanted her to do, and if she didn't cooperate, how she could expect to spend the rest of her twenties and thirties.

"The drug charges against you are still pending," he added, "but I can make them disappear, if you do what I ask."

McDonald told her to go back to Tehran, accept the job with her father, and she would be contacted.

She settled into a routine: living in an apartment, working for her father with overseas customers that used all her languages, and riding every day.

Then late one evening, a few months later, her doorbell rang. Opening the door, she found only a note, with a name, a time, and a location.

"I hoped McDonald had forgotten me," she said. "But he hadn't."

Terrified McDonald would carry out his threat, she followed the directions on the note. "That's how I first made contact," she added.

For the next twelve months, Sam began to slowly infiltrate the terrorist cell.

"When they realized I could be trusted and seemed to have the same fanatical goals, they gave me more to do."

At first, Sam fed them information. They questioned her regularly about life in the U.S.

"I even taught them common words and phrases. It nearly killed me, knowing that they were going to use this information against Americans. But I didn't know how or where."

Then McDonald made direct contact, posing as a wealthy British rug buyer.

A week later, under the guise that she was going to cement a new and prosperous deal for her father's business, she flew to London.

"McDonald was at the airport, and he took me straight to a hotel. I spent three days there going over everything," she said.

Then McDonald applied more pressure. "Unless you want to spend the best years of your life at Her Majesty's pleasure?" he'd added.

From then on, Sam flew on a regular basis to London, Paris, Rome, and Berlin.

"Most Germans speak English," she said. "So that wasn't a problem."

"How did you explain that to your father?" Michael asked.

"We had clients in all those countries. I persuaded him to let me go to increase sales."

"Did you?"

"Yes. I was quite successful."

Michael didn't doubt it.

As McDonald predicted, the terrorist network soon began using her as a courier.

"That's when I first met Jarrah." She didn't know what was in the packages she carried, and opening them to find out wasn't an option. "They were wrapped in such a way that they'd know if someone tampered with them," she said.

On her frequent trips to London, McDonald began to train her in several undercover and surveillance techniques. She'd even learned how to shoot.

"I didn't want to, but he told me it could save my life. What life?"

When McDonald told her to get close to Jarrah, she at first refused.

"Do it," he said. "I don't care how. Seduce the bastard if necessary." He then waved an official-looking document under her nose. "Otherwise, it only takes a phone call."

But Sam didn't have to seduce Jarrah.

"He liked women, and women liked him," she said.

But the decision for her to act as his wife hadn't been his idea.

"It came from someone else," she added.

"Who?" Michael asked.

"I don't know. Most of his meetings were held in secret. He never mentioned names in front of me. But he did tell me I'd been chosen because of my knowledge of the U.S." She put her head in her hands. "Can we do the rest of this later? I'm really tired."

"How much more is there?"

"Not much. Most of the rest you seem to know." Sam looked around. "I thought we were really attracted to each other. Or was that all part of your plan too?"

"No."

Finally, she pointed at the Beretta. "Would you have shot me?"

"Yes. If I had to."

"You don't have to. I'm no threat to you or anyone else. But the next time you aim a loaded gun, make sure the safety's off."

"It was, but the mag's empty," Michael lied.

She shuddered, and there were several seconds of silence before she looked up. "What happens now?"

"I've got to take you in."

"I'm going to jail?"

"No. You're going to tell some people I know what you've just told me."

She got slowly to her feet. "Good thing I didn't unpack."

As she passed him, Michael reached for her arm. "I'm sorry, Sam. Time's running out. If there'd been another way …"

She faced him. "You've known all along who I was?"

"Yes."

"So why didn't you take me in the day we met?"

He didn't reply.

"Michael? Why? Why go through this charade?"

"It wasn't a charade."

She touched his cheek. "What are you trying to say?"

"You're not making this easy."

She slid both arms around his neck. "Then let me make it easier. I would never do anything to hurt you. Does that help?"

"It helps."

"Then you've made this nightmare a tad more bearable."

"The nightmare's going to end. I promise," he said. Then against his better judgment, he kissed her.

"I'll get my bags," she said eventually.

"In the morning. Right now, you need to get some sleep. Alone."

She began to leave the room. "Are you going to lock me in?"

"No."

She faced him again, stepping closer. "You trust me?"

He nodded. "And you'd better learn to trust me too. I mean that, Sam."

"I do, Michael," she said softly.

Eagles Nest, Somewhere off Route 301, the Eastern Shore, Maryland
Tuesday, March 25, 2003

Michael was in the kitchen when Sam appeared.

"What's going to happen?" she asked, beginning to pour a cup of coffee.

"I'm taking you to a meeting with me and two of the team."

"Are they as good as you?"

"In certain things, yes."

She reached out to touch him. "And in others?"

Michael backed away. "Don't go there, Sam. Now's not the time."

At around the same time in Georgia, FBI agents from the local Savannah office arrived at Highland Farm with a search warrant. They told the astonished MacFarlands that a Samantha Conti, an employee, had been stopped at B.W.I., about to board a flight to Atlanta.

"Her brother's a wanted fugitive," one of the agents told Stella MacFarland. "This warrant covers her personal effects and her car."

Stella showed them to the trailer. "I didn't know she had a brother. I just don't believe this. It's all a terrible mistake. When will she be back?"

"Don't count on her coming back, ma'am," was the reply.

Michael's Office, G Street, Washington, D.C.
Two hours later

They'd hardly spoken on the drive from Eagles Nest, and as soon as they entered the suite of offices, Sam couldn't help but notice that Michael was all business.

After introducing Brian and Dan, he told her to sit.

Then, to her increasing dismay, she was fingerprinted and photographed. Then her bags were searched. They found nothing of any relevance.

"You understand why you're here?" Michael asked when they'd finished.

Sam only nodded.

"You also understand that this interview will be taped?"

Sam nodded again.

"To ensure we correctly interpret your information, please speak your replies."

"I understand."

"Are you ready?"

"Yes."

Michael turned on the tape recorder. "Tuesday, March 25, 2003. Interview with Samin Fareed commencing 1030 hours. Present in the room are Lieutenant Colonel Michael Correa, Brian Mullen, and Dan Whitney." Michael faced her. "Please state your name, age, and country of birth for the record."

"My name is Samin Fareed. I'm twenty-eight. I was born in Iran on June 12, 1975 ..." she began.

For the next two hours, Sam answered all of Michael's questions, and apart from a few dates and irrelevant names, she told them very little that they didn't already know.

At 12:30 p.m., Michael signaled for Brian to take over.

"Tell us about your relationship with Jarrah," Brian said.

"He's a sadistic pig. I was terrified of him. He treated me like dirt. I was a cook and a housekeeper. Nothing more than a slave."

"But you did have sex with him?"

Sam didn't reply. Instead she turned to Michael. "Why is that important?"

"We're trying to establish your ties to him. That's all."

"So if I tell you I had sex with him, you'll think I've been lying?"

"Not necessarily. But please answer the question."

She faced Brian. "Yes, I had sex with him. He raped me whenever he felt like it. Does that answer your question?"

In the silence that followed, they could all have heard a pin drop.

Michael turned off the tape recorder. "I'm sorry, Sam," he said. "We've got to know everything. Want to take a short break?"

She nodded.

He pressed the intercom button. "Molly? Two coffees, please." Then he faced Brian and Dan. "Come back in fifteen minutes."

Dan got to his feet.

Reluctantly, Brian followed, and the look Michael got left him in no doubt as to what Brian was thinking.

"Goddamn him," Brian muttered in the safety of his office. "Why can't he keep his fuckin' dick in his pants?"

"I heard that," Dan said from the doorway. "That's what you think?"

Brian motioned to him to close the door. "That's what I know. It's Kathryn again. Only worse."

"What about Kathryn?"

Brian sat at his desk. "Forget it. But I do know the boss man ain't goin' to be too objective."

"That doesn't sound like him."

"Trust me. I know better. And don't ask. One day, when we're poppin' bonbons 'cause there ain't nothin' better to do, I'll tell you."

"But what she's told us so far fits."

"Maybe too well," Brian replied.

"How are you holding up?" Michael asked.

Sam took a sip of coffee. "I'm okay. I just wish I hadn't been asked those last questions." She cradled the coffee mug, her voice low. "I wanted to tell you last night about my relationship with Jarrah." She looked up. "I'm so sorry, Michael."

He remained where he was, leaning against his desk. "So we've both been around the block."

She gave a small smile. "Thank you."

He returned her smile. "Don't thank me yet. I've got to remain impartial. It could get rougher. Just tell us the truth, and it'll soon be over."

"Then what?"

The knock on the door prevented his reply.

After Brian and Dan took their seats, Michael turned on the tape machine. "Interview with Samin Fareed resuming at 1245 hours. Also present with Michael Correa are Brian Mullen and Dan Whitney."

"Before the break, you told us Jarrah raped you," Brian said. "The children are the result?"

"No. They're not mine. I took birth control pills. You can check with my doctor in Bradenton ..." Sam replied. "...and Jarrah believed that most normal American families had two kids, but I didn't know how seriously he took it until the baby arrived one afternoon. She was only a few weeks old. I named her Susie."

"Where are the children now?"

Here we go, Michael thought.

"They're safe."

Michael could see Brian wasn't about to let that go. "Move on, Brian," he ordered.

"You said you rarely mixed with the neighbors. But how did you explain the sudden arrival of a baby?"

"Jarrah made me wear awful tent dresses. I could have been a size four or a size fourteen. No one could tell. And some women don't look that pregnant. I could easily have hidden it." She gave Brian a very direct look. "I gave them no reason to think I was lying."

Brian continued to question her about her relationship with Jarrah, trying to trip her up, but Sam never wavered from her original answers.

"We were told the neighbors in Florida thought Jarrah was an airline pilot. Is that true?"

"No, it isn't," she said. "It was the story he told them."

"You're sure?"

"Yes, I'm sure. Although I wasn't included in any of his secretive meetings, I'd have known if he was really flying."

"How?"

"I was acting as his wife. I did the washing and cleaning, and we did have some conversations."

"About what?"

"The children, paying bills, all the usual stuff, and he'd ask me about things in the U.S. that he didn't understand."

"Like what?"

"Lifestyles, mostly. Nothing in particular."

"How did he spend his time?"

"He took up scuba diving."

"When?"

"Shortly after we arrived. July, I think. He must have gone to a local school, because one morning he was in a hurry and said he had a lesson in thirty minutes."

"Did he get certified?"

"When I asked him, he told me he wasn't going to take the final exam. But he did dive a lot in the beginning. He was out there two or three times a week. I thought he'd found a hobby."

"Anything else?" Brian asked.

"He took a boating safety course."

"Where?"

"In Bradenton, I suppose."

"You suppose?"

"He didn't say."

"Did he have a boat?"

"Not that I saw. I think if he had, he'd have told me."

"When was this course?"

"Sometime in November 2001."

"Did he pass?"

"He got a certificate. Then he signed up for a captain's course."

"How long was that?"

"He did the day course. I think it was about three weeks."

Michael was making notes.

"Did he pass?"

"Yes. He was really excited. He went out to celebrate and came back two days later."

"Did you ask where he'd been?"

Sam shook her head. "I told you, we didn't have a close relationship. I was just useful window dressing."

"Was he still diving?"

"Yes."

"Who did he dive with?"

"He said with people he'd met on the course."

"Did you ever meet them?"

"No."

"Did they come to the house?"

"I don't think so." Sam's eyes fixed on Brian. "You have to understand, I was a nobody in his eyes. Women are excluded from almost everything male."

"Except the sex?"

"Yes, except that," she said quietly.

Michael held up his hand. "Interview will resume after lunch."

He switched off the tape recorder and got to his feet. "We all need a break. Sam will be going with Molly."

With only a few hungry tourists as competition, they found two outside tables at a cafe around the corner from the Department of Justice building.

"I'd love to be a fly on the wall," Brian said, watching Molly and Sam in conversation but out of earshot.

"No need," Michael replied. "Our fly's right there."

Brian chuckled. "Clever. You think she'll tell Molly somethin' we don't know?"

"Maybe. Who knows what women talk about when they're together." Michael faced him. "I know what you think. But this time you're wrong.

Any relationship I've got with Sam won't interfere with this investigation. The stakes are far too high."

"If you say so."

"I do say so."

"How are you doing?" Molly asked.

"Okay, I suppose," Sam said. "After what I've been through, it's almost a relief to finally tell someone. Have you any idea what it's like to live in fear every day?"

"Not every day, no."

"I was terrified for the children," Sam continued. "I didn't realize how attached I'd become. I'm the only mother Susie has ever known. That's scary. I didn't think I had a maternal bone in my body."

"All women do. It's one of the crosses we have to bear. Husbands, sons, boyfriends. They all bring out the mothering instinct in us to some degree or other." Molly took a sip of iced tea. "The older child's called John?"

Sam nodded, her mouth full of food. She swallowed. "He's a super little boy. Heaven knows what he went through. When he was first delivered to me, he didn't talk."

"At all?"

"Not a word. I'd no idea what language he spoke. But now he speaks English like a native."

"Like you."

Sam smiled. "That's what happens when you spend your teenage years in Britain."

"I think it sounds wonderful," Molly said. "I wish we could all speak like you."

"Thank you," Sam said quietly.

"You knew nothin' prior to the attacks on the World Trade Center and the Pentagon?" Brian asked as soon as the interrogation resumed.

"No, nothing. If I'd known, I would have told McDonald." Sam turned to Michael. "I watched it on TV like everyone else. Jarrah reacted as though he'd won the lottery. It was awful. For the first time in my life, I knew what it felt like to want to kill someone."

"Then what happened?"

"He was glued to the TV for several hours. After the second tower fell, he told me he was leaving. He didn't say where, and I knew not to ask. He got back late, in a really up mood. He spent the rest of the night at the computer. I went to bed. He was still there in the morning."

"How did you contact McDonald?"

"Jarrah was away a lot, so I was able to use a telephone."

"He didn't check the phone bills?"

"It wouldn't have made a difference. I used a toll free number and an access code. McDonald told me the calls were automatically rerouted. If I didn't get through to him the first time, I was to keep trying every hour. Sometimes I could; sometimes I couldn't. Jarrah would never tell me how long he'd be gone."

"What information did you pass to McDonald?"

"Very little. There wasn't much to tell."

"More than you've told us?"

"Less."

"Why did you call McDonald a two-faced weasel?"

Sam then explained that not long after the attacks on 9/11, they flew to Germany. "My mother hadn't been well," she said, "so I went home for a few days and left the children in Berlin."

When she arrived in Tehran, she was amazed to see McDonald deep in conversation with another man in the airport terminal. She recognized the man from photographs McDonald had once shown her. "Remember these faces," he'd said. "If you ever see any of them, I want to know."

"Who was he?" Michael asked.

"I don't know. I just remember the face."

"Middle Eastern?"

"Yes, as far as I could tell."

"Would you recognize him again?"

"Probably."

It was the last place she ever expected to see McDonald, and as he had no way of knowing that she'd be there, she managed to avoid detection.

"He told me he was trying to catch this man, so what was he doing there, and why was he talking to him?" Sam added.

I don't know either, Michael thought. "Did you stay for the outcome of this meeting?"

"No. But they were sitting in the lounge area, having drinks. It didn't look like McDonald was arresting him. Could he even do that?"

"Not without permission from the Iranian authorities."

"That's what I thought."

From then on, Sam told them, she stopped trusting McDonald. As she didn't want him to know that she saw him, she continued to make the calls to the toll free number, but, as usual, there was very little to report. Until the night of September 14, 2002.

"Jarrah took a phone call around ten. I overheard bits and pieces. Someone had been taken into custody. I don't know who."

I'll bet I do, Michael thought.

"Jarrah swore a lot," she continued. "He was madder than I'd ever seen him. The next thing I knew, he slammed down the phone and told me we were leaving."

She hadn't immediately realized that Jarrah meant they were leaving for good. But within two hours, she had packed all the children's clothes and her own, and was driving to the airport in Tampa. According to the instructions Jarrah gave her, she was to leave the minivan in long-term parking, buy a ticket to New York, and get a connecting flight to Berlin, Germany. She was then to wait at the apartment there for further instructions.

"I was terrified," she said. "I didn't know what to do, so I called McDonald and told him what was happening. He said he'd arrange to have tickets waiting for me at the British Airways desk at JFK and that I was to fly to London instead."

"But you didn't fly from Tampa or catch any connecting flight, did you?"

"No." Sam then confirmed that she'd taken a cab back to the local airport in Sarasota and got on the first morning commuter flight to Newark, New Jersey.

"Did you go to New York?" Michael asked.

"Yes. I really was going to fly to London, but by then I'd had time to think. The children were my priority, and I realized that I still might not be safe, so I made arrangements for them and disappeared. Until you found me."

"Where are the children now?"

"I can't tell you."

"You've got to."

She shook her head. "I won't."

Michael reached into a desk drawer and pulled out the enlarged photograph Brian had taken of Sis Matthews-Boyd and the children at the school in Bedminster, Pennsylvania.

"Maybe this will help," Michael added, sliding the picture toward her.

Sam didn't pick it up, but from her reaction, they could tell she had no clue that they already knew. "You're no better than McDonald. You bastard!"

"Not according to my birth certificate." Michael turned to Brian and Dan. "I think we can safely assume that Miss Fareed has just identified the photograph of Sis Matthews-Boyd, her child, and the two children that Miss Fareed said were given to her."

Sam wiped her eyes and blew her nose. "How could you," she said quietly.

"Are they the children in question?" Brian asked.

"You know they are. Please don't hurt them."

"I don't know who you think you're talkin' to, Miss Fareed. But we're not in the business of harmin' kids," Brian said. "Regardless of who they are."

"Or the people who cooperate," Michael added.

"Will Sis get into trouble?"

"I don't see why," Michael replied. "As long as you've told us the truth."

"I have."

"How much does Mrs. Matthews-Boyd know about all this?"

"Nothing. She knew I was living with someone, but she didn't know who. When I arrived on her doorstep, I told her that I'd found out he was a big-time drug dealer, and as I knew too much, he'd threatened to kill me and the children."

"She didn't question it?"

"Sis is not only my best friend, but she's also quite naive. Of course she believed me."

"Who did she think the children belonged to?"

"I told her this drug dealer, from a previous marriage. She knew they weren't mine; otherwise, I'd have been pregnant at Wharton, wouldn't I."

"Why didn't you stay with the Boyds?"

Sam stared at the photograph, still on Michael's desk. "You eventually traced the children to her. I would have been next. I didn't want Sis mixed up in this."

"So what was your excuse for leaving them?"

"That I was on the run, and until he was caught, I wouldn't be safe. Getting a job with horses was actually Sis's idea."

"How did you disappear so successfully?"

Sam said that even though McDonald told her he'd take care of everything, she'd concealed a considerable amount of cash. Money from her father, who, having agreed that she needed to learn Spanish in order to open up a South American market for his rug business, consented to her going back to America and signing up for an online Spanish course at the University of Florida.

Smart, Michael thought.

They'd already confirmed she'd withdrawn most of the money in her bank accounts in the name of Sabrina Armond from an ATM at the Tampa airport.

After leaving JFK and handing over the children to Sis Matthews-Boyd, Sam had gone to a New York police precinct to report her pocketbook stolen.

"You can call the 20th Precinct," she said. "They should still have the list I gave them, including my fictitious Italian passport."

After filing the police report, she'd gone to the Italian Embassy, who eventually gave her a temporary visa, until a new passport could be issued.

"I was just another body in the system. No one thought to check," she added. "Luckily for me, I don't think the Italians are the greatest at keeping records."

She'd stayed in the New York area, changing hotels every few days, until the passport arrived.

Now, as a legitimate Italian citizen in the U.S. on an extended visit, getting a social security number and opening another bank account had been relatively easy. Sam took a driving test in Pennsylvania and got her license using Sis Matthews-Boyd's address. Then she bought a used Ford Escort for cash at one of the many car dealerships in Lancaster.

"How much money did you have?" Michael asked.

"I took about $80,000 to New York," Sam replied, to astonished looks. "My father wire transferred three thousand dollars a month for over two years to the local Western Union. I took the money in cash. I didn't touch a penny, and Jarrah never knew."

It hadn't been all luck that she'd ended up working for the MacFarlands. Having initially got a job at a stud farm in Lexington, Kentucky, Sam heard via Sis that there was an opening for a groom at their estate.

She faced Michael. "I'd been there seven months when you found me."

"And if I hadn't found you?"

"I don't know. I'd still be working there, I guess."

"Were you expecting to see Sis and the children this past weekend?"

Sam nodded. "Yes."

"Were you surprised when they didn't show up?"

"At first I was. But then I asked one of Arnold Matthews' grooms, and he told me Sis had a cold. Was that true?"

"Yes. It's true. You spent your time at Wharton in the company of Sis Matthews-Boyd?"

"Yes."

"And at the Matthews' estate in Pennsylvania?"

"Every chance we got."

"So how come Arnold Matthews didn't recognize you at the MacFarlands?"

From her expression, Michael concluded that she thought it was a stupid question.

"The last time I saw him, before this past weekend, was the summer of '98. You seem to know him. Does he strike you as the kind of man who'd pay that much attention to his daughter's friends? Plus, we hardly ever saw him. Look at me. I doubt my own father would recognize me, let alone Arnold Matthews."

She's got a point, Michael thought. "Where's Jarrah?"

"I really don't know."

"Could you find him?"

Sam didn't reply.

At the end of the day, and despite Brian's vehement objection, Michael took Sam back to his townhouse in Alexandria.

"Sleepin' with the enemy," Brian muttered, not caring who overheard, as the couple left the suite of offices.

"He is?" Dan asked after the door closed.

"I doubt it," Molly said before Brian could respond. "Michael's way too professional for that."

"Yeah, right." Brian's sarcastic reply left them in no doubt as to how he felt.

"I've seen the way she looks at him too," Molly continued. "But he wouldn't jeopardize all we've done so far just because he's attracted to her."

"God, I hope you're right."

"I am," Molly replied.

Michael's Townhouse, Duke Street, Old Town, Alexandria, Virginia
Later that evening

After putting Sam's bags in the guestroom, Michael ordered food to be delivered.

Back in the living room, Sam cradled a drink before the food arrived and then ate in silence.

"Nothing to say?" Michael asked when they'd finished eating.

"It's been a long day. I'm exhausted."

"Sorry to put you through it. It had to be done."

"I understand. It is over?"

The perfect opening. "Not exactly."

She faced him. "Why am I not surprised. What do you want now?"

"I want you to find Jarrah for me."

"You're joking?"

"No."

Sam stayed silent, but her eyes never left his. "On one condition," she said eventually. "I want to see the children first."

"After you find him."

"No, before." She got to her feet. "Otherwise, forget it. I'm going to bed."

"Before you go, how did you stay in contact with Sis?"

"She called me on my cell phone once a week."

"How come we couldn't trace it?"

Sam managed a small smile. "She never left a message. Just let it ring a couple of times. We programmed the phone to have a certain ring when she called. That's how I knew it was her and the children were okay. Occasionally, I'd get a letter that she mailed from her father's estate."

"Is that how she contacted you about the opening at the MacFarlands?"

"No, she called. There's a separate phone line for her father's stables. Sis still goes there on weekends to ride. Whoever does Arnold Matthews' books was hardly going to notice a call to Kentucky, even if they'd checked, which I doubt. They get calls from there all the time, and from all over the world."

Sam turned to go. "Are you coming with me?"

Michael shook his head. "It's complicated enough without us getting more involved."

"So just forget about you?"

"I didn't say that. We've got to wait until all this is over."

Sam studied him for a moment. "I believe you."

"Good. It's the smart thing to do."

The Rental Cottage, Cedar Lane, Bedminster, Pennsylvania
Wednesday, March 26, 2003

For the last few weeks, with Brian and Dan needed elsewhere, Michael was forced to cut back on surveillance. Only the CIA agents had been monitoring Sis.

"If I'd known I was going to spend almost six months in a bird hide, I'd have decorated and hung pictures," Bentley said at one point.

Consequently, Michael's early morning call to Eden gave them all hope that this particular assignment was fast coming to an end.

"Michael will be here this afternoon. After the boy gets back from school," Eden told Hunter and Bentley. "He's bringing the kids' mother with him."

"The suspected terrorist?" Bentley asked.

"I guess," he replied. "All I know is that if necessary we have to break cover and keep our subject from leaving the house."

"Oh, great," Bentley muttered.

"Look on the bright side," Hunter said. "It means we're probably finished here."

Michael's Office, G Street, Washington, D.C.
The same morning

At 8:15 a.m., Michael called a friend at the FBI.

"I need a favor," he said. "I've got fingerprints and some photographs..."

"Can you do it?" he asked after he'd finished explaining.

"No problem. Just get me what you've got, and I'll do the rest."

Fifteen minutes later, Dan found Sam sitting in the reception area, drinking a cup of coffee.

"Michael wants to see you," Molly said immediately. "He said to go straight in."

"Close the door," Michael said after Dan entered his office. "We're taking Sam to see the kids in Pennsylvania. I want you there to put the fear of God into Sis Matthews-Boyd."

"Then what?"

"The children stay with the Boyds."

"And Fareed?"

"I'm letting her go. She's going to find Jarrah for us."

Dan imagined too clearly what Brian would say. "Is that wise?" he said instead.

"It's my risk. My decision. Is that understood?"

Dan nodded. "I hope you know what you're doing."

Before they left the office, Michael handed Molly a business-sized envelope with a note attached.

"Can you take care of that?" he asked.

She quickly read his handwriting. "Lunchtime okay?"

"Perfect," he said.

The Matthews-Boyd Home, Spruce Hill Lane, Bedminster, Pennsylvania
Late afternoon

Michael's cell phone rang a few minutes from his destination.

"Subject's just arrived home with the children," Eden told him. "We're at the end of the driveway, in case she decides to leave."

"Stay there," Michael said. "I'm on my way."

Sis Matthews-Boyd's surprise was genuine as she opened the door to see Samin Fareed.

"Oh, my God! Sam!"

As the women embraced, tears already flowing, Michael stepped into view.

When Sis saw him, she took a step back. "You're—"

"Lieutenant Colonel Michael Correa," Sam interrupted. "And I think you've met Dan Whitney. They're with the Department of Justice."

"Dan?"

"Good afternoon, ma'am."

Sis could only shake her head.

"Where are the children?" Sam asked.

"In the kitchen," Sis replied. "Will someone please tell me what's going on?"

As Sam disappeared, Michael followed Sis into the foyer, while Dan signaled to the agents and then closed the front door.

"We need to talk, Mrs. Boyd," Michael said, as Sis was about to return to the kitchen, and handed her his card. "Let's use the living room. Sam needs some time with the children."

Sis ran a hand through her hair, hardly glancing at the card. "Er, yes, of course. This way."

She sat in stunned silence as Michael spun a very plausible story. Even Dan was impressed.

"... so if you'll continue to take care of the children, I know Sam would appreciate it."

"Yes. That won't be a problem."

She finally faced Dan. "You're not Dan Olsen?"

"No."

"Did you go to Princeton?"

Dan shook his head. "I drove through it once."

"Why did you lie to us?"

"Sam needed to know the children were really okay," Michael said quickly. "We had to get someone inside your house, without arousing suspicion, in case you were being watched."

"Oh, no! We're in danger?"

"Not at all. But now you know about Sam, I'm leaving the agents with you, until her assignment is over."

"Is that really necessary?" she asked.

"A precaution, that's all. Now please call your husband. We need him here."

Mark Boyd appeared as stunned as his wife, but seemed satisfied with Michael's answers to his few questions.

"So there's no danger if we keep the children?" he finally asked.

"No," Michael said. "Look at the agents as a tax-free safeguard." He got to his feet. "Let me introduce you to them."

"I miss seeing you at the bar," Boyd said quietly as Dan passed.

"Maybe I'll stop in sometime," he replied.

While Sam helped Sis put the baby to bed, Mark Boyd met agents Hunter, Eden, and Bentley. "One of them will be with your wife and the children at all times," Michael said.

"So much for our fast track outta here," Eden muttered.

Finally ready to leave, everyone gathered in the foyer.

Leave the best for last. Michael faced Sis. "You can call my office with any news of the children. It will then be passed on to Sam. Other than that, you'll have no contact with her. Is that clearly understood?"

Sis nodded.

He faced both Boyds. "If you have any concerns, talk to the agents. They're here for you." He turned to go. "One more thing," he added, addressing Sis. "Your father and I were at the MacFarlands' over the weekend. You are not, under any circumstances, to tell him who I am. Neither are you to mention my visit here with Miss Fareed. Do you understand?"

She nodded.

"Good. As we speak, FBI agents are with him explaining that you and your husband received a death threat. They even have the note. The FBI doesn't take kindly to threats like that. It's being done to protect you. And it will hold up under scrutiny."

Still trembling, Sis hugged Sam goodbye, while Michael motioned to the agents to follow him outside.

"Work out your own shifts," he said. "Leave the monitoring equipment and phone tap in place. Just in case."

"The bird hides?" Eden asked.

"Tom Morgan can pick them up. Look on the bright side. No more sneaking around."

"Sis Boyd's still our main subject?" Bentley said.

"Yes," Michael replied. "And don't let her ride roughshod over you."

"Won't happen."

"Did you really call in the FBI?" Bentley asked.

"Affirmative," he said. "We've come too far for this to get screwed up now. And yes, they know about you."

Unlike the ride to Pennsylvania, Sam rode back to D.C. in the passenger seat. Classical music played softly, and Dan's only comment from the Suburban's rear seat, before he fell asleep, was "Mark Boyd's an idiot."

Michael didn't disagree, but kept his opinion to himself.

"You okay?" he eventually said to Sam, after many miles.

"I'm fine."

"How were the children?"

"They hardly recognized me."

"You've changed your appearance."

"That's not it. Sis has been a good mother to them for almost seven months. They're very adaptable at that age, especially Susie. John has Sis's daughter to play with and enjoys his new school. It's a far better home environment than I could have given them." She stared through the side window at the passing night. "You terrified Sis."

"It was intentional."

Sam turned back. "She asked me twice if I was really working for you and the Department of Justice."

"What did you tell her?"

"I told her yes twice."

"Smart. And true."

"I assume that little stunt of getting Sis to call you was to keep me in line?"

I wondered when we'd get to that. "'Stunt' isn't the word I'd use."

"No, I don't suppose it is."

"Call it added insurance. If anything goes wrong, it's my head on the chopping block."

"I know," she said.

After leaving Dan and the Suburban in the office parking lot, Michael changed vehicles and drove with Sam to Alexandria, Virginia.

Michael's Townhouse, Duke Street, Old Town, Alexandria, Virginia
Later that night

"You kept your promise," Sam said.

"Did you doubt it?"

"Not really. Is it time to keep mine?"

"If you think you can find Jarrah without endangering yourself, yes."

"Where Jarrah's concerned there's always danger."

"We'll be monitoring you from the get-go."

She shook her head. "That's the fastest way to get me killed." She could tell from Michael's expression that he was having a hard time believing her.

"He's not a peasant," she continued. "He's well educated, intelligent, and crafty as a fox. I've seen the FBI's Most Wanted posters. Don't you think, with that kind of money being offered, that someone would have turned him in? It hasn't happened, because he's surrounded by fanatics like himself, and they're all just as capable as you of using high-tech toys. Unlike westerners, they don't care if they die. If I find him, I'll be searched and scanned, and if I survive his interrogation, I'll be watched like a hawk. He can spot surveillance a mile away."

Michael studied her. "So what you're saying is I let you go. No strings. You just disappear again?"

"It's the only way."

Sam refused his offer of a drink. He poured himself a Glenfiddich on the rocks, lit a small cigar, and took the chair opposite. "Do you know where he is?"

"No. But I know where I'd start."

"Go on."

"First of all ..." Sam began.

Michael listened to what she had to say and finished his drink. "I'll probably end up in Leavenworth," he said. "But you make a valid case."

"Then you agree?"

"Maybe."

"What about McDonald?" she asked. "According to you, he's looking for me too."

"Leave the two-faced weasel to me," he said. "What he doesn't know won't hurt him."

Michael's Office, G Street, Washington, D.C.
Thursday, March 27, 2003

When Michael did eventually arrive, he told Molly he needed to see Brian and Dan immediately.

They appeared within a minute, and Michael motioned for them to close the door.

As he anticipated, Brian was the first to speak. "Where's Miss Fareed?"

"Gone."

"She escaped?" Dan said.

Brian knew better. "I'm bettin' he let her go. Right, Michael?"

Before Michael could reply, Dan continued, "You can't be serious?"

"John McEnroe said it better. Brian's right. She's gone to find Jarrah for us."

"Like hell she has," Brian said.

Michael glared. "You're really beginning to piss me off. I took her to the airport this morning. And no, I'm not telling you which one, until I know I've got your cooperation on this."

"But we are monitoring her?" Dan asked.

"No."

Brian sat in a chair across from Michael's desk. "We know you're the big risk taker, but isn't this way over the top?"

"I don't think so, or I'd never have agreed."

"So what happens now?" Brian asked. "We sit around, twiddlin' our thumbs, on the unlikely event she's goin' to call?"

"No. You're going to Savannah. Talk to the Georgia Ports Authority. I want to know, as best you can determine, if that's where Jarrah's men and Wentworth's crates came in. Then I want you to find D.J. Perkins again and get those names he mentioned."

"What about me?" Dan asked.

"You and I ..."

There was a knock at the door, and Molly's head appeared. "Sorry to interrupt, but your father's on line two. He says it's urgent."

Michael picked up the receiver.

"I need to see you now," Francis said. "So unless you're meeting the president, this can't wait." He sounded angry.

"Fine. Where?"

"Langley. Soon as you can."

Then there was dial tone.

Michael got to his feet and picked up his jacket. "Gotta go. Brian, get packing for Savannah. Dan, we'll talk later."

Then he was gone.

"That didn't sound good," Dan said quietly as he heard the outer office door close.

"If this keeps up, we'll all be lookin' through the classifieds," Brian muttered. "I reckon Michael's stepped way over the line this time. And there ain't a damn thing we can do about it."

"Yes, there is. We can support him."

"You're kiddin'?"

"What he's done makes perfect sense, if you really think about it."

"How so?"

"If the terrorists are as good as we're beginning to believe, they'd spot a bug or a tail in an instant. You even commented about the way Fareed looks at him. I don't think it was an act. If she feels that strongly, I think she'll do it."

"If she can find Jarrah, and when she does, he don't kill her."

Dan hesitated. "True. But doesn't that prove Michael's point? She's risking her life to do this."

"I'm not convinced." Brian began to leave. "At least I get to go travelin' again. I gotta feelin' that this part of D.C.'s about to get real uncomfortable."

CIA Headquarters, Langley, Virginia
Early afternoon

On his arrival, Michael picked up his Visitor's Pass and headed directly to his father's office.

Mary Howard looked up as he came through the door. "Go straight in," she said. "He's waiting."

Francis was behind his desk. "Close the door," he said.

Michael did, and when he turned back, Francis was on his feet holding an 8 x 10 photograph.

"What the fuck is this?" Francis's voice rose dramatically as he waved the photograph. "What the fuck were you doing at Dulles this morning?" He threw the photograph at Michael. "I want an explanation. And I want it now!"

Silently, Michael studied the photograph. He wasn't big on public displays of affection, but when the airport's broadcast system announced the last call for Sam's flight, she turned to him. "I know you said we have to wait, but please kiss me goodbye. We might never see each other again."

The same thought had crossed his mind, so Michael honored her request, and it was no peck on the cheek. In fact, as Francis threw several more photographs in his direction, Michael hadn't realized they'd kissed for that long or, apparently, that passionately.

He now kicked himself for being so stupid. It would make perfect sense that an international airport as busy as Dulles would be under constant surveillance.

"We look good," he said, hoping some levity would calm his angry father.

It had the opposite effect.

"She's a goddamn terrorist! You've been sleeping with the enemy!"

Michael noticed it wasn't a question, and before he had time to reply, Francis leaped to his feet and exploded.

As he circled his desk, he began with "Asshole!" and by the time he finished with "Stupid sonofabitch!" he'd completed several circuits.

Michael remained seated and realized that there were very few letters of the alphabet his father had left out. He's also couldn't remember seeing him this angry. Francis was now a couple of shades shy of fire-engine red and was shaking when he finally sat again.

"You goddamn oversexed sorry excuse for a son!" he snapped. "You should be court-martialed. And I'll be the first in line to recommend it."

"I'm not. I shouldn't. And you can't be," Michael replied.

"You should be horsewhipped, before walking the plank!"

"That's the Navy, Dad. I'm Army."

Francis began to rise. "Any more lip from you, mister, and I'll have you dragged outta here in handcuffs!"

"I'd like to see you try."

"Don't you threaten me!"

"I didn't sleep with her," Michael added quietly. "It crossed my mind, but I didn't."

"You're a barefaced liar!"

Michael stood. "Great. My own father doesn't believe me. So from now on, if the president wants you informed, he's going to have to tell you himself." He turned to go. "Don't expect a Christmas card either."

"Sit down!"

"Go fuck yourself, Dad," Michael added, scooping up the photographs before opening the office door and leaving it that way as he left.

"Oh, shit," Francis muttered, watching him go.

Before Michael left the parking lot, he dialed a familiar number.

"Good afternoon, Colonel," the male voice said. "Do you need to speak with the president?"

"Yes," Michael replied. "I need to brief him in person."

"I'll make sure he knows."

"Thank you," Michael said and hung up.

He didn't make his second call until after he'd left Langley.

"Doing anything for dinner?" he asked when Dan answered.

"Nothing planned," Dan said.

"My place?" Michael added. "We need to talk."

"Sounds good. I'll call you when I'm leaving."

"And tell Molly I won't be back."

"Sure thing," Dan replied and hung up. *This really doesn't sound good.*

Michael's Townhouse, Duke Street, Old Town, Alexandria, Virginia
Later that evening

Dan couldn't stop laughing. Considering the seriousness of the situation, Michael thought it was a peculiar reaction, to say the very least. But Dan's laughter as he viewed the photographs was infectious.

Dan wiped his eyes. "You've got the complete set. You could have them framed." He swiveled on the barstool. "That wall would be great. Or sell them on eBay." He turned back. "What was your father's reaction?"

"Nothing like yours." Michael chuckled as he stirred a pot on the stove. "The opposite, in fact."

"How was it left?"

"I think my last words to him were 'go fuck yourself, Dad.'"

"That's not good. Pissing off the director of the CIA, who just happens to be your father. Double whammy." Dan took a drink of his beer. "What now?"

"Before you arrived, I got a call. I meet with the president in the morning. After that, if I still have a job, we need to find Sadilov. Agreed?" Michael spooned the contents of the pot onto two plates. "Hope you're hungry?"

"I didn't know you could cook like that," Dan said, finishing the last mouthful of food. "You'd make someone a great wife."

"If it doesn't go well tomorrow, it could well come to that. A cook in Leavenworth's canteen."

"Why Leavenworth?"

"Right now, that's where my father thinks I belong."

"Jesus. You really did piss him off."

Michael nodded. "The press would have a field day if they knew the returning director of the CIA can sound like a foul-mouthed drunken grunt in an Army barracks brawl. Sadilov?"

"They appear to be heading south. Although I did think about the 'red herring' angle. What do you think?"

"South. But if I'm right, what's their target? If they've planned for this long, it's gotta be something big. Nothing on a major holiday. They're too smart for that."

"I've looked at the map," Dan said. "And I agree with you. There's a lot of military bases in and around Georgia. But with the war in Afghanistan and Iraq, most of our troops are being deployed. They've already hit the heart of New York. Security in D.C. is on high alert. There's not a nuclear power plant anywhere close. That leaves?"

"I wish I knew."

"The G-8 Summit. Isn't that being held in Savannah?"

"In 2004. So why would they snatch Sadilov more than a year in advance?"

"But they'd take out the leaders and the senior members of their cabinets of the eight most powerful nations on earth. That would cause unbelievable chaos."

"Good point." Michael got to his feet. "Coffee?"

Dan nodded. "Then I've got to go. Do I pack for tomorrow?"

"Hold off, until after my meeting."

As he was leaving, Dan picked up one of the photographs of Michael and Sam.

"When you've got some time, I'd like to know how you do this."

Then he grinned broadly and escaped through the door, a second before Michael was about to throw an empty beer can in his direction.

Rome, Italy
Friday, March 28, 2003

Sam's Alitalia flight arrived at Leonardo Da Vinci at 7:45 a.m., Rome time.

Her Continental flight from Dulles to Newark the previous morning left her with only a four-hour wait before boarding the nonstop flight to Rome. Both she and Michael agreed that waiting for any connecting flight was dangerous, but he hoped to lower the odds of her detection by using the New Jersey airport. Although she was traveling on her Samantha Conti passport and her appearance was very different from the way she'd looked when McDonald last saw her, Michael didn't want to take any chances that the man from MI-6 could well have spies in place, regardless of the fact he had no jurisdiction.

After clearing customs, Sam picked up her one piece of checked luggage and headed for the nearest payphone.

When Michael and his team searched her bags in D.C. and found nothing, she was sure they'd been looking for something like a little black book, with names and telephone numbers. She had one. In her head. Figures came naturally to her, and being able to remember countless long numbers was one of the reasons she'd been chosen to pose as Jarrah's wife. She'd been initially surprised, as they seemed to know so much about her, that no one, including Michael, had connected that possibility to her Wharton accounting degree.

She now dialed the only person in Rome she knew she could trust.

The phone rang seven times. Then a sleepy male voice answered.

"It's Samin," she said.

There was a pause. "Samin? Il miei bello e seductive, Samin." Alberto switched to heavily accented English. "How long I have waited. I knew you'd come back to me. Where are you?"

"The airport."

"I will come for you, si?"

Sam thought she heard a female voice in the background. "No, Alberto, I'll take a taxi. It sounds as though you have company."

Alberto gave a theatrical sigh. "She is nothing compared to you," he whispered. "She will be gone by the time you arrive."

Sam gave the cab driver the address to Alberto's villa on the outskirts of Rome, in fluent Italian. The son of a very wealthy Italian industrialist, Alberto had far too much money and time at his disposal when she'd first met him. He was, in her mind, almost too pretty for a man, and the word "playboy" was particularly apt. After he'd tried unsuccessfully to romance her, they became friends. He'd never given up on the idea that one day she'd be his prize, but Sam had no intention of joining the very long list of Alberto's conquests. She knew he wasn't gay, but she suspected that he could very well be bisexual. And with his money and looks, he could take his pick of either sex.

It was a business-savvy girlfriend who suggested to Alberto that he open a designer furniture and accessories boutique catering to Europe's young and wealthy. Lending his name to the overpriced items would only attract more business, she said. To Alberto, it had been just another toy to play with, until the company became an overnight success. With an ever-increasing "money no object" clientele, Sam gladly supplied him with exquisite and grossly expensive Persian rugs.

He was waiting on the steps to the villa, having buzzed the cab through the ornate security gates, and Sam's first reaction was he looked as though he'd been poured into his skin-tight leather pants.

Alberto kissed her on both cheeks. Then he hugged her and kissed her again before paying for the cab.

Sam tried to protest.

Alberto flung his hands in the air. "It is nothing," he said. "I would have bought you an airplane if I thought you would come." He picked up her bag and put his arm through hers. "Why are you here?"

As they entered the villa, Sam began to explain.

She'd slept on the overnight flight. So after a long lunch with Alberto, with the excuse that she had to go clothes shopping, she temporarily left him on a downtown street.

"We meet again later, yes?" he said as she was about to enter a Gucci boutique. He waved his arm. "At my place? It is beautiful, yes?"

She turned to the store opposite. "Yes, Alberto, it's beautiful."

He beamed and kissed her hand. "I will be waiting."

Via the plate-glass windows of the Gucci boutique, she watched him cross the street and disappear before beginning her search for a payphone.

When she found one, Sam punched a long series of digits that accessed not only a calling card, but also a German telephone number.

A woman answered on the fifth ring.

"It's Nina," Sam said in English. A woman had never answered before, and although she'd memorized the password, it had been so long.

Think. Think. "I need to speak with Isabelle," Sam continued as the name flashed into her head.

"This is Isabelle."

"I would like to visit," she added. "How's the weather?"

"The weather is very mixed."

"Shall I call again?"

"Tomorrow. It might have improved."

"Thank you. I'll do that." Sam hung up. *Damn!*

If the authorities were monitoring the call, unless they'd gotten a lot better, they'd have no idea that Sam was being told it was unsafe for her to visit. "The weather is very mixed" meant the group or an individual was under possible surveillance. The code had worked well for several years, and as Sam left the phone booth, she was grateful that the number still worked. If it hadn't, her chances of finding Jarrah would have dramatically decreased.

Another day with Alberto, she thought. *I can live with that. Now I really need to go shopping.*

The White House, Pennsylvania Avenue, Washington, D.C.
The same morning, Eastern Standard Time

Michael arrived in plenty of time and was escorted to the basement-level room where he and Makepeace had viewed the videotape. This time, the Secret Service agent told him the president apologized for the delay then closed the door, leaving Michael alone.

Michael looked around, thankful the screen wasn't immediately visible, unsure whether to sit or stand.

As the minutes ticked by, he finally sat. In the soundproof room, he wasn't able to hear anything beyond the door, but he felt sure he'd hear the door opening.

When it did, Michael was on his feet in an instant.

Makepeace entered alone, and someone immediately closed the door behind him.

He held out his hand. "Michael, sorry to keep you waiting." He then placed a black folder on a small table. "It's been a helluva morning."

"I won't keep you, sir. But there've been some developments. I thought a briefing face to face was in order."

Makepeace half sat on the table. "What's going on?"

Michael's briefing was short and to the point, although he left out a few minor details.

"You trust this woman?" Makepeace asked when he'd finished.

"Yes, sir, I do."

Makepeace flipped open the black folder and picked up the photograph inside. "I guess she trusts you."

When Michael saw the image, he wanted a large hole to swallow him. *I'm dead.*

"When you've had enough of Special Ops, I suggest you try Hollywood. You'll make a fortune." Makepeace waved the photograph. "No wonder women fall at your feet." He then grinned broadly. "Got my blood racing."

Michael couldn't remember a time when he'd been this embarrassed. "My father thinks I should be sent to Leavenworth, sir."

Makepeace laughed. "He does, does he? Typical father reaction. I can assure you that the only time I envisage you going to Leavenworth is to interrogate prisoners."

"I sincerely apologize, sir."

"What for? If the first lady sees this, she'll want your autograph."

Michael was horrified. "She's not going to see it, is she, sir?"

Makepeace replaced the photograph in the folder. "Not on my watch. Or anyone else's." He was back to business. "I assume from your comment that Francis knows?"

"Yes, sir. Our meeting yesterday didn't go well."

Makepeace raised an eyebrow. "He disapproves of your decision?"

"In the strongest possible terms, sir."

The president studied an expression that was unreadable. "But you feel you've done the right thing?"

"Yes, sir. I take full responsibility. It was my decision and mine alone. If I thought there was another way, I'd have found it. She's taking a phenomenal risk on our behalf."

Makepeace grunted. "How's the head? Matthews and MacFarland were most concerned."

"It was nothing, sir."

"Maybe not to you. But thanks anyway. They feel so badly, it's swelled the campaign coffers."

"Glad I could help, sir."

"They don't suspect a thing. Haven't a clue who you really are. I'll make sure it stays that way."

"Thank you, sir."

Makepeace turned to leave. "I fully support what you're doing in a tough situation." He reached the door. "And stay away from my daughter." He opened the door. "Just joking," he added with a grin, disappearing from view.

The Secret Service agent appeared immediately. "Ready, Colonel?"

Michael could only nod.

He never smoked in the car, but Michael was puffing on a small cigar as he swept through the private entrance and out into Washington's lunchtime traffic.

Michael's Office, G Street, Washington, D.C.
A short time later

To Dan's surprise, when he entered Michael's office, Michael was drinking something that looked remarkably like scotch.

"Stockade?" Dan asked.

"Celebration," Michael replied. "I got the president's approval."

Dan sat, still eyeing the drink. "Still, you never drink at lunchtime."

"Makepeace had a copy of the photograph."

"In that case, pour a bigger one."

Michael finished the scotch. "Before anyone changes their mind, I think we should get the hell outta D.C."

"I'm with you there. When?"

"Tonight or tomorrow. I haven't decided."

"If we went tonight, you could see Lynn."

"What about you?"

"I'm sure there are hotels in Columbia." Dan stopped. "How's Sam going to get in touch with you?"

"Call my cell phone."

"What if they find the number?"

"She didn't write it down. She said she was good at numbers and would remember it." Michael stopped. "Oh, fuck," he added quietly. "I think I've just made a monumental error in judgment. Did you hear what I said?"

"I'm not following."

"What are my cell phone numbers?"

Dan shrugged. "They're programmed on speed dial." He flipped open his cell phone.

"Stop," Michael said. "Don't look. Tell me."

"I can't."

"Exactly. How many numbers do you know?"

Dan closed his eyes. "Not that many."

"Get my point? We didn't find an address book, or anything remotely like one. Why? Because she memorizes everything. And I'll bet that includes not only telephone numbers and addresses, but bank accounts, credit cards, God knows what."

"Shit," Dan said. "Now what do we do? Follow her and get her back?"

"She's long gone. How could I have been this stupid." He faced Dan. "Don't answer that."

"I wasn't going to."

"Hold the fort," Michael said to Molly thirty minutes later. "We're leaving. I'll be in touch."

"Will you be gone long?"

"Can't say. Could be a few days."

"Or even years," Dan muttered.

"What should I do if anyone needs to speak with you?"

"Take messages."

"From your father too?"

"Especially him."

Something's going on, Molly thought, watching them leave. *They didn't even tell me where they were going, or why.*

Outside, in the parking lot, Michael pointed to the Suburban that Dan normally drove.

"Get everything you need. We're going to Baltimore to get another vehicle."

"Reason?" Dan asked.

"I don't trust my father. He's so pissed off, I wouldn't put it past him to try to have me tailed. I've got enough problems without him bugging my ass."

"Fine with me," Dan said. "He doesn't know about the warehouse?"

"I hope not. How soon can you pack?"

"Won't take long."

"Good," Michael replied. "Your place first."

After leaving Dan's apartment, he'd expected they'd go to Baltimore and pick up a nondescript car from the warehouse. Then head south. He was wrong on both counts.

A Classified Address, Baltimore, Maryland
Late afternoon

Having told Boost what he wanted, Michael then scanned the two rows of vehicles.

"See anything you like, Colonel?" the corporal asked.

Michael shook his head and kept on walking.

Now almost at the end of the warehouse, he stopped. "What's that?" He turned back to Boost. "Saving the best for last?"

It was the only vehicle Dan could see that was protected by a dust cover.

Boost removed the cover.

"That's more like it," Michael said.

Dan eyed the car. "Sweet wheels. And the perfect place to park it. How many explosives are behind that wall?"

"Enough to take out several city blocks, Mr. Whitney," Boost replied.

"Did Tom call Picatinny?" Michael asked him.

"Yessir. They're coming Monday."

Michael circled the car. "What's the lowdown?"

"2001 Aston Martin DB7 12-cylinder Vantage coupe. Less than 7,000 miles. Got Touchtronic transmission, a premium audio system, and goes like the wind." Boost turned back to the car. "She's perfect for you, sir. That's Jaguar Regent Gray paintwork, and the interior's charcoal and stone leather."

Michael opened the driver's door and slid inside.

"See, Colonel, she fits you like a glove."

"I didn't know they made gloves that expensive," Dan said.

Michael ran his hands around the wheel. "History? And it better be legal."

"It is, sir. From a real bad ass in Long Island. I had to do a helluva deal to get it away from the Feds."

"How much of a deal?"

"Nothing I can't find again, sir."

"You're sure?"

"Yessir. I'm real sure."

"Fine, I'll take it. Keep the Jag. And keep it off the road until I give the OK."

"Understood, sir." Boost ran his hand over the immaculate high-gloss fender. "Tags, Colonel? Take your pick."

"Connecticut and Florida," Michael replied. "With all the relevant documents. Just in case."

"It'll take a few minutes, sir." And without waiting for Michael's reply, the corporal broke into a jog, heading toward the office at the other end of the warehouse.

Dan sat in the passenger seat. "Now this is what I call the perfect undercover vehicle. Costs more than most homes, and I'll bet they only sell a few hundred a year in the entire United States."

"It's gray."

"I'd noticed. Well, so much for keeping a low profile, Mr. Bond."

Michael laughed. "Want that Chevy back there?"

Dan shook his head. "If we're going down, let's do it in style."

"My thoughts exactly."

Instead of heading back to D.C. on I-95, Michael headed east.

"We're going to Eagles Nest for the weekend," Michael said when Dan asked. "I need the break, and so do you. Plus, I don't want to be stuck in Friday traffic heading south. This'll be bad enough."

They crawled in three lines of bumper-to-bumper traffic on Route 50 toward the Chesapeake Bay Bridge.

"I could get used to this," Dan commented at one point. "This car's a big-time chick magnet."

"So you don't think I'm crazy?"

Dan smiled at a young blonde behind the wheel of a BMW convertible in the next lane. "I didn't say that."

Michael's cell phone rang.

"It's Molly," he said before flipping it open.

Dan listened to the one-sided conversation.

"How gruesome?" Michael asked a minute into the conversation.

"Good," he said after the reply. "Wait 'til I give you a green light. Then send them." He snapped the phone shut. "I've got to call McDonald in the morning," Michael continued before Dan had time to ask. "That's going to be fun."

Then he explained.

Eagles Nest, Somewhere off Route 301, the Eastern Shore, Maryland
That night

"The boat will be here tomorrow, according to Tom," Michael said, stroking Delta's nose. "I'll be with this guy in the morning. So kick back. I'm hoping the downtime will give us some new ideas."

It was obvious to Dan that Michael was very attached to the horse. "Fine with me. Got a fishing pole?"

"Several."

"Then I'll fish. You ride."

"Okay by me."

Rome, Italy
Saturday, March 29, 2003

Alberto insisted that Sam meet a group of his friends at a well-known downtown ristoranti, where wealthy Romans and visitors alike went to see and be seen. With tables and chairs spilling onto the cobbled piazza, it was a mecca for paparazzi, and the last place she wanted or needed to be. With cameras continually being pointed in their direction, she couldn't wait to escape. On the other hand, Alberto basked in the limelight.

With flashbulbs popping, and Alberto distracted, Sam made her way to the restroom and hopefully a payphone.

She found one in a narrow passageway. Surrounded by men and women constantly coming and going, her first thought was what the English referred to as a "public telephone" was the perfect name.

She made the call. Like the previous day, her conversation was brief. According to Isabelle, "the weather is still mixed."

After Sam hung up, she wondered how long she should wait in Rome, or whether she should just risk going to Berlin.

She looked up to see Alberto. "I thought you had left me again, il miei bello?" he said.

"I would never do that," she lied.

Eagles Nest, Somewhere off Route 301, the Eastern Shore, Maryland
Early the same morning

Michael took his coffee onto the deck and dialed one of the numbers McDonald had given him. It was 1:00 p.m. in England, and he hoped he was interrupting McDonald's lunch or maybe a golf game, although he wasn't sure if the British spymaster was the type to play golf.

"I've found Fareed," Michael said after McDonald answered on the second ring.

"Fantastic, old boy," McDonald replied. "Are you keeping her? Or sending her to us?"

Michael couldn't control a smile. "She's no good to us. She's yours if you want her." He could almost hear McDonald thinking.

"Did she tell you anything?"

"Nothing."

"She'll talk to me."

"Don't bet on it," Michael said.

"Oh, we've been at this a little longer than you. We've got all sorts of tricks up our sleeve."

Arrogant SOB. "Really? Do those 'tricks' include a medium?"

McDonald hesitated. "I'm not sure I'm understanding you?"

"We think it's simple," Michael continued. "She's dead."

McDonald almost shouted, "How?"

"Auto accident in West Virginia. The state police think she fell asleep at the wheel. There was an eighteen-wheeler stopped on the hard shoulder. When they eventually extracted what was left of the car, the body inside was unrecognizable. It could only be identified through fingerprints."

"How did they get her fingerprints?"

Michael sounded bored. "From the hands."

"No, no," McDonald said. "How did they know it was her?"

"They didn't. Someone in my office regularly checks on police reports. The body matched her description. We asked the local coroner for a copy of his report. That's when we knew."

"How did you get her fingerprints?"

"That's classified. Even to you."

"When was this?"

"About a month ago," Michael said casually.

McDonald raised his voice. "And you're only telling me now!" He was, Michael thought, beginning to sound like his father.

"I've been busy."

"Bollocks! I want to see the remains."

"Not possible. West Virginia doesn't store unclaimed bodies. She was cremated."

"How convenient."

"Sorry," Michael said. "But I've got copies of the autopsy photographs and the coroner's report I can send you. Did you know she took drugs?"

"Drugs? What drugs?"

Michael was enjoying himself. "According to the report, the blood analysis showed large amounts of cocaine in her system."

"That's not possible."

"Why's that?"

"Never mind," McDonald said. "Send me everything you've got."

"Sure," Michael replied. "No problem. Sorry it didn't pan out. Maybe we can collaborate again sometime?"

McDonald had to force the words "I'll look forward to it."

Michael snapped his cell phone shut. "Gotcha."

On the other side of the Atlantic, McDonald replaced his phone in his pocket. *Bloody hell,* he thought. *I think I've just been outplayed at my own game.*

Michael was smiling all the way to Delta's stable, and he wasn't quite sure how the horse knew he was in a good mood. Delta was in high spirits but behaved perfectly, and for the first time, Michael understood what Sally Ridgeway had kept telling him: "Become one with the horse."

"You looked good out there," Dan said several hours later, having watched horse and rider from the bedroom window. "When the president first suggested it, I never thought you'd take it this far."

"Neither did I," Michael said. "But everyone needs a hobby. Right?"

Dan looked toward the Bay. "What do you call that then?"

Michael turned to see his boat approaching, with Tom at the helm. "That's the hole in the water, surrounded by fiberglass, into which I pour money."

"Stupid of me. I hadn't realized Delta, the stables, miles of paddock fencing, new Suburban and two-horse trailer, and general upkeep were on clearance at Sam's Club."

Michael laughed. "Okay, two hobbies. Want to buy a boat?"

"Not after what you've just said." Dan eyed the forty-six-foot Viking as Tom came alongside the dock. "I'd need to win the lottery before I could afford the gas."

"It's only money," Michael replied, stepping onboard. "How's she running, Tom?"

They spent the afternoon on Chesapeake Bay.

Dan was feeling no pain after several beers, and as the afternoon wore on, a cold March wind and the medium chop seemed to melt away.

Back on dry land, Dan and Tom were left to barbecue, while Michael checked on Delta.

"He seems more relaxed," Dan said.

"'Bout time," Tom replied. "This mission's really got to him. He's not used to coming up empty like this. He needs the downtime. So do you."

Dan kept forgetting that Tom had been with Michael since his Army career began. He looked around. "I know it's none of my business, but how does he afford all this?"

Tom chuckled. "He never told you?"

"No. But then I've never asked."

"You don't really know what he used to do, before all this civilian crap, do you?"

Dan shook his head. "I hear bits and pieces."

"Let's just say, he got well rewarded for taking huge risks. And he earned every penny. But most of the money comes from his maternal grandfather's estate. Wealthy family." Tom flipped the steaks. "The fast cars, the boat, and the women, that's his way of letting off steam. Most of the time, he's consumed with the job. Mind you, that horse has bin good for him. Never thought I'd see the day."

Tom lowered his voice. "His father plays strictly by the book. Michael's mother was a different story. That's where I reckon he gets it, and why he and his dad clash."

"You heard about that?"

"There's not much I don't know," Tom added. "Remember that."

Tybee Island, Georgia
The same day

Brian couldn't be bothered to get another flight and rental car, so he drove to Savannah, checking in at the Ocean Plaza for the third time.

Even though it was well past midnight, the same young woman was on the front desk.

"Welcome back again, Mr. Mullen," she said.

"Good to be back. You ever leave?"

She laughed. "The night guy called in sick, and I can always use the extra money."

Brian slept in, and after a hearty breakfast, he drove down Butler Avenue toward the north end of the island.

It is good to be back, he thought, turning into the small trailer park and stopping at Leisha Johnson's mobile home.

A young woman was hanging washing on a clothesline, and as Brian approached, she turned.

"Mr. Brian? Otis didn't say nothin' 'bout you coming."

He hardly recognized her. Gone was the flamboyant outfit and jewelry and elaborate hairstyle. Instead, Leisha wore a tee shirt and shorts, her long black hair in a ponytail, and her face was devoid of any makeup. She looked, Brian thought, like a beautiful young girl.

"He didn't know, Ms. Johnson. It was goin' to be a surprise." And wondered which of them was the most surprised.

"He'll be awful happy you're here."

"Where is he?"

She picked up the empty clothesbasket. "Library. He rides that bicycle you got him for Christmas everywhere."

She looked at her watch, and he noticed the "talons" were gone too. "He should be back soon." She lowered her voice, although Brian didn't know why. "He's doing real good in school."

"Pleased to hear it. How about you?"

"I got a job," she said. "The Wal-Mart on Whitemarsh Island. I get one Saturday off a month. This is it." She hesitated. "You can wait inside."

Brian followed her into the trailer and looked around. "How are the boyfriends?"

She fixed on him with her almond-shaped eyes. "I don't do that no more. You can sit down, if you like."

It was obvious to Brian that was all she was going to say on the subject. And it was all she needed to say.

He sat. "I need to ask you ..." he began.

"You don't have to," she said when he'd finished.

"I know. But I'd like to."

"That's real nice, thank you. Otis never stops talkin' 'bout you. It's like he's a changed boy."

When Otis did appear, he jumped up and down, and to Brian's amazement, still holding several library books, he gave Brian a hug.

That afternoon, Brian drove him into Savannah, and with Leisha's permission, they returned to the trailer with a new computer.

Brian spent the rest of the weekend hooking up the computer and loading educational software.

"No games," Brian told him. "This isn't a toy."

"You listen to Mr. Brian," Leisha said. "Don't you let him down now. He ain't foolin' with you, Otis."

On Sunday evening, Otis tried to stop Brian from leaving. "I gotta work tomorrow, son. But I'll see you after school. How's that?"

Reluctantly, Otis agreed.

Brian then drove straight to Skipper's, but D.J. Perkins wasn't there.

"Haven't seen him for a few days," the barmaid said. "Try back tomorrow."

Chapter Twenty-Five

Rome, Italy
Monday, March 31, 2003

Sam was exhausted. Spending the weekend with Alberto was bad enough. Losing an hour's sleep due to European Daylight Saving just compounded the problem. She knew Alberto slept. She just wasn't sure when. Since late Saturday afternoon it seemed to her that most of the patrons from the downtown ristoranti where they'd had lunch began arriving at the villa, and the party, where wine and hard liquor flowed like water, hadn't stopped until the early hours of Monday morning.

I have to get out of here, she thought, now alone in the kitchen. *Sex, drugs, and rock and roll isn't for me.* She was immediately reminded of Michael.

Almost sure at that time of the morning she would remain undisturbed, she took the risk and picked up the nearest telephone.

The same woman answered on the third ring.

Sam asked again about the weather. Unlike her first two abortive attempts, this time she got the reply, "The weather is fine."

Having had the previous two days to fully remember the code, Sam continued, "I would like to visit."

"We would like that," Isabelle said.

"I enjoy the theater. May I see the leading production?"

"I will arrange it."

"Thank you," Sam said. "I will call again to confirm my arrival."

"We will look forward to it," Isabelle replied, before hanging up.

When Sam replaced the receiver, she was smiling. Her hunch had paid off. According to the conversation, it was safe to go, Jarrah was there, and best of all, he was expecting her.

She left the kitchen. *All I have to do now is get a car.*

An hour later, Alberto found her sitting by the pool.

Dressed in a bathrobe and wearing very dark glasses, his hair was a mess, and he hadn't shaved. He sat opposite her and groaned, "Oh, my poor head."

Sam only laughed.

"I keep doing this. Why do I keep doing this?"

His question didn't need a reply. "Alberto, I need a favor," Sam said instead.

He lifted his glasses and squinted at her with bloodshot eyes. "For you, il mio amore, anything."

Now dressed and shaved, Alberto waved his hand at the vehicles in front of them. "Choose the one you like."

Sam eyed his collection of expensive and exotic cars. "The Mercedes."

"No," he said. "It is a car for donna anziana." He kissed her hand. "And you are not an old woman."

Sam thought the black E-Class four-door sedan, although luxurious, was still nicely understated.

Alberto pointed to the bright yellow Porsche Carrera. "That is the one for you." He caressed the fender. "This one is perfect, si?"

Sam was almost tempted. "No, Alberto, it isn't. I would like to borrow the Mercedes."

He attempted to shake his head, but his hangover got the better of him. "Take it," he said. "It is yours."

"I can't do that."

"Yes," he said, throwing her the keys. "I am glad to be rid of it. Now I will have space for a better one, si?"

After two cups of very strong coffee, Alberto looked and was feeling marginally better. But as hard as he tried, he couldn't stop Sam from leaving.

"I'll return the car," she said.

"It is yours. Keep it. My gift to you." Then he hesitated. "You will come back to me, yes?"

Sam smiled. "Of course."

He was still watching from the steps of the villa as Sam turned through the gates and out of sight.

When she felt she was far enough away, she pulled over and stopped. She'd really done a lot of clothes shopping, and her bags had swelled to three. On top of one bag was a map.

After studying it again for some time, she finally put the Mercedes in gear and headed out of Rome.

Eagles Nest, Somewhere off Route 301, the Eastern Shore, Maryland
The same morning

Dan found Michael on the deck.

"You were up early," Dan said.

"Thought I'd take a ride before we left."

"I've been thinking about that. Where exactly are we going?"

"South."

"Where south? And how do we start?"

"Beats me," Michael replied. "I hoped you'd have got some ideas by now."

Dan laughed and looked around. "Nothing that strikes me. Mind you, it's a nice day for a drive."

Michael grinned. "That's a fact."

Michael's cell phone rang. "It's my father again. He's already called twice."

"You're not going to answer it?"

"Hell, no. Let him stew."

As Michael turned to go, Dan was left to wonder if ignoring the director of the CIA was a smart thing to do, even if he was your father.

"Now that's what I call a good-looking hunk of metal," Tom said in the driveway, eyeing the Aston Martin.

Michael slid behind the wheel.

"You take care, sir," Tom continued. "Delta will be fine. Call if you need me."

"Thanks, Tom."

"Let's take the scenic route," Michael said at the end of the long driveway, "301 to Norfolk. In the meantime, think fast."

Georgia Ports Authority, Route 25, Port Wentworth, Georgia
An hour later

At the red brick building with a circular drive, Brian entered through the double glass doors and flashed his ID at the uniformed Ports Authority police officer behind the reception desk.

"I got an appointment with the chief," Brian said.

After signing in, he was given directions, and after showing his ID to the guard at Gate 5, he easily found the Ports Authority police building.

"What's this about, Mr. Mullen?" the chief asked, studying Brian's business card. "You're a long way from D.C."

"We suspect that members of al Qaeda came in through this port," Brian said. "Would that have been possible before 9/11?"

"Unfortunately, yes. The crews on the container ships were basically free to come and go as they pleased."

"And after 9/11?"

"Like everyone else, we stepped up security, and continue to do so. As long as they had some form of ID, we wouldn't have questioned it. Of course, like I said, that's all changing."

"What about a container from the Port of London, cleared by British customs, say toward the end of 2002?"

"What was in this container?"

"Manifest said household items."

"That would have been arranged by an agent. Then collected by truck and taken to its destination. We don't get many of those. Most of the port's containers go to large distribution centers. We even have our own train terminal."

"So it wouldn't have raised any red flags?"

The chief lowered his voice. "With the volume handled here on a daily basis, right now, we check roughly ten percent." He paused. "We're more inclined to check containers from the Middle East, and a few other places, rather than Great Britain."

"What other places?"

"South America, for starters." He hesitated. "Is there something I should know about? It's not often DoJ comes to visit."

Brian got to his feet. "I was just checkin', that's all." He stopped at the door. "Just keep doin' what you're doin', Chief."

Damn it! Brian thought as he drove away. *With these guys' expertise in usin' fake documents, I'll bet this is where they came in. The container was a risk that paid off.*

Parkhotel Leipzigerhof, Defreggerstrasse 13, Innsbruck, Austria
Late that night, Austrian time

Before leaving Rome, Sam made the reservation. She knew, if needed, she could get to Berlin in about thirteen and a half hours, without holdups or lengthy stops for gas, but due to Alberto's raging hangover, she lost her early start.

Although she made good time, it wasn't until she got on the Autostrada Del Sole, north of Firenze, that her pace rapidly increased. Whenever possible, she set the cruise control to 161 kph, on a road surface that put America's interstates to shame. The Mercedes was designed for driver and passenger comfort at speeds that stateside would probably have got her thrown in jail. Consequently, this Mercedes was nothing like the "mobile kitchens" that the American public had come to expect from their automobiles. Unlike its U.S. counterpart, there were no cup holders.

As the car ate up the kilometers, Sam tried hard to forget why she was heading toward the Alps and fervently hoped that she wasn't racing toward the gates of hell.

At the spectacular Brenner Pass, she crossed the border into Austria and stopped at a scenic rest area to stretch her legs and take full advantage of the pure mountain air. Had the reason for her journey not been so dangerous, Sam knew she'd be enjoying herself far more.

She checked in to the Best Western-owned hotel around 7:00 p.m. and made her way directly to a Defreggerstube restaurant, complete with a beer garden and cozy bar.

Being a Monday night, the restaurant was relatively quiet, and she sat alone and undisturbed at a corner table. She'd picked up a German newspaper in the lobby, and after placing her order with a waiter who spoke English, she scanned the first page of the *Berliner Morganpost*. Although her spoken German was sporadic at best, she could understand the written word far better.

To her horror, in one of the articles, she saw a name she knew. Marokkaner Mounir al-Motassadeq.[12] He'd been arrested by the German authorities in Hamburg, suspected of being part of the 9/11 attacks on the World Trade Center and the Pentagon, and went on trial in February. Sam couldn't understand whether he'd been sentenced or was still in custody. Not that it mattered. Because now, according to the newspaper's reporter, another possible terrorist suspect had been arrested in Berlin late the previous night. But this time, no name was given. All it said, as far as Sam could tell, was a man in his mid-thirties.

Shivers ran down her spine. *Did I call Isabelle before or after the arrest? Is there any connection to Jarrah? Is it still safe to go? Am I driving into a trap?*

Sam swallowed hard and took a large gulp of wine. *If I get into trouble, can Michael save me?*

When her dinner order arrived, she could hardly eat, but could only thank her lucky stars that she'd stopped overnight.

After making a decision, she did eat her meal and then left the hotel on foot.

With the Parkhotel Leipzigerhof being so close to the center of Innsbruck, it didn't take her long to find a payphone.

She placed the call. As the woman who answered sounded familiar, Sam assumed that she was again speaking with Isabelle.

Sam asked the same questions and still got the "all clear" replies. Then she broke code and added, "Are you absolutely sure?"

There was a long hesitation. "I am sure."

"I read the morning paper," Sam continued. "I can delay my visit, if necessary."

Again there was an agonizing delay. "There is no need. You are expected."

By whom? she thought, hanging up.

Wishing she had a laptop to surf the web, she began to leave the phone booth. *I should have bought one in Rome,* she thought. *I have plenty of money.* Then she stopped. *What an idiot I am.*

Sam turned back to the phone and dialed an even longer series of numbers. The phone rang four times before the connection was made.

---

12 After a second trial, in Hamburg, Germany, he was eventually convicted
   in August 2005 for his part in the 9/11 attacks on the World Trade Center.
   Sentenced to seven years.

En route to Georgia, USA

Now on I-95, Michael stopped at the same truck stop that Brian had used and got gas.

"Want something to drink at Denny's?" he asked Dan.

"Why not? We'll give the place some class."

"I doubt we will. The car might."

They had just taken a booth, with the Aston Martin in full view through the window, when Michael's second cell phone rang. He doubted anyone was calling Fulton Industries, but it was the number he'd given Sam.

He flipped open the phone and pressed the TALK button.

"Michael, it's Sam."

He plugged in the headset and got to his feet. "Where are you?" Gesticulating for Dan to stay put, he walked back outside.

"Austria. The clocks went forward at the weekend. I'm now seven hours ahead."

He leaned against the side of the car. "Are you okay?"

"Yes, but I need your help ..." She then explained about what she'd read on the front page of the *Berliner Morganpost*. "I need to know who this man is," she continued. "If it's Jarrah, I'm walking into a trap."

"I'll get back to you."

"You can't," she said. "I'll call from the road tomorrow."

"Before Berlin?"

"Long before that."

"The two-faced weasel thinks you're dead."

"How did you manage that?"

"I'll tell you, when I see you."

"Oh, I hope so," she replied.

"Sleep well, Sam."

"I miss you, Michael."

The line went dead.

"Coffee to go?" Dan asked as Michael sat down again.

He took a good look around. At that time of the afternoon, Denny's was practically deserted, but Michael knew it wouldn't stay that way for long. "Not yet. Call Bruyere. Wake him up if you have to. We need info on a suspected terrorist caught in Berlin last night. Especially the name."

"I'm on it," Dan said, flipping open his cell phone.

"Take it outside," Michael said. "There's a better signal."

He watched Dan leave as the waitress arrived with their coffee. "You're like a couple of jack-in-the-boxes," she said. "First you. Then him. I keep telling them we need outside tables."

"It's business," Michael said. "You know how that goes."

She eyed the car through the window and turned back to Michael. "Looks like you're successful at it. Whatever it is."

Michael smiled. "We like to think so."

Dan arrived back at the table. "It wasn't Jarrah," he said quietly. "Bruyere says they're getting so skittish that every suspicious-looking Middle-Eastern man is being hauled in for questioning. The media overreacted again. They're as bad if not worse than ours."

"Sam's in the clear?"

"I wouldn't say that."

"You know what I mean."

"Yes, I know what you mean." Dan took a long drink of coffee. "I assume that was her calling?"

"Affirmative."

I knew Brian was wrong. "How did she sound?"

"Nervous."

"Want to go over a plan of action?"

"Not now. We've got a nosy waitress. Drink up. No cup holders."

Dan settled in his seat, eyes half closed, as the Aston Martin purred down I-95.

"Stopping to see Lynn?" he asked as the sign, "Welcome to South Carolina," flashed past.

"No," Michael said. "She's a distraction I don't need right now."

"I don't mind."

"You don't get it, do you," Michael continued, never taking his eyes off the road. "You're as bad as Brian. The mission comes first, no matter what. I don't get sidetracked by beautiful women, regardless of what you think. We need Sam's cooperation, so I'll use whatever means possible. Got that?"

"Got that. Brian thinks—"

"I know what Brian thinks," Michael interrupted. "And he's wrong. Now do me a favor and find us somewhere decent to stay tonight."

Harbour View Inn, Vendue Range, Charleston, South Carolina
Late afternoon

Using a satellite link from his laptop in the car, Dan accessed a list of hotels. He was somewhat surprised when Michael chose four-star accommodations.

"We'll stand out like a sore thumb using a Motel 6," he said when Dan asked. "How much does it cost?"

"Good," he added after Dan told him. "I'll put it on the CIA's tab."

Michael checked the Aston Martin into the valet parking garage, and in his room, with views of Charleston's harbor, he stood silently by the window.

"Something's been bugging me," he said eventually. "Did it occur to you that we were able to play the videotape?"

"I'm not following."

"Unless something's changed that I don't know about, that tape was American, shot on American equipment. We use NTSC. The Europeans use PAL."

"What's the difference?"

"The way the signal's formatted."

"So that means they're going back and forth undetected?"

"Looks that way. But how, with our beefed-up security?"

"Boat?"

Michael shrugged. "Possible. But think of the time factor. No, I think they're successfully slipping through the net some other way."

"I can only think of two. Canada and Mexico."

"Agreed. I'm almost inclined to rule out Canada. They're getting as good, if not better than we are."

"Mexico then?"

"That's my guess. And it's only a guess."

"Make a call?"

Michael shook his head. "Not yet. We've got no proof. And even if we did, we don't want them spooked before we find that bomb."

"Good point."

"There's free wine and cheese in the lobby," Michael added. "Wanna grab some before we get dinner?"

"Sure."

I'd hardly call it "free," Dan thought as they left Michael's room. *At these nightly rates, they should be paying for dinner too.*

Dan was soon to discover that Michael was more of a "chick magnet" than the car. By the time they'd finished eating at a local bar/restaurant, they'd been joined by what Dan thought of as "four gorgeous women."

The young women were obviously disappointed when Michael and Dan left the bar without them.

"You could take your pick," Dan said on the sidewalk.

"So could you." Michael began to walk away. "Personally, I'm not into one-night stands. But go ahead, if that's what you want."

Dan caught up. "Can't, even if it did cross my mind."

Michael stopped. "Why's that?"

"I forget sometimes why I'm with you."

"Not that bodyguard crap?"

Dan only nodded.

"I told Collins from the start, I didn't need one. It was true then. It's true now."

Michael began to walk again. "You're more useful to me as part of the team."

Dan caught up. "That's how you think of me? Part of the team?"

"And a friend. You watch my six. I watch yours." He stopped to light a small cigar. "While we're on the subject, want some action?"

"What kinda action?"

"Not those babes back there, if that's what you're thinking. The military kind."

"Keep talking."

"Something tells me this current situation's going to get hot. When it does, speed and precision will be imperative. Law enforcement, I don't care how good, hasn't got the expertise. Special Ops does."

"You think Sam will come through?"

Michael nodded. "Or die in the attempt. But I've still got to be ready at a moment's notice. If you want in, you'd better get in shape."

"I am in shape."

"Not for this mission." He grinned. "Flexing a few muscles at some pretty Charleston ladies isn't what I had in mind."

"You're going to lead this, aren't you?"

Michael puffed on the cigar. "Affirmative. Even though I'm an old man."

"Jesus. That's scary. What about Brian?"

"What about him? If I'm too old at thirty-six, he's got one foot in the grave. Plus, I don't need that kinda obstruction."

Dan stopped. "You've done this before, haven't you?"

"Didn't Collins tell you anything?"

"Very little. I didn't question his original request, seeing as who he is."

"Then, yes, I've done this before. Except we called them the enemy, not terrorists." Michael hesitated. "And they didn't have their hands on a nuclear bomb attempting to blow up civilians on U.S. soil, maybe crippling our economy, and not caring if they die in the process. Other than that, it's a piece of cake."

"I feel so much better knowing that," Dan replied. "What now? Apart from a grueling keep-fit schedule."

"Pack a bag and keep it within arm's reach. When I give the order to go, there'll be no stopping to pack anything. We leave. Got that?"

"I'm beginning to. When?"

"How the hell should I know? It could be days, weeks, or even months."

"Or maybe never."

"Somehow," Michael said, "I don't think that's going to be an option."

God. I hope he's wrong, Dan thought.

Chapter Twenty-Six

Parkhotel Leipzigerhof, Defreggerstrasse 13, Innsbruck, Austria
Tuesday, April 1, 2003

Sam checked out early, grateful that Europe had switched to Euros. It made buying traveler's checks so much easier. And she could cross borders too, without a passport and the fear of being monitored.

Leaving the Alps behind, she entered Germany and reached Munich. From there, according to the map, it was a straight shot to Berlin.

That's not a good way to describe it, she thought. *I really don't want to die.*

After another two hundred miles, at 1:30 p.m., she pulled off the highway to get gas and use a payphone.

The Harbour View Inn, Vendue Range, Charleston, South Carolina

Michael's second cell phone rang only twice before he answered it.

"Michael, it's Sam."

He glanced at the bedside clock. It read 6:30 a.m.

"Did I wake you?" she added.

He sat up, rapidly trying to clear his head. "It's okay. It wasn't Jarrah ..." he began.

"Thank goodness," she said when he'd finished. "Then it's still plan A?"

"Correct."

She hesitated. "It could be awhile before I call again. I hope you understand that?"

"Understood. Sam? If there's the slightest hint of trouble, I want you to call this number." Michael then gave her Bruyere's number in France and explained who he was.

"... and store the number in that brain of yours."

She swallowed. "You worked it out?"

"Yes, Sam, I worked it out."

"Well, I guess you know everything then."

Michael gave a low chuckle. "Why am I having a hard time believing you?"

"I have no idea."

"Why didn't you tell us?"

"You never asked."

That's what Otis said. "Anything else I didn't ask?"

"I don't think so."

"Watch your back."

"I will. Michael? I'm not going to say goodbye; it sounds too permanent. Au revoir, instead."

"Au revoir, Sam. Bonne chance," he said in perfect French before hanging up. Then he swung his feet over the side of the bed, and after reaching for the hotel phone, he dialed Dan's room. "You awake?" he asked when Dan answered.

"I am now."

"Good. Let's go for a run. Meet you in five."

"Is this an April Fool's joke?"

"No, it's not."

They ran for roughly five miles, and before entering the hotel, Dan stopped. "See. I am in good shape."

Michael chuckled. "Really? Then next time, we'll do it wearing full body armor and carrying an eighty-five-pound pack."

Michael's Office, G Street, Washington, D.C.
Midmorning

Line one to the phone on Molly's desk rang.

"Michael Correa's office," she answered.

"It's Francis Correa. Is my son there?"

"No, sir, he's not."

"Where is he?"

"I don't know, sir." *Wow, he sounds pissed.*

"I thought you were his personal assistant?"

"I am, sir. But he doesn't tell me everything."

"Great," Francis muttered. "Got any idea why he's not answering his cell phone?"

"No, sir, I don't."

"Can you reach him?"

"I can try for you, sir. That's the best I can do."

"Well, if you reach him, tell him I need to speak with him. It's urgent."

"Yes, sir. I'll do that."

Francis was about to hang up. "When did you last see him?"

"Friday, mid-afternoon."

Francis's voice rose. "He's been gone since Friday?"

Molly remained calm. "Yes, sir, since Friday."

She thought she heard him mutter, "Damn him!" Then there was dial tone.

At least he makes his own phone calls, she thought, beginning to dial Michael's cell phone number.

"Your father just called," she said when Michael answered. "He says it's urgent that he speak with you."

"How did he sound?"

"Never having met him, I'd still say really pissed off. Excuse my language."

Michael chuckled. "Sorry to burden you with him. I'll make sure he apologizes when all this is over."

"There's no need."

"Yes, there is."

"He's the director of the CIA."

"So? If he calls again, tell him to go jump in the lake."

"I can't do that!"

"Sure you can."

Berlin, Germany
Early evening

On the outskirts of Berlin, Sam found a payphone.

"I have arrived," Sam said when Isabelle answered.

"In the city area Mitte, there is a newsstand on the corner of Alexander Platz and Karl Marx Allee. Ask for a March copy of *Brigitte*. It will tell you everything you need to know."

Sam was about to say more when the line went dead.

Using a Berlin city street map, she easily found the newsstand.

When she asked the elderly vendor for the magazine, she felt as though she should be wearing a trench coat and dark glasses. But he silently handed her a copy from a shelf beneath his cart and turned immediately to other customers.

Sam returned to the Mercedes.

With the doors locked and the engine running, she flipped through the magazine.

Carefully hidden between two of the pages was a typed list of instructions in English, and according to them, her destination wasn't far.

Hotel Arcotel Velvet, Oranienburger Strabe 52, Berlin, Germany
A short time later

Following the instructions, Sam left the Mercedes in the hotel's garage, and after asking for the key to room 315 at the front desk, it was handed to her without comment.

"Enjoy your stay with us," the desk clerk said in perfect English.

As she headed toward the elevator with her bags on a cart, she realized that she had no idea how long she'd be staying, and asking him didn't seem to be an option.

In her room, complete with mini bar and big TV, she scanned the hotel's brochure.

Looks like I have everything I need, including a restaurant, she thought. *Just as well.* The instructions made it quite clear that she could not leave the hotel, under any circumstances, until after she was contacted. But they did not stipulate whether it would be hours or even days.

Guess I'll just have to wait.

Tybee Island, Georgia
That night

By 7:00 p.m., Brian was again at Skipper's on Butler Avenue.

"Still no sign of D.J.?" he asked.

The barmaid shook her head.

"You looking for D.J.?" asked a man, three seats down.

"Sure am."

The man played with his bottled beer. "Haven't seen him for the past few days. Could be his former missus is back in town. It's about that time of year." He took a swig from the bottle and faced Brian. "He's probably at home."

After some persuading, the man gave Brian directions. "It's an older home, so it's got no numbers. Built back when we didn't need 'em. Look for a large tree and a Ford pickup."

Seeing the man was serious, Brian suppressed a smile and thanked him.

No sooner had Brian found the house than he heard a dog with a very deep bark.

The noise grew louder as he approached the front door. Lights were on inside, and through some flimsy drapes, he could make out the screen of a large TV.

Before Brian could ring the bell, D.J. opened the door, and at his side was a dog with the biggest head Brian had ever seen.

D.J. grabbed a huge leather collar. "Can I help you?" He didn't sound friendly.

"It's Brian. Brian Mullen. We met at—"

"Course it is. Sorry. I thought you'd gone for good. What a surprise. Come on in."

Brian entered the house, following D.J. into a living room that, apart from the flat-screen TV, looked as though it had been furnished with rejects from Goodwill. Brian's immediate thought was that the folks from HGTV would have one helluva makeover.

"Beer?" D.J. asked.

"Sure," Brian replied.

"Sit where you want," D.J. added. "Curly here won't bother you."

Brian sat on the cleanest chair he could find. The entire room was a mishmash of tattered furniture that looked destined for the dump long ago. Curly sat in front of Brian, drooling from an enormous mouth, and the dog's eyes never left Brian's.

That's not a good sign, he thought. *One chomp, and I'm history.*

With a can of beer, D.J. took the chair opposite and pushed some escaped stuffing back into the dirty fabric. "Thought you'd changed your mind about buying a place here, seeing as I haven't seen you around. What's it been? Six months?"

"Seven. I've bin tryin' to find you for the last few days."

"Well, I'm here. Not going anywhere, until the bitch has gone again."

"You lost me."

"Look at all this crap," D.J. continued. "I used to have nice stuff. I replaced the TV, but until I know the bitch is dead, I'm living in this squalor."

Brian was soon to discover that D.J. had, after many years together, finally married his longtime girlfriend.

"She was the nicest lady you could possibly meet," he said. "Until that ring went on her finger. Did a complete one-eighty." He looked up. "You married, Brian?"

"Not yet."

D.J. snorted. "Don't."

According to D.J., soon after the wedding, the relationship went rapidly downhill. Within months of the marriage, she hired a high-priced attorney, filed for divorce, and tried to take not only D.J.'s house, but also his shrimp boat.

"When the dust finally settled," he continued, "she left for Kansas." He popped the tab off another beer. "Her sister lives in Richmond Hill. And once a year the bitch comes to visit for a week. Last year, she came with a truck. Cleaned me out."

He waved his arm. "This garbage was given to me by friends on the island, so temporarily I'd have somewhere to sit." He took a long swig from the can. "It's amazing what you can get used to. So until I know for sure she's in hell, it stays."

"Apart from the TV, what's left?"

"Curly. She gave him to me when he was a puppy. I was hoping he might bite her head off. But if he did, Animal Control wouldn't take too kindly. He'd probably be put to sleep. That's what they should do to her."

"She's got a sense of humor," Brian said, eyeing the smooth-coated monster.

For a moment, he didn't think D.J. understood.

Then D.J. laughed. "See what I mean? Who in their right mind would name a Rottweiler Curly?" He got up to get another beer. "You say you've been trying to find me?"

Brian nodded. "Remember the bomb, and our conversation? You said you knew a coupla guys who might, for the right price, help get it." Brian was hoping that this approach might work.

It didn't.

D.J. straightened, and his voice became hard. "I don't know who the hell you are, mister. But I reckon you'd better leave, before I call the cops."

Brian flipped open his ID. "I am 'the cops.'" Then he handed an astonished D.J. a business card. "I'm with the Department of Justice."

"I can see that," D.J. said, looking at the card. "So us meeting at Skipper's was a ruse?"

"No. Coincidence. And I'm back on the island 'cause I really need those names."

"The local shrimping business is a small community, so they'll probably find out if I tell you. Right now, I've got enough problems."

Brian shook his head. "Trust me; they won't. We can get real creative when it comes to interviewin' people of interest."

"I don't know." He stopped, obviously thinking. "Now it makes sense. The cop from D.C. You're the Mr. Brian that Otis is always going on about?"

Brian nodded. "Guilty. How do you know that?"

"Like I said when we met, this's a small island."

No shit, Brian thought. *Rollins said the exact same thing.*

"The kid's doing great," D.J. continued. "Like night and day from the way he was. And so goddamn proud of that bicycle, you'd think it was the only one in Georgia. Even his sister's got her act together. It was real nice of you to help him out."

Brian shrugged. "He's basically a good kid. Just needed a push in the right direction. Now, about those names?"

An hour later, Brian drove back to the Ocean Plaza with two names.

"Don't know the addresses," D.J. told him. "But with your resources, I don't expect you'll have any trouble finding them."

"When the 'bitch' has gone, call me," Brian said as he was leaving. "My cell is on the card. Dinner, my dime. I'd like to stay in touch. And it's got nothin' to do with my work."

"Thanks. I'll do that," D.J. replied.

Ocean Plaza Beach Resort, 15th Street & Oceanfront, Tybee Island, Georgia
A few minutes later

In the parking lot, Brian left his car next to a late-model Aston Martin.

Jeeze, that's one helluva fancy car, he thought, checking out the Florida license plate. *If I'm goin' to buy on the island, I'd better get my act together. Those are rich folks's wheels.*

In the lobby, the young woman behind the desk, whom he now knew as Trish, waved at him.

"Mr. Mullen, there's two gentlemen waiting for you in the bar."

"Waitin' for me?"

She nodded. "They checked in late this afternoon."

Michael and Dan were seated at a small table, two beers in front of them.

Brian took the third chair. "You checkin' up on me?" he asked Michael.

"What makes you think that?"

"I'm surprised, that's all. Molly tell you I was here?"

"Affirmative. And I thought it was time to recon the area, as Dan and I have never been."

Brian ordered a coffee from the bartender. "Fareed call?"

"Twice."

Here we go, Dan thought.

"Anythin' interestin'?"

"She made initial contact. Now we wait."

Ocean Plaza Beach Resort, 15th Street & Oceanfront, Tybee Island, Georgia
Wednesday, April 2, 2003

Brian yawned and stretched.

I could get real used to this, he thought, scanning the smooth Atlantic from his bedroom window. The beach was almost empty, but he could see two men in shorts and tee shirts running toward the hotel from the north end of the island. *That's Michael and Dan.* He turned back to the clock; 7:00 a.m. *They were up early.*

Brian took his time to shave and dress, but he still beat them down to breakfast.

He was halfway through eating when Michael and Dan sat down.

"Bring me up to date," Michael said.

In between mouthfuls, Brian told him of his visit to the Georgia Ports Authority.

"... they're no different from any other large container port," he finished. "They're beefin' up security, but from what we now know, it's like shuttin' the stable door after the horse has bolted."

"Let's assume—"

"Always dangerous," Brian interrupted.

"Let's assume," Michael began again, "that they did come in here. Where would they go? Is there a large Muslim population in Savannah?"

"Beats me."

Michael turned to Dan. "We could find out after we've eaten."

"Sure. And talking of horses, I could eat one right now."

"Try cow," Michael said. "I'd feel better."

"You brought your bag of tricks?" Brian asked Dan. "I didn't see the Suburban in the parkin' lot."

"We changed vehicles," he replied.

"How come?"

"Michael managed to royally piss off his father."

Brian faced him. "That so? How?"

"You don't want to know," Michael said.

"So this recon was just an excuse?"

"You're half right."

Their breakfast order arrived and effectively stopped Michael from having to say any more.

"I need to talk to you," Brian said to him when breakfast was over. "Walk me to my car?"

Dan got the message as Michael got to his feet. "I'll meet you outside."

"Do that. See you in five."

In the parking lot, Michael headed toward Brian's car.

"So talk to me," he said, deliberately leaning against the side of the Aston Martin.

Brian eyed the car and had to force himself from commenting. *I hope the owner don't see him. If that was mine, I'd be real pissed.* He cleared his throat. "I'm gettin' the impression that you don't trust me. And that I'm bein' excluded from the team."

"I don't. And you are."

Brian was stunned. "Well, that was easy."

"You asked. I told you."

"Do you want me to resign?"

"No. If I'd wanted you out, you'd be gone."

Brian believed him. "Where do we go from here?"

"You tell me. I made a tough decision. The president supported it."

"He did?"

"Yes. And if you hadn't spent so much goddamn time commenting on my relationship with Sam, you'd know that."

"Well, I—"

"I'm through with excuses. In the military, you learn to follow orders. Regardless of what they are. If you don't trust me by now, I'll find someone who does."

Brian was about to reply when Michael's cell phone rang.

For a second, Brian didn't think he was going to answer it.

After several rings, Michael finally flipped it open. "What the hell do you want?" he snapped.

"I met with the president yesterday," Francis said. "Apparently, he approves of what you've done. I may have overreacted."

"No shit? Calling me a barefaced liar? It's going to take more than 'I may have overreacted,' Dad."

"What do you want me to say? Sorry? I apologize?"

"That's a start. But right now, I'm busy."

"We'll talk later?"

"No, Dad. I've got nothing to say." Michael paused. "Cancel that. In future, stay the hell out of my way." He snapped the phone shut and turned back to Brian. "Where were we? Ah, yes, a replacement."

"That won't be necessary," Brian said quickly. "You've got my full cooperation."

"And trust?"

"That too." Brian lowered his voice. "You sure ain't anythin' like Evan Gage."

Michael finally grinned. "Who?"

Before Brian could continue, Dan appeared.

"Want Dan and I to check out one of those leads?" Michael asked.

"Sure. Take your pick."

He wrote down a name. "Ready?" he said to Dan.

"When you are."

Michael opened the driver's door to the Aston Martin. "Meet back here later," he added to Brian.

He watched them leave. *I did underestimate you. He leaned against the car to test me. Thank God I didn't open my big mouth again. Dan was right. He does know what he's doin'.*

At the last traffic light on Butler Avenue, Michael's cell phone rang again.

He quickly checked to see who was calling before pressing the TALK button.

"Correa."

"Michael, it's John LaRoche from SLED. Your assistant said I could reach you on this number. Is this a bad time?"

The light turned green. "Go ahead," Michael said.

"I got to thinking what little evidence was found at Wentworth's house in Camden. As the case is still open, I went back there with a Hepa filter vacuum cleaner. I just got the results. Did you go to the beach in March?"

"No."

"And neither did we. I vacuumed each room separately. Most of the grit was sand. The kind you find at the ocean. Don't know if that helps?"

"I'm not sure either."

"I told Lynn I was calling. She said to say 'hi.'"

"Thanks. Did the analysis narrow it down?"

"'Fraid not. Beach sand/ocean is about as far as they could go without an exact comparison."

Michael thanked him again and hung up, and as he did, he saw the sign for Dolphin Cruises and Cafe Loco.

Taking a fast left turn, he stopped in the sandy area outside the ship's store.

"LaRoche found beach sand," Michael said, getting out of the car.

Dan looked around, kicking up some dirt. "What do you think this is?"

"Looks like sand to me."

"Want to look around while I find this guy?"

"Sure."

Dan plugged in the laptop and checked the name Michael had handed him. *Okay, Mr. Buck "Bubba" Conway. Let's see where you live.*

He found Michael on the dock, smoking a small cigar.

"Bubba Conway lives at Isle of Hope," Dan said, looking around. "Is this where Otis said they came in?"

Michael nodded. "Over there's the public boat ramp."

"I can see why they chose this place."

"Me too. Let's go find Bubba."

They retraced their steps along the boardwalk past Cafe Loco.

"This guy's really known as Bubba?" Dan said. "Do you believe that?"

Michael stubbed out the cigar butt. "Welcome to the South."

"Isn't that 'welcome to the South, y'all'?"

Michael was grinning as he slid behind the wheel again. "Remind me to introduce you to Bonnie Chase."

"Who's Bonnie Chase?"

"A very rich Southern belle."

"Why do I think I'm going to regret this? We need G.P.S."

"We don't. That's why I've got you."

Isle of Hope, Savannah, Georgia
Thirty minutes later

They found Bubba Conway's home with no difficulty.

"Looks normal to me," Michael said, driving slowly past.

"I can see a swingset."

"He's got kids?"

Dan checked his notes. "Two. Aged two and seven months. They could have threatened him like they did Sadilov."

Michael did a three-point turn on the narrow street. "Let's ask the neighbors."

Dan had to admit that Michael could really turn on the charm when he had to. Leaving the Aston Martin parked as far off the road as he could, he knocked on several doors. In two cases, no one was home, but three were, including the neighbors on either side.

By the time they finished, they knew Conway's life history, going back as far as the grandparents.

"He were real wild. Always gitting in trouble," one neighbor said. "But once he married that Nancy, he changed. Straightened right up, he did. He's a great dad too. Works hard and keeps the place real nice. Well, you can see for yourself."

Michael thanked him and headed for the car.

"That's it," he said to Dan. "He's not our guy. But it scares me that these people are so trusting."

"You don't look like a criminal."

"That's good to know. Let's hope Brian's having more luck."

Thunderbolt, Savannah, Georgia
Midmorning

Brian did his own research to find an address for Edward Slycroft but almost missed his house as he cruised slowly down a side street of old and, for the most part, small 1940s-style ranchers. On the remains of a concrete slab driveway with more weeds than hard surface was a tow truck and a man in a uniform beginning to winch a new-looking Dodge pickup onto the flatbed.

Brian parked on the overgrown grass close to the rusty chain-link fence and approached the man. "Excuse me, sir?"

The man turned, and on seeing Brian, he immediately pulled a piece of paper from his pocket. "Let's do this the easy way," he said, waving the paper and making a quick grab for a hidden baseball bat. "I got all the legal documents. So unless you want to dig an even deeper hole for yourself, stand back and let me do my job."

He took a step toward Brian, swinging the bat. "It only takes a phone call to get the cops out here."

Brian held his ID in clear view. "No need."

The man stepped closer and peered at the ID. "Sorry. I thought you was him." He lowered the bat. "Jesus, what's he got himself into this time? DoJ? The guy's a fucking asshole."

"You've met him?"

"No, thank God. When we get repossessions, we try and time it so they're not home."

"You said, 'this time.' You've been here before?"

"Yeah," the man replied. "Coupla years back. Soon as I drove into the street, I remembered. It was our third attempt. One of the first guys who tried got a beatin'. He refused to come back. So they sent me."

"Were you successful?"

The man grinned. "Second time I was."

"And now?"

"Just got the order. I like it when they're this easy."

"So what did he do?"

"Didn't pay." He turned away. "Nice-looking truck too. A lot of what we get is beaten to hell."

"Any idea why?"

The man turned back. "It's only a rumor, but I hear he's got a big gambling problem. He paid cash for this truck. Then months later, he took a loan against it. Dumb shit. Now he's lost it."

"What else do you know about him?"

"Not much." He turned to the house. "Look at it. What a god-awful mess." He studied the legal papers. "Says here he's a shrimp boat captain. That's no excuse. It's not like they're gone for months at a time. I'm surprised the neighbors haven't complained."

Brian could find no reason to disagree.

"Thanks for the information," he said. "Don't mind me. I'm goin' to take a look through the windows."

"Help yourself," the man replied. "It's probably empty. The vehicle's usually the last to go."

But from what little Brian could see through the filthy windows and broken screens, the house was far from empty. In fact, he caught a glimpse of some very high-end electronics. By the time he finished his snooping, the tow truck driver was getting ready to leave.

Brian waved. "Thanks for your help."

"You're welcome. Hope you've got something on him. Guys like that shouldn't be allowed on the streets."

I'm bettin' Michael would agree with you, Brian thought, getting back in his car.

He flipped open his cell phone.

"Any luck?" he asked when Michael answered.

"No. Bubba's not our guy. What about you?"

"I gotta funny feelin' I hit pay dirt."

Ocean Plaza Beach Resort, 15th Street & Oceanfront, Tybee Island, Georgia
Early afternoon

"Brian's right," Dan said in Michael's room, turning the laptop toward them. "Slycroft's got just the kind of track record that al Qaeda would pick up on. Huge gambling debts that mysteriously got paid off. His house and shrimp boat were mortgaged to the hilt. Then those loans were drastically reduced. He paid cash for the truck. Now it seems he's slipping back into old habits."

Michael went to the window, staring at the view. "We're going to pay him a visit."

"When?" Dan asked.

"Tonight. Late. I knew I should have brought my other kit bag."

"What do you need?"

Michael ran through the short list.

"You can get all that at Wal-Mart," Brian said. "On Whitemarsh Island."

"How do you know that?"

"Otis's sister works there now." He looked at his watch. "I gotta go. I promised I'd pick him up from school."

"He's back in school?" Michael asked.

"Yeah. Doin' real well. He's a bright kid."

"You've been helping him out?"

Brian shrugged. "Now and then. Yes."

"How big's this Slycroft?" Michael asked after Brian had gone.

"His gun permit says five foot ten inches. Weight: One hundred and ninety pounds."

"He's got a gun permit? I'm going to enjoy this. And 190 I can handle."

"What exactly are you going to do?"

"Scare the shit outta him."

Slycroft's House, Gilbert Street, Thunderbolt, Savannah, Georgia
Almost midnight

After getting Otis from school, Brian had guided him through his homework before driving to Whitemarsh Island to pick up Leisha. Then buying the items on Michael's list at Wal-Mart, Brian had taken them both to dinner.

He'd arrived on Slycroft's street just after 11:00 p.m. to see the Aston Martin parked under some trees, half off the dark road.

"Any luck?" Brian asked.

"Not yet," Michael said. "He's not home. We've been staking out the place since 2200."

"We should call the Thunderbolt cops. We've got no authorization."

"To hell with authorization. I'm only going to talk to him."

It was a few minutes to midnight when a cab stopped outside Slycroft's house.

"That's him," Dan said, watching as a man then entered the house.

Michael immediately got out of the car. "Time to rock and roll."

"What exactly are we goin' to do?" Brian asked.

"You're doing nothing until I get inside. Stay out of my way. Got that?"

Dan shrugged as Brian muttered, "Got that."

They waited in the shadows until Michael crossed the street. Then he signaled them to follow and wait behind some overgrown shrubs by the side of the front door.

As soon as they were in place, Michael rang the bell, and didn't stop.

They all heard an angry voice saying, "Jesus! I'm coming. I'm coming! I'm frickin' coming!"

Slycroft flung open the door.

When he saw Michael, it was already too late.

Giving Slycroft no time to react, Michael pounced and spun him back into the hallway, forcing him to his knees in a powerful chokehold. Seconds later, Brian and Dan saw Slycroft's head already beginning to sag toward his chest as Michael applied pressure with his free hand. When moments later Slycroft slumped forward, Michael let him go.

"Got the duct tape?" he said.

"What did you do to him?" Brian asked.

"Knocked him out the easy way. Let's get him tied up before he regains consciousness."

"That was pretty impressive," Dan said quietly as they dragged Slycroft's limp body into what looked like a living room. "I'd no idea you were that good. Or that fast."

Michael didn't comment.

Using the duct tape, they tightly bound Slycroft to a dining chair, and following Michael's instructions, they also taped his mouth and pulled a wool cap over his eyes. Having rigged a clip-on garage-type light with a 200 watt bulb and extension cord, Michael fixed it to the back of another chair and sat down, facing the still-unconscious Slycroft.

"To hell with this," he said after a couple of minutes and disappeared into the kitchen.

"Kill the lights," he added when he returned and threw a full pitcher of cold water at Slycroft's face.

Slycroft immediately tried to cough and move, and got so violent when he realized he was tied up that Brian had to hold on to the back of his chair to stop it from tipping over.

Michael turned on the spotlight. "Can you hear me?" he asked.

Slycroft moved his head and tried to mumble something through the duct tape.

"If you can hear me, nod your head."

Slycroft nodded.

"If I remove the tape, you are not to speak until I tell you. Understand?"

Slycroft nodded again.

"If you do, it's going to go rapidly downhill. Understand that?"

This time, Slycroft nodded violently.

Michael signaled to Brian, and the next thing Slycroft knew was the tape was being ripped from his mouth.

I'll bet that hurt, Dan thought from the shadows.

"As long as you tell me the truth, I'll let you live. Lie to me, and I will kill you."

This time, Brian noticed that Slycroft froze.

"When did al Qaeda first contact you?"

Before Slycroft could answer, he heard the distinctive sound of a hammer being cocked.

"November 2001," he said hurriedly.

"An exact date?"

"I dunno. I'd have to look at a calendar. Before Thanksgiving."

"Did you know who they were?"

"Not at first, I swear."

"When did you find out?"

"After they told me what they wanted me to do."

"And you didn't think to turn them in?"

"I was going to lose everything. Two hundred and fifty grand's a lot of money."

"Where's the money now?"

"I spent it."

"All of it?"

"Yes," Slycroft said quietly.

"Can you identify them?"

"Possibly."

"Shoot him and get it over with," Dan commented.

Slycroft frantically turned his head to hear where the other voice was coming from. "I'll do anything. Don't kill me. Please, don't kill me."

"Why waste a good bullet," Michael said. "I'll just slit his throat."

"Oh, God, no. Please. Please."

Suddenly a large dark stain appeared on Slycroft's crotch, and a trickle of urine began to spread across the dirty hardwood floor.

Michael continued to question him and was getting no more relevant information until he asked about names and places.

"I heard one of them ask about Port Wentworth."

"What about it?"

Slycroft hesitated. "I think he wanted to know how far it was."

"Why?"

"I don't know. Honest, I don't know."

After Brian pulled back the wool cap covering his eyes, all Slycroft saw was a very bright light and the dark barrel of a handgun aimed directly at his head. Another hand, from somewhere behind him, then showed him photographs one at a time. In the end, Slycroft identified Jarrah as the man who paid him and appeared to be the leader, and As'ad Rashid, but no one else.

"Kill him now?" Dan said when they got all Michael thought they were going to get.

"There's already enough trash in the streets," he replied. "Are you listening, Slycroft?"

"Yes, I'm listening."

"Step one foot outside this house, and you will die," Michael continued. "Some men are coming for you. When they do, you'll give them your full cooperation. Otherwise, when I'm done with you, you'll be begging me to end it. Got that?"

Slycroft could only nod as the puddle on the floor grew larger.

It took them less than a minute to dismantle the spotlight and leave the house. As Michael had insisted they all wear latex gloves, their fingerprints weren't a problem.

"You'd have killed him, wouldn't you?" Dan asked as they drove away, with Brian following.

"If I had to."

"It wouldn't be the first time?"

"Affirmative."

Dan didn't speak again until they'd reached the Ocean Plaza parking lot. "We left him tied up. When do you plan on calling the Feds?"

"When I get around to it," was the reply.

Ocean Plaza Beach Resort, 15th Street & Oceanfront, Tybee Island, Georgia
Thursday, April 3, 2003

Dan's cell phone rang at 6:00 a.m.

When he heard what the caller had to say, he got out of bed and woke Michael.

"Bruyere just called," Dan said. "He's got the DNA results back on the dead kid in Haguenau. It's not a perfect match to the DNA SLED got from the guest bath drain hairs in Camden, but they are related."

"So it was Sadilov's son?"

"Looks that way. What do you want to do now?"

Michael looked at the bedside clock. "Early breakfast. Then get the hell outta here."

"What about Port Wentworth?"

"We'll drive through it before we leave."

Port Wentworth, Georgia
Two hours later

"Slow down," Dan said. "Look right."

Having just crested the railroad bridge beyond the entrance to the Georgia Ports Authority on Route 25, Michael slowed.

Set back from the road and partly hidden by old palm trees growing in the sand and grass frontage was a small warehouse-type building. A narrow awning ran the width of the building, giving some shade to both the single access and two sets of double loading doors.

"You could easily hide a boat and trailer in there," Dan added.

Michael didn't disagree, but with an eighteen-wheeler now on his rear bumper, he put the Aston Martin into second gear and pulled away.

They spent the better part of an hour cruising up and down side streets.

"This's a total waste of our time," Michael said, having seen yet another blue marker for I-95. "We've passed more than a dozen buildings. Any one of which could hide the bomb. And just because Slycroft overheard them ask about Port Wentworth doesn't mean the bomb's here."

"At least we gave it the once-over."

"I'll grant you that. But now it's time to get back to D.C."

Hotel Arcotel Velvet, Oranienburger Strabe 52, Berlin, Germany
Friday, April 4, 2003

Sam had now been confined to the hotel for three days.

Sometimes she wandered through the lobby and bought a magazine or picked up sightseeing brochures, staring into the street beyond the windows. But never once did she step outside.

The hotel staff all seemed to be both friendly and bilingual. But after getting the same waiter two nights in a row at her table in the restaurant, she decided that it would be better if she ate in her room. She was sure he was just being hospitable, but she had no answers to his many questions about her visit to Berlin.

For the most part, she just read or watched TV. With both Internet access and a telephone available, she mentally kicked herself again for not buying a laptop in Rome. Although, using the telephone was something she dare not risk. She was, for all intents and purposes, a four-star hotel prisoner. But a captive nonetheless.

At noon, the telephone rang, making her jump.

Tentatively, she answered, "Hello?"

"This is the front desk," a man said in English. "A gentleman is here to see you. A Mr. Rossi. May I send him up?"

Sam swallowed. "Of course. Thank you."

Her hands were damp as she paced the room, and it seemed like an eternity until there was a knock on her door.

She looked through the spyhole, but the man was unrecognizable.

Deciding that the chain wasn't going to save her if whoever he was intended causing her serious harm, she tentatively opened the door.

"Hello, Samin. I thought you were dead."

She was speechless.

"Are you going to ask me in? Or do I have to stay in the corridor?"

She grabbed his arm and pulled him inside.

The door closed, and she was in his arms.

He gave her a long kiss then nuzzled her neck. "I never expected to see you again," he whispered.

Holding both his hands, she stepped back. "You look so different. Even your own mother would pass you on the street."

He threw his topcoat from his shoulders and held her again. "That's the idea. I've missed you."

She pulled back, staring into eyes partially hidden by blue-tinted glasses. "I've missed you too, Hamza. You'll never know how much."

He took her hand and led her to the bed. "Show me how much."

She was smiling broadly as she stripped.

"You did miss me," Jarrah said, several hours later. "We should be apart this long more often."

"No, no, no," Sam replied. "I've lived a nightmare without you."

"Ah, yes," he said, propping himself on one elbow, looking down. "What happened? Something went wrong?"

"Very wrong," she replied. "It's a long story."

He kissed her. "Tell me. For you, I have all the time in the world."

Since leaving Newark on her Rome flight, Sam had almost seven days in which to think and plan. She'd lied to Michael about the amount of time she'd spent with McDonald in London. It was three months, not three weeks, and she took the gamble that Michael would never check. His disdain for the British spymaster was obvious. McDonald taught her a lot in that time, and she'd put it all to good use for Jarrah. But lying to him could still cost her

her life. She'd seen what he did to people who betrayed him, and for most of them, death was a welcome relief. *Just tell him the truth.*

She now slipped naked off the bed, and after putting on a robe, she sat across from him in a comfortable chair.

"When we split up, I didn't fly to New York; I took a cab back to Sarasota..." she began.

Jarrah listened, never once interrupting, until she finished, "...so here I am, finally reunited with the love of my life."

Jarrah grinned. "The children?"

"Gone, like you told me."

"And this American colonel, Michael?"

"Correa," she said. "Thinks he's a knight in shining armor, out to save the world." She lowered her voice, leaning forward. "But be warned, Hamza, despite everything we know and learned, I think he could be a very dangerous man."

"You do?"

Sam got to her feet. "Yes. Even though we both feel the same way about Americans. We lived among them for over two years, and me for even longer. They are like little children. Big and playful, they want everyone to like them and have convinced themselves, and some other western nations, that the rest of us want to live like they do. Hah!"

She spat. "They think they are the great saviors of the world, and we should be indebted to them for eternity."

Sam knelt by the foot of the bed. "But we know better, don't we."

Jarrah got off the bed and began to dress. "I hope Allah hears your words of wisdom," he said. "You deserve a far greater reward than me."

"How did you leave it with this Michael Correa?" he asked from the bathroom.

"He sent me to find you. I've called him twice. All from payphones."

"Does he know where you are?"

"The last he heard, I was headed for Berlin."

"Does he expect you to keep calling?"

"Yes. But I told him it might be some time."

"Good. Then keep him waiting." Jarrah stopped. "He didn't arrange for the car?"

"No, I told you, it was a gift to me from that idiot playboy in Rome."

Jarrah laughed and checked his appearance in the full-length bedroom mirror. "How do I look?"

She studied him. "The ponytail suits you. I like the brown hair and blond highlights. The pencil-thin mustache and goatee are so masculine. You remind me of a successful movie producer."

"Italian?"

"Perfect."

"Get dressed," he said. "We are going to dinner."

"Is it safe?"

"This American colonel must trust you. We know you weren't followed. There is no surveillance. The car is clean. There's nothing in your luggage, and now I know there's nothing on you except beautiful silky skin."

"And the German authorities?"

"Too busy chasing every Middle-Eastern man they see." He flicked through her clothes hanging in the closet. "Wear that," he added, handing her a dress. "I like you in Valentino." He faced her. "They expect us to hide in caves and behind rocks in the mountains. Not travel first class and be flamboyant in the process."

Sam slipped the dress over her head. "You're a genius," she said. "It's the last thing they'd expect."

"No. You are the genius," he said, kissing her hand.

Over dinner, at one of Berlin's most expensive restaurants, Sam discovered that the apartment where she'd first met Jarrah was still being used. When she asked if that's where they were going, he replied, "No. A four-star hotel. Some sightseeing together. We still have time."

Chapter Twenty-Seven

Michael's Office, G Street, Washington, D.C.
Thursday, April 10, 2003

Michael hadn't only stepped up the keep-fit regime for himself and Dan, but also insisted that they get more range practice.

"You're already a crack shot," Dan said.

"And I need to keep it that way," Michael replied. "Practice, practice, practice. Don't underestimate our enemy."

They were just about to leave for the indoor shooting range when his second cell phone rang.

"Michael, it's Sam."

He let out a short breath. "You're okay?"

"I'm fine. I found Jarrah."

He closed his eyes. *Thank God.* "Where?"

"Here in Berlin. This's the first chance I've had to call you. Sorry."

"Don't be sorry. You're sure you're okay?"

"Yes. As I suspected, he had the place I was staying under surveillance, and when he knew it was safe, he showed up."

"Did he interrogate you?"

"For several hours."

"Did he hurt you?"

Sam imagined Jarrah. "No, he didn't hurt me. I'm far too useful to him."

"He believed what you told him?"

"Absolutely."

"Where are you?"

She looked around. "At a payphone, near some downtown shops."

"Where's Jarrah?"

"I don't know. I've spent the last week sightseeing and shopping. He's been with me most of the time. This morning, he told me he had a meeting. I've got no idea where or what it's about. Like I told you, I was never privy to that kind of information. Nothing's changed."

"He's been sightseeing?"

"And shopping."

This doesn't sound right. "How?"

Sam's voice dropped to a whisper. "I've got to go. I've just seen him. Sorry."

Then there was dial tone.

Michael flipped his cell phone shut.

"Sam?" Dan asked.

Michael nodded. "Something's wrong. Are the Germans blind? According to her, before she abruptly hung up, Jarrah's in plain sight. How's that possible?"

"He's changed his appearance?"

"That's all I can come up with. But she didn't have time to tell me. Shit."

Downtown Berlin, Germany
Less than a minute later

After picking up her shopping bags, Sam crossed the street.

"Spending money again?" Jarrah asked as she reached him.

She smiled. "It's something I'm good at."

"If you don't stop, we'll need our own airplane to carry it all."

"Oh? We're leaving?"

"Soon," Jarrah replied. "I want you to be packed and ready. Lunch?"

Chapter Twenty-Eight

Michael's Townhouse, Duke Street, Old Town, Alexandria, Virginia
Thursday, May 1, 2003

Michael had just turned on the eleven o'clock news when his second cell phone rang.

He hit the MUTE button to the TV and flipped open the phone.

"It's Sam. Sorry, it's late."

"Better late than never. Where are you?"

"On a street in Malaga."

"You're in Spain?"

"For almost two weeks."

"What's going on?"

"I'm not sure ..." she began.

She went on to explain that on Wednesday, April 23, she and Jarrah drove to the airport in Berlin, using the Mercedes that Alberto gave her. Then, leaving the car in long-term parking, Jarrah tossed the keys into a trashcan before boarding a 12:35 p.m. Iberia flight to Madrid. They'd flown first class. At the airport, a man she soon found out was called 'Asim was waiting. He then drove them to a large apartment between Sol and Plaza Santa Ana in downtown Madrid. Sam spent most of the next seven days in the apartment, but whenever Jarrah told her to go either shopping or sightseeing, she was accompanied by 'Asim.

"Jarrah wanted me out of the way," she said. "It was just like Florida. But this time, I was never alone."

"Go on."

According to Sam, the following Thursday, "It was April 29ᵗʰ," 'Asim drove her to a villa on the Costa del Sol. "It took less than seven hours to get here, and I've been here ever since," she ended.

"Where's 'Asim now?"

Sam chuckled. "He got tired of my shopping trips. This's the first time, apart from sleeping, that I've been out of his sight since arriving in Spain."

"Jarrah doesn't trust you?"

"He doesn't trust anyone."

"Have you spoken to him?"

"Not since leaving Madrid. The villa is lovely, and I don't think it's a rental. The car 'Asim drove certainly isn't. But I can't ask questions. 'Asim's worse than Jarrah. He normally sticks to me like glue."

"Does 'Asim have a last name?"

"Of course. But I don't know what it is, and I'm not going to ask. He carries a gun, if that gives you any idea of how I'm living. He's definitely not friendly."

She hesitated. "I've got to go. I told him I was buying another bikini, and I wouldn't be long. It's obvious that he thoroughly disapproves of me, and I'm sure that if I give him the slightest provocation, he'll kill me."

"Sam? Before you hang up, who else was at the Madrid apartment?"

Jarrah, 'Asim, and me. I was hustled out of there by 'Asim at all times of the day and night. If Jarrah was meeting someone, I don't know who or if there was more than one person. I really do have to go. I don't want a bullet in me."

She hung up before Michael could reply.

Michael's Office, G Street, Washington, D.C.
Friday, May 2, 2003

At 8:30 a.m., Brian, Dan, and Molly were listening to Michael's account of Sam's nighttime phone call.

"Check the airlines," he told Molly when he'd finished. "She was very specific."

"She coulda got that information off the web," Brian said. "I do it all the time."

"After the fact?" Michael replied. "But let's say you're right; how do you explain a Malaga prefix to the number she called from?"

Brian stayed silent.

Michael pointed to the world map on his office wall. "If she's telling the truth, look where she is. Across the Straits of Gibraltar is Morocco. Now they're real friendly toward us." He moved his finger. "And that's Rota. One of our most strategically placed military bases in the Med."

"You think it's a foreign target?" Dan asked, but before Michael could reply, he added, "They've had enough time to get it there."

Michael shook his head. "No. That's not it, and I can't tell you why. Call Bruyere. Ask him if they've got wind of anything going on in Madrid. I doubt Jarrah's there on vacation."

He scribbled something on a piece of paper. "That's all the address Sam gave me. And if she's telling us the truth, tell him Jarrah dumped the Mercedes."

"Or he wanted her to think that. There could still be a spare set of keys."

Michael closed his eyes. "I'm getting really tired of this. How do you fight this kinda enemy? Don't bother to answer that."

Dan shrugged. "I would if I could."

Now alone in his office, Michael put his feet up on the desk, and leaning back, he studied the world map.

From Rome to Berlin. From Berlin to Madrid. Let's say they really did dump the car. That means he's probably not going back. Sam's in Malaga, out of the way by the sound of it. So what's the next move? Goddamnit! It's like trying to play chess blindfolded.

There was a knock on his door, and Molly's head appeared.

Michael waved her inside.

"From what I've been told, those flights were genuine," she said. "I also checked names on the terrorist suspect list. There's no 'Asim anything."

"That figures."

"But it does mean 'protector' or 'guardian' in Arabic. Not that it helps."

Eagles Nest, Somewhere off Route 301, the Eastern Shore, Maryland
Saturday, May 3, 2003

By mid-afternoon, with Michael at the helm of the Viking and Tom by his side, they were cruising Chesapeake Bay.

In Tom's opinion, Michael had been strangely quiet since arriving the night before. He'd spent the morning riding Delta, and it was almost as an afterthought that he'd mentioned taking the boat out.

From the flying bridge, Michael began to slowly increase the Viking's speed. "How fast will she go?"

"Don't rightly know, sir. We've never tried."

The bay ahead of them was clear of sailboats, and there was only a slight chop.

"Let's find out," Michael added.

Tom glanced over his shoulder. As the sportfisherman went up on plane, the wake from the two Detroit Diesel engines was huge.

"Glad I'm not waterskiing," Tom commented and turned back to see the needles on the rev counters rapidly rising. He thought they were hovering dangerously close to the red line when Michael began to ease back on the throttles.

"The specs were right," he said. "Top speed is about thirty-two knots."

Tom did a rough calculation. "Why'd you want to go almost thirty-seven miles an hour in a boat like this? If you want breakneck speed, sell it and get a cigarette boat."

Michael stared at the horizon. "Is she in good shape?"

"Tiptop, you know that, sir."

Michael spun the wheel, and the boat began turning for home. "Could Boost get more outta her?"

Tom's eyes narrowed. "Maybe. He'd have to take a look. Why?"

"Just curious," he replied, effectively ending the conversation.

It wasn't until after they docked and hosed down the boat that Michael took a beer from the refrigerator and sat on the gunwale.

Tom sat across from him and popped the tab off his beer. "Something's bugging you, sir. I can read you like a book."

"One of the few that can."

"So talk to me."

Michael began at the beginning. Some of what he said Tom already knew, but he never once interrupted.

"… so here I am, almost a year later, knowing a lot more, but no closer."

Tom was about to say something when Michael continued, "Brian said when you hit a brick wall, go back to the beginning."

"To Worcek?" Tom asked.

"Not that far. But you're right; something is bugging me. In the investigative process, we never found Jarrah's boat."

"You didn't find his car either."

"That's different," Michael replied. "Thousands of BMWs are sold each year in the U.S. Compared to the cost of a fifty-two-foot Egg Harbor, they're not even close to being in the same league."

"Golden Egg, sir. That model's called a Golden Egg."

Michael's eyes narrowed. "You did some research?"

"Sure. They're big bucks, even used. Sorry, didn't mean to interrupt, sir."

"You didn't. But see where I'm going? Sam meets Sis at Wharton and spends the next four years with the wealthy and influential Matthews family. She goes straight to Rome and that playboy Alberto, and yes, we checked him out through Interpol. He's the real deal. Now she's in Malaga, playground of the British and Europeans. Most of the al Qaeda operatives who've been found so far were in inner cities, mixing with or doing blue-collar-type work. This's the first time to my knowledge that a woman has been this close to any form of their leadership. They see us as decadent and spoiled. What better place to hide than amongst the so-called elite."

"Now I understand."

Michael took a swig of beer. "If what we suspect is true, they took the bomb away by boat."

"But wasn't that on a trailer, sir?"

"So we think. My gut's still telling me we should look for the Egg. As Dan said, they've had enough time to get it practically anywhere. But if that's the case, why buy a fifty-two-foot Egg Harbor here? There's plenty of luxury power boats available worldwide."

"Didn't you tell me the FBI checked out all the sales over the last four years and came up empty?"

"That's sales they could trace through dealerships. Not private sales."

"But didn't they check out marinas?"

"What if it isn't being kept in a marina?"

"Where they going to hide a boat that size?"

All Michael did was look around.

"Oh, shit," Tom added. "Moored at a private dock, just like this."

"Correct."

"But where, sir?"

"If I could answer that, I'd be a happy man right now."

"They coulda scuttled her?"

"I don't think so. Jarrah had other ways to escape from Florida. And if he didn't need a big boat, why spend that kinda money on one and take a captain's course for a 50-ton license?"

"Good point. There's always aerial surveillance?"

"It briefly crossed my mind. But how can I mobilize the Coast Guard and Air Force, and God knows who else, spending millions of dollars and tying up badly needed manpower on a gut feeling?"

"You've done it before."

"There was a bit more to it than my gut, Tom."

"Sorry, sir. What other way is there?" He hesitated. "We could always get a helo and do it ourselves."

"And where would we start? Let's say they took the bomb last July, as we believe. They've had almost eleven months to get it where they want it."

"So look at it backwards," Tom said. "How far can you take an Egg Harbor without gassing up? Not across the Atlantic or Pacific. You'd have to stay relatively close to the coast around the Gulf of Mexico. Check to see if one went through the Panama Canal. If it didn't, it's still on the East Coast."

"Don't forget the Great Lakes."

Tom gave a small smile. "I was hoping you had, sir."

"That still leaves us thousands of miles to cover." Michael finished his beer. "We're beginning to learn more and more about the way al Qaeda operates. They plan, sometimes for years. They've got almost unlimited resources when it comes to money and equipment. They get trained at camps in Afghanistan, Pakistan, Somalia, the Philippines, etc. Then they're let loose to live among us. So why do I keep coming back to whatever they're planning is the last place we'd think to look?"

Tom glanced at his watch and got to his feet. "I dunno, sir. But my gut's telling me it's time to eat. You need to check on Delta. I'll finish up here and put something on the grill."

"Thanks, Tom."

"You're welcome, sir."

Tom watched Michael go back down the dock. *If he don't quit worrying soon, he's going to grind himself into an early grave.*

Michael finished the last mouthful from his plate and sat back.

"That was great, Tom. What will I do if the Army ever lets you go?"

Tom chuckled. "I got the impression when I signed on with you, it was for life. You ain't getting rid of me that easy. Army or no Army."

Michael grinned. "Cigar?"

"Don't mind if I do, sir." Tom lit the cigar and took a deep puff. "You never did answer my question."

"What question was that?"

"Why you want Boost to check out the Viking."

Michael poured two glasses of Glenfiddich on the rocks, handing one to Tom. "I want to see if he can tweak her."

"Knowing Boost, he probably can. But at what cost to fuel economy? I thought that's why you got her with diesels."

"But back then I wasn't planning on running down a fifty-two-foot Egg Harbor."

Tom chuckled. "Now I get it."

"If I can locate Jarrah and the Egg, it's doubtful he'd suspect anyone with a similar-size boat. Forget the Marines. We play him at his own game."

"The Navy and the Coast Guard have got some pretty fast boats, sir."

"I know. But Sam said he could spot surveillance a mile away. They don't care if they die. One whiff of him being exposed, and he could trigger God knows what. I daren't risk it."

"I'll get Boost out here Monday, sir."

That night, Michael constantly tossed and turned in his sleep. His dreams were a never-ending slide show of Sam; Jarrah's face from the only known photograph; sandy, sun-kissed beaches; a fast sportfisherman; snapshots of Rome, Berlin, and Madrid; and his father's angry face. Somewhere in the jumbled mix, he thought he saw Lynn, but the image was far too vague.

Chapter Twenty-Nine

Michael's Office, G Street, Washington, D.C.
Wednesday, May 14, 2003

Dan entered Michael's office just before 10:00 a.m.

"I've just got off the phone with Bruyere," he said.

Michael motioned to him to sit. "Good or bad?"

Dan shrugged. "Could be either. He's got someone in Madrid checking out apartments in the area of the address Sam gave you. So far, nothing. But FTF did find the Mercedes in long-term parking at the Berlin airport. They haven't touched it, but they've now got someone keeping watch, in case anyone comes back."

"So Sam told the truth about the car?"

"Looks that way. It does get better. Bruyere tracked down the flight attendants on the Iberia flight to Madrid. Two of them share an apartment in Berlin. The first one couldn't remember seeing a couple matching that description, and the second one was out playing tennis. She showed up just as they were leaving. Her station's in first class, and the only reason she remembered them was although they looked Italian and had an Italian last name, because she checked the passenger list, was that they spoke English. She thought it odd."

"Really?"

"Apparently, that flight's first-class passengers are usually business people. This couple definitely wasn't."

"Did Bruyere get the name?"

Dan smiled. "Raimondo and Susana Rossi. From what she could remember, he had a brown ponytail, and the woman's hair was straight and blonde."

Then according to Dan, Bruyere got the woman to help with an identikit of Jarrah before she left for her scheduled Iberian airways route that morning.

"This is how she identified him." Dan held up a piece of paper. "It just came via e-mail."

Michael studied the face. "His own mother wouldn't recognize him."

"That's what I thought. But it doesn't mean that's what he looks like now."

"I know."

"But just to be sure, Bruyere's sent the identikit to his people in Madrid. Maybe we'll get lucky?"

"That would make a change."

Chapter Thirty

Michael's Office, G Street, Washington, D.C.
Tuesday, May 20, 2003

Dan took the call at 9:10 a.m.

According to Bruyere, the latest identikit of Jarrah, compiled with the help of the Iberian airways' flight attendant, had finally produced results. With hundreds of apartments within the area of the street names Sam gave Michael, FTF agents made the decision that adequate surveillance would take too much time and manpower. So they resorted to searching the old-fashioned way. They went door to door. Several of the residents in one building thought they recognized the identikit of Jarrah. That was the good news.

The bad news was that after watching the suspect apartment for twenty-four hours, with no signs of life, Bruyere gave the order to break down the door. But they were too late. Whoever had been there was already gone. And the news was about to get worse.

"For the last two days, we've studied all the Madrid airport surveillance tapes," Bruyere said. "No Jarrah. And no one who looks like him. We went through all the airline passenger lists too. No Rossi either. He could be anywhere."

"What about the woman in Malaga?"

"Have you any idea how many villas are in the area? We could search for months and still not find her. If she's still there. We'll keep looking."

Dan passed on the news to Michael. And to Dan's surprise, he didn't comment.

But after Dan closed the door, leaving Michael alone, he stared again at the world map on his office wall.

When Sam calls, she's giving me tidbits of information. Enough to know she's telling me the truth, because she knows I'll check, but not enough for us to do anything about it. And when we do, it's always after the fact. Why do I feel I'm being played, goddamnit!

Michael got to his feet, running a hand through his short hair, and studied the map more closely. But although he traced the route Sam had already taken, his eyes kept moving back to the East Coast of the U.S., and Savannah, Georgia, in particular.

Chapter Thirty-One

Michael's Office, G Street, Washington, D.C.
Wednesday, June 4, 2003

"There's a Jason Burrows on line one," Molly told Michael. "He's says he's a CIA analyst with the bin Laden Issue Unit.[13]"

"Put him through."

The line clicked. "Colonel Correa?"

"Speaking."

"Could we meet, off campus? There's something I think you should know."

"You work for my father?"

"We all do, indirectly, sir. This has got nothing to do with him personally."

Michael's interest was piqued. "Where and when?"

"I don't know. Somewhere we can talk freely."

"Roosevelt Memorial. 1300."

Burrows checked his computer clock. "I know it, sir. I'll be there. I'll be wearing—"

"I'll know what you look like," Michael interrupted.

Burrows swallowed. "Thank you, sir."

Before Michael left the office with Dan on their now-daily run, he'd not only checked the CIA employee directory, but also had a copy of Burrows' driver's license.

---

13 A twenty-five person unit within the CIA, who monitor anything of relevance to Osama bin Laden. Known internally as 'The Manson Family.'

"We're meeting this guy," he said to Dan, showing him Burrows' photograph and explaining the earlier phone call.

"Do you know what he wants?"

"No clue. Except he sounded nervous. Watch my six. I wouldn't put it past my father to set some kinda trap."

"Great," Dan muttered. "We're not only fighting terrorists, but the CIA. How perfect is that."

The Roosevelt Memorial, Washington, D.C.
Lunchtime

Despite the milling tourists, thirty-eight-year-old Burrows was easy to find. Wearing an open-neck checked shirt and khaki slacks, he was slightly built with thinning brown hair and a small goatee.

Michael stopped in front of him and wiped his face with a towel. "I'm Michael."

Burrows nodded and looked around. "I know."

Dan reached Michael's side. "I need to check you out."

Burrows shuffled his feet. "Is this really necessary?"

"If you want to speak to the colonel, it is."

"He's Secret Service," Michael said in way of explanation as Dan quickly, and for the most part unnoticed by passersby, ran a scanner over Burrows.

"He's clean."

"I made sure I wasn't followed," Burrows said. "I really do have a dentist appointment, so they knew I'd be leaving."

Michael pointed to the path. "Let's walk. What's this about?"

Burrows glanced pointedly at Dan.

"He's with me," Michael added. "You speak freely to both of us. Or forget it."

"I'm with a twenty-five-person unit at the agency," Burrows began hurriedly. "They call us 'The Manson Family.' We monitor anything with relevance to Osama bin Laden." Burrows slowed, looking around. "If I'm caught talking to you, it could cost me my career."

"We're all on the same side," Michael said. "Or hasn't anyone noticed? Go on."

"Last month, we got wind of a fatwa issued to bin Laden on May 21st by a prominent Saudi cleric. In a nutshell, it grants bin Laden permission to use nuclear and chemical weapons against the U.S. and her allies."

Michael stopped. "Why are you telling me this?"

Burrows lowered his voice. "Someone at a pay scale far in excess of mine has made the decision that we should keep it quiet. I think it's a terrible mistake. I've been with the unit since the mid-nineties, and bin Laden's used every fatwa that's been issued. It's well documented."

Burrows dropped his voice to almost a whisper. "Rumors get around. We know some of your background and who you really work for. Keeping this information under wraps from the commander in chief, I believe, is a monumental error in judgment."

"Who is this Saudi cleric?"

Burrows pulled a small piece of paper from his pants pocket. "Sheik Nasir bin Hamid al Fahd.[14] I wrote it down."

Michael took the paper. "Thanks. Does this fatwa give any clue as to where or when?"

Burrows shook his head. "No. But it does say as we 'infidels' have killed millions of Muslims, and as they consider this a 'holy' act, they've got carte blanche to take out as many men, women, and children as possible. I think ten million was mentioned."

Michael's expression gave nothing away. "Any idea where they're going to get a weapon like that?"

Burrows shook his head. "Our best guess is Russia. They've got everything they'd need." He held out his hand. "I've got to go. Thank you for seeing me. I've got no idea what you're going to do with the information, but please, keep my name out of it. I've got a wife and three children."

Michael returned a surprisingly firm handshake. "Rest assured, your name will never be mentioned, and this meeting didn't happen."

"Thank you, Colonel," Burrows replied.

Michael and Dan both watched him go.

"After what we just heard, you're taking it remarkably calmly," Dan said.

"Yeah, right. My guts are turning to mush as we speak."

"Mine too. I gotta sit down."

"Ten million?" Dan added from the nearest bench as Michael sat beside him. "Tell me this isn't happening."

"I can't. But you'd better start praying to every God you know, and a few more you don't, that we stop this in time. Otherwise, this is going to make 9/11 look like a walk in the park."

"Considering where we are, that's a real bad analogy."

---

14 Saudi-born cleric who issued the May 21, 2003 fatwa to Osama bin Laden, virtually giving him 'carte blanche' to use weapons of mass destruction against the U.S. at home and abroad, and our allies. He, along with two other sheiks, was arrested at Mecca in June 2003, after their fatwas were linked to acts of terrorism.

As they ran silently back to the office, all Michael could think was, *Call me, Sam. For God's sake, call me.*

Michael's Townhouse, Duke Street, Old Town, Alexandria, Virginia
Later that night

After eating leftovers, Michael stretched out on the sofa with the TV remote. He channel surfed for a couple of hours before finally hitting the OFF button in disgust.

His afternoon meeting with Burrows had rattled him more than he cared to admit. A Glenfiddich on the rocks and his favorite brand of cigar didn't help. Neither did a long hot shower.

Falling into bed, he tossed and turned for another hour before reaching for his cell phone.

"Hey, lady," he said.

"Hi, stranger," a very sleepy voice replied.

"I woke you? I'm sorry."

"It's okay," Lynn said, trying to focus on her bedside clock. 11:35 p.m.

"Go back to sleep."

She sat up, turning on the light. "No, don't hang up. I'm awake now. Has something happened?"

"Nothing."

"Are you all right?"

"I'm fine."

"Stop giving me off-the-shelf answers."

"I'm an off-the-shelf kinda guy."

"Yes, and I'm the Venus de Milo. Tell me what's going on?"

"I can't. You know that."

"Yes, I do know, but there is something, isn't there?"

"Maybe."

"Is it dangerous?"

"Depends."

Although they now spoke several times a week, Lynn hadn't seen Michael since the middle of March. But their relationship had definitely grown, so over the next hour, she eventually managed to get more out of him than one-word sentences.

"If I don't see you soon, I'll forget what you look like," she said at one point.

"I haven't forgotten you," he replied.

"Good. Because I really want to see you."

"As soon as I can, I promise."

"I'll hold you to that."

"I hope you will."

Michael sounded far more relaxed when they finally hung up, but as Lynn finally replaced the receiver, she knew something was very wrong.

SLED, Computer Crime Center, West Park Blvd., Columbia, South Carolina
Thursday, June 5, 2003

By midmorning, Lynn had gotten very little work done.

She felt sick to her stomach, and unable to concentrate, she was just staring at a blank computer screen when Boswick's head appeared around her office door.

"Morning, Lynn," he said. "Still seeing the pretty-boy colonel?"

She swiveled her chair to face him. "Stop calling him that. I'm sick of it!" She noticed his cheeky grin was fast disappearing. "I took an oath to protect and serve. I'm not sure about you—"

"That was a cheap shot," he interrupted.

"It was meant to be. Michael's Special Forces," she continued. "Unlike us, they purposely put themselves in harm's way so that we'll all be safe."

Realizing what she'd just said, she sprang to her feet and rushed out of the office.

"Oh, shit," Boswick muttered, as he watched her hastily retreating down the corridor.

In the ladies' room, Lynn locked herself in a stall and let the tears flow. She tried to tell herself that she was just another temporary woman in Michael's life, and it was true that he'd never said anything to make her think otherwise. It didn't help.

I don't care about me. But please, God, keep him safe. Don't let anything happen to him. And then decided that she'd make a pact with the devil, if she thought it would help.

She wasn't sure how long she'd been gone, but after splashing cold water on her face and blowing her nose several times, she went back to her office.

To her surprise and annoyance, Boswick was still there, and it was obvious to him she'd been crying.

"Are you okay?" he asked.

"Do I look okay?" she snapped.

"I didn't mean to upset you."

"You didn't. Well, no more than usual."

"I hadn't realized you were so serious about him."

"I'm not."

Boswick didn't comment. Instead, he cleared his throat. "Let me take you to dinner tonight?"

She was about to reply.

"No funny stuff," he added quickly. "I promise. One friend to another, that's all. It looks like you could use one right now."

He thought he was about to get another earful, but to his surprise, Lynn wiped her eyes and quietly said, "Thanks, Charlie. Maybe, it's what I need."

On the verge of leaving, he hesitated. "I'm guessing that Michael's doing something dangerous?"

She faced him, her eyes full of tears again. "He called late last night. He can't tell me, and I can't ask. Right now, I'm so scared for him, I just want to die."

Michael's Office, G Street, Washington, D.C.
Late afternoon

Michael was about to leave when his second cell phone rang.

"It's Sam," she said. "I have to be quick. I'm in a bar in Amsterdam with a group of people."

Michael could hear music and people talking in the background, and they weren't speaking English.

"What are you doing there?"

"I'm not sure. I flew out of Madrid a few days ago. I've been staying at this house here. It's the first chance I've had to use a phone."

"Where's Jarrah?"

"I don't know. 'Asim said he'd meet me, when he put me on the plane. I didn't even know where I was going, until I got to the airport."

"Where's 'Asim now?"

"Still in Spain, I guess. I've got to go. Sorry, Michael."

All he heard was dial tone.

He turned back to the world map on his wall. *Amsterdam? What the hell's she doing in Amsterdam?*

He seriously thought about getting Dan to call Bruyere again but decided against it.

All the FTF has done for us is chase all over Europe with zero results. No, this time I'll wait.

Chapter Thirty-Two

Michael's Office, G Street, Washington, D.C.
Monday, June 9, 2003

"SAC Fuller's on line one," Molly said a little after 10:00 a.m.

Michael hit a button on the phone pad. "Correa."

"Don't know how you do it," Fuller said. "But that anonymous tip you got was right on the money."

"Good."

"The guy's singing like a canary. How did you say you found out about him?"

"One of my guys was on Tybee Island. Slycroft's name came up in conversation at a local bar."

"Do you know if your guy acted on it?"

"No, he didn't. He just informed me."

"Really?" Fuller continued. "Because someone got to him before we did. He was scared shitless. Our agents had to throw him in the shower before they'd let him inside their vehicle. Someone had tied him up and left him. He was so pleased to see them, he was begging to be taken in. You wouldn't know anything about that?"

"Why would you think that?"

Fuller gave a low chuckle. "Well, thanks anyway. We're getting names, dates, a shitload of stuff. I'll pass it on, even though it's of no interest to you. Correct?"

"Thanks. I'm always looking for more paperwork."

"That's what I figured."

Michael's Office, G Street, Washington, D.C.
Thursday, June 12, 2003

Michael's second cell phone rang as he was arriving back from his run.

"I'm in Cancun," Sam said.

"Mexico? What are you doing in Mexico?"

"I don't know. But I'm at the airport, waiting for Jarrah."

"When did you get to Cancun?"

"Monday night. I'm staying at this resort, but I don't know for how long. I think I'm going to be moved again. One of Jarrah's men is looking out for me, but the idiot drank the water, so now he's stuck in a bathroom at the hotel. That's why I'm finally alone."

"You flew there from Amsterdam?"

"Yes, on US Airways. It was a one-way ticket."

"And Jarrah wasn't with you?"

"I told you that. I haven't seen him since Madrid."

Michael could hear noise in the background.

"I've got to go," Sam continued. "His flight's already landed, and he'll be coming through customs any minute."

"Flight from where?" Michael asked.

But she'd already hung up.

"Goddamnit!" He hit the desktop so hard with his fist that Molly heard it through the closed solid-wood door.

Michael got to his feet, staring yet again at the world map on his office wall. *Rome, Berlin, Madrid, Amsterdam, Cancun, Mexico. He's getting closer. A roundabout route, but he's definitely getting closer. But where did he go between Madrid and Cancun?*

He flipped open his laptop.

Using the times Sam gave him, Michael found a matching US Airways flight from Amsterdam that connected in Philadelphia. But he continued to surf. By the time he'd finished checking, one thing became clear; if she told the truth, her flight hadn't been the cheapest, but it was the fastest.

He'd planned on getting Brian or Molly to check incoming flights to Cancun for Jarrah, but having already seen a small number of possibilities from all over the world, he decided against it. *Our priority's to find where he's going. Not where he's been.*

Chapter Thirty-Three

En Route to Michael's Office, Washington, D.C.
Wednesday, June 25, 2003

For the past few days, in Molly's opinion, Michael had gone from a bear with a sore head to a caged lion. In his frustration, when he wasn't in his office with the door closed, he'd pace, stopping in the middle of a conversation every time a phone rang.

At 7:30 a.m., his second cell phone rang in heavy commuter traffic on I-395.

This time, Sam didn't even bother to say who it was. "Check the NOAA[15] web site," she said quietly. "He's been studying weather."

"Weather where?" Michael asked as the car in front of him began to brake hard. "Sam? Weather where?"

"I don't know. I overheard him say 'lambs.'"

Then all Michael heard was dial tone.

Michael's Office, G Street, Washington, D.C.
Thirty minutes later

Molly looked up as he came flying through the outer door.

"Everyone in my office. Now," he ordered, not slowing down.

"Molly, pull up the NOAA web site," Michael said when they were assembled. "See what's happening. I want to know."

---

15 National Oceanic & Atmospheric Administration.

Brian and Dan watched her leave.

"Sam called," Michael continued. "Jarrah's watching the weather. She heard him say 'lambs.' Mean anything to you?"

"As in sheep?" Dan asked.

Michael shrugged. "Lambs to the slaughter."

"This doesn't sound good."

"I need you to think. Fast."

"I'm goin' to surf Google," Brian said. "See if I can get some ideas."

As Brian left Michael's office, Molly reentered carrying a wireless remote laptop and placed it on his desk. "That's the NOAA site. There's nothing there. See for yourself."

Michael studied the screen. "I want this monitored 24/7. Until further notice."

"The whole world?" she asked.

Michael turned to the wall map. "The Gulf of Mexico and the East Coast."

"Well, it is hurricane season, I suppose."

Michael didn't reply. Seconds ticked by before he finally faced her. "That's it. He's waiting for bad weather. Good work."

She beamed.

Brian appeared in the doorway. "All I'm gettin' is references to nursery rhymes. We gotta narrow the search."

"No," Michael said. "Widen it. 'Lambs' is something. What?"

"A hotel. A restaurant. A shopping mall," Dan suggested.

"Fine," Michael replied. "Try anything. Dan take Texas. Brian, Mississippi, and get Molly started on Louisiana. And keep watching the weather."

"Gulf states?" Brian asked.

Michael nodded. "One at a time. I'll check Florida."

But before he did, he called Tom. "How's the boat?"

"She's running great, sir."

"Get her ready. All the supplies we discussed. He doesn't know it yet, but Dan's coming with you."

"Where to, sir?"

"South."

"How far south?"

"I'll let you know."

"If Dan takes the helm, we can keep on cruising. I just gotta get a list of marinas along the way to gas her up."

"What did you say?"

"If Dan—"

"No, after that."

"I just gotta get a list of marinas ..."

"Thanks, Tom. I'll call you later."

"You're welcome, sir." But Tom was talking to dial tone.

Michael opened his laptop and did his own Google search, trying to ignore the fact that there were over four hundred thousand listings. But he was only halfway down the first page when something caught his eye.

He stared again at the map before doing another search. Then he reached for the telephone and made several urgent calls; the last one, and by far the most important, was to the Naval Air Station, Jacksonville, Florida.

Eventually hanging up, he let out a long sigh. *I pray to God I'm right,* he thought before dialing Dan's extension.

"You find something?" Dan asked from the doorway moments later.

Michael motioned to him to close the door.

"I think I know the target," he said. "Are you packed?"

"Ready to go, when you give the word." Dan moved closer. "So what is it?"

Michael pointed at the map. "There."

Dan stared. "You're kidding? Why there?"

"If Sam's telling the truth and Molly's right, Jarrah's waiting for bad weather. Tropical storms and hurricanes spin counterclockwise in the northern hemisphere. If one hits just right, it'll carry the fallout westward. Like a cork in a bottle. No escape."

Dan stepped closer to the map. "You're right. I bet that's the target. The last place anyone would think. These guys are smart. What now?"

"I've got a P-3[16] beginning aerial surveillance around the clock."

"How many millions is that costing?"

"Considering what's at stake, it's a bargain."

"Point taken. What are they looking for?"

"An Egg Harbor headed toward a marina."

"A marina called Lambs?"

"Affirmative. Now go. Get to the Eagles Nest as fast as you can. Tom's waiting. Use cell phones, until you board."

As Dan left his office, Michael was again reaching for the telephone.

Ten minutes later, Brian and Molly were standing in front of him.

"I'm leaving," Michael said, zipping up the case to his laptop. "I don't know when I'll be back."

---

16 The Navy's four-engine turboprop anti-submarine and maritime surveillance aircraft.

"Leaving for where?" Molly asked.

"I'm flying to Bragg."

Brian looked around. "Where's Dan?"

"Gone."

"Gone where?"

Michael took his shoulder holster and Beretta out of a desk drawer. "I don't have time to explain." He faced Molly. "Unless the president wants me, take messages. You don't know where I am. Keep monitoring the weather. I'll only answer my cell phone for you. Understood?"

"Yes, sir. Understood."

"And help her out, Brian. I need you here."

"How you gettin' to Bragg?"

"Helo from Andrews," Michael replied, heading for the door.

Then he was gone, leaving Molly and Brian alone.

Brian stood in front of the map. "Michael's bin studyin' this for weeks. I reckon he knows where Jarrah's headin'."

"Why not tell us?"

He faced her. "If I'm right, this is where Special Ops takes over."

"Then how do you explain Dan leaving too?"

"I can't. And that's the truth."

Eagles Nest, Somewhere off Route 301, the Eastern Shore, Maryland
An hour and a half later

As Dan ran down the dock, he could clearly hear the rumble of diesel engines.

He found Tom in the salon, surrounded by black canvas bags.

"We starting a war?" Dan asked.

"Finishing one I hope, Mr. Whitney. Dump your bag in a stateroom. We gotta get going." He hesitated. "There's Dramamine in the cabinet in the guest head."

Dan swallowed. "Thanks."

Ten minutes later, they were cruising down Chesapeake Bay.

"The colonel know the target?" Tom asked.

"He thinks it's ..." Dan began.

Tom was already nodding as Dan finished. "I'm betting he's right on the money. He's rarely wrong, if ever, when it comes to the mission. Course his women are a different story. Makes a lot of mistakes with them. You ready for boating 101, Mr. Whitney?"

"Only if you'll call me Dan, Master Sergeant. It's about time."

"You gotta deal. Now stand here and push the throttles forward together. Don't worry, you've got clear passage."

Dan took the helm.

"Keep going, Dan. We gotta be down there before Christmas."

He was gripping the wheel as the Viking went up on plane.

"Just remember," Tom added. "It's like driving a car with no brakes and real poor response."

"That's comforting," Dan replied. "How fast will she go?"

"Since Boost worked his magic, we can cruise at thirty-eight knots."

"You did say cruise at thirty-eight?"

Tom grinned. "There's plenty more if we need it."

Fort Bragg, North Carolina
Early afternoon

The UH-60 Black Hawk landed at 12:45 p.m. The Air Force sergeant on duty who'd caught Michael's car keys before he boarded at Andrews, followed by the words "take care of it," eyed the Aston Martin as though he'd won the lottery.

Less than an hour later, Michael entered a two-storey building left over from World War II days.

On the second floor, in the once-familiar room, he was reunited with some of his former company team.

"It's good to see you again, Michael, sir," the assistant detachment commander said with a big grin. He eyed Michael's suit. "You the pinup boy for corporate America now?"

Michael took off his jacket and tie, and threw them over the back of a chair.

"Welcome back, sir," added the master sergeant, eyeing the shoulder holster. "The M-9[17] adds a nice touch. You look like a goddamn cop."

"It's good to be back," he replied. "Now I know why I miss you guys." He patted the Beretta. "D.C.'s a dangerous place. But you should see the car."

---

17 Beretta's military issue 9 mm semi-automatic since 1990.

Within minutes, after setting up the equipment, Michael was all business, and two large images of Hamza Jarrah and As'ad Rashid were projected onto a wall.

"Gentlemen, our target ..." he began.

For an hour and a half, the twelve men of Alpha team ignored the desks and gathered around Michael. Using a five-paragraph operations order, or OPORD, he briefed them using his laptop, an overhead projector, and butcher block paper on all the possible scenarios.

When it came to paragraph three, Execution, which included the Brevity Codes, he got his first interruption.

"Use characters from *Sesame Street,* sir," the senior communications sergeant said.

"I like it," the junior weapons sergeant added. "Cookie Monster in my crosshairs."

"In that case," Michael said, "Jarrah's Big Bird. And he's mine. Got that?"

"Got that," the senior weapons sergeant replied.

"You want these assholes alive?" the intelligence sergeant asked.

Michael shrugged. "I want them taken down. Clear?"

Several heads nodded.

"If I'm right, they'll be five or six of them." He turned back to the laptop. "Paragraph four: we've got no service support." Then he looked around. "We can do this with one hand tied behind our backs."

"It's fuckin' payback time," he heard the assistant operations and intelligence sergeant mutter at one point. Michael didn't disagree.

When the briefing was finally over, using DoD software, Michael obliterated all the information from the laptop's hard drive. Permanently. But he was left in no doubt that the team couldn't wait to get their hands on Jarrah and his operatives. They'd said very little, but the atmosphere in the room had changed dramatically after Michael explained the mission. All they had to do now was wait.

Fort Bragg, North Carolina
Saturday, June 28, 2003

Dressed in fatigues, Michael was in the team room when he took the call on a secure satellite phone at 1800.

"We've got movement, sir," the communications officer aboard the P-3 Orion told him. "An Egg Harbor sportfisherman leaving a private dock south of Jacksonville, heading due north. I'm sending pictures."

"Do that," Michael replied, turning on the team's laptop.

"There's a single male at the helm on the flying bridge," the communications officer continued. "Looks like one passenger ... no, make that two, sir. One male, one female."

That's got to be Sam, Michael thought.

"No positive ID on any of the individuals, sir. Sorry."

"What color's the female's hair?"

There was a pause. "Black, sir."

"Is it short?"

"Yes, sir."

"That's the target. Trust me."

There was another pause. "One unidentified male just seen carrying an automatic weapon. Looks like a Mac-10.[18]"

"Don't let them out of your sight. And keep me informed. Got that?"

"Got that, sir."

The team gathered around Michael as one by one, photographs from the P-3 via a secure satellite feed began to appear on the laptop's screen.

Michael pointed to one of them. "If I'm right, that's Jarrah at the helm."

"Big Bird, sir?"

Michael grinned at the master sergeant. "You got it."

He pointed at another photograph of a bearded man with a lightning bolt scar, half concealing a Mac-10, he immediately recognized as As'ad Rashid. "And there's Oscar the Grouch."

"And the woman, Michael?" the detachment commander asked.

"Won't be a factor," he replied. "Concentrate on the mission."

For the next two hours, the P-3 continued to transmit photographs, but Michael hadn't seen Sam again.

When the Egg Harbor finally docked, and he was sent photographs of Jarrah and Rashid securing the lines, there was still no sign of her.

---

18 Military Armament Corporation's highly compact select fire machine pistol.

Fort Bragg, North Carolina
Sunday, June 29, 2003

The Nightstalker's MH-60 Black Hawk arrived from Hunter Army Airfield in Savannah the previous night. So when Michael's second cell phone rang at 9:00 a.m., the team was ready to go. It was probably the most important phone call he'd ever received. It was also the shortest. But he finally got the confirmation that he'd been right about Jarrah's target as Sam whispered one word before hanging up.

Within minutes, the team was aboard, and the Black Hawk lifted off, heading back the way it came.

Within an hour of flight time, Michael got word through the chain of command that Posse Comitatus[19] for this particular mission had been waived.

"We've got a green light," he told the men, hanging up the secure satellite phone before making another call.

Somewhere in the Atlantic Ocean, off the Coast of South Carolina

Using a secure Iridium Satphone to communicate with Michael to and from the Viking, Tom was now grinning as he clicked off. "We got company coming."

Dan looked around at the vast expanse of ocean, with no other ships or land in sight. "We're going to shore?"

Tom shook his head. "Take too much time. Keep an eye out beyond the stern. Their ETA is 1035."

Dan checked his watch. "In twenty minutes?"

"You'll see. I'm staying at the helm. You'll need these," he added, handing Dan a pair of Army-issue M2 rubber-cased binoculars. "When they get closer, you let me know."

---

19 Means 'the power of the country,' and the act was originally passed in 1878, with the intent of removing the Army from domestic law enforcement. For the last twenty years, it has become more of a procedural formality, but it does prevent the unauthorized deployment of troops at a local level for civilian law enforcement. The National Command Authority (the president) still has considerable control to use the military in the war on terrorism, etc.

Dan scanned the horizon behind the Viking for ten minutes before he saw a small black dot. As the dot grew larger, he could hear and see a military-style helicopter, flying low and directly toward them.

"You're kidding?" he said loudly to Tom. "That's our passenger?"

Tom only nodded before easing back on the throttles to decrease the Viking's speed to fifteen knots.

The boat slowed, beginning to roll more dramatically in the swells.

The helicopter got a lot closer.

"Better get your butt up here with me," Tom shouted down. "Or get inside. You sure don't want to be on the sundeck."

Grabbing the handrail, Dan chose the flying bridge with Tom.

Now hovering seventy-five feet above the Viking, the downdraft kept to a minimum, the first thing Dan saw was a thick rope from the Black Hawk landing on the sundeck. When he looked up, a figure in a helmet and fatigues jumped from the helicopter's open doorway onto the rope. His "fast rope" descent, without a safety harness, only took four seconds. The moment he was onboard, he signaled to the Black Hawk, and the helicopter rose to one hundred and fifty feet, taking the three-inch-diameter rope with it. As soon as the rope was clear of the Viking on the leeward side, the line was released into the sea, and the Black Hawk banked sharply away.

Immediately, the Viking's speed increased again.

That looked like a stunt from a Hollywood movie, Dan thought, trying to steady himself, as the figure climbed the ladder to the flying bridge.

"Welcome aboard, sir!" Tom said as Michael reached him and took off his helmet.

"Good to be aboard, Tom," he replied.

"That was quite an entrance," Dan commented.

"There was no other way. We've got Jarrah cornered."

Lambs Yacht Center, Lakeshore Blvd., Jacksonville, Florida

By the time they reached their visitor slip, it was getting dark.

As Michael, now dressed in a tee shirt and shorts, eased the Viking alongside the dock, anyone watching could have easily been fooled into thinking they were three men on a fishing trip. Had anyone been allowed inside the salon, the arsenal of weapons told a totally different story.

He cut the engines as Dan and Tom secured the lines.

Dan had just finished when he saw Jarrah coming toward him along the dock.

"Evening," Dan said as Jarrah got closer. He pointed at the Egg Harbor. "Nice boat."

Jarrah smiled. "It suits my purpose."

"You a live-aboard?"

"No. Visiting."

"Yeah. Us too. Staying long?"

Jarrah shrugged. "Probably not."

"Know what you mean. The fishing's been lousy." Dan began to board the Viking. "Nice meeting you. Gotta go. I've got a cold beer waiting."

Jarrah only nodded and turned his back.

Inside the salon, Dan sat in a chair and swallowed. "You couldn't get any closer?" he asked quietly as Michael handed him a beer. "Jesus! He's docked in the next slip."

Michael sat opposite. "Good planning. How was our terrorist?"

"Sorta friendly. He speaks English like a native."

Tom grabbed a beer from the refrigerator in the galley. "If you don't mind me saying, sir, I think you should keep a low profile. Just in case."

"Good point."

Within an hour of them docking, the captain and senior intel sergeant arrived onboard. Dressed in civilian clothes and carrying four large pizzas and six packs of beer, they looked just like a couple of guys ready to party.

In the salon, after Dan was introduced, they ate the pizza and drank one beer before dividing up the next few hours into who would stand watch. Although they could see dim lights from inside the Egg Harbor, since Dan had seen Jarrah earlier, no one else had appeared. But on Michael's orders, using a laptop on a counter in the galley, they constantly monitored the NOAA web site. And when he did sleep, Michael's loaded Beretta was within easy reach.

Chapter Thirty-Four

Lambs Yacht Center, Lakeshore Blvd., Jacksonville, Florida
Monday, June 30, 2003

"Wake up, sir. We've got something."

Michael opened his eyes to see Tom in the master stateroom.

"You need to look at NOAA," Tom added. "Looks like you got your storm."

Still dressed, Michael rolled off the bed and checked his watch: 7:30 a.m.

In the galley, with a strong cup of coffee, Michael stared at the laptop's screen. A tropical depression already named Bill was rapidly forming in the Gulf and expected to hit Louisiana later that day.

Michael turned. "Any movement from the Egg?"

The captain shook his head. "Nada. But the team's on standby. He's got to make his move sometime today, don't you think?"

Michael peered through the blinds. Outside, the sky was already gray and overcast, and as he turned back, large drops of rain were beginning to strike the windows.

He nodded. "Tonight. Under cover of darkness. That's what I'd do."

The captain and the intel sergeant got ready to leave. But before they did, due to the security risks of transmitting in the open, they re-checked the frequency to their communications gear, predetermined at Michael's Friday afternoon briefing. Using blue dot secure speech to communicate, their equipment was known in the business as 'blue dot Motorolas.'

The captain was about to open the door to the sundeck when he stepped back.

"Oscar's on the move," he said quietly.

Michael quickly cracked a blind in the salon to see Rashid walking rapidly down the dock, away from the Egg Harbor.

The intel sergeant immediately picked up the empty pizza boxes and stepped into the rain. "We're on him," he said, followed by the captain. "Looks like it's started."

Michael watched them leave.

"There's no other movement on the Egg," Dan said as Tom began loading trash into a large plastic bag.

Then Tom put on foul-weather gear. "I'm taking this to the dumpster, sir. See what I can see."

As he opened the door to the sundeck, a strong gust of wind hit the Viking. "Perfect boating weather," he added before climbing off the boat.

But Tom had nothing unusual to report on his return.

As the day wore on, the Viking began moving gently against the dock as the rain got heavier, driven by ever-increasing strong gusts of wind.

"You okay?" Michael asked Dan halfway through the afternoon.

Dan nodded. "Finally getting my sea legs, I hope."

Michael peered through the blinds at the Egg Harbor for the umpteenth time. "Let's hope it lasts."

"Unsub coming along the dock," Dan said suddenly around 7:00 p.m. He waited until the individual got a little closer. The sheeting rain didn't help, but the man's face was effectively hidden by a hooded rain slicker, and he was carrying what looked like two large plastic bags of takeout.

"Could be a food delivery," he added as the man climbed aboard the Egg Harbor and disappeared from view.

But an hour later, the "delivery" man had still to reappear.

"Reckon he's one of Jarrah's men," Tom said to Dan. "When this goes down, you make sure you watch Michael's six."

Dan turned back to the salon window. "Got it covered. Where is he?"

"Talking to the team." Tom checked his watch. "I gotta get my gear."

As he left the salon, Michael came up the steps from the galley.

Dan's first thought was that if Molly or Brian could see him they'd probably be surprised. Dressed in black ACUs,[20] an assault vest, and boots, wearing a headset and throat microphone, and carrying a helmet, he now looked like the soldier he was.

"Anything from the Egg?" he asked, bending down to one of the black canvas bags on the salon carpet.

"Nothing."

Michael got to his feet and pocketed several fifteen-round magazines for his Beretta. Then he picked up an M-4.[21] "Want one?" he asked.

Dan took a quick look at the rifle. "I'll stick with my Glock. Okay?"

"Whatever makes you comfortable."

"Right now, that would be a decent meal and a cold beer."

The Viking was suddenly buffeted violently against the fenders.

Michael grinned. "What's wrong with our MREs?[22]"

Then he headed for the door.

"Where are you going?"

Michael stopped. "Up top."

"Not without me."

"Not dressed like that. There's some gear in your cabin. Put it on."

But Michael waited until Tom reappeared from below decks.

"I'll secure the area," Tom said at the salon door.

Michael had every reason to agree. Just because they hadn't seen any activity onboard the Egg Harbor didn't mean that Jarrah had dropped his guard.

"No point in fucking this up now, sir," Tom added quietly before slipping into the night.

Getting the "all clear" signal, Michael quickly climbed the ladder to the flying bridge, followed a few minutes later by Dan, now dressed in ACUs and an assault vest. The storm had intensified, and he had to brace himself as another strong wind gust hit the boat. In the salon and below decks, the storm hadn't seemed that bad, but being so far above the waterline only accentuated the roll.

---

20 Advance Combat Uniform.

21 Colt's gas operated, semi/full automatic assault rifle. Introduced into service in 1997.

22 Meals Ready to Eat.

The Plexiglas and canvas sides to the enclosure were holding back the worst of the weather, but the rain beating on the fiberglass hardtop made normal conversation almost impossible.

At least we're dry, Dan thought.

Unlike the team.

Taking Sam's words seriously that "Jarrah can spot surveillance a mile away," and with twenty-four hours to recon the area, Michael and the team had stayed in constant touch using the secure blue dot Motorolas. As the closest public boat ramp was ten minutes from Lambs, they'd decided it was the most likely launch point. Consequently, although Dan didn't know it, the team had been in place for several hours. Michael wasn't taking any chances. The Quick Reaction Force, or QRF, was now effectively hidden in the entrance to a privately owned boathouse directly across the Ortega River on the Viking's port side. Driven by the junior engineer, the F-470 Zodiac with a suppressed 35 HP Evinrude outboard also had onboard the junior medic and the team's master sergeant. Using 'brevity codes,' their call signs were respectively Turkey, Hawk, and Swan. And to cover all bases, if something should go wrong, the 'Go-to-Hell' site was approximately three hundred and fifty yards off the Viking's stern, by the bridge to the old Roosevelt Highway. Despite the worsening weather, it was still extremely doubtful that an unmarked panel van in the unofficial parking area would attract any attention.

The assault team, consisting of the warrant officer, the senior weapons sergeant, the senior engineer, the senior medic, and the senior com, known as Pigeon, Falcon, Buzzard, Dove, and Oriole, were aboard the second Zodiac, with another suppressed Evinrude, in the Cedar River. Well concealed behind the heavy wooden pilings that supported the San Juan Avenue bridge, the team was approximately fifty yards from the boat ramp at Lighthouse Marine Park.

In truth, the park was just a large gravel area where cover was minimal at best. Eagle, the junior weapons sergeant and sniper, along with Finch, the junior com sergeant acting as his spotter, finally decided to climb onto the dilapidated roof of a nearby derelict boat storage building and were now unseen from their perilous perch in an over-watch position at two o'clock. To their right, at ten o'clock, hidden beside a concrete parapet to the road bridge and helped by a large bushy palm, but still with clear sight of the boat ramp, were Raven, the team captain, and Sparrow, the intel sergeant.

Regardless of how good Jarrah's operatives were, the team had no doubts about their ability to launch a surprise high-speed assault. The darkness helped. And in their minds, Tropical Storm Bill was the added bonus.

At 11:00 p.m., the storm intensified, making Michael and the team think that if Jarrah was going to make a move, it wouldn't be much longer.

Conversation on the Viking's flying bridge had been almost nonexistent. Taking his cue from Michael's silence, Dan had refrained from asking where Tom was. He knew Michael was in contact with the team, but there'd been no indication. What Dan didn't know was that when the assault took place, any communication would be kept to the bare minimum.

At 11:30 p.m., the gusting wind and driving rain got even worse, but it wasn't sufficient to stop Finch, the sniper's spotter, from seeing headlights approaching on San Juan. After the vehicle turned into the park, he waited a few more seconds to confirm the large dark pickup with four men inside was towing a boat on a trailer before communicating, "Finch. Tango Alpha."

Michael and the team knew immediately that "Tango Alpha" meant "target arriving."

No one moved as the pickup stopped in the gravel area, and three men got out. Then with two of them directing the driver, the pickup began to back slowly down the ramp. The third man positioned himself at the rear of the boat trailer as it edged closer to the water.

The team's 'standard operating procedure,' or SOP, called for the sniper to initiate the assault, even though the team in the vicinity had all eyes on the target.

Eagle waited for the perfect shot.

The team's headsets hissed.

"Oscar has landed," he said quietly.

Seconds later, the pickup's windshield exploded, and with a dead driver at the wheel, the vehicle began to roll backward. Jarrah's three other operatives hadn't heard the suppressed M-24[23] as Eagle squeezed the trigger, and their immediate reaction was to grab the boat trailer. As they did, the assault team's Zodiac came out of nowhere. Speeding to the bottom of the ramp, from his lead position in the bow, Falcon felled the figure at the rear of the

---

23 Bolt-action sniper system. Caliber: 7.62 mm, five-round magazine.

trailer with an M-249,[24] while Raven and Sparrow laid down well-aimed suppressive fire.

By now, the third operative was also down, and although the fourth man had been hit, he somehow managed to roll partway under the trailer. Falcon was almost on top of him, but before he fired again, he saw a handheld radio in the man's hand.

On the Viking's flying bridge, Michael's headset came alive again.

"Condor. Condor. Big Bird's squawked, over," Falcon quickly warned.

Turning toward the Egg Harbor, Michael had no time to reply as Jarrah suddenly appeared on the sundeck, a Mac-10 in his hand.

From his elevated position in the open entrance directly above the ladder, but with no time to put on his helmet and no space to handle the M-4, Michael took the risk.

"Jarrah!" he shouted, the Beretta already in his hand.

Immediately, Jarrah began an indiscriminate burst of automatic fire, and as he spun and looked up, he saw Michael.

In the split second it took Michael to aim and squeeze the trigger, Sam came flying into view. As she lunged at Jarrah, he heard her yell, "No!"

But it was too late.

Facing forward and rapidly descending the ladder, Michael saw the bullets from Jarrah's weapon hit her as Jarrah fell. In that millisecond, Sam jerked like a limp rag doll. Then she was gone.

At the same exact moment, an upward spray of bullets struck the Viking.

From his place of concealment on the floor of the flying bridge, to save Michael before he too was hit, Dan felt he had no alternative and thrust forcibly forward with both feet. The soles of his boots hit Michael squarely on the shoulders. It was so sudden, and with only a wet stainless steel handrail to hold on to, Michael lost what little grip he had and flew headfirst toward the sundeck below. He heard bullets whistling past him, and his only thought was that he was going to die by a dead man's hand. Landing partway on the gunwale, he knew he'd been hit more than once, but he also heard and felt a nasty crack as his head and shoulder took the brunt of the fall. But instead of landing inside the boat, the speed and momentum of his nosedive catapulted him over the side.

---

24 Squad Automatic Weapon. Made by FN Manufacturing, this gas-operated, one-man, portable automatic weapon was introduced into service in 1987. With various magazines available, it is capable of firing up to 750 rounds per minute.

The last thing he remembered, before hitting the water, was the searing pain.

Then everything went black.

Dan heard Michael hit the water and in an instant was on his feet. He came down the ladder so fast that he lost his footing on the wet teak treads but managed to partly save himself by grabbing the handrail. It only slowed his fall. He pitched face down, slamming his head against a cleat on the gunwale. But he didn't hesitate and rolled off the boat into the water. As he did, he heard another burst of automatic fire.

From his well-hidden vantage point on the Viking's bow, Tom was about to leap over the railing when one of Jarrah's men suddenly appeared from around the far side of the Egg Harbor's flying bridge, aiming in Tom's direction. With a burst of automatic fire, Tom cut him down, hesitating for less than a second to see, even in the storm-driven rain, blood and human tissue splatter the white fiberglass. Then, still holding the M-4, Tom dove overboard.

To everyone involved, what had taken mere seconds seemed more like slow motion.

"I can't find him!" Tom heard Dan shout as he surfaced.

Below the hull of the Viking, away from the cabin and dock lights, Tom's first impression was that he was swimming in black ink. Toward the stern of the boat, he could just make out Dan about to dive for a second time.

As Tom reached the stern, Dan surfaced again, and Tom could now see a mixture of water and blood covering his face.

With one hand holding on to the swim platform, Dan took a huge breath. "I can't find him," he said again.

But before Tom could reply, Dan took another huge intake of breath and disappeared below the surface.

The QRF heard Falcon's warning to Michael, immediately followed by automatic gunfire, and as Tom was now about to dive, the F-470 Zodiac was speeding in his general direction.

He got ready to shout when a powerful spotlight hit him.

Waving his arm instead, the boat did a fast turn, coming to a rapid stop beside him.

"We've got a man in the water," he said breathlessly, bobbing up and down in the wake, just as Dan appeared on the surface again.

In an instant, Hawk and Swan were over the side.

"You okay, Tom?" Turkey asked.

Tom nodded, now holding on to a rope attached to the inflatable. "It's Michael. We gotta find him."

"Oh, shit."

Tom threw the M-4 into the Zodiac and was about to let go of the rope when he heard a male voice.

"We got him!"

Immediately, Tom swam to help Hawk and Swan, and with Dan following, they brought Michael's lifeless body toward the boat.

He was still motionless as they pulled him onboard, and while Tom hauled himself into the boat, Turkey was already calling for help.

Tom's first thought on seeing Michael was that he was dead.

Swan, the junior medic, was already beginning CPR as Dan was pulled from the water.

"This weren't supposed to happen," Tom muttered. "Not to the colonel. This ain't right."

At the dock, they lifted a wet and still unconscious Michael onto a stretcher and immediately placed an oxygen mask over his nose and mouth.

Holding a bloodied bandage to his chin, Dan refused all offers of help and climbed unassisted after Michael into the waiting ambulance.

The assembled team could only watch as the doors then closed, and the ambulance drove swiftly away, sirens blaring.

"He was breathing," Swan said quietly.

Tom didn't comment, and as far as he was concerned, their remaining silence said it all.

By the time local law enforcement and the FBI arrived on the scene, there was no sign of the team, Tom, or the Viking.

St. Vincent's Hospital, Barrs Street, Jacksonville, Florida
Wednesday, July 2, 2003

Michael opened his eyes to see a woman in uniform at the end of his bed. It took him a moment to realize where he was.

His head was thundering, his shoulder throbbing, and his ribs ached, but he managed to move his arms and legs.

"You're finally awake," the nurse said. "How do you feel?"

He wanted to say, "like shit." He didn't. "I've been worse. What happened?"

She put back his chart. "Dislocated collarbone, three cracked ribs, and we suspect a concussion. How's the head?"

"It hurts."

"Well, now that you're back in the land of the living, I'll get the doctor, Mr. Doe."

She turned to leave.

"What did you call me?"

She stopped. "Mr. Doe. I've got no idea who you are, but there's a guard outside your door."

"What kinda guard?"

She shrugged. "He's got a dark suit and an earpiece."

"Secret Service?"

"Could be. But if you're a criminal, why would the Secret Service be here?" She hesitated. "You robbed a bank?"

"No, I didn't. That would be FBI."

"Well, you must have done something."

If you only knew. "Do I look like a criminal to you?"

She took a small step toward him. "Not really. But then Ted Bundy was very good looking too."

"Thanks."

The door opened and immediately closed before he could say any more.

Michael could vaguely hear voices coming from outside, but he couldn't make out any of the conversation. Looking around his obviously private room, the window blinds were drawn on both sides, although he got the impression that it was daylight outside.

Where the hell am I? Attempting to sit up, he noticed the intravenous needle in his left arm. *What's that for?*

His headache was now so bad that he lay back and closed his eyes.

Michael had no idea how long he'd been asleep, because the next thing he knew, a man in a white coat, followed by his father, were in his room.

"I'm Jack Roberts, your physician. How are you feeling?"

With no women present, Michael did reply, "Like shit."

Roberts laughed. "I'm not surprised. Your father's here."

"I can see that. Hello, Dad."

"You gave us a real scare," Francis said. "I'm pleased to see you're finally awake."

Roberts picked up Michael's chart. "Now tell me how you really feel?"

"My head hurts like hell, and my body feels like it's been kicked by a mule and stung by angry bees."

"Good analogy. Bullets will do that. The vest you were wearing saved you."

Michael pointed at the intravenous. "What's that for?"

"We needed to keep you quiet."

"Sedation?"

"Correct."

Michael slowly faced his father. "That your idea?"

"No, it was mine," Roberts said quickly.

"Really? When can I leave?"

"We'd like to keep you a few more days for observation. Just in case."

He tried to sit up. "I need to speak with my father. Alone."

Roberts turned to go. "Fine with me. Don't stay too long," he added to Francis.

Francis waited until the door closed, then pulled a chair to the side of the bed.

"Did we get them?" Michael asked.

"No, you got them," Francis replied. "Jarrah's dead, thanks to you. One bullet straight between the eyes."

"And the others?"

"One survived. But they don't think he'll make it."

"And Sam?"

Francis hesitated. "We can talk about her later."

"No. Now."

Francis cleared his throat. "I'm sorry, Michael."

"She's dead?"

Francis nodded. "According to the report I got, she jumped in front of Jarrah as he began firing at you. She could well have saved your life."

"Think that makes me feel any better?"

"Probably not."

"I want to be left alone now, Dad."

Francis got to his feet. "I'll stop in later. See how you're doing. In the meantime, get some rest."

Michael's tears didn't start until after the door closed.

It was some time later, Michael wasn't sure how long, when the door opened again, and Dan appeared.

"You okay?" he asked.

"Thanks to you. I owe you."

Dan limped to the bed. "No, you don't. You'd have done the same for me. Sorry about the collarbone and head."

Michael studied him. One eye was swollen shut and already beginning to turn various shades of blue and yellow. Dan's nose looked as though it could have been broken, and there were stitches in the large gash on his chin.

"You look like I feel," Michael said. "Wonder what those babes in Charleston would think now?"

"I don't think they'd be so eager." Dan hesitated. "Do you know about Sam?"

"My father told me. What's he doing here?"

"Probably waiting for the president."

Carefully, Michael sat up. "You gotta be kidding? He's expected here? Why?"

Dan grinned. "You're a hero. The hospital's all abuzz."

"Shit. My nurse thinks I'm a serial killer."

Dan chuckled. "She probably saw Jarrah's body."

"God, I hope not."

Michael attempted to swing his legs out of bed.

"Hold on," Dan said. "Where do you think you're going?"

"Outta here. Can you unhook an IV?"

"Yes. But I'm not going to."

"Thanks, friend. Then see if you can find my cell phones."

Dan looked through the ACUs Michael was wearing when they pulled him out of the water.

"They're here," he said. "But the batteries are dead. I don't think they're designed to be submerged for long periods."

"Great. Lend me yours."

Reluctantly, Dan handed it over.

Michael pressed some buttons. Then a voice he recognized answered.

"How's the boat, Tom?"

"More to the point, how are you, sir? It's good to hear your voice. You gave us some anxious moments back there."

"I'm fine. The boat?"

"Bullets and fiberglass don't mix, sir. But the good news is the holes can be fixed."

"Is she seaworthy?"

"Sure. It's mostly cosmetic."

"Good. Then this is what we're going to do ..."

"You're not serious?" Dan asked when Michael hung up.

"Deadly. And you're going to help me ..."

"On one condition," Dan said when he'd finished. "Wait 'til tomorrow. Otherwise, no deal."

Michael closed his eyes. "Deal."

Suddenly, there was a lot of movement beyond the door, and Makepeace entered the room.

Dan managed to get to his feet.

"Good to see you, Whitney. Great job. Very well done."

"Thank you, Mr. President."

"Give me a moment?" Makepeace asked.

"Of course, sir."

"Don't forget," Michael said as Dan reached the door.

"I won't." He faced Makepeace. "Mr. President."

As Dan left, the door immediately closed.

"So, Michael," Makepeace said, sitting on Dan's vacated chair. "You gave us one helluva scare. But a phenomenal job. Just phenomenal."

"Thank you, sir."

"You're getting a medal, I hope you realize that?"

"There's no need, sir."

"Course there is. You deserve it."

"I didn't do this alone, sir. It was teamwork."

"I realize that. But it was your outstanding leadership that brought all this to a happy conclusion."

"I really don't want a big fuss, sir."

Makepeace chuckled. "It'll be a private ceremony. Otherwise, we'll blow your cover. Can't have that."

Then what do you think this is? "Thank you, sir."

"Still seeing the pretty lieutenant from SLED?"

"I'd like to think I am, sir."

"Good. Bring her along. When you're feeling better. I want to meet her, remember?"

"Yes, sir. I remember."

"Do you feel up to telling me?"

"Yes, sir. When I got the phone call ..."

"... and that's the last thing I remember, until I woke up here. Whitney saved my life."

Makepeace grunted. "So I understand. Sorry about Fareed. But she came through, just as you predicted." He got to his feet and held out his hand. "Thank you, Michael. I thank you. This country thanks you."

Michael returned the firm handshake. "Excuse me for not getting up, sir."

Makepeace chuckled. "Patience, Michael. All in good time."

At the door, he stopped. "Behave yourself," he added before he left.

"Don't bet on it, Mr. President," Michael said quietly to an empty room.

He closed his eyes. *So much for keeping a low profile.*

Michael's room door opened again, and this time the nurse appeared.

It's like Grand Central Station.

"Did you see who was here?" she said. "At this hospital. Did you see? The president came to see you, didn't he?"

"Yes. Still think I'm a serial killer?"

She put her hand on her chest. "I'm so sorry. Forgive me, whoever you are. I feel so stupid."

"Don't."

She began to straighten the bed. "Anything you want, anything, you just ask."

Michael grinned. "Good. Get this IV out of my arm; otherwise, I'll pull it out myself."

"I can't do that."

"Sure you can. I'll put in a good word for you with the president."

Her eyes narrowed. "You know him well, don't you?"

Michael crossed two fingers. "Like that."

"IV coming out," she said. "I don't know why they had you sedated in the first place."

I can think of a few reasons.

St. Vincent's Hospital, Barrs Street, Jacksonville, Florida
Thursday, July 3, 2003

Michael was aware that over a period of time, he didn't know how long, but he suspected overnight, people had entered his room.

When he finally opened his eyes again, it was daylight, and Francis was sitting by the bed.

"How long have you been there?" Michael asked.

Francis shrugged. "Not long."

"The president get off okay?"

"Yes. Because he thinks so highly of you, he insisted on flying down here to make sure you're all right. And to thank you in person."

"Do you think highly of me, Dad?"

"Of course. I'm very proud of you."

"Really? You think I did a great job?"

"You know I do."

"Do you think I'm the best at what I do?"

"Without question. And so does the president. I thought you understood that?"

"Just making sure. So when did you plan on telling me the bomb was useless?"

Francis didn't reply but instead studied his son.

Michael pulled himself into a sitting position. "Whenever you're ready."

Francis cleared his throat. "How long have you known?"

"Long enough."

"Does your team know?"

"No. I never told them."

"Don't you trust them?"

"Implicitly."

"Then why?"

"The main target was Jarrah. The bomb was just added incentive. By the time I knew for sure the terrorists would never be able to use it with any effectiveness, if at all, we were in too deep. If I'd broken the team's trust, we'd have lost our edge."

"Are you going to tell them?"

"Probably not."

"How did you find out?"

"I had plenty of time to think about it over Christmas. How many Mark 15 thermonuclear bombs from 1958 do we have left in our arsenal? The answer's none. Same deal with the triggering devices. If it had no capsule, what good was it to them? Even though we'd got nowhere at that point, I realized it was only a matter of time before someone suggested we research the original crew. Especially as Brian said, 'When you hit a wall, go back and start over.' When the subject did come up, I told him I'd already checked. Worcek was the only one left. But to be sure I'd got it right, I contacted the pilot of the B-47 who jettisoned the bomb. He signed for it. He told me it wasn't armed."

Francis blinked, his voice rising. "He told you! You said he was dead. Some experimental aircraft crash."

"You believed me?"

Francis glared. "Why would I think otherwise?"

"You tell me." Michael looked toward the ceiling. "Mind you, Brian never thought to question it either." He faced his father again, and this time his voice had a definite edge. "Why would he? We're all on the same side. What possible reason could I have for lying to someone this nation's security and my life may depend on?"

Francis got abruptly to his feet. "I can see you're feeling better."

"Yes, Dad. A lot better. What happened to Sadilov?"

"It's not important." He hesitated. "Did the co-pilot die in Vietnam?"

"No. He flew commercially for American Airlines, until he retired. He lives in the Midwest."

"Anything else you failed to tell me?"

From Michael's silence and expression, Francis assumed correctly that he was getting nothing more.

On his way to the door, he pointed at an oversized fruit basket that had been delivered when Michael was asleep. "That's from McDonald," he added. "God knows why he'd want to send you the biggest goddamn basket I've ever seen."

"Is there a card?" Michael asked.

Francis found the card. "Yes. It says, 'You won this round. Delighted you survived to fight another day.' What the hell does he mean by that?"

"Haven't got a clue. Bye, Dad."

"I'll see you back in D.C."

As Francis left the room, it occurred to him that he'd not only been outsmarted by his own son but probably outplayed too.

But by the time he strode out of the hospital to his waiting car, he was grinning. *I'll be damned. A real chip off the old block.*

Michael hit the remote to the TV, just as the female morning newscaster faced the camera, obviously reading from a teleprompter.

"... severe flooding from Tropical Storm Bill continues in the neighboring states of Louisiana, Alabama, and Georgia, leaving thousands still without power. And in a follow-up to the strange story we brought you yesterday, where a military-style raid was carried out at Lambs Yacht Center on Lakeshore Boulevard on Monday night, a spokesperson for Lambs said in a written statement to News 4, 'We knew about the raid. But more than that we cannot comment.'"

The screen changed to a videotape of an overweight man in a golf shirt, shorts, and boat shoes, standing in front of a large motor yacht. The caption along the bottom of the screen read, "Frank Siddons of Jacksonville."

Siddons didn't know whether to look at the camera or the reporter. "I don't care what they say," he said. "We heard and saw automatic gunfire. If it was a military exercise, like we've been told, they were using live ammunition. I took my wife, and we hid below decks. There was definitely something going on. When the gunfire stopped, we saw the flashing lights of an ambulance leaving. Ask anyone who was here."

The camera panned back to a young male reporter. "We've tried to interview several of the other boat owners who were at Lambs on Monday night, but so far no one is willing to talk on camera."

The camera panned again to the long dock and two slips that were now empty.

Where's my boat? Michael thought.

"According to the people who did talk to us," the reporter continued, "all the action took place over there. But as you can see, there's no sign of anything unusual."

He looked down at his notes. "All we've been able to determine from the Jacksonville police was that they also knew about this exercise. I've been told that if everyone staying overnight at Lambs had been given a warning that it was going to take place, this military-style raid would have lost its authenticity."

The reporter faced the camera. "As the war on terrorism continues, according to my sources, the public can expect more of this kind of thing."

The female newscaster appeared again, looking straight at the camera. "Thanks, Roy. If we get any more information, WJXT will of course bring it to you. In other local news ..."

Smiling, Michael hit the OFF button.

When his nurse entered the room an hour later, she found him with Dan, out of bed and dressed in a shirt and shorts, his arm in a sling and wearing dark glasses.

"What do you think you're doing?" she asked.

"Leaving," Michael replied.

"You can't."

"Watch me."

She eyed him. "Where did you get those clothes?"

"I brought them," Dan said. "He can't walk out of here wearing wet ACUs and Kevlar."

She began to argue again, but Michael cut her off. "Either you let me leave or ..." He stopped in mid-sentence, turning to Dan. "Got your weapon on you?"

Dan produced a Glock.

"We shoot the guy outside," Michael finished.

Horrified, the nurse stepped hastily back. "You wouldn't?"

Michael moved toward her. "Try me."

"Okay," she said finally. "But you'll need some pain medication and a wheelchair."

Dan was about to protest.

"Fine," Michael interrupted. "We'll take both. And get rid of the guy outside. Where's the service elevator?"

Ten minutes later, they were in the large elevator.

"We look like the walking wounded," Dan said and eyed the oversized basket of fruit. "Smart to use the wheelchair."

Michael grinned. "We couldn't carry it. And I wasn't going to leave it. They can keep the flowers. My room was beginning to look like a funeral parlor."

As Dan had arranged, a cab was waiting.

"Tom's expecting us?" Michael asked, sliding onto the back seat.

"Ready to go when you are."

"Then let's get the hell outta here."

Lambs Yacht Center, Lakeshore Blvd., Jacksonville, Florida
Thirty minutes later

"It's real good to see you again, sir," Tom said as Michael reached the boat. "How you feeling?"

"Better, now I'm here." He took a good look at the Viking's fiberglass hull and the flying bridge. "How many holes?"

"A few, sir. Nothing that can't be fixed."

Michael studied the spray pattern of bullet holes before looking across the marina at the two empty slips on either side of a dock. "What happened to the Egg?"

"The Feds took it away, sir. Bodies and all." He hesitated. "I'm real sorry about Miss Fareed. She was a real brave woman to do what she did."

Michael only nodded. "Can you give Dan a hand? We brought extra rations for the trip."

"Beats MREs," Tom commented, eyeing the oversized fruit basket.

Within minutes, the lines were secured, and with the rumble of diesel engines, Tom eased the Viking out of the slip.

"Choice is yours, sir," Tom called down from the flying bridge, the boat already heading toward the river. "Long way or short way home?"

"I don't care," Michael replied. "I'm just along for the ride."

Charleston Harbor, South Carolina
Early evening

Cruising at top speed, Tom easily made it to Charleston, even though Michael and Dan needed the downtime. Michael more so than Dan. The sea was calm, much to Dan's relief, and so far Michael had slept for the better part of the journey.

At the Charleston gas dock, they filled up, the stars and stripes already flying everywhere.

Michael could see Dan on his cell phone, and after flipping it closed, he heard him say to Tom, "About ten minutes."

Wearing only swim trunks, Michael lay back down on the sun lounger and closed his eyes.

The next thing he knew, he was gently being kissed.

"Very festive," Lynn said, getting to her feet and studying the large areas of bruising on his torso as he slowly sat up. "Between you and Dan, you'd make one decent body."

Michael stood.

She moved closer.

"Don't hug me," he said.

"It's good to see you too."

Michael eyed her two large bags as Dan lifted them onboard. "Plan on taking a boat trip?"

"That was the general idea." She hesitated. "If you don't want me here, I can get Charlie back."

"Boswick?"

"The same. He drove me." She turned to go. "It's not too late."

"No. I want you to stay."

She turned back. "Sure?"

"Very sure."

After moving the boat to a temporary visitor's slip, and with what Michael considered to be the weakest excuse, Tom and Dan left them alone.

"Don't be mad, but Dan called me," Lynn said, watching them leave. "I wanted to come to the hospital, but apparently you had enough visitors."

"I'm not mad. He still wants to meet you."

"The president remembered?"

"Of course."

She moved much closer. "I don't know what you went through, and I'm not going to ask. The fact that the president flew to Jacksonville to see you is enough." She slid her arms gently around his neck. "But in my opinion, what you need now is some good ol'-fashioned loving."

When she kissed him this time, he responded like the Michael she knew.

He held her with his one good arm. "I don't know how."

She took his hand. "You'll find out I can be real creative. Where's the largest bunk?"

Michael led her to the master stateroom, where she smiled at the queen-size bed.

"The largest bunk," he said and grinned. "What were you expecting, hammocks in the galley?"

She laughed and lay down. "Come here, good looking. It's not polite to keep a lady waiting, even in your battered state."

Michael discovered during the next two hours just how "creative" Lynn could be. And when he did finally sleep, wrapped in her arms, it was the most peaceful sleep he'd had in a very long time.

Chapter Thirty-Five

Friday, July 4 Through Sunday, July 20, 2003

They celebrated the Fourth of July at sea.

"Thought you'd like this back, sir," Tom said on the afternoon of the Fourth, handing Michael his Beretta as they cruised up the Carolina coast. "It landed on the sundeck."

Michael handled the gun. "You cleaned it?"

Tom grinned. "Sure. Know how much it means to you, sir."

Over the years, Michael had taken a lot of good-natured ribbing over his choice of weapon. But the Beretta had saved his life on more than one occasion, and he'd been secretly disheartened at its possible loss. To him, it was not only his constant companion, but he also considered it good luck.

Lynn stayed at Eagles Nest for almost two weeks and later referred to it as "our two weeks of lust." She wasn't surprised to see Michael disobeying doctor's orders and ride Delta on a daily basis with his arm still in a sling, but she decided not to comment.

Two days after arriving in Maryland, Dan, with Tom's help, drove out to Andrews to pick up the Aston Martin. The car had been stored in a hangar, and from what they could tell from its immaculate appearance, the Air Force sergeant on duty that day had taken Michael's words very seriously.

By the time Michael was ready to drive Lynn back to Columbia early on the morning of Sunday, July 20th, he was suntanned and fit, and making it very obvious that he wanted to get back to work.

"Are you staying?" she asked when they reached her condo, shortly after lunchtime.

Michael shook his head. "I can't. I'm expected at Bragg later."

She took the risk. "Another mission?"

"No. A sort of 'thank you' party for the guys."

As Michael swept out of the parking lot, Lynn realized that if their relationship was going to last, she'd better get used to the fact there were certain areas of his life that were always going to be off-limits.

Fort Bragg, North Carolina
Later that afternoon

In a simple no-frills ceremony in the team room, Michael awarded all twelve men the Bronze Star. There were salutes and handshakes and congratulations, but each one of them knew that outside those four walls, the mission would rarely, if ever, be mentioned again.

Later, at the Green Beret Club, Michael placed three hundred dollars on the horseshoe-shaped bar. The inside of the club had changed very little since he was last there, except for the large pink plastic palm tree just beyond the deck.

"Where did that come from?" he asked the master sergeant.

The master sergeant grinned. "Dunno, sir. It just appeared one night. You know how it is."

There was a lot of laughter, bawdy jokes, and general camaraderie, but after two beers with the team, Michael quietly said goodbye and left.

On his drive back to Alexandria, his shoulder now throbbing, he knew that this mission was over for the team. But in his mind, there were still some loose ends to tie up, and he surprised himself that he was actually looking forward to Monday morning.

Chapter Thirty-Six

Michael's Office, G Street, Washington, D.C.
Monday, July 21, 2003

"Welcome back, sir," Molly said. "We missed you."

"Thanks, Molly. It's good to be back."

She handed Michael a sheet of paper. "Those are all your messages. If you don't mind me saying, I think calling the State Department should be a priority."

"Maynard Abernathy? When did he call?"

"Friday, sir."

"You should have called me at home."

"I wasn't going to do that. You needed the rest. Anyway, he knew you were on leave."

"He did? Who is he?"

"The assistant to the deputy director of the Office of the Coordinator for Counterterrorism. He said to tell you it was about Dr. Sadilov."

Sounds like a typical State Department title, Michael thought, already reaching for his phone. "Thanks, Molly. We'll go through the rest later."

"Very good, sir," she said, turning to leave.

Michael assumed Abernathy had a direct line as he answered his own phone.

"It's Michael Correa. I understand you want to talk to me?"

"Thanks for calling back, Colonel. Your assistant made it very clear that you were not to be disturbed last week."

Michael didn't react. "Sadilov?" he said instead.

"Ah, yes. We're assisting Dr. Sadilov. But apparently, he's not willing to speak with anyone but you. Do you know why?"

Michael had no clue, but he wasn't about to tell Abernathy that. "I've got a good idea."

"Can you help us out?"

"Of course. Where is he?"

"Here in D.C. When and if we can debrief him, he'll be rejoining his family."

"You've got them too?"

"Not here. The wife and daughter are presently undergoing therapy. I understand that they went through a horrifying ordeal."

Michael wasn't about to comment. "So when can I see Sadilov?" he asked.

"As soon as you're able."

"How about now?"

Abernathy gave him an address. "Thank you, Colonel. I'll let them know you're coming. I can't stress enough how important this is."

Michael hung up and checked the address again. *Is it a coincidence that it's so close to the Russian Embassy? So Sadilov is alive. But why does he want to see me?*

"I'm not sure when I'll be back," he told Molly a few minutes later. "Hold all my calls."

An address on Columbia Rd. NW, Washington, D.C.
Thirty-five minutes later

It was obvious to Michael, as he waited in an antique-filled living room, that the house was not only an upscale bed and breakfast, but it had been taken over by either State Department or DoJ personnel. He wasn't going to ask, but they were clearly expecting him.

A few minutes later, when Dr. Dimitri Sadilov appeared, he immediately reminded Michael of a World War II Holocaust victim. Although his once-shaved head now had a noticeable amount of dark peach fuzz, his cheeks were hollow and his face gaunt.

Michael held out his hand. "Dr. Sadilov, je suis Michael Correa."

Regardless of his emaciated appearance, Sadilov had a firm handshake. "I recognize you, Colonel, with Sam's telling me," he replied in halting English.

"Préféreriez-vous parler français?"

Sadilov gave a small smile. "Thank you, no. I need practice my English. You not need practice your French. You speak much good."

"Thank you." Michael then handed him a piece of paper with a handwritten note, also in French.

Sadilov read the note. "Yes, I like. It is best?"

Michael nodded.

"We're going for a walk," he told the man just beyond the doorway. "Follow if you must, but give me some space." Opening his jacket, the shoulder holster and the grip of the Beretta were clearly visible. "Is that clearly understood?"

The man nodded. "Understood, sir."

Michael and Sadilov headed slowly toward Dupont Circle.

"Sam said you are man to trust ..." Sadilov began.

It became apparent to Michael as the Russian continued his halting story, only reverting to graphic French when denouncing Jarrah and his al Qaeda operatives, that to get him to cooperate, they'd raped his wife and daughter and murdered his son, and to make sure he didn't forget, they taped it. That much, Michael was only too aware. Had Sadilov still refused to help them, his wife and daughter would have been next. After separating them in Haguenau, Sadilov had been given a fake passport and was then accompanied by one of Jarrah's men all the way to Charleston, South Carolina. At the airport, Sadilov was met by Grigori Kolesnikov. The two men didn't know each other, but there was an immediate affinity as both were originally Russian. Sadilov was soon to discover that the former KGB agent, now a U.S. citizen, had been tracked down by al Qaeda while working under the name George Tyson at the New Canaan, Connecticut, private school. According to Sadilov, Tyson had actually thought that after giving al Qaeda the information on the Tybee Island bomb for a large sum of money that would be the end of it. He was very wrong. When he realized they weren't going to let him off the hook, fear took over. Using the name Harold Wentworth, an alias left over from his Cold War days, and with his genuine love and aptitude for antiques, he hoped to disappear again.

When Michael asked, Sadilov said that Wentworth never did find out how al Qaeda found him again.

"He much scared, like me," Sadilov said.

Michael asked, "Why were you taken to Camden?"

Sadilov replied, "A hold me place."

"A place to wait?"

"Yes. That is it. A place to wait. Until they ready."

Sadilov and Wentworth had planned behind al Qaeda's back. "When Harold see the tape, he was telling the authorities about them," Sadilov said.

"He like America much. When they come for me at night, they think I have tape. They find out I do not later. They want tape. But Harold not give it back. They cut his throat."

"You saw them?"

"No, no. They tell me. Show me picture." Sadilov slowly shook his head. "So much death. So much."

"Do you know where they took you?"

"Savannah, Georgia. They have bomb in small warehouse in Port Wentworth. I see it, try not to laugh."

"Because it was too old and no good?"

Sadilov nodded. "They think bomb is fine to work. It have no capsule. But I tell them, need engineer to make part for trigger device."

But when al Qaeda didn't find him an engineer, convinced that Sadilov was stalling, Sadilov had to learn how to make a detonator. "I'm scientist, not engineer. It take long time," he said, but he also saw an opportunity to delay them as long as possible, in the hope that he might be rescued, along with his wife and daughter. "They not too clever with bomb," he added. "They should believe me."

Sadilov didn't see his wife and daughter until after he was rescued, but he insisted that he have proof they were still alive. Consequently, at the beginning of each week, he was handed a photograph of them holding that day's newspaper. "Every week for seven months."

"They're safe now. And so are you."

"Yes. Thank you."

"When did you meet Sam?"

"In Florida." Sadilov went on to say that he finally ran out of ideas and time on how to stall Jarrah and was convinced if he told them the truth about the bomb, they'd definitely kill him. His hope was that if he told them it was ready, and they tried to detonate it and failed, he could still escape.

"I think Sam is Jarrah's wife," Sadilov said. "But she is not. She hate him, she telling me. She also telling me about you. She say if we live, we must find you. You will help."

"Do you know what happened to Sam?"

Sadilov nodded. "I was on boat. I saw."

Michael was surprised. "You were there?"

"Jarrah expect all to die. You shoot much good."

"Thanks."

"You get hurt, yes? You are better now?"

"I'm fine, thank you."

After seeing Michael pushed out of the line of fire by Dan and falling into the water, at the same time Sam was gunned down by Jarrah, Sadilov hid. It wasn't until Federal agents had quickly removed the Egg Harbor from its slip, along with all the bodies, that they found Sadilov in a closet. He was whisked away to a private hospital where, less than twenty-four hours later, he was reunited with his surviving family.

It hadn't taken Sadilov's wife and daughter long to figure out that on the morning of July 1st, their captors weren't coming back. When Sadilov's daughter found a TV in the house and turned on the morning news, she told her mother they were leaving. Within the hour, they'd managed to stop a Jacksonville police car. As English was taught in French schools, it hadn't taken the daughter long to explain to the Jacksonville police who they were.

"They were in Jacksonville all that time?"

"Yes. Jarrah expect bomb go boom! Nothing left."

Sam arrived in Jacksonville only two days before the bomb was due to go off. When she'd asked him if it would explode, Sadilov lied and said yes, still thinking she was with Jarrah. At that point, she told him they had to escape, but he'd refused. He couldn't tell her that the likelihood of the bomb detonating was slim to none. He dare not trust her, and even though she told him about Michael, he'd only realized whose side she was truly on when she tried to stop Jarrah. With fatal results.

"What do you need me to do for you, Dr. Sadilov?" Michael asked.

"Your government make promise my family and me can stay in United States. I like that. Harold, he like it here too. They want for me to say everything. Do I do that?"

"Yes. You can tell them everything."

"It is not problem? My wife, my daughter, they go through so much."

"If you and your family would like to live in the U.S., I'll make it happen. They'll give you new names, a new home, and a new beginning."

Sadilov stopped and faced him, tears in his eyes. "You will do this for us?"

"Yes. And I'm very sorry about your son."

"Thank you. You know what happened?"

"Yes, I know."

Sadilov put his hand on Michael's arm. "Please, Colonel, I speak with your State Department, if you are there."

That's going to be fun. "I'll be there."

"Sam tell me true. You are good man. I am sorry she die."

"Me too."

With Sadilov returned to his secure accommodations, Michael headed back to his office.

Michael's Office, G Street, Washington, D.C.
Early afternoon

"The White House has called twice," Molly said as he came through the door. "How was the meeting?"

"Interesting."

She began to stand with the telephone notes in her hand.

"Not now, Molly. We'll go through those later."

He called the White House.

"Good afternoon, Colonel. Are you feeling better?" the familiar male voice asked.

"I'm fine, thanks."

"That's good to know. The president asked that I arrange a date for the award ceremony."

"Is this really necessary? I don't need a medal."

"There are some who would strongly disagree with you. Look at it this way, you're collecting the set."

Michael had to laugh. "Fine. Pick a date."

"Don't forget that the president wants to meet Lieutenant Tillman. Would you like me to coordinate that for you?"

"No thanks, I'll do it."

He gave Michael several dates, with the promise that Michael would call him back ASAP.

Then Michael dialed Abernathy's number.

"I met with Sadilov," he said. "He'll talk to you, no problem, as long as I'm present."

"That's highly irregular. I'm not even sure it's possible."

Michael had no idea of his status in the whole Jarrah affair, but dealing with pompous State Department bureaucrats was not his strong point.

"Fine," he replied. "No me, no Sadilov. Unless, of course, you'd like me to arrange another Special Op on U.S. soil? Having seen your setup, I doubt the body count would be that high."

"Are you threatening me?"

"What possible reason would I have for doing that? A promise, maybe. Think about it. The man's been through hell."

Michael replaced the receiver. *Fuck him.*

Then, lighting a small cigar, he leaned back in his chair and closed his eyes. *Enough of the desk jockey. Just let me get back to active duty.*

The cigar had burnt out in the ashtray when his phone rang.

"Your father's on line one," Molly said. "Don't you think it's time to plug in your secure phone again?"

"Not right now. I'll take it." He picked up the receiver. "Yes, Dad?"

"How long have you been back?" Francis snapped. "Less than a day? And yet you've managed to piss off most of the upper echelon at the State Department. What the hell are you doing?"

"My job."

"Your job! I'm told you threatened them. What kinda job is that?"

"Mine, apparently. Sadilov will only talk to them if I'm there. How's that so difficult? Seeing as I brought down these guys, it's not as if I'd be learning something I didn't already know. It's a load of bureaucratic bullshit. And I hope you've got them on a conference call. This way, I won't have to repeat myself. I've got more important things to do. Bye, Dad."

Michael hung up.

CIA Headquarters, Langley, Virginia

Francis cleared his throat. "Did you hear all that?"

"Loud and clear," a man's voice replied.

"I did warn you," Francis continued. "But he's got a point. He probably knows more than you do."

"Are you saying yes to this?"

"What's the alternative? My son's not known for his patience. Give him an answer, or he'll have Sadilov out of there and gone before you know what hit you."

"What if we move him?"

Francis gave a short laugh. "He chased Jarrah halfway around the world and got him. What chance do you think you'll have?"

"He'd do that?"

"Very possibly. And he's got the president's ear. If this gets out, I don't want to be first in line for the fallout. You know what he's like."

"What a fuckin' nightmare," the man muttered. "I hope your son doesn't ever plan on running for political office. He doesn't know the meaning of the word 'diplomacy.'"

"Years ago, we used to say that about Makepeace, remember?" Francis realized what he'd just said. "Oh, shit."

There was a long pause. "When this is over, maybe we can get him sent to Iraq?"

"Now, there's a thought," Francis replied. "And I know exactly who can arrange it."

"Who's that?"

"Brigadier General Joshua Collins."

There was a chuckle. "Perfect."

Michael's Office, G Street, Washington, D.C.
Tuesday, July 22, 2003

This time, Michael called Bruyere.

"I want to personally thank you for your cooperation and hard work on our behalf," Michael said in fluent French.

"There's no need to thank me, Colonel. It was a pleasure to help. I am very happy that you caught them."

"It's Michael. And it was a team effort."

Bruyere chuckled and switched to English. "Under your leadership, Michael. Dan has always spoken very highly of you. I am beginning to understand why. You speak French like a native. And please call me Henri."

"Thanks, Henri. What kind of car do you drive?"

There was a pause. "I am guessing you have a good reason for asking?"

"I do."

"A 1994 Citron. It gets me from A to B, I think you say?"

"How about an almost-new Mercedes E-Class?"

"That would be very nice. But far too expensive on my salary."

"Not necessarily. There's a car just like it in long-term parking at the Berlin airport. Call a local Mercedes dealership. They'll open it and get you some new keys. Then, it's yours."

"You mean ...?"

"Yes, that one. No point in breaking in. You won't find anything, and even if you did, it's now after the fact. The owner doesn't want it back, and it's no good to us. So you'll be doing me a favor if you'll take it. Call it the spoils of war."

Bruyere laughed. "Thank you, Michael. I very much hope that one day you and I meet."

"I'll look forward to it, Henri."

Chapter Thirty-Seven

An Undisclosed Location, Washington, D.C.
Monday, July 28, 2003

Early in his Army career, Michael got a well-deserved reputation for pushing the envelope.

Driving the Aston Martin and wearing a very expensive dark gray suit, he arrived at the address he'd been given to quizzical looks from the agents on duty.

"Lieutenant colonels in Army Special Forces must make a lot more than I thought," one agent commented, watching Michael enter the building.

In a room with a long conference table, Michael saw Dr. Dimitri Sadilov was already seated at the far end.

"Maynard Abernathy," he said, stepping forward to shake Michael's hand. "Glad you could join us, Colonel."

"Wouldn't have missed it," Michael replied, returning the handshake with a crushing grip.

Still wincing, Abernathy introduced the five other men. And the only thing of note, in Michael's mind, was they all seemed reluctant to shake his hand. All five had equally long titles that he immediately forgot, but he did store some of the names.

Then without waiting for any instructions, he headed toward Sadilov.

"Good thing we brought a male stenographer," one of the men commented quietly. "That's Francis's son?"

"Probably takes after his mother," was the whispered reply.

Reaching Sadilov, Michael shook his already damp hand and sat down.

"Dobroye den, Dr. Sadilov," he said quietly, then switched to French. "There's nothing to fear from them. They'll ask questions. You answer."

"Are we ready?" asked the man at the head of the table.

"We are," Michael replied.

"Dr. Sadilov, please state your full name for the record ..."

It became apparent from the start that Sadilov's nervousness had greatly affected his ability to speak English. After several questions, with painfully slow and jumbled answers, Michael translated the next one into French.

Sadilov appeared extremely relieved and rattled off his reply, which Michael then translated to astonished looks.

Abernathy immediately stopped the interview.

"Why didn't you tell us we needed an interpreter?" he asked Michael. "We thought Dr. Sadilov spoke English."

"It's neither his first or second language," Michael said. "Under these circumstances, being questioned by the State Department's version of the Spanish Inquisition, I'd be having trouble." *That's just made me a few enemies,* he thought, noting their expressions. "I'll translate. It'll go much faster. Ready?"

"You speak French?" Abernathy asked.

"Fluently. Or Russian, if you'd prefer."

He watched them talking softly amongst themselves at the far end of the table, while off in one corner, the stenographer seemed to be quietly enjoying their indecision.

Michael whispered to Sadilov, "Stay seated." Then he got to his feet. "I'm on a time crunch here," he added. "So make up your minds, or I'm leaving."

The man at the head of the table looked up. "Sit down, Colonel. You can translate."

It was over in less than an hour. One thing that Michael learned was that all of Sadilov's luggage was monogrammed with a large D.S. The al Qaeda operatives had, at the last minute, realized this and changed his fake documents to the name Denis Savin. *And that answers that,* Michael thought.

Michael shook Sadilov's hand. "I wish you and your family well in your new life."

"I thank you much, Colonel. We look forward to new beginning in Chicago suburb."

"I'm not supposed to know that," Michael said quietly.

Sadilov nodded. "I know. Sam give me your numbers. I write them down." He glanced toward the far end of the room. "They never know."

Michael grinned. "Use them if you need to. Udachi, Dr. Sadilov."

"Do svidaniya, Colonel," Sadilov replied.

Michael left him where he was, and as he was passing the stenographer, the man looked up, smiling. "Thanks for a memorable morning, Colonel," he said, barely audible.

"Did you get it all?"

"Oh, yes."

As Michael got to the door, he stopped to face the small group of officials. "Be nice to him," he said. "Nuclear physicists of his caliber don't grow on trees."

Chapter Thirty-Eight

Eagles Nest, Somewhere off Route 301, the Eastern Shore, Maryland
Friday, August 1, 2003

Lynn heard Michael enter the bedroom.

"Zip me up?" she asked.

The next thing she knew, her dress was fastened, and Michael was kissing the nape of her neck.

"Don't stop," she added, before finally turning to face him.

She stared and took a step back, silently scanning him from head to toe.

"Is my zipper undone?" he said.

"No, but it should be." She gave him a very seductive smile. "You know what they say about women and men in uniform."

Michael grinned and stepped toward her. "We've got time for a quickie."

"I can't," she said. "Not because I don't want to have outrageous sex with you, but because we're due at the White House in less than three hours. I'm nervous enough as it is, without meeting the president knowing what we just did."

"Did you say outrageous sex?"

She nodded.

"Promise?"

"Definitely."

She looked more closely at his chest. "When presidents leave office, they usually open a library. When you retire, what are you going to do, open a museum?"

Michael only shrugged.

"Don't tell me," she continued. "You got all those patches and medals for doing a little bit of this and a little bit of that in places you can't talk about. Right?"

"Close."

En Route to Washington, D.C.

During the drive, Lynn took furtive glances at Michael. She knew he was Special Forces, but until a short time ago, never having seen him in uniform, let alone a dress uniform, she realized she'd really pushed that fact to the back of her mind.

"Is something wrong?" Michael asked, never taking his eyes off the road.

"No. I was thinking how good you look. Dark green suits you."

The White House, Pennsylvania Ave., Washington, D.C.
Early afternoon

As Michael predicted, the award ceremony was short and to the point.

Makepeace made a brief speech, congratulating him with words that Lynn thought were very flattering and without a doubt all true. After awarding Michael the Distinguished Service Cross, ending with the words, "... in keeping with the finest traditions of military service and reflecting great credit upon himself, this Command, and the United States Army," the president then pinned the medal on Michael's chest.

Michael snapped to attention and saluted.

At that point, Lynn was bursting with pride.

Then Makepeace shook Michael's hand and, almost as an afterthought, added for the few dignitaries in attendance to hear, "Congratulations too on the promotion. You just made 'full bird colonel.'"

"Thank you, sir."

Makepeace leaned forward. "If I had my way, you'd be wearing stars," he added quietly, adding the Eagles to Michael's shoulder epaulets.

Then he turned to those in attendance. "Would you excuse us please? I need some time with the new colonel."

Very effectively dismissing them all, including his father to Michael's relief, the invited guests filed out of the Oval Office, and the door closed, leaving Makepeace and Michael alone.

"Sit," Makepeace said, gesturing at a sofa. "If it weren't for the group outside, I'd light a cigar." He sat opposite. "Of course, the first lady would kill me."

Michael smiled. "When you feel that desperate, sir, there's always Eagles Nest."

For a second, the president closed his eyes. "Ah, yes. What I wouldn't give for an afternoon there, right now." He leaned forward. "Would you stop me from having a cigar on that boat of yours?"

"No, sir. I'd join you. A good cigar and ten-year-old Glenfiddich are my weakness, sir."

Makepeace had a broad grin. "Bullshit. From what I can tell, you don't have any weaknesses." He lowered his voice. "Unless, of course, it's that pretty lieutenant. In which case, I wouldn't blame you."

Michael was beginning to wonder when the ball was going to drop. He didn't have long to wait.

Makepeace leaned back, studying Michael's chest. "You're an outstanding credit to the uniform. But I guess we'll have to think of something else the next time. You've run out of room."

Here we go. "What next time, sir?"

"You were in the middle of an investigation before that terrorist Jarrah, and now I'd like you to finish it. There's an election next year, and I don't want to take any chances. I've still got a lot to accomplish. I don't want any hidden surprises that I can't handle. Understood?"

"Understood perfectly, sir."

"Good. Take some more time off. That's an order, Colonel. Then get back to work."

Michael stood. "Very good, sir."

Makepeace got to his feet. "Did you mean what you said about Eagles Nest?"

"Yes, sir. You're welcome anytime. I thought you realized that?"

"I'm going to take you up on it."

"Do that, sir."

Makepeace was at the door. "Send in Lieutenant Tillman," he said to someone outside.

Moments later, Lynn entered the room.

Makepeace held out his hand. "I'm delighted to finally meet you," he said as she took the president's hand. Then taking her arm, he steered her toward the sofa.

Lynn dutifully sat. "Thank you, Mr. President."

"For God's sake, Michael, sit," Makepeace added.

Michael sat next to her, and he could sense how uncomfortable she was.

"I can at last thank you in person," Makepeace continued, "for an extraordinary piece of police work. Michael tells me it was you who found the e-mails. Very well done."

"Thank you, Mr. President. I was just doing my job."

"You're being far too modest. Isn't she, Michael?"

Lynn couldn't help but notice that he seemed perfectly at home with the most powerful man of the world's great superpower.

"I totally agree, sir. We'd still be looking if it wasn't for Lieutenant Tillman."

Makepeace studied her for a moment. "It was great work. If you ever want a private tour of the White House, let Michael know. I'll arrange it."

"Thank you, Mr. President. I'd like that very much."

"Good." Makepeace got to his feet.

Michael and Lynn immediately stood.

"Have you learned to control him yet?" Makepeace suddenly asked.

Lynn swallowed. "No, Mr. President."

"Pity. I was hoping I'd found someone who could."

Lynn said a quick prayer. "Give me time, Mr. President?"

Makepeace laughed. "Excellent. Take all the time you need." He turned to Michael. "I hope you heard that?"

"Every word, sir. When did you say you wanted that cigar?"

"That was below the belt."

"It was meant to be, sir."

Makepeace held out his hand. "A pleasure as always, Michael. Congratulations again."

Then he thanked Lynn one more time, and the next thing she knew, she was holding Michael's hand, walking down a long carpeted corridor. Unbeknown to her, Michael had purposely used a different exit to avoid running into his father.

She didn't speak until she was strapped into the passenger seat of the Aston Martin.

"Did I make a fool of myself?" she asked. "I was terrified."

"You did fine," Michael said. "He's human you know."

"But he's the president."

"So? I'm betting we both put our pants on the same way."

She finally laughed. "I wonder if he takes them off the same way?"

"Meaning?"

"Have I got plans for you."

Michael was grinning. "Good. I thought you might have forgotten."

"Trust me. I didn't forget."

There was a point on Route 50, heading toward the Bay Bridge, that Lynn thought if Michael was stopped for speeding, they'd be thrown in jail, regardless of the fact there was no traffic.

"Stop worrying," he said as the odometer climbed to well over 100. "I'll just flash my military ID."

"I suppose having the president as your best friend can't hurt either."

"That too."

At Eagles Nest, Lynn made good on her promise, and it was some of the most erotic sex Michael could ever remember.

"Remind me to wear my uniform around you more often," he said sleepily, many hours later.

"I will. That's a promise," she murmured.

Chapter Thirty-Nine

Michael's Office, G Street, Washington, D.C.
Thursday, August 8, 2003

"You've got to do something," Molly said to Brian. "He's been moping around for days. It's not right."

"You tell him."

"I'm a woman. He won't listen to me. He finds it impossible to share."

"It's the way he was trained."

"He's very smart. He can be retrained."

"Kathryn couldn't do it."

Molly began to sort some papers on her desk. "Maybe she didn't know how."

"If you're right, what makes you think he'll listen to me?"

"I know all about his reputation, and so do you. As you're a man, it'll sound better coming from you. All he's done since Sam was killed is work and spend time with that horse. Even it's a male."

"A neutered one."

"That's not funny. Talk to him. We're all beginning to suffer."

Later that morning, Brian opened Michael's door and stepped inside.

"Goin' for your run?" he asked.

Michael looked up from his paperwork. "Of course."

"Want some company?"

"You're serious? You really want to run?"

"Nah. I was thinkin' of sittin' on a park bench and watchin'."

Michael checked his watch. "Get your gear. We leave in fifteen minutes."

The Lincoln Memorial, Washington, D.C.
Some time later

Michael stopped at the drinking fountain. "You're in better shape than I thought," he said. "Want to keep going?"

Brian shook his head. "It's time for the park bench. You too. There's somethin' I gotta say."

Michael sat.

"I'm real sorry Sam was killed," Brian added. "But it's time to move on."

Michael wiped his face with a towel. "So that's it. The fatherly lecture."

"No. Just one friend to another. We're concerned. That's all."

To Brian's surprise, Michael leaned over, his face covered by the towel.

"Sam got herself killed savin' you," Brian continued. "So I reckon she'd want to see you get on with your life. I know you had strong feelin's for her too, but the mournin's over. We need you back. Think about it? That's all I've gotta say."

Michael turned his head. "That's what you think?"

Brian only nodded.

"If I'd slept with every woman who showed an interest in me, I'd have been dead from exhaustion a long time ago."

"But we all thought—"

Michael interrupted, "I'll grant you that given a very different set of circumstances, and if I wasn't already involved with someone else, I probably wouldn't have turned Sam down. She was a beautiful, intelligent woman. But like I told you from the start, I don't necessarily play by the rules. We needed her cooperation. I was going to use every means possible."

"Molly thinks you're depressed."

"Possible. Sam's death could have been avoided. It was my fault."

"Bullshit!"

"You think?"

"I know. Did you feel this way about losin' men in battle? I doubt it. Sadness, deep regret, yes. No one wants to see anyone die. But this's a different kinda war. We're fightin' civilians too. That's justa fact of life. So now that's bin cleared up, what else is wrong?"

"Post mission blues. Happens all the time."

"I get it. Like a big fancy weddin' and the huge party afterward. When the bride and groom have gone, all that's left is this big empty space."

Michael grinned. "Affirmative. And talking of weddings, what's going on with you and Pauline?"

Brian hesitated. "I decided there's no need to rush into anythin' yet."

"How long have you been together?"

"Fifteen years."

"Good luck explaining that."

"She'll be okay with it."

Michael grinned. "Like hell she will." He checked his watch and got to his feet. "Trust me."

"You're probably right," Brian replied. "You goin' to call Lynn?"

"Yes. Not that it's any of your business."

"She understands you."

"Maybe."

"There's nothin' 'maybe' about it. She's good for you. And I ain't racin' you back to the office. There've been enough deaths."

Michael's Office, G Street, Washington, D.C.
Later that afternoon

After his talk with Brian, Michael felt considerably better. So much so, his first phone call was to Lynn. After a lengthy conversation, during which he managed to truthfully say, "I miss you," she'd readily agreed to come for a long weekend at Eagles Nest.

"I don't see a problem, so expect me tomorrow lunchtime, or sooner," she said. "That okay with you?"

"Sounds great," Michael replied. "See you tomorrow."

He made several more phone calls before calling a meeting in his office.

With Brian, Dan, and Molly all seated, Michael leaned against his desk.

"It's time to wrap this up ..." he began.

"... and according to Sadilov, he was moved, along with the bomb, to a waterfront house south of Jacksonville right before it was due to go off. A pickup towing a boat on a trailer heading south down 1-95 on a Saturday morning wasn't going to attract any attention. Sam arrived later in the day."

"The same house that they were holdin' his wife and daughter?" Brian asked.

"No. Jarrah rented a much larger one with a dock. We assume it's where he took the Egg Harbor right before the raid in Bradenton."

"No wonder we couldn't find it," Dan said.

"In plain sight," Michael continued. "According to the owner of the house, he thought Jarrah was a wealthy Italian when he signed a two-year lease. As the owner lives abroad, the managing agent would check from time to time. The place always looked good, and the rent was paid promptly. No red flags. Any more questions?"

"Where did they store the bomb?" Brian asked.

Michael handed him a map and pointed. "Right there."

Brian stared and then looked up. "You're kiddin'? In Port Wentworth? That's right over the bridge from the Georgia Ports Authority. I was there. Less than a quarter of a mile away."

"Don't feel bad," Michael said. "Dan and I drove past it. Dan even made a comment."

"They bought the place?"

"No, rented. The landlord never went there. His checks were always on time."

"Why did they choose Jacksonville, sir?"

"Good question, Molly. If the bomb had exploded during the storm, the fallout would have gone west, basically cutting off Florida. That would have affected not only a slew of military installations, including SOCOM, but also the interstate, train terminals, the power distribution grid, and even Cape Canaveral. Like a cork in a bottle. They gave the target a lot of thought."

"What happens to the children?"

"As no one knows where they came from, the Boyds have agreed to keep them. The State Department's doing the paperwork. And while I'm on the subject of loose ends, two days ago, the FBI finally raided Applegate's paramilitary organization. Slycroft told them al Qaeda was training there. Applegate was killed in a firefight. But don't expect to see anything on the news."

Michael got to his feet. "If there's nothing else, we're done. I'm taking a long weekend, and you're all doing the same."

Molly was about to interrupt.

"You too," he added. "There's nothing that can't wait until Monday. Then, we have to finish what we started before all this began." He paused. "Thanks for all the help and support. I couldn't have done it without you. Actually, I couldn't have done it. Period. You're the best. Now get outta here. I'm locking up."

He watched them leave. *Thank God it's over.*

Eagles Nest, Somewhere off Route 301, the Eastern Shore, Maryland
Late afternoon

As Michael drove up the driveway, he could see Delta already waiting by the gate.

I've got time for a ride, he thought, and after putting the car in the garage, he went directly inside to change.

A short time later, he entered the tack room attached to the stable to pick up the grooming kit. On a peg above Delta's saddle hung his bridle, and draped over the noseband was a length of brightly colored fabric.

What the? Michael thought, wondering why it looked familiar.

Then it hit him.

He inhaled. The scent was unmistakable, but to be sure, he searched for a label. *Hermes, Paris; 100% silk.*

The last time he saw it, it was draped around the neck of a certain individual on a Sunday afternoon in March at a millionaire's waterfront estate in coastal Georgia.

It isn't over? This stinks of the CIA and my father's involvement. I'll deal with him later. Michael took a quick look around before pocketing the scarf. *But thanks, Sam. I got the message.*

Afterword

The truth is that after the midair collision between the B-47 and the F-86L aircraft on February 5, 1958, we thought the media story would be that the B-47 and crew landed safely, and the fighter pilot had been found and was recovering in a hospital. However, all subsequent references were articles about the weapon and its possible hazards, regardless of the fact that the weapon did not have the necessary capsule inserted to make it a nuclear device. The capsule wasn't even on board the aircraft when it left our home base of Homestead Air Force Base, Florida.

Photograph courtesy of Clarence Stewart

It was later proved that these capsules had not even arrived there, making a nuclear explosion impossible. Despite this, some local individuals who knew better have deliberately kept alive the rumor that a terrible detonation was possible and that it could not only devastate Savannah, Georgia, but the surrounding area, as well as the entire East Coast. Closely tagging along were a few of the news media who would not investigate the available data. They kept to their motto: "Don't let the facts stand in the way of a good story."

The United States Air Force has made two assessments with experts and has published reports on April 12, 2001 and May 31, 2005. Their summary statement is as follows:

> "The Air Force has consistently asserted that the best course of action in this matter is to discontinue to search for the bomb and leave the property in place. The Air Force also continues to reject an offer of salvage."

The living crew of the B-47 and the fighter pilot hope that their endorsement of this book will finally put an end to speculation about the incident.

Photograph courtesy of Col. Howard Richardson

Howard Richardson
Colonel, USAF (Retired)

About the Author

Born in England, Rowan Wolfe is now a United States citizen. After working for several years as a marketing director in Connecticut, Rowan moved to Maryland to focus on her writing, and won the Maryland Writers' Association Annual Fiction Contest in 1999. Wolfe published her first novel, *The Trial of Evan Gage*, in 2003. She lives and writes in Savannah, Georgia.

Printed in the United States
59868LVS00001B/73-1209

9 781600 080012